DOUBLE TAKE

Books by Judy Mercer

Fast Forward
Double Take

Published by POCKET BOOKS

DOUBLE TAKE

JUDY MERCER

POCKET BOOKS
New York London Toronto Sydney Tokyo Singapore

This book is a work of fiction. Names, characters, places and incidents are products of the author's imagination or are used fictitiously. Any resemblance to actual events or locales or persons living or dead is entirely coincidental.

POCKET BOOKS, a division of Simon & Schuster Inc.
1230 Avenue of the Americas, New York, NY 10020

ISBN: 0-671-55707-6

Printed in the U.S.A.

For Maizelle Woodward Mercer,
remembered with love, admiration, and gratitude,
and for Arthur Adolph Mercer, *Doc* . . .
to whom I don't express those things often enough

With thanks to Henry Dearing, Attorney at Law and master of encouragement, and Kate Grimm, intrepid researcher; and to Phil French; Mike Hope; Ken Sorensen; John Harris; Andy Roeser; Brad Sargent; Ellen Mason, Editorial Producer, *Dateline NBC;* Rich Camgros, Operations Manager, Shamrock Materials, Marin County; Ken Holmes, Assistant Coroner, Marin County; Detective III Dennis Tilton, Missing Persons Unit, Los Angeles Police Department; Amy Blyth, Director of Media and Public Relations, Charleston Trident Convention and Visitors Bureau; Greg Davy, Media Relations Representative, Metropolitan Transportation Authority; Peter Hidalgo, Manager, Metrolink Media Communications; Rick Yatman, Acey Decy Lighting, Los Angeles; the Atchison, Topeka and Santa Fe Railway Company; Southern Pacific Lines; Forest Lawn Memorial Parks and Mortuaries; and with special thanks to Larry, for helping me believe in magic and in myself.

An honorable murderer, if you will;
For naught I did in hate, but all in honor.

—Shakespeare, *Othello,* V, ii

DOUBLE TAKE

1

"BUT YOU'RE DEAD!"

The lone woman crouching on the beach started violently, overbalancing. Her palms hit sand, hard, and the shell she'd been about to pick up, a small but perfect conch, bit into her knee as she fell. Above her small cry of pain and alarm, she heard the voice again, a strangled, inarticulate sound somewhere in the darkness behind her, louder, nearer.

Her head snapped erect as her legs tensed for flight. There was nothing in her field of vision but ocean, white foam soughing into the lazy arcs of low tide, and sand, an endless, empty stretch to either side. It was one o'clock in the morning. There was no one to help and nowhere to run.

She dug the conch from under her knee, a feeble weapon. In that millisecond, her mind raced through options. How near was he? Could she charge him? It *was* a him, no question. A man's voice, thick with menace.

Half erect and off balance, she planted her feet like a clumsy sprinter on the blocks and pivoted toward her attacker, still ten or so feet away but closing in. It was then that mental tumblers clicked into place. It wasn't menace she'd heard. It was shock. And the man wasn't running; he looked as if he were being pulled forward against his will.

Ariel Gold came to her feet. Wind whipped hair into her eyes, but she slung her head, stood her ground, and waited.

The man was a stranger, but that was hardly surprising since she'd arrived on the island only an hour before. He was fair, slightly built, in his late thirties, she guessed. His tie was undone, his suit jacket unbuttoned, he was barefoot. All those impressions came and went in an instant. What struck Ariel was his expression. The cold silver of a full moon showed her a face riveted by fear, pain, and something more complex: something like wonder. He looked as if he'd come face-to-face with a ghost.

One hand reached toward her, hesitantly.

"Jane?" he said.

2

ARIEL EXPELLED A LONG, RAGGED BREATH AND FELT HER BODY RELAX a millimeter. The man had a right to look unstrung.

"I think," she said, "you've mistaken me for my sister."

Even now, six months after she'd learned that she'd had an identical twin who'd died unknown to her, who'd died instead of her, it hurt to hear the name. It was tough to think about the nightmare that had almost brought them together. It wasn't getting much easier.

"Jane sometimes spent summers here on Kiawah," Ariel said gently. "I guess you knew her?"

The obviousness of the question seemed to be lost on her companion. She wasn't even sure he'd heard it—or anything else she'd said. He'd come to a standstill several feet away, as if it were too terrible to approach her further. His eyes explored her face, her hair, her body, with a hunger that would have been frightening if it hadn't been so incredulous.

Ariel's knee had begun to throb. Her thumb, she realized, was nervously tracing the curve of the shell she still held, and her calf was threatening to go into a cramp from the fight-or-flight stance she'd forgotten to come out of. The man had yet to respond in any reasonable way, and if his silent scrutiny wasn't actually scary, it was unnerving. She slipped the shell into her pocket, wiped sandy palms against her shorts, and held out her hand.

"Ariel Gold. And you're . . . ?"

The skin below his pale eyes fluttered, a tiny tic constricting his lower lids. In the space of a second he seemed to draw into himself in some way, actually to diminish in size.

"You look," he said, "so much like . . ."

"So I'm told." Ariel dropped her unacknowledged hand. "Did you know her well?"

He frowned. "Jane didn't have a sister. Jane didn't have any siblings at all, and her mother was dead. In fact, her father was dead." The words were accusatory; the tone wasn't. He spoke with the same distinctive drawl Ariel had heard at the Charleston airport: soft, rich as loam, and, in this case, puzzled. "I don't understand who you are," he said simply.

"You do know a lot about her." Ariel sighed. "Did you also know, then, that her mother—our mother—died when Jane was a baby? That Jane was raised by our grandfather?" She paused. "You know B.F.?"

He inclined his head in what might have been a nod, but a wait of several seconds produced no other response. Ariel glanced out at the Atlantic. It looked as if it was going to be tit for tat, and curiosity about her sister, a deep need to talk to someone who'd known her, took over. As if it were perfectly natural to stand chatting with this stranger while sane people slept, as if their presence on the beach at that hour wasn't questionable in itself, and as if her explanation were unremarkable, she answered his implied question.

"It's a long story. What B.F. didn't know was that there'd been two babies. Twins. I was left behind because . . . well, I'll make it a short story. I was raised by adoptive parents in California. I never met Jane. I didn't know anything about my birth parents until a few months ago."

Seeing his puzzled frown turn into what looked like skepticism, Ariel said, "I'm not making this up, you know. Babies do get separated at birth, more often than you imagine, and—"

"I didn't say I didn't believe you," he cut in mildly. "Your face is pretty irrefutable evidence, isn't it? No, I was just thinking, Jane was right. She tried to describe something to me once. She said she'd always felt a kind of incompleteness—her 'inner space,' she called it—in some deep, inaccessible place. Hattie told her . . ." He smiled. "Is dear Hattie still around?"

So enrapt was Ariel that it took her a moment to register the question. "Hattie?" She blinked. "Oh. Sure."

He nodded and walked the few steps to where the surf nibbled at the sand. He dropped to one knee, unmindful of the wet that immediately soaked his pant leg, and picked up what looked like the broken shaft of a child's shovel. Absently, he began to peel at its jagged tip.

"Hattie told her," he said, "that was the way with some 'females,' that one of these days she'd meet some man or other—'probably some no-'count rascal,' she said—'then you'll be whole as Sears when Roebuck came along.' " He chuckled. "Not a very romantic image, is it? But then, I don't think Hattie had any great opinion of romance. Hattie, that once at any rate, was wrong."

He'd begun drawing or writing something in the damp sand. Holding the five inches of splintered stick in his fist as a child holds a crayon, he made deliberate, deep gouges that appeared to absorb his attention. He seemed hardly aware of what he was saying.

"*I* knew what Jane meant. That incompleteness wasn't going to be filled by someone she hadn't met; it was left by someone who'd already gone. Loneliness is what it was, and need. The void that's left when grief and shame and fear eat a hole in your guts."

Ariel edged closer to where he knelt. His face, long and rather thin even full on, was almost spectral from her perspective. Shadow sculpted his cheek and hollowed the temples of his broad forehead. She saw a flash of reflected moonlight at his wrist—something metallic that slipped into sight and was hidden again when his arm moved. She couldn't make out what he was so intently carving into the sand.

"Is it Jane you're talking about?" she asked quietly.

He lifted his head and gave her an appraising look, one eyebrow raised. At that moment, it occurred to Ariel, he was actually looking at *her,* seeing not the woman he remembered but the one who was there. The moment passed. As he began to talk again, she had a sudden, vivid sensation of being present yet apart, of seeing the two of them from above, tiny figures in vast, quiet emptiness, isolated as a moonscape. A curious intimacy bound them. His accent was to her ears as exotic as myrrh, and as he drew her into memory, the past became more real than the present.

"Jane turned nine the summer I met her," he began. "I was thirteen. We had a great deal in common, even with the disparity in our ages, and there was a little pocket of time, before she made friends hereabouts, when we were inseparable. She had no father or mother. I had no father and no mother to speak of. She had no brothers or sisters and never would have. . . . Well, so she believed.

"I was a lone child, too, and young for my age, a misfit right down to the ground. I wanted to be anybody but me, anywhere but here, so I contrived to be elsewhere, living in my imagination. Jane fell right into my make-believe world. In fact, she led. She was so quick. So . . ." He paused, seeking the words to bring a long-ago little girl to life again. "Jane read voraciously, and she was full of words and stories and romantic ideals.

"That first summer she was into mythology, knights and damsels and ogres, you know, and she decided that we were Epimetheus and Pandora—since they were both fatherless and motherless, too. You know the legend? *The Paradise of Children?* In our games, though, we were able to get the troubles back into the box, or we found ways to vanquish them and be heroes—defeating disease and conquering evil and so on. Sometimes Jane got impatient with playing Pandora—she was a bit of a pill, wasn't she?—and cast herself as Hope. We made up little dramas, with the squirreliest cast of characters you can imagine, and she managed to work Hope, at least as a bit player, into most of them. Even the *Odyssey,* as I recall." He gave a little laugh. "Lordy, we were young! So terribly, achingly innocent. Such a long, long time ago."

"When 'there was no danger, nor trouble of any kind,' " murmured Ariel.

He started, his chin dropping, and the mood was broken. "How on earth—? That's from the story, isn't it?" In some agitation, he said, "Jane did that! Did you know that? She could remember whole snatches of stories, and she'd work them verbatim into the dialogue of our plays, and then she couldn't understand why I couldn't do it, too. She'd get so outdone with me when I couldn't remember the lines she'd given me!"

Ariel squatted beside him. "Tell me more about Jane."

"Amazing," he said. He shook his head as if to clear it, and when he picked up his narrative, his almost trancelike reverie was gone.

"There's not a lot more to tell. By the next summer she had more friends than she knew what to do with, and even though she tried to get me to join their little crabbing parties and oyster roasts and so on, I was too old for them. The age difference had kicked in and, truth is, no one but Jane wanted me around anyway.

"Whenever she was here during the next two or three years, I didn't happen to be, and the next time I saw her she wasn't a child anymore, and I was a man." His expression had turned brooding. "Or they were trying to make me into one. I'd been shipped off to military school early on. By then I'd had a year at the Citadel, and I was . . ." He shrugged and tossed the stick away. "Jane tried and, Lord knows, nobody but her could've made that summer bearable. We talked for hours on end." He looked around him, getting his bearings. "Probably right on this spot more times than once.

"She'd try to tease me out of my misery, Jane did. She had a remarkably sophisticated sense of humor for her age. Droll. When that didn't work, she'd try to convince me to stop worrying about what other people thought. She'd quote somebody or other—one of her favorites was something like 'The formula for failure is trying to please everybody'—and tell me to listen to my own drummer. Can you imagine? She must've been all of fourteen or fifteen at the time. She still believed in good and evil and happily ever after, and here I was, supposedly an adult, wanting to buy into the myth."

He glanced at Ariel and away again. "I went to her wedding. We'd kept in touch through the years, mostly her doing. Said she couldn't afford to lose the only 'brother' she had. And then we did lose touch—thanks to her husband, I imagine. It happens," he said matter-of-factly.

There was a stretch of silence while Ariel waited for him to go on and, when it appeared that he had nothing more to say, she prodded.

"You never answered me a while ago. You were talking about the 'incompleteness' Jane felt? You said something about fear. Whose?"

Abruptly he stood and became busy brushing sand from his trousers.

"Fear? Lord knows Jane didn't have anything to be afraid of. Not with B.F. guarding the gates. If he wasn't exactly a father, the man damn sure gave new meaning to the term 'father-protector.' "

"So?" Ariel bristled, reflexively leaping to her grandfather's defense. "Give him credit for trying, then, since ultimately even he couldn't protect her, could he? Not from murder."

His hands, like his manner, became very still.

"No. Murder, like God, is no respecter of persons."

He gave his pants a last tired swipe. "My dear, funny, beautiful Jane. You were right before, of course. The fear wasn't hers."

Before Ariel could scramble to her feet, he was walking back in the direction from which he'd come, and when she started to call out to him, she realized that she didn't know his name.

"Hey!" she shouted. "Will you wait a minute?"

She looked around for her sandals and, snatching them up, ran toward the distant dunes. When she topped them, he was gone.

She hurried back to the water's edge, but the tide was beginning to come in. Whatever he'd written was gone, too.

3

THE SUN WAS HIGH IN THE SKY WHEN ARIEL FINALLY PEELED OPEN bleary eyes. Quickly, they closed against the hot light streaming through the bedroom's open windows and, just as quickly, they snapped open again. It wasn't the glare that had dragged her into consciousness. It was a noise, a metallic clang.

She shot upright and, fighting pinging needles of alarm, tried to bring her brain into play. She was on Kiawah Island, South Carolina. She'd gone to bed in an empty house, B.F.'s house, but B.F. wasn't here—wasn't due until this evening. Worse, her dogs were back in California. She desperately regretted that fact.

Had the clatter she'd heard come from outside? Had she dreamed it? She raised anxious eyes to the ceiling fan whirring overhead. Was the thing about to cut loose from its moorings and launch itself? A similar noise at just that moment made short work of conjecture. Ariel cocked her head, listening with every cell.

The noise had come from inside the house. From the floor below. Quietly retrieving her robe, she tried to envision the downstairs floor plan, but it was a blur. She'd explored only a few rooms of the big old house last night before heading for the beach.

The man on the beach! Could he have followed her here? She sensed the wrongness of the thought almost before it flashed through her mind. He'd had no interest in her at all, only in the sister whose memory she evoked. And he'd been harmless; she was sure of it. She sniffed. She smelled coffee. Someone had broken in and made coffee? She sniffed again. And bacon?

Ariel firmly belted her robe and found her glasses. She went to the top of the stairs, crept down, following the sounds to the kitchen. She stopped just outside the door and peered into the huge, old-fashioned room.

Hattie Best clapped a cast iron skillet onto the stove's red-hot eye, not gently. "Did I wake you up?" she said. "Sorry. I was tryin' to be quiet—for the last three hours."

Hattie's stiff back was to the door. How she'd heard Ariel's approach was a mystery, but then a great deal about B.F.'s housekeeper and old friend remained a mystery.

The spare, seventyish woman flipped a last thick slab of bacon onto what looked like a paper grocery bag, broke eggs into the skillet, and, her swift copper-colored hands wasting no motion, began to stir something white and grainy in a saucepan.

"Good morning," Ariel said. "When did you get here?" She cleared hoarse gravel from her throat. "What's that you're making?"

"Three hours ago, like I just told you. And what I'm makin's breakfast—though it's nearer dinnertime."

Ariel glanced at her watch. "Not according to my body. It's not even seven o'clock in California. I meant what's that you're fixing there. Cream of Wheat?"

"You're not *in* California, and it's not Cream of Wheat. It's grits." With a squint-eyed glance at Ariel's puffy eyes and her hair, a shock of which was standing straight up like Alfalfa's, Hattie nodded toward the percolator and a mug waiting beside it.

Ariel poured strong coffee and wandered to the open back door. For a time she watched a quarrelsome squirrel chattering at his partner, who was busy with some sort of scrap and disinclined to respond. Ariel glanced at Hattie. There was a definite resemblance.

Yawning, she wandered back and sat at one of two places laid at the table. As if she were a hostess with a difficult guest, she began to make conversation.

"I didn't get here until midnight, and I was too keyed up to sleep so I walked down to the beach. My flight took forever, and there was a glitch with the car rental and then that drive over from Charleston . . ." She blew into her mug. Expecting no comment and getting none, she said, "I kept thinking I was lost, and there was nobody on the road but me. I mean, I never saw one human from the time I hit the island until . . . Actually, that's not true! Hattie, there was a man on the beach last night—well, this morning, to be accurate—who knows you and B.F. He and Jane were friends back when they were kids. Do you have any idea who he is? A thinnish, fair-haired man in his late thirties?"

Hattie set a plate in front of Ariel and filled her own. "You manage to forget his name, too, did you?" she asked slyly.

Ariel stilled. The question, put to the average person, might have been innocent. But since she remembered absolutely nothing beyond six months before, Ariel didn't fit into the category of average.

While her grandfather had never doubted her, in regard to her identity or her amnesia, the same couldn't be said for this woman who had raised Jane. If Hattie's suspicions hadn't been voiced the few times Ariel had been in her company, they'd been felt.

Deliberately, Ariel picked up her fork and began eating. "The man didn't give me his name," she said. "You can't think who he might be?"

"Jane had lots of friends, most of which I haven't seen since they got grown, so I wouldn't know 'em now. Look here, what you do is your business, but it's not too smart to be talkin' to strange men in the middle of the night. With the dope fiends and such out there, your vacation might end up shorter than you planned on."

Ariel didn't know how to reply to that. "Ah . . . what do you put on grits?" she asked. "They seem to, uh, need something."

Hattie shrugged. "Salt. pepper."

Ariel seasoned the mushy stuff liberally and mixed it with her eggs. The food staples Hattie had brought were still lined up on an old Hoosier cabinet nearby, and Ariel reached for a bottle of Worcestershire sauce. "May I?" she asked and added a dollop.

"Better," she pronounced. "Good."

There was, for several moments, no sound but that of Ariel's enjoyment of her food. She was about to refill her coffee cup when she realized that she was the only one eating.

"What?" She swallowed. "What's the matter?"

Hattie's hooded eyes were black as basalt and no less hard. "Worcestershire sauce" was all she said.

Ariel's teeth clamped her lower lip. Had she committed some breach of Southern etiquette? "Yes?" she asked.

"You put it on your grits."

"I did," Ariel admitted.

"Jane did that. Jane was the only one I ever knew to do that."

"Oh," Ariel said. Feeling very ill at ease, she studied the woman across from her.

The stony face was scored with deep lines, particularly from the nose to the sides of the downturned mouth. Ariel wondered if the creases were new, if they'd been etched by sorrow at Jane's pointless death. The nose was hawklike, and the planes of the cheeks were flat, the bones unusually prominent. Not for the first time, Ariel wondered at the antecedents who had combined to make such a strong, distinctive face. An oil hanging above B.F.'s fireplace in Los Angeles came to her mind. The subject was an Indian, a Seminole, whose immense dignity and still, waiting carriage were not dissimilar to Hattie's. Whose narrowed eyes waited, too.

"My presence must be hard for you," Ariel said. "A stranger. Reminding you of Jane."

"You don't," Hattie said and left the table. As she wrapped her almost untouched food with foil, there was no haste to her movements, and no concession.

"Even with those contact lenses you been wearin' and copyin' her hair and losin' all that weight . . ." She stole a glance to see how that set with Ariel. It didn't set well. "I'd sure be interested to learn, though, how you come to know some of the things you do. Like the Worcestershire sauce." Her stolid look was a challenge. "B.F. don't need any more grief," she said flatly.

Ariel opened her mouth to protest, but coincidence and the uncanny similarities of twins and all the other arguments so familiar to her—she used them on herself, frequently—flew from her thoughts.

"Wait a minute. Where *is* B.F.? I'd assumed you all were coming here together."

With one last piercing look, a sort of visual last word, Hattie hefted the skillet from the stove, drowned it in hot suds, and began to scour it into sublimate surrender. "Changed his plans," she grunted. "He's in New York."

"In New—you mean he's not coming?"

"Said something about a hostile take-on or take-out or whatever that came up, but I 'spec he'll get here when he can. Sooner or later."

Ariel considered throwing her yolk-smeared plate against the wall. She considered throwing it at Hattie.

"Why—just out of curiosity—didn't you tell me? When did he know about these 'changed plans'?"

"I heard yesterday. You'd left already. You just got up. I just told you. He's got the plane up yonder with him, and he'll probably turn up anytime, so don't get on my neck about it."

Ariel's annoyance fizzled. She'd worked like a coolie overachiever for the past four months, and she was not going to spend this long, hot holiday weekend in a sparring match. She was going to enjoy it if it killed her.

"If you'll excuse me," she said, "I'm going to cover myself with sunscreen and go see how the Atlantic compares to the Pacific."

Ariel had gotten to the staircase when Hattie called her name. The woman was drying her hands on a dish towel, and she was concentrating on the task as intently as a surgeon scrubbing up. "B.F. said tell you he'd get here quick as he could. Told me he called a man about bringin' over some shrimp. He said fix Frogmore stew for supper."

Ariel nodded. "Fine. Thanks." She didn't know what Frogmore stew was, but she knew how to quit when she was ahead. She started up the stairs.

"It'll be ready at seven," Hattie called after her, "and it don't keep."

4

HENRY HELLER PUNCHED THE DISCONNECT BUTTON ON THE RE-ceiver with all the vehemence he could invest in such a dinky gesture and regretted that he was using a plastic portable.

He'd get an old-fashioned telephone, he told himself, a solid, black phone with a rotary dial. He'd get a separate line, limited exclusively to communicating with his ex-wife—to one particular ex-wife, the mother of his son. The measured pace of dialing, unlike pecking at push buttons, would be suitably ominous. The shrill ring on his end would be appropriately alarming. Best of all, it would be so satisfying to slam the receiver into the cradle, which he invariably did after a conversation with Emily.

Henry slid down in his chair, stretching out his long legs and further abusing his perennially aching back. It was a lot easier, he was aware, to wool-gather about telephones than to decide what to do about the latest and, so far, worst problem with Sam.

Their son, according to Emily, had become a thief. Nothing big, just a little petty shoplifting, a couple of CDs—but, oh, did Henry despise a thief! And he wasn't crazy about the kid's taste, either. Pearl Jam and Smashing Pumpkins?

Surprising, Henry reflected. If Sam was going to do something as stupid as stealing, Henry would've sworn he'd pocket Van Cliburn or even Elton John, for pity's sake! The thirteen-year-old loved the piano with a consuming and genetically unexplainable passion. When he wasn't playing whatever sport was in season, he was feeding one pianist or another into his ears via his Discman or he was seated at the keyboard, his long, nimble fingers dancing through anything from Liszt to "Great Balls of Fire."

Much more troubling than the boy's taste was why he'd felt the need to steal at all. Moral considerations aside, Henry thought, the child support he paid every month would preclude the need for such a reckless act of . . . what? Rebellion? Was that what it was? Some pubescent rite of passage as unavoidable as acne?

The crushing burden of being thirteen had never reduced *him* to delinquency, Henry assured himself righteously. On the other hand, there was that time when . . . He grimaced as a few adolescent memories rose to haunt him. Nothing in more than thirty hard-lived years since came close for sheer reckless stupidity. And he had to admit it: aside from rioting hormones, he'd had no reason to rebel. He'd never wanted for friends, for modest luxuries, for parental affection. Hell, the Cleaver clan had been dysfunctional compared to his family! Henry fingered his short graying beard and followed the thought: his *two*-parent family. Was Sam's theft, like a number of increasingly serious misdeeds in the two years since his parents had split, an expression of the boy's anger? Insecurity? A cry for attention?

Henry harrumphed. Enough with the armchair psychology; this called for professional advice. He made a note to call his friend and former brother-in-law—brother of a different ex—and having mentally relegated the problem to the capable Dr. David Friedman, he suddenly remembered the time.

He scooped up a hodgepodge of papers, grabbed his hat, and hurried to his car. With his usual disregard for such constraints as speed limits, he gunned it. He was late for a conference that he himself had called at the studio, and a lot of high-priced talent, producers, correspondents, and bean counters for *The Open File* would not be pleased to be kept waiting.

According to the latest ratings, the Woolf Television newsmagazine show of which Henry was supervising producer had taken a slight upswing. Although he was privately a bit superstitious about examining gift-horse molars, an embarrassing and unprofessional failing he'd never admit, Henry was expected to pinpoint the factor or combination of factors that had produced this unexpected uptrend and capitalize on it.

He had his theories.

A not unimportant factor, in his opinion, was gadding about the Lowcountry of South Carolina right about now, living high on the hog in one of her filthy-rich grandfather's houses, the exact number of which Henry hadn't gotten straight. Ariel Gold had always been an able and hardworking producer for the show. Lately, however—in fact, ever since the events of the previous winter when in hardly more than a fell swoop she'd lost her memory and found an identity and an identical twin she'd never known existed—Ariel had become first-rate. Her twin was dead and so, in a sense, was the old Ariel Gold.

The events had been life altering, and Henry still couldn't explain the sea change Ariel had undergone. Neither could she, but she'd chosen not to deal with it, an anomaly for one of the most relentlessly inquisitive people Henry knew. The old Ariel had been remote and rather grim, a low-profile loner camouflaged by excess flesh, Clark Kent glasses, and a wardrobe Elizabeth II would consider frumpy.

Her twin had been a successful fashion model.

Ariel had relearned the ropes of her profession with the zeal of a televangelist. She'd tackled the dreariest jobs without complaint. She'd mastered her nemesis, the computer. She'd watched and listened and studied the techniques and procedures of her coworkers. She'd become a living encyclopedia of facts about the competition. She pored over newspapers and periodicals searching for any incident or subject that could possibly provide one of the unresolved stories in which *The Open File* specialized, and with her nearly photographic memory, she could recite the assimilated information at will.

From the earliest days of her personal cataclysm, Ariel had looked different. At first, the changes had been as subtle as a lift to her carriage, a nuance of body language. Henry could swear she even smelled different—like some kind of special soap. Or some elusive, almost-remembered thing: rain on forest flowers, maybe, or . . . He shifted in his seat.

New little touches, Henry recalled, had been added to her clothes: a pin or scarf or belt worn in a deceptively offhand way.

Then, as the extra pounds had begun to disappear, the clothes themselves had changed, as had the face.

Henry was convinced that the unprecedented facility with hair and makeup as well as the attention to grooming—the shaping of eyebrows, manicuring of nails, and whatever other arcane things it is that women do to themselves—wasn't the result of some mysterious zap of knowledge. Any halfway-intelligent woman who reads umpteen magazines every month must pick up that stuff, and a few things are going to be obvious if she simply looks in the mirror. Henry believed the old Ariel had avoided just that. She no longer did, and that, he contended, was the mysterious factor.

He didn't contend it to Ariel; she didn't want to hear it.

The changes in Ariel were no more baffling to Henry than the changes in himself—or more accurately, in his feelings toward her. He knew she was no longer just somebody who worked for him; he wasn't sure what she was.

He hadn't opened that can of worms with himself, let alone with Ariel.

5

THE DAY BEFORE, ARIEL HAD LEARNED TWO THINGS THAT DIFFERENTiate the Atlantic and Pacific coasts. The first thing was obvious; 98 percent humidity is hard to ignore. The second was that even if the Atlantic's warmer—it was off South Carolina, anyway—you still spend a lot more time in the water trying to cool off. That led to a third painful lesson: when you're back and forth into the ocean like a sweat-slick yo-yo, not all "waterproof" sunscreens live up to their advertising.

Ariel squirmed at the breakfast table, trying to find some position in which the backs of her angry red thighs didn't come in contact with the cane seat of the chair. She reeked of Noxzema, she was sending off heat waves like a Roman candle (legal in this state, she'd noticed), and she felt as if she'd slept on 60 grit sandpaper. At least Hattie wasn't there to abrade her even further.

On rising, she'd found an empty house and a terse note informing her that the housekeeper would be spending the day with a cousin in Beaufort. "Back after supper," Hattie had written in an incongruously elegant script. "Crab salad in the icebox if you want it."

Ariel had been relieved to find the woman gone; on the other hand, it was awfully quiet.

Listlessly, she sliced a peach onto her cereal, licked sweet juice from her fingers, and listened to the ceiling fan whir. She hoped this wasn't to be the pattern for the whole long, unseasonably torrid weekend. What, she wondered, would she do with herself? She didn't know anybody. It was too hot to go into Charleston, and she couldn't go back to the beach.

She peeled the T-shirt from her parboiled upper body to let in a little air. She wished she'd lost more than the thirty pounds she had; there'd be less skin to hurt. She wished that this particular weekend hadn't been targeted for a record-breaking heat wave. She wished she hadn't let B.F. pester her into coming here.

"Poor, poor pitiful me," she sang off-key, and ate her cereal.

It was nearly sundown when Ariel put aside an acrostic puzzle that refused to be solved and considered going into the house for something cool to drink. Instead, she pushed herself to and fro in her chair, one of several white rockers that lined the wide wraparound porch, and gazed out into the yard, a lush, peaceful, and somewhat untamed jungle of palmettos and giant live oaks dripping Spanish moss. Today had been just what she'd needed: uninterrupted inertia. She rested her head against the chair's high back and listened to a distant, solemn rumble. The thunder didn't alarm her; it had been grumbling throughout the afternoon like a querulous giant. Now, however, Ariel saw that a large, very black cloud had stolen in from somewhere. The last, dazzling shafts of sunlight streaked from behind it, bathing a delicate pink sky with gold.

The next thunderclap was louder, a roll of bass drums echoing and reechoing into the distance. The voice that came from behind Ariel was almost as deep. She shrieked like a peacock, sprang from her chair, and spun around.

"Whoa, now, Ariel Gold!" B.F. Coulter exclaimed as he pushed open the screen door. "You like to fell off the porch!"

One hand to her chest, her mouth an O of shock, Ariel grasped the porch rail for support. A number of possible responses suggested themselves, but as her heartbeat throttled down to normal, she glared at the huge white-haired old man and merely said, "You know, you talk like somebody who's never seen indoor plumbing. Isn't that kind of strange considering you just got off your own private jet?"

"Stop makin' light of plain English and come here to me."

"Watch out for the sunburn," Ariel said and stepped into her grandfather's grizzly-bear embrace.

* * *

"How come Hattie to go off and leave you?" B.F. asked, glowering at the crab salad on his plate. "I wouldn't of let Sarge go over to Monroe's if I'd known there wasn't anybody here to cook something substantial." He forked in a mouthful of the offending salad. "How'd you like that Frogmore stew, by the way?"

"I imagine she went because she preferred her cousin's company to mine." Ariel flinched as a particularly loud boom of thunder followed within seconds of a lightning flash. "And *I* can cook, you know, but there's nothing wrong with this. It's good, and so was the stew, even though it wasn't a stew at all. Why do they call it that? And who is '*Mun*-roe'?" she asked, imitating her grandfather's pronunciation.

"Fellow that sees after the property and the car and so on. His wife's been down with something, and Sarge brought 'em some vegetables and—I don't know—some other stuff he put up." B.F. waved his fork, dismissing the caretaker as well as Sarge, the retired L.A.P.D. detective who was his cook and bodyguard. "I don't appreciate Hattie leavin' you by yourself," he complained, "and you not knowin' anybody. I didn't get her up here from Florida to visit her kinfolks."

"Let it be, okay? Hattie's concerned about you. Thinks I'm a fortune hunter. Maybe she'll come around in time."

"Listen," B.F. said. "It's startin'." He cocked an ear, smiling into space as first tiny pings and then hard bullets of rain began to drum against the tin roof of the house. "How in the world you can live in L.A. and not hear a good downpour from one year to the next is beyond me.

"Okay." He pointed the tines of his fork toward Ariel, pinning her to a bargain. "I won't say anything to Hattie. But you got to promise you won't put up with any guff from that ornery old woman. She takes too much on herself—always has. Her and confounded Sarge McManus both."

Ariel heard noises and, on cue, that gentleman came in from the kitchen, drying his sparse, graying crew cut with a dish towel and carrying a Coca-Cola.

"Starting to come down," Sarge informed them. The short, square, and formidably solid man nodded hello to Ariel.

"You never heard of basal cell carcinoma?" he asked.

It took Ariel a long, puzzled moment to connect the question to her sunburn, a condition for which B.F. had already chastised her. "Evening, Sarge," she said. "How's Mrs. Monroe?"

"Nothing wrong with her that not having six kids wouldn't cure. That peckerwood of a husband of hers ought to take up a hobby and keep his . . ." Hearing his own unintended pun and clearly not knowing where to go with the rest of his comment, Sarge reddened from his broad face to his nonexistent neck, looking like a tinted concrete block.

Quickly, he turned to his employer. "B.F.," he began and then jutted his lower lip belligerently. The old man's big shoulders were shaking with laughter.

"I wouldn't be usin' terms like 'peckerwood' if I were you," B.F. advised. "People hereabouts are bound to take offense at some near-Yankee comin' down here low-ratin' 'em."

"Monroe said there's been some burglaries in the area recently," Sarge said, ignoring the gibe. "In the summer houses. A man over on Edisto Island walked in on one in progress, and whoever it was put him in the hospital. Bashed him on the head."

"What man on Edisto?" B.F. asked, completely serious now.

"Nobody we know. A doctor from, I think, New Jersey, and unfortunately, he didn't get a good look at anybody. The talk is it's local boys, but none of the stuff that's been taken has turned up, so who knows.

"B.F., it's long past time to get a security system in here, and we're not arguing anymore about it. Now, I'm going into Charleston tomorrow to take care of it, and once the thing's installed, I want both of you"—he included Ariel in his order—"to make sure you keep it activated."

When the telephone rang, Ariel realized that it was the first time she'd heard it since she'd been here. Almost before she could place where the ringing was coming from, Sarge was on his way to the kitchen. He was gone for quite a while, and when he returned, his face was pale. He licked his lips and made one or two false starts before he could speak.

"That was Foy down at the tackle shop," he told B.F. "Somebody came in there and told him that John William's been found dead." He crossed his arms in front of his chest as if to block the bad news he'd already heard. "He said it was suicide."

Ariel looked from Sarge to her grandfather and saw the same anguish. In a small voice, she asked, "Who's John William?"

6

"LORD HAVE MERCY. I CAN'T BELIEVE IT'S HAPPENED AGAIN!"

Ariel found B.F. slouched low in a wing chair, staring at his stockinged feet and muttering to himself. Chin on chest, long, thick legs planted on a footstool, he cradled a snifter of brandy. It appeared to be untasted, perhaps forgotten.

Following Sarge's obviously traumatic announcement, the two men had stared long and hard at each other, and after giving Ariel's hand an absentminded pat, B.F. had taken the younger man into the kitchen, where they'd briefly conferred. She'd heard the back door close, and B.F. had returned alone, shaking his head sadly. He hadn't seemed disposed to talking, and Ariel had busied herself clearing dinner away. She still didn't know who John William was.

"B.F.," she began and halted when she heard footsteps in the hall. She turned to see Hattie in the living room doorway, patting at her wet face with a big, man-sized handkerchief. Ariel could see droplets of rain sparkling on her coarse gray hair.

"I heard," Hattie told B.F.

Without raising his eyes, he murmured, "Yep."

"They're sayin' he took his own life."

"Humph."

Evidently regarding his grunt as a request for information, Hattie said, "At the Barron house in Charleston. In his car, closed up in the garage, they say." As awful as this pronouncement would be in any circumstances, the words seemed to Ariel to be weighted with extra significance. She looked to see what B.F.'s reaction would be.

With the smallest twitch of the head, he merely closed his eyes. After several seconds he whispered something that sounded like "Lord have mercy."

Hattie crumpled the damp handkerchief in her fist and studied her employer, her face a scowl of anxious concern. Then, with a glance at Ariel, she left in the direction of the kitchen. Since it didn't look as if she was going to get anything out of B.F., Ariel considered going after Hattie. That idea was quickly dismissed. She settled in a chair facing his and, busying herself with needlework, she waited.

A petit point lily had blossomed before B.F. roused himself.

"Small-town grapevines," he grumbled, apparently to divert himself from more painful lines of thought. He took the first sip of the brandy. "By midnight they'll have that poor soul neck deep in some kind of scandal. Dealin' dope or some such hogwash, I wouldn't be surprised." He glanced at Ariel, and his lips folded onto each other in a weary, humorless smile. "John William was a druggist," he explained. "A pharmacist."

His gaze fell on the needlepoint, and he sighed. "Jane used to do that kind of stuff, did I ever tell you that? I swear, I wish you two could've known one another! Wouldn't it be something if you could both be here? Sewin' on your little doilies together?"

"It's not a doily." Seeing her grandfather slipping deeper into gloom, Ariel was brisk. "B.F., tell me what this John William was to you. Who was he?"

The old man set his glass on the piecrust table beside him. Laboriously, he bent over to loosen his socks, tugging them away from his toes, which he wiggled luxuriously.

"John William Barron was Sarge's nephew. I've known him forever. Knew his father, too—Sarge's brother. You recall that oil over my fireplace in L.A.? The one you admired? It was John Barron, John *Early* Barron, that painted it, and John Early Barron was John William's daddy."

"Now wait. How come Sarge *McManus* has a brother named Barron? And another thing, when I asked you who the subject of the painting was, didn't you say, 'He'd be a very old man by now, or dead'? The man in the painting was young, like maybe twenty. Surely the artist was at least that age, but Sarge is only—what? Sixty?"

B.F. held up three fingers.

"Okay, sixty-three." Ariel gave her head a little shake to rattle her brain into accurate mathematics. "His brother must have started painting awfully young. Or he must have been a good bit older than Sarge or . . . ? I'm getting myself confused."

B.F. chuckled. "Always the analytical investigator, aren't you? No, you're right. John would be over eighty if he was livin', and he was actually Sarge's stepbrother. He was more like a second daddy, though, and Sarge worshiped and adored him. You know, it kind of ran in that family," he mused, "havin' kids way apart in age, I mean. Same thing happened with John."

"B.F., could you start at the beginning? This isn't getting any clearer."

"It's not complicated. John Barron's father died, and his mother got remarried to Jackson McManus, Sarge's daddy. He was a widower, okay?"

"So far, so good."

"Sarge wasn't but a little guy, I reckon maybe two or three. John would've been about grown, though—painting already—and it couldn't have been too very many years later that he got married himself. That first wife wasn't exactly on the same footing as John—society-wise, if you follow what I mean—and I hardly even knew the girl. The marriage lasted just about long enough for their daughter to be born before the mama ran off with a drummer." He smirked. "The travelin' salesman type, not the musician type. Now, I tell you what's the truth: that *was* a scandal! The Barrons were an old family in these parts, real aristocracy." B.F. shook his head, remembering. "It was right about that time, right before the girl flew the coop, when I got to be friends with John. Would've been about nineteen forty or not too much later. John held up his head, faced 'em all down, and raised his daughter—as stiff-necked as if his wife had just stepped out to a meeting of the missionary society. But he was a different man after that."

"Stop right there. You've never told me, you know, how you came to know Sarge or that he came from this part of the country—or that you did, for that matter."

"I didn't. Your grandmother was from Charleston. Family home there fell to the wrecker's ball, but this house we're sittin' in was originally her family's, too, their summer home. She inherited it. She was always the happiest when we were here, I think."

Ariel's eye went to a cluster of framed photographs she'd examined earlier. There were several of two girls in various stages of growing up. Jane, of course, and B.F.'s daughter, Suzanne, Jane's and Ariel's mother. It wasn't these she studied now but an older, tinted portrait of a pretty young woman with softly waved brown hair and a small bouquet of gardenias at her breast.

"How did you meet your—meet my grandmother?"

"Atlanta. That's where I met Miss Margaret." B.F. seemed more than willing to be diverted to a more cheerful tale.

"She was visitin' cousins down there. The father was a big banker. I was lookin' for a loan. He invited me home to dinner. He had two daughters, unmarried then and now—for pretty obvious reasons. They looked like bulldogs and sounded like Chihuahuas and didn't have as much sense as either one. Anyhow, despite the fact that I wasn't too prosperous at that time, I reckon he was of the opinion that I'd amount to something. Or, more likely, he was just desperate for some sap to marry one of those two poor mongrels off to. It didn't work out like he had in mind, though. I met Margaret.

"Her family had plenty—old money—and they weren't exactly tickled at me courtin' her; they didn't see me as the chalk the banker did—"

"The what?"

"The chalk. The hot pick. You know, a good prospect. You're not into the sport of kings, I take it?"

"Get on with your story."

B.F. swallowed brandy and shrugged. "That's about the size of it. Margaret, for one of the few times in her sweet, vague life, put her back up. She was bound and determined to have me, and have me she did, for twenty-four years—and pretty fair ones they were." He grinned a slow grin. "Margaret, like the banker, knew how to pick 'em."

Ariel gave her grandfather a long-suffering look. "Maybe we should get back to the Barrons."

B.F. blew out a lungful of air and reluctantly said, "That was the story I was tellin', wasn't it? John's story, and John William's.

As of tonight, we know that the son's has got no happier an ending than the father's." The old man took a sip of brandy and smoothed white hair as wispy as dandelion fuzz. "Where was I?"

"The wife had run off with a drummer, and John was painting and raising his daughter, and it was somewhere around nineteen forty."

B.F. nodded, thought for a minute, and took up his narrative.

"John Barron eventually got to be well known, and I don't mean just hereabouts. Truth is, I halfway expected you to know the name. His work's been shown all over the country—the world, for that matter—and since there's not a whole lot of it around, it's hard to come by. Bad thing is, all this appreciation came too late.

"Not bein' a success while he was livin' wasn't a financial problem for John. He'd inherited a right smart from his mama and invested very well. It did make him a melancholy sort of person, though. Moody. Had spells of bad headaches, as I recall, and he got to be something of a hermit. The irony is, that worked for him posthumously—made for kind of a 'mystique,' you know what I mean? Eccentric, tragic artist that shunned the limelight, blah, blah, blah. It wasn't just hype. There wasn't but a few of us could say we knew him—or thought we did. But I'm gettin' ahead of myself.

"After years of John bein' a loner, like I say, it seemed like things were lookin' up. When he was in his forties, he married again. Grace." B.F. sighed. "Ah, me!" he said, and a tired smile lit his face. "Amazin' Grace!"

He drained the last of his brandy and glanced at the lamp beside him, which, like all the lights in the house just then, dimmed, failed for a second, and then buzzed back into life.

"Might ought to get out some candles if this storm keeps up," he said. The admonition had hardly been voiced when Hattie came in bearing a kerosene lantern and matches. She placed them handy to B.F. and, without comment, left again. As if there had been no interruption, B.F. continued.

"Grace was from away. John met her, as I recall, up North, and a gorgeous thing she was! A little bit unpolished right at first, I s'pose, but, Lord! Hair black as night but the bluest eyes . . . You know that kind of beauty? You couldn't blame John for bein' foolish enough to marry a girl young enough to be his daughter. She *wasn't* that much older than Halley, matter of fact, but—"

"Who's Halley?"

"John's daughter. I already told you about her."

"But you didn't— Never mind. Go on."

"Well, some would disagree, but it looked to me like John did all right marryin' Grace. What happened couldn't be laid at her feet. Girl was like sunshine! Tried her best to get John to lighten up and seemed like she was makin' headway. I saw him a time or two that year they were together, and I'd have sworn he was happy."

B.F. stopped talking and stared, preoccupied, into the distance behind Ariel.

"What happened?" she finally asked.

"Same thing as tonight. Different car, same result. One cold fall night John Barron closed the garage door, got into his brand new nineteen fifty-six Buick Roadmaster, and turned on the engine."

"Oh, dear." Ariel digested the information. "I wondered why everyone was so sure what happened tonight wasn't an accident."

B.F.'s mouth twitched as if he was about to say more. When he didn't, Ariel put aside the needlework she'd long since forgotten, moved to his chair, and began to massage his shoulders. She was kneading the back of his neck, pondering his recollections, when the lights went out, this time for good.

In the pitch black she heard a match being struck, and the lantern flared to life just as brilliance flashed outside the big living room windows. The echoing thunder was dying when Ariel said, "Wait a minute! Didn't you leave out something kind of germane here? What about John William? Where'd he come from?"

B.F. set the lantern on the table and settled back, requesting with an impatient hitch of his shoulder that she get back to the job at hand.

"He was born about seven or eight months after his daddy died," he said. "For all I know, John didn't even know he was on the way."

He glanced over his shoulder and, his voice dry, said, "Don't waste your time thinkin' it. John William Barron didn't just favor his daddy; he was John's spittin' image. There wasn't any question about that from the day he was born. Unfortunately," he added, "he inherited more from John than his looks."

7

"HENRY? IT'S ARIEL."

"I know who you are. What's wrong?"

"How do you know something's wrong?"

"Why don't you just tell me."

The telephone, which had died along with the power the night before, had finally been resuscitated, and Ariel had wasted no time in calling Los Angeles. Even though it was Saturday, she'd found Henry at his desk, a not uncommon occurrence. He sounded as if something was stuffed in his mouth, also not uncommon.

"What are you eating?"

"Tofu. Stop asking silly questions and get to the point."

"I won't be back on Tuesday. It seems I'm going to be going to a funeral right about then."

"Good God! It's not B.F.?"

"No, no!"

"Who?"

"A man named John William Barron. Somebody I never met."

"I'm not sure I want to hear the answer to this, but why are you going to the funeral of a man you never met? Is that some kind of Southern thing?"

Ariel gave the receiver a look. She'd been adamant at first. When B.F. had begged her to stay over and go with him to the services, she'd said "absolutely not." She hadn't brought anything suitable to wear, she'd said. "Buy something," B.F. had said. She hadn't known the man, she'd said; his people would resent some stranger at the funeral. "He didn't have that many people," B.F. had said, "and neither do I. You're about the only people I've got left," he'd said. That had pretty much cinched it.

"They're doing an autopsy," she told Henry now, "so we're not sure when the services will be, but I think Tuesday. And, listen, do me a favor; get somebody on an artist, a painter named John Early Barron, okay? He committed suicide in nineteen fifty-six, in Charleston."

Ariel could almost hear the blood starting to pump in Henry's brain.

"You said this newly deceased person was named Barron, too, didn't you? What's the connection? How'd he die? Why are they doing an autopsy? Who's John Early Barron?"

Ariel couldn't help grinning. She knew exactly what Henry's eyes looked like right now. His hand would be reaching for a pencil. She could also picture the crumbs—from a cinnamon bun or a doughnut—caught in his beard. "Cool your jets, Henry. This isn't grist for the *Open File* mill. I'm just curious."

"That's a new quality."

" 'A man should live if only to satisfy his curiosity,' " Ariel pontificated, still grinning.

"To what sage are we indebted for that gem of wisdom?"

"I think it's a Yiddish proverb."

"Oy! A Yiddish proverb in a cornpone accent! Speaking of which, how's it going with Daddy Warbucks down there in Dixieland—other than an apparent dearth of entertainment? I have to assume that's why you're dropping in on strangers' funerals?"

"It got off to a slow start, but even with this death you're poking fun at—which is a tragic business—I'm glad I came. For the first time I can remember, not being *able* to remember isn't a problem. I was never here before and never knew any of these folks before I lost my memory marbles, so I'm not at the disadvantage I am back there. It's a huge relief, to tell you the truth."

"Speaking of which, again, I suppose it's a waste to ask whether you remember a story we were putting together about nine months ago? Disappearance that got a lot of play at the time? The computer tycoon?"

"Can't say that I do." Ariel smiled at Hattie, who trudged by pushing an antique vacuum cleaner. Hattie grimaced back with something that might pass for a smile. "And," Ariel said into the phone, "in these last months I've looked at every *Open File* that ever aired."

"This one didn't air."

"Oh. Was it one of my segments?"

"No. It was Richard Cummings's. He left the show before you came—or came back, so to speak. Before the amnesia."

"Why are you asking about it?"

"No reason. Look, I've got to go. Are you going to be back on Wednesday or when?"

"I'll call you," Ariel said.

Henry grunted something unintelligible and disconnected.

"Yeah," Ariel said to the dead line. "It was good to talk to you, too."

The instant she replaced the receiver, a deafening roar started up in the dining room, and almost before it began, an even greater roar came from the living room.

"Cut that confounded Hoover off!" B.F. bellowed.

The heavy, eight-foot-high pocket doors that separated the two rooms—solid heart pine, according to B.F.—slid closed, and the roar became a muffled hum.

"Have you ever considered getting this house air-conditioned?" Ariel asked, joining her grandfather and pouring herself a glass of tea from a pitcher beside him.

"Nope."

"I see." She plucked the last cube from a vintage aluminum ice bucket and cooled her forehead with it before surrendering it to the glass.

"You'd think the rain would've broken the heat, wouldn't you?" she asked rhetorically and then, seeing the newspaper on his lap, asked, "Anything in there about John William?"

"Just a little ol' story on page two. No obituary. Guess it was too late to get much in."

Ariel took the main news section he offered, found the story, and, in a brief first paragraph, read that the body of John William Barron, thirty-six, a Charleston pharmacist and lifelong resident of the city, had been found at his home the night before and that the cause of death was under investigation. The remaining, longer paragraphs detailed that the deceased had been the son of "a Charleston painter of international renown."

John Early Barron, according to the article, had achieved little recognition during his lifetime, "struggling as a plein air painter of Lowcountry landscapes and a portraitist in an era dominated by Abstract Expressionism."

Posthumous acclaim, it seemed, had come primarily through "his legacy of stirring portraits." The Native Americans of the Southeast, particularly the Cherokee and the Seminole, had been favored subjects; " 'But,' " Ariel read aloud, " 'it was with Barron's portraits of the Gullah people of the Sea Islands that he truly came into his own.' What's Gullah?"

"Black folks hereabout. Their language. Creole, it is, and sweet as blackstrap to hear. Kin to Geechee."

"What's . . . Never mind." Ariel returned to the paper. She read that Barron's work was in great demand by present-day collectors and that "public collections in which his work is represented include the Charleston Museum locally and the Cleveland Museum of Art, the Art Institute of Chicago and Vose Galleries of Boston."

The article closed by reporting that "the artist's poignant narrative style is thought to provide insight into his own troubled life, which ended tragically early, surrounded by rumor and speculation." John Early Barron had died at his home in Charleston in nineteen fifty-six, a suicide. He was forty-four.

"Wow! Your old friend's not small potatoes, is he?"

Getting no comment but a shrug of the eyebrows from B.F., Ariel asked, "What 'rumor and speculation'?"

"People kill themselves, buzzards gather."

"They do everything here but say John William killed himself, too, don't they? I wonder if he left a note. Hey!" She'd just realized what wasn't in the newspaper. "You flaked out on me before you finished your story last night. Did John William have a family? Was he married?"

"Was once. Lasted about as long as his daddy's marriages did, only there weren't any children to this one. The Barrons were a proud and fruitful family in the old days, but it looks like they're about played out."

The doors rumbled open, and there was a momentary surge of vacuum cleaner racket before Sarge, wincing, slid them shut.

"Autopsy's later today," he said. "Funeral's Tuesday."

B.F. nodded. "They find a note?"

"Nope."

"Surprisin'. I haven't seen a lot of John William in the last few years, but I wouldn't have thought he'd changed that much."

Sarge let out a mirthless laugh. "He did love to make the most of a dramatic moment."

"Get right down to it, though, it's pretty unusual for *any* suicide not to write himself a eulogy—or an excuse. Any luck locatin' Grace or Halley?"

"Yeah, John William had their numbers in his book. Living in Savannah, both of them." Sarge had poured himself tea, but finding only water in the ice bucket, he set the glass down and crammed his hands into his pockets. "All those years being a cop, and telling the next of kin's still rotten. More fool me to volunteer."

The distant snore of the vacuum cleaner ceased, and in the profound silence that settled, Sarge wandered to one of the windows overlooking the front porch. The dull light of the overcast afternoon filtered through the old glass, tinting his face gray.

"I'm not sure Grace even understood what I was telling her," he said. "She got weepy but not like you'd think, you know? Hearing her only son was dead? I haven't laid eyes on the woman in thirty years, so I can't judge, but I'd swear she was loaded."

"What about Halley?" B.F. asked. "How'd she take it?"

Sarge frowned. "Different story altogether. From all the reaction I got, I could've been calling to remind her that her subscription to *Reader's Digest* was running out."

"Didn't you tell me she and her brother were close?"

"*He* thought so. Maybe it was one-sided. I haven't seen Halley any more recently than Grace. Fact is, I don't think I'd know her if I ran into her on the street."

"Grief takes people in different ways," B.F. remarked, "and Halley's got Barron blood. If she's turned out anything like her daddy—proud as a sultan, John was—she could be in mortal anguish and act like she was at a garden party."

Just then there came a faint ringing from the upper story of the house. Before Ariel could identify the sound, B.F. muttered, "Fax." He pushed himself up from the wing chair and, taking a moment to get his balance, declared, "I'll probably be on the phone awhile. Call me when supper's ready."

"Let me get you some ice," Ariel suggested to Sarge and took the bucket. When she'd returned and filled his glass, she said, "I'm very sorry about your nephew."

"Yeah. Thanks."

"I gather you two were close?"

Sarge held the glass to his cheek in a gesture not unlike her own earlier attempt to combat the oppressive mugginess.

"You could say that. I didn't see him that often, and we had about as much in common as . . ." Unable to think of a better analogy, he shrugged and said, "We were different as night and day, but I tried to, like they say, 'be there for him.' "

"B.F. said he didn't have a family."

"That's right."

"Do you have any idea—does anyone have any idea what made him do this thing?"

The burly man's jaw muscle worked convulsively for long seconds. He was biting back, Ariel thought, the strong desire to tell her to mind her own business. In the end he simply said, "A note would've been helpful."

Ariel thought, "When a man despairs, he does not write; he commits suicide." Aloud she said, "It's a puzzle, isn't it, that he didn't leave one?"

"Yes."

This last was said with a certain amount of finality, and Ariel changed direction. "I hadn't known that you grew up around here. How'd you happen to end up in L.A.?"

"It was about the most distance I could put between myself and here without leaving the country."

"B.F. said he'd known you pretty much all your life, but he didn't say how you came to be working for him."

"It's no big deal. He told you about my brother?"

Ariel nodded.

"When John died—the way he died—I couldn't stay around here. I cut out. Got into the police academy in L.A., got married, got divorced, got shot by a punk in a Seven-Eleven. I was off-duty, buying a pack of cigarettes; he was holding it up. I got disability, got early retirement. End of story."

"Why do I think you've skipped a few chapters? From what I

know of your career, it was distinguished by several commendations along the way to retirement."

"Okay," Sarge said, "I was a regular Joe Friday."

"To go from the L.A.P.D. to being B.F.'s personal Paul Prudhomme and Punjab—which is a weird combination, if you don't mind my saying so . . . that's kind of a big leap."

As if the question had served to remind him of his duties, he said, "I've got a flounder to stuff."

The unlikely-looking cook headed for the kitchen. He didn't ask Ariel to follow along, but then he didn't ask her not to.

She watched, reverently, while he chopped onions, celery, and red pepper with the lethal-looking skill of a Benihana chef, performed what amounted to a surgical procedure on the fish, and diced country ham into little more than atoms. He was whipping eggs, his granite biceps bulging under his shirt sleeve, when he finally responded to her last comment.

"I didn't go to work for B.F. directly from the job. I had some money from my dad—nothing like what John inherited from his mother, but enough to open a small restaurant in West L.A. I'd always loved to cook, and I had an idea that good food, well prepared and reasonably priced, would go over."

He dropped butter into a big iron skillet. "Take my advice," he said. "Don't open a restaurant."

"It should've worked."

"It didn't. B.F. bailed me out of some heavy debts. Then he got sick and—"

"What do you mean, 'got sick'? How sick?"

Dumping the vegetables into the pan, Sarge stirred, squinting over his shoulder at her. "Bypass. He didn't tell you about that?"

"He did not."

"I don't watch his diet because I want to deny him pleasure."

Ariel got to her feet abruptly and, arms crossed, walked away from this unwelcome knowledge. After several minutes of staring out at the backyard, she asked, "Is he all right now?"

"Better than he deserves to be." Sarge set the pan on a cool burner. "We all have our vices," he said, and with that, pulled an unfiltered cigarette from his pocket and went past her into the yard. He struck a light, inhaled with obvious pleasure, and after three or four deep drags, ground the cigarette under his feet.

There was a touching delicacy and embarrassment about the way he pincered the butt and deposited it in a nearby trash can.

"Three a day, tops," he said, and went back to work.

"B.F. did something for me when John died," he presently said, "something big, and I never forgot it. It wasn't the first thing, and the bailout wasn't the last. I paid back the financial debt a long time ago, but I won't be going anywhere very far away as long as he's around." His frankness invited an observation.

"You don't still mistrust me, do you," Ariel commented.

"Nope. I checked you out."

"You—" She closed her lips.

"It was Hattie's idea, but I would've anyway. I went after you like I was back in harness, trying to poke holes in some suspect's story. I checked it all: the commune where you and Jane were born, your being taken by the Children's Services people, your adoption, your marriage, your husband getting wasted. It was all like you claimed. Trust me, you wouldn't be sitting in B.F. Coulter's kitchen otherwise."

Ariel didn't waste time resenting his witch-hunt; she was glad of it. "Did you find out anything I hadn't?"

"Not as far as I know." Sarge took in her disappointment and smiled crookedly. "There is one thing I want to ask you, though."

"What's that?"

"Prudhomme I know, but who's Punjab?"

It took Ariel a few seconds to remember the reference. She laughed. "You never read *Little Orphan Annie?* The big guy . . . Daddy Warbucks's fearless bodyguard?"

"Go get your granddaddy," Sarge said. "Tell him dinner's on."

8

John William Barron's funeral was held in Charleston's Saint Michael's Episcopal Church, where (as B.F. had informed Ariel during a carriage ride through the city) George Washington and Robert E. Lee had each worshiped during visits.

The attendance this day wasn't that notable, nor was it large. A quietly dressed group of mourners—neighbors, local business-people, and customers of the pharmacy John William had owned, as speculated by B.F.—dotted the pews of the historic church.

Ariel saw none of the people she'd met at a dinner party she and her grandfather had attended the night before. Few of that group had known the dead man, and even they hadn't known him well. She herself, Jane nearly reincarnate, had been of much greater interest than had poor John William. She'd practically been able to see thought balloons bubbling up from their heads: *Not as slender as Jane by a long shot. . . . Not as charmin' as her sister was; must come from bein' raised up North or wherever. . . . Reckon why the girl didn't get that little gap between her front teeth fixed? . . . What d'you reckon this one did to her nose? Looks like she stole it from Vivien Leigh!*

Ariel couldn't blame people for making comparisons; she did it herself. She rubbed her sunburned, too perfect, surgically altered nose and wondered what it would have been like to grow up with Jane. Would she have been jealous, always trying to live up to that unstudied perfection? But if she'd been raised with the love and approval lavished on Jane, would she have had reason to *be* jealous? What would she be like today? What if? What if? As she'd heard Hattie say, "If frogs had wings they wouldn't bump their butts so much."

Hattie had declined to attend the funeral, saying she'd been to too many in her life. Ariel noticed that there were no black people in the church, and she wondered if that was an indication of a more genuine reason.

She looked around to see if, on the off chance, the man from that first night on the beach was there. He wasn't. The tragedy of the suicide and a full social and sight-seeing schedule had driven that surreal encounter from her mind, but she made a mental note to ask B.F. later if he knew who the man could be.

Other than Sarge, the only family member in attendance was a single woman who, it was whispered, must be the sister, Halley. She'd arrived only moments before the service began and taken a seat, alone, on the front pew. She wore a black suit and a hat with an almost opaque black veil. She kept her head bowed. If she wept, she did so without movement or sound, and never once did she look openly at the casket.

The casket was closed. While Ariel had had no desire to see the body, the fact that John William remained faceless in her mind made her feel even more detached. She wondered whether his manner of death had discouraged a larger crowd or whether he simply hadn't had a great many friends. She wondered why life had been unendurable to so young a man—a troubled man, Sarge and B.F. had both implied. What Ariel wondered most was: where was the mother?

Sarge still knew a few people "downtown," and his years in the L.A.P.D. were common knowledge here on his old stamping ground. Since the discovery of the body, he'd kept himself—if not in the thick of things—at least on the fringe.

He'd learned the first night that the rumors Hattie reported were true: his nephew had, to all appearances, died of carbon monoxide poisoning. The body had been found facedown across the front seat of the car. There'd been vomit on the floor. Particularly terrible had been the fact that the upper torso was hanging out the open front door, wedging it open, and one hand was extended, fingers touching the concrete floor as if reaching for help that hadn't come.

Although the coroner's report wasn't yet in, Sarge had heard that the blood and tissues had been found to be bright red. Like the nausea, the color indicated chemical asphyxiation.

The car had been in Park gear, the motor dead, the gas gauge on empty. Judging by the relatively low level of carbon monoxide remaining in the garage, the car had run out of gas hours before.

Word hadn't come down regarding estimated time of death, but it hadn't taken too much brainpower to deduce that John William had been dead for a while. From what Sarge had learned working out at a local gym with officers responding to the call, he put death a good twelve hours—maybe more—before 6:30 P.M. Friday, when the body had been found by an employee of John William, a pharmacist named Grover Washburn.

Washburn told police that he hadn't been concerned when John William wasn't at work on Friday morning, that it was often left to him to open up. He did admit to being a trifle miffed since he'd worked the previous evening, but, he'd said, John William was the boss. If he wanted to take a morning off, it was his right. When he did, he customarily gave advance notice. This time he'd left a note. Washburn found it in the ornate antique cash register at the soda fountain, an equally venerable marble-and-oak affair.

According to Sarge's sources, Washburn had gone on to say that the cash drawer had been used as a message center before. Since putting money in was one of the first duties on opening, it was a logical place to leave a note you wanted found right away. No, he'd said, no money was missing.

When his employer hadn't turned up or called by the afternoon, Washburn had grown concerned. He called the Barron home. There was no answer. Then there was a spurt of customers, one after the other. Washburn was busy all afternoon and annoyed to be left in the lurch. When he closed for the day, he detoured by the house to see what the problem was and, he was frank to say, to sound off a little. He found the door unlocked, the house empty. He walked through, calling out. Finally, he went into the garage.

B.F. nudged Ariel out of her reflections. The service was over, the mourners stirring. The minister was departing through a side door, ushering the black-shrouded Halley Barron before him.

Sarge was emerging from his position all alone in the second pew.

"Where's John William's mother?" Ariel asked her grandfather. "Where's Grace?"

B.F. shrugged, asked Sarge, and got a similar answer.

"Are we going to the cemetery?" Ariel asked.

"You didn't hear?" B.F.'s white beetle brows came together. "I'm the one s'posed to be hard of hearing. Preacher said interment's private. 'Friends' are invited to this fellow Washburn's out in Mount Pleasant." To Sarge he said, "What you reckon this private interment's about? I never heard of such a thing."

"Could be the heat. Or maybe it's got to do with Grace? Not up to seeing people and wanting to say her good-byes without looky-loos?" Sarge's lip curled. "The rumors about why he 'did it' are already flying, of course."

When they emerged from the church, Ariel was profoundly grateful that they wouldn't have to endure a graveside ceremony in the blast furnace the day had become. By the time Sarge brought B.F.'s Lincoln around, she was "glowing," as she'd heard one of the female partygoers express it the previous evening. B.F. was just plain sweating. The car's air-conditioner was in high gear, and she was glad to get the red-faced old man into the cool interior.

On the way to the suburb of Mount Pleasant, Ariel made a personal discovery. They were crossing what had to be the highest, narrowest, and most interminable bridge on the planet when she added acrophobia to what she hadn't known about herself. She clamped her eyes shut and fought light-headedness.

"Something wrong?" asked B.F. from beside her.

"Not a thing. Sun's in my eyes."

"You're wearin' sunglasses, and the windows are tinted. Jane was afraid of heights, too."

Ariel felt a change of surface under the tires, and B.F. said, "You can open 'em now."

The wake didn't resemble anything Ariel associated with a funereal gathering. Grover Washburn seemed more interested in one of the guests than in hosting, and all the guests seemed more interested in the buffet than in the dear departed. Ariel was almost run down by a portly man who was after the last deviled egg.

To give them credit, some attendees tried to adopt solemn tones, but Ariel saw more than one ill-disguised smirk and she didn't miss the whispered speculation about the absent mother.

The black-veiled woman from the church wasn't there.

"I came here to pay my respects, but I don't know who I'm s'posed to be payin' 'em *to.*" B.F. rattled the ice cubes in his glass and grumbled. "Let's go on home."

Early that evening Ariel and her grandfather were meandering the trails near his house. It would be their last walk before Ariel left for the airport, Los Angeles, and real life.

As they crossed a small wooden bridge that arced over a trickle of brackish water, a huge live oak rustled moss-draped branches above them. A bird—a hawk, B.F. said—called in the gathering dusk, and something furtive disturbed the heavy undergrowth just beyond the bridge.

"River otter," B.F. said. "Mama and babies, looks like."

Ariel saw nothing but a branch snapping back into place. She looked up to where stars had begun to prick the sky. "I'll miss all the stars," she said. "You'd never know they existed in L.A."

"You don't have to go back, you know. You'd never have to work again if you'd quit bein' so stubborn about money."

"Don't start. If you're so anxious to spend your filthy lucre, call the humane society or UNICEF or somebody."

"Well, then, at least let me fly you back."

"No." Ariel linked her arm in his. "Now, come on and let's walk over to the water. I want one more look."

The beach, consumed by a greedy high tide, was considerably shallower than on Ariel's first night on the island.

"B.F.," she said, "I met a man down here who knew you. He was . . ." When she tried to envision the face from five nights before, Ariel found that the image was no longer quite sharp. Fleetingly, she had the notion that she'd imagined the entire encounter. "He was fair, medium height. He and Jane were friends from back when they were kids, he said."

"Jane had a lot of friends, honey. I don't know . . ."

Ariel searched her mind for clues. "He was an only child, I think he said. Oh! And he went to the Citadel."

"That doesn't exactly pin him down, Ariel Gold. Why in the world didn't you just ask this fellow what his name was?"

"I did, but he . . . Never mind. It's not important. What's that?" Ariel pointed toward a small dark form at the water's edge. She took off her sneakers and plodded through the loose sand of the dunes onto the beach, but she knew before she reached it that what she'd seen was only a dead gull. The sad carcass lay with one wing outspread as if in final supplication.

Maybe it was a mood brought on by the funeral or the dying day. Maybe it was leaving her grandfather. For whatever reason, Ariel felt melancholy. Before she turned back to where he waited, she cast one last look at the shimmering water, and fragments of a poem came to her mind. "The sea," it went, "Delaying not, hurrying not/Whispered me through the night. . . . Lisped to me the low and delicious word death."

Ariel was thirty thousand feet over the Mississippi when she jerked awake from a light doze, activated her overhead light, and asked a passing flight attendant for a cup of coffee. She'd been lucky and gotten both side seats to herself. She searched her tote bag for the Charleston *Post & Courier* she'd bought at the airport.

After her hiatus on Kiawah, the headlines seemed more depressing than usual. "Can't let you out of my sight for a minute," she mumbled to the world at large, putting aside the first section for something lighter. A headline in the arts and leisure section caught her eye. "A Legacy of Despair?" it inquired, and beneath it was a human-interest piece on the renowned artist John Early Barron: his mysterious life, his great promise thwarted by a tragic early death, his only son's identical end.

The photograph that accompanied the story was that of the father, but Ariel didn't need to see the son. B.F. had said John William Barron looked like his father from the day he was born. The light eyes, the fair hair, the broad forehead, the ascetic planes of the face, were the same. The face Ariel had been unable to describe to her grandfather was once again sharp in her mind and, somehow, it was no surprise that the man on the beach had been John William.

9

"You must be Sam Heller," Ariel said to the dark-haired adolescent in Henry's office.

It was a safe guess. While the boy's eyes were light rather than dark, they were deep-set like Henry's. He also had Henry's lanky frame—an inch of wrist protruded beyond his shirt cuffs—but it was the ill-humored expression that was a dead giveaway. He offered Ariel a "what's it to you?" look and hunched over long, knobby-knuckled hands propped on bony knees. His chair creaked when he turned, ever so slightly, away.

"Is your dad around?" Ariel asked.

"Yeah. Somewhere."

Either Sam's voice had settled to maturity or he was making an effort to keep it in the baritone range.

"He didn't happen to say when he'd be back from 'somewhere'?"

"Nah."

"What's that you've got?" Ariel had just noticed the object loosely clutched in Sam's fingers.

"A CD." The boy raised martyred eyes to the ceiling.

"That much I'd figured out." Ariel craned to make out "Jerry Lee." Sam's thumb obscured the rest of the name.

"Lewis?" she asked.

He looked down as if he didn't remember which CD he had with him. "Yeah."

"I would've thought Jerry Lee Lewis was a little before your time. He was before *my* time."

A tiny spark of interest lit Sam's eyes. "Yeah, the rock and roll, sure, but you must've listened to him when he went country. That was in the nineteen sixties."

Ariel suppressed a grin. His tone suggested it was when mastodons roamed the earth. "Right. I was a big country music fan about the time I started grammar school." She folded her arms and leaned against Henry's door. "Speaking of school, hasn't it started? How'd you luck out and get the day off?"

The boy was instantly sullen again. "Dad's taking me to see a judge."

Ariel stopped herself from asking the obvious question and returned to safer ground. "Do you just absorb the music through your fingertips?"

Sam's expression turned blacker. "My Discman's *busted.*" His voice cracked on the emphatic last word, and he turned away again, this time with finality.

Oops, thought Ariel. Good thing I didn't go for something controversial like What grade are you in? What she didn't know and likely never had known about teenage boys was everything.

"Well," she said, "I can see you've got things on your mind, so I'll just mosey on back to my desk. When your dad comes back, ask him to see Ariel, would you please?"

She'd then been back at work for only two hours, and it felt as if she'd never left. The marshes and palmettos, piazzas and wrought iron of the Carolina Lowcountry seemed a century as well as a continent away, and the doomed man on the beach seemed even less real. The fact that he'd figured in a dream she'd had the night before—the granddaddy of all bizarre dreams—added to his insubstantiality.

It had been far too late to call B.F. when she'd gotten in the previous night, and in the flurry of picking up the dogs at the kennel this morning, she hadn't had time. Ariel was haunted by the possibility that she might have been the last person to see John William Barron alive, yet she didn't know what difference that really made. She felt that the Charleston authorities should be told, but what they could do with the information she didn't know. He'd certainly said nothing that night to indicate his intentions, and if he'd said anything she should report, she couldn't think what it might be.

She looked at her watch and then at her phone. She knew B.F. had flown to New York today. She punched in the number of his Manhattan condominium. There was no answer. The obstinate old walrus wouldn't hear of getting an answering machine for his personal line; on that issue he was illogical but immovable. Ariel left a message at his corporate office, where he might or might not call in during his trip, and gave up the effort. She went back to work on the idea she'd wanted to see Henry about.

After her weird dream had awakened her at dawn, she'd been unable to go back to sleep. As was her habit, she'd reached for a magazine from the stack on the bedstand, a stack that had grown to Tower of Pisa proportions with the arrivals during her absence. A report in an obscure medical publication had brought her fully awake. It was on her desk now, and Ariel was feeling the exhilaration that always came with new story ideas for *The Open File.*

The report was the work of a psychiatrist whose patient's supposed memory retrieval had led her to implicate herself in a long-unsolved murder. If the details were sketchy, they didn't contradict the evidence. The patient was a respectable citizen with nothing to gain and everything to lose. The doctor sounded a little too eager, but the ink was still wet on his report. It was new, and hot, and Ariel couldn't believe it hadn't yet been picked up. She'd gotten a booker working on locking it up first thing. It would be the hook of her piece: a look at current, sometimes controversial therapies for anxiety disorders and the impact on their beneficiaries (or victims, depending on one's point of view). After several exploratory calls, Ariel was even more fascinated by her subject.

This piece, if it came to fruition, would have nothing to do with her own situation: the amnesia that had wiped out her first thirty-one years. The exhaustive research done in aid of her own situation, however, did come in handy.

She was adding to her scribbled list of buzz phrases—post-traumatic stress disorder; false memory syndrome; EMDR, short for Eye Movement Desensitization and Reprocessing; cognitive therapy; exposure therapy—when she felt a presence at her elbow, and a curious frisson in her middle. She was caught off guard, not by the presence but by that little thrill.

"Well, hey," she said and found herself scowling for no explainable reason. "Be careful, would you?"

Henry Heller had pushed Ariel's notes to one side as he parked his behind on her desk. "I hear you met Sam," he said. "Winsome little rascal, isn't he?"

"Takes after his father." Ariel adjusted her expression. "So. I'm back."

"At last, honey chile. 'Absence makes the heart grow fonder,' et cetera. See? I can do the quotation shtick, too."

" 'Failing to be there when a man wants her is a woman's greatest sin, except to be there when he doesn't want her.' Don't do dueling quotations with me, boss; I'll mop up the floor with you."

"You got some sun."

"And I'm beginning to molt. Really ap*peal*ing, pun intended."

Henry looked at the perfect pink nose, the fine brows, and the changeable eyes that today looked green. . . . In the days when they'd hidden behind heavy, unbecoming glasses, they could've been olive drab for all he'd noticed. He took in the cheekbones, of which there'd been no vestige until recently; the wide mouth turned up in a self-deprecating grin; the healthy hair, highlighted now by the sun as well as L'Oréal or whatever. He cleared his throat. "Aaaah, you look okay."

Ariel explained the idea she was exploring and listened to congratulations for finding the obscure case study, reservations regarding overexposure of the whole memory retrieval bit, and, more enthusiastically, suggestions for a slightly different slant.

"Dad?"

Sam stood in the hallway just outside Henry's office, with his hands stuffed into the back pockets of his jeans and an impatient frown on his face. He shifted his weight from one foot to the other and said, "Aren't we supposed to be over there at eleven-thirty?"

"Right, son. Be there in a second." Distractedly, Henry began to paw through his coat pockets.

"Sam said you're taking him to see a judge?"

"Yeah. You don't happen to know the address of Judge O'Connell's office? I've got it here somewhere."

Squinting, Henry held a scrap of paper at arm's length. With his other hand he patted the same pockets he'd just been rifling.

"Here." Ariel handed Henry the reading glasses he'd dropped on her desk and asked, "Is this some kind of career counseling appointment? Is Sam interested in becoming a judge?"

Henry snorted. "Judg*ee,* more likely. O'Connell's a friend of a friend who suggested I get the judge to talk to Sam—a little 'tough love' strategy."

"Uh-oh! What's the kid done? He's not on drugs, is he?"

"Not that I know of. God, I hope not! No, Sam just decided to embark on a life of crime is all. He found some CDs he admired, and it slipped his mind he was supposed to pay for them. We returned the merchandise, and Sam apologized. The store's not pressing charges."

"Ah . . ." Ariel grimaced. "Well, you can't say he doesn't appreciate music, anyway. Just out of curiosity, what happened to his CD player?"

"I smashed it with a hammer," Henry said. "He made me mad."

Still rummaging through his pockets, he got to his feet.

"Oh, yeah. We didn't find much on that artist you wanted researched, but the folder's on my desk. Feel free to look for it."

"Right," Ariel said. The odds of locating anything in the maelstrom that was Henry's desk ranked with stumbling onto Atlantis.

She watched as he reluctantly joined his son, draping one long arm over the boy's shoulders. With neither of them looking at the other or saying a word, they left to see the judge.

10

"YOU STILL MAD AT ME?"

Ariel held the squirming, licking, frenetic mass of happiness that was Stonewall and inquired of Jessie whether she'd been forgiven.

The big German shepherd had been distant when Ariel had picked up the two dogs that morning. She'd averted her gaze whenever Ariel had tried to look her in the eye and, with immense dignity and the occasional sigh, had made it plain that she considered imprisonment in the kennel a personal betrayal.

"Guess you are. Let's get dinner in your bowl and see how things go from there."

Ariel gave Stonewall a gentle scratch above the tawny nose that matched the rest of him and released him, whereupon he cut dizzy circles from his water bowl to her shins to a disgusting, half-chewed, often buried rawhide bone he offered to share. The scruffy mutt had belonged to her twin, and B.F. had more or less forced him on Ariel after Jane died. In truth, it hadn't required all that much arm-twisting. Stonewall had claimed Ariel for his own the moment he first laid golden eyes on her. His wholeheartedness, Ariel sometimes speculated, had suggested some sort of primal, instinctive recognition. Or maybe, she thought now, he'd simply recognized the main chance.

"Yeah, yeah, yeah," she told him. "You love me, you missed me, and there's not a fickle bone in your body."

It wasn't until after Ariel had fed the dogs, checked her answering machine (on which there was no message from B.F.), gone through the accumulated mail, and sat down with her own dinner that Jessie made her first oblique move toward reconciliation. Returning from a reconnaissance trip to the backyard, she strolled over to the canister of dog treats Ariel kept on the kitchen counter. She contemplated it for a meaningful moment and then, nonchalantly, peered over her shoulder at her mistress.

"A little demonstration of who's boss, is it? I'm supposed to interrupt my dinner when you deign to acknowledge my presence?"

Jessie's eyes went back to the canister.

"You win." Ariel gave a treat to the shepherd as well as to Stonewall, who'd come tearing through the dog door the second the lid came off the canister. The smaller dog inhaled his; Jessie crunched hers politely, cleaned up a fallen crumb, and returned her gaze to the canister.

"Don't push it."

By the time Ariel had finished dinner, Stonewall had disappeared, probably to somewhere forbidden like the chaise longue in the bedroom, and Jessie was napping at Ariel's feet.

While she'd inherited Stonewall from her sister, she'd inherited Jessie from herself. She'd found the shepherd shut up here in this kitchen six months before when she'd awakened with no idea of who she was or what she was doing in this house.

The fierce-looking dog had been no more familiar to her than her own strange face, and it was hard to say which had frightened her more. Queerly, Jessie hadn't immediately seemed to recognize her, either. Long, frozen seconds of terror had passed before the dog relaxed muscles tensed for attack, pricked her ears, and allowed her fur to settle.

Ariel stroked the dog's smooth black-and-tan fur with her bare foot and with her toes scratched the pink belly. The scar there vividly recalled a time Jessie had saved her mistress's life. Jessie had survived; the attacker hadn't.

Queasiness stirred through Ariel's own belly at the memory of the dead man's face, the inert body sprawled a few feet from where she now sat.

Another image flitted through her mind. The thin, expressive face of John William Barron as it must have looked frozen in death. She thought of a lonely young misfit who'd yearned for the father he'd never known, who'd taken refuge in an imaginary world, who'd grown into a melancholy man beset by "grief and shame and fear."

Abruptly, Ariel called out to Stonewall. Before she could retrieve the dogs' leashes from their nearby hook, Jessie was by her side, and in short order the three of them were out the front door and perambulating the quiet, dark neighborhood.

Ariel paused for a brief chat with a pug-walking neighbor, a Tweedledee-shaped gentleman who looked unnervingly like his dog. Jessie paused for a briefer encounter with a fleet cat, and both dogs paused all too often to check out every new smell accumulated during their kennel incarceration.

Ariel tried, but she couldn't banish the specter of the Barron man from her mind. The devils that had plagued him seemed to have found a new host, and she was haunted by the provocative words she was fairly sure she remembered accurately.

That he felt "grief" she could understand, but what about "shame"? Well, the sins of the father, perhaps . . . a father who'd taken his own life. And where did "fear" figure in? John William had never said what it was that frightened him, she recalled, but he'd as much as said that he was afraid of *something,* and a few hours later he was dead.

A young man trotted toward her pushing a three-wheeled "baby jogger," from which the small passenger joyfully exclaimed "Dog!" and reached out a chubby hand to grab fur. Ariel smiled as the little girl was whisked past. Her smile faded with the runner's echoing footsteps.

How likely was it, she wondered, that a person whose life was scarred by suicide would commit that dreadful, most irrevocable of acts, in exactly the same way and even the same place! Could a person who'd suffered that pain be so callous as to inflict it on others? Maybe the children of suicides, like those of alcoholics and batterers, were especially susceptible. Perhaps, because they know from personal experience that it's a real and possible option, they're more apt to exercise that option themselves.

Or perhaps not.

Ariel returned home, released the dogs, and dialed New York.

* * *

"This better be important," B.F.'s sleep-rasped voice said.

"I'm sorry. Did I wake you up?"

"No. Yes." Ariel heard a grumbled, froggy harrumph and the abrupt cessation of background noise before B.F. said, "I was watchin' the Braves and the Mets, but I reckon I dropped off. Who won, do you know?"

"Sorry again. Listen, B.F., I've got some, well, morbid news, and I need your advice. That man I met on the beach . . . you remember the one I was asking you about? Well, I'm ninety-nine percent sure he was John William Barron." Ariel was actually positive, but leaving the tiny window of doubt somehow seemed a mitigation. "The night I met him was the night he died," she added. There was a bottomless silence before B.F. spoke.

"God bless America," he said on a long exhalation, and then, "What makes you say so?"

"I saw a newspaper picture of his father. What I wanted to ask is, do you think there's any point in my contacting the police in Charleston?"

"Did the boy say anything to you that might bear on his actions?"

"No . . . not really."

"But?"

"Have they held the inquest yet? Have they definitely ruled suicide?"

"Not till Friday, Sarge said, but if you know something—or suspect something—that might alter that judgment, it wouldn't matter if they had. What is it?"

"Probably nothing. Look, tell Sarge to tell his friends in the police that John William was on the beach at Kiawah at one in the morning—from about one o'clock until one-thirty that I know of—and that he mentioned being afraid. He didn't say what of, and I can't guarantee he meant it in the sense of being afraid for his life."

"What in the world did you two talk about?"

"Mostly he just reminisced about Jane. He did, ah, kind of indicate that maybe you and he hadn't seen eye-to-eye on something or other."

"What we didn't see eye-to-eye on was his hanging around Jane."

As Ariel had noticed more than once when B.F. got down to

business, the drawling cadence of his speech vanished. "John William was a weak-minded, mixed-up kid who suffered an identity crisis every day of his life," he said bluntly. "I don't say it was his fault—he inherited a bad set of circumstances—and I don't deny that I was protective of Jane." He cleared his throat, and more mildly, said, "I don't make any apologies. John William liked to dramatize things. He courted disaster. I didn't want him creating some tragedy for a sensitive, nurturing girl like Jane to deal with, and my instincts were borne out, weren't they? I don't know what kind of 'fears' he had in mind when he talked to you, but I wouldn't be surprised if they were bogeymen."

"Goodness." Ariel blinked.

"I'll tell Sarge what you said and to give his pals your number if they want it, but I don't want you sucked into his fantasies now that he's dead any more than I wanted him doing it to Jane when he was alive."

Ariel listened to a few seconds of heavy breathing before she said, "Are you all right?"

"Couldn't be better if I had good sense. Now get off the phone and let an old man get some sleep. And, hey—you stay in touch, you hear?"

"Yes, sir. Sleep well."

Softly, she replaced the receiver. She decided to follow her grandfather's example. Her body was still hovering somewhere between Eastern and Pacific time, and (as she'd heard it put in Charleston) she hadn't "gotten her nap out" the night before.

She checked the burglar alarm and, after prodding Jessie from a dream that had her hind legs quivering in pursuit of phantom prey, turned off the lights. The shepherd roused herself and looked around blankly, perhaps wondering where the fleeing rabbit had gone. After a moment she yawned and stretched and followed her mistress to the bedroom.

11

Henry looked distracted. Ariel had noticed it on and off all day Thursday. It wasn't the vague look he got when he was hatching a new idea for the show. It wasn't the crazed look that came next, if the idea had really begun to percolate. And it wasn't the heedless preoccupation with which he drove, too fast, when he appeared to be thinking about everything except where he was pointing the car, reducing any passenger to wobbly-kneed aspic.

"How's it going with Sam?" she asked him that evening when they happened to be leaving the studio at the same time. "Have you had any more problems?"

Henry stared at Ariel for longer than it should have taken him to recollect who his son was. "No, it's okay. For now, anyway. Wait here a second, will you?"

He returned to his office and when he came back, he had a file folder under his arm that hadn't been there before.

"Homework?" Ariel asked.

"Let's go get something to eat, you want to? You're not busy, are you?"

"Oh, Henry, I'm so sorry—I do wish you'd asked sooner! I'm afraid I'm off to the opera tonight. I'd cancel, but François will be by in the limo in just a little while, and plans are all made to meet Pavarotti afterward for a late dinner."

Henry couldn't have looked more startled if she'd flapped her arms and clucked.

"Okay, okay," he said, scowling. "I guess that wasn't the right way to ask."

"No, but it was truly flattering that you believed me for two whole seconds. I'm in the mood for something greasy. Where's that chili place you go?"

"Somewhere you can't take your car unless you're tired of everything on it that's detachable. Come on. I'll drive."

Ariel briefly debated which she valued more: her new minivan or her life.

"Let's compromise. We'll take your car, but I'll drive."

"Suit yourself. You can't do anything to it that parking lot jockeys and a hundred fifty thousand miles haven't already done. But watch the clutch. It's got a personality."

After a short, sedate drive during which Henry spoke only to give directions, they were soon settled in the corner booth of a Hollywood diner Ariel was pretty sure hadn't attracted too many stars—of the celebrity or the culinary award variety—in its patently long history.

The leatherette that covered the seats was the color of dried blood and as brittle as ancient parchment, the Formica tabletop retained its faint marbleized pattern only in the center, and everything in the joint that wasn't stainless steel was red or yellow—or had been once. But there was no lack of customers, and the smells, a combination of fried foods that definitely included onions, released a spurt of saliva in Ariel's mouth.

"Bet you get a good cup of java here," she said with a grin. Then, more quickly than she'd propped her forearms on the table, she yanked them up and, snatching a napkin from the dispenser, began to wipe arms and then table.

"Well, I said I was in the mood for something greasy, didn't I?" She dropped the napkin in the ashtray and wiped her fingers against each other. "This place is really a lab for the Center for Science in the Public Interest, right? How high can your cholesterol count actually soar without turning your arteries to stone like Lot's wife . . . that kind of stuff, right? How long does ptomaine take to kill? Can you taste E. coli?"

"Lot's wife didn't turn to stone." Henry held up two fingers, a signal someone in the bedlam of the exposed kitchen must have picked up, since Henry flashed a quick salute before turning back to Ariel.

"That mind-and-memory show's looking like a go," he said, referring to the segment Ariel was developing on unorthodox psychotherapies. "What about the interview with the woman who implicated herself in the murder? Is that on?"

"The booker's got exclusivity pretty much nailed down," Ariel said, "but our lawyers are still negotiating with her lawyers. I think they think there's a movie of the week in it, much more profitable than one piddly little ol' interview. We've lined up two other cases with definite potential. One involves TA, transactional analysis, and the other's a real cheerleader for EMDR, the rapid eye movement therapy, but in my opinion—"

"Acronyms are dandy, and the issue makes a dandy background," Henry lectured, "but keep in mind, it *is* just background, the cement that holds the story together. It's the story itself, the characters, that keep the audience's fingers off all those remote clickers out there. People don't want to be educated; they want to watch people."

"Yessir." Ariel had heard the "character-driven" speech before.

"What about that Barron data we got together for you?" Henry asked. "That artist? Is that something I need to know about?"

"No. Just a personal thing." Ariel was arranging the condiments into a neat line with the napkin dispenser. She made a minute adjustment to the ketchup. "But thanks."

The information gathered by *Open File* production assistants had included nothing she hadn't previously known, a waste of everybody's time—as had been, it seemed, her phone call to B.F.

She'd heard from a Charleston detective named Newton. He'd taken down her statement and thanked her and that was the end of that. She was trying not to feel like a sensation seeker, those publicity parasites who slither out of the woodwork with eyewitness tales and "best friend" confidences after every tragedy.

"The artist, John Early Barron," she explained to Henry, "was a friend of B.F., and B.F. had known John William Barron, his son, his whole life. The sad truth seems to be that suicide runs in the family." She gave a glum little lopsided grin and asked, "What are we really here to talk about? What's in that file you've got there?"

"You remember I said something on the phone about a piece we worked on a while back—one we didn't air?"

"The one I *don't* remember? Sure. What about it?"

"I want you to look at something." He shuffled through a few papers and handed Ariel four 8 × 10 photos. She gave Henry a puzzled look before glancing at them one by one.

"So?" she asked, no more enlightened than she had been.

"I take it you don't recognize anybody?"

Ariel hesitated, decided to postpone questions, and looked through the pictures again, more carefully. She shrugged and shook her head.

Henry tapped the top photo, that of a man of thirty plus in front of a multicolumned, official-looking building. The look on his face, startled and less than pleased, suggested that the camera had caught him off guard, and to judge by the blur of his legs, he'd been moving fast. The man was attractive, Ariel thought. More than attractive. Especially if you liked intense types. Tall, rangy, dark intense types.

"Grant Lacy," Henry said.

"Lacy? Lacy . . . ? Oh! The one who took off or went missing or whatever? I saw the odd article about him in my very early days." Ariel studied the photo even more intently. "I sure never saw his picture, though."

"Camera shy."

"That whole thing—all the brouhaha—was before my time. When was it again?"

"Nine months ago."

"Right. That's right, so I missed the blitz. He'd turned up . . . or, wait . . . What was it that happened?"

"He didn't turn up, and nothing's happened."

Ariel closed her eyes, dredging her memory. "Boy genius. Started his own computer company. Micro-something? Star. MicroStar. Low-profile type. Ultra-eccentric."

"Yeah, the wizard of odd. Made it big by the time he was twenty-five; that'd be seven or eight years ago. Millionaire umpteen times over when, according to his wife, he went jogging one evening, never to be seen again. Well, he was 'seen' everyplace from a McDonald's in Poughkeepsie to a mall in Fort Worth, mostly by the literati who do their reading in the grocery checkout line."

"I guarantee one thing: if you did see him, you'd remember him," Ariel murmured with another appreciative gander at the photo. "Even *I* might remember *him.*" She raised her eyes to see Henry frowning at her. "What?" she asked and, without waiting for a reply, flipped to the next photo, a tearsheet from a glossy society publication. "Lacy's wife?"

"Yeah. She controls MicroStar now. Nominally anyway. She's conservator."

Mrs. Lacy was blond, pretty, and tanned. Her gown had the look of an original, and the jewels that glittered on her bare throat looked genuine. Her smile didn't. "She looks expensive."

"The lady's rumored to be worth a paltry few million her own self, but nothing like what she'd have had if Lacy'd turned up dead. Either she had nothing to do with his disappearance or somebody made a mistake or she's not greedy."

There was no guessing from Mrs. Lacy's public smile whether she was innocent, inept, or avaricious. Ariel moved on to the third shot, which had a grainy dot pattern indicating reproduction from a newspaper.

"That," Henry said, "is the guy who really runs the company since Lacy disappeared. Clifford Gilroy, formerly chief financial officer. MicroStar's not on the leading edge innovation-wise right now, but word is it's in a better position fiscally than it used to be."

"Solid-looking citizen," Ariel said. "A 'suit.' But you still haven't said—" Her question was interrupted by the waitress bearing thick mugs of coffee and white crockery bowls of steaming chili. They made room for the food, which Henry eyed with manifest lust. Ariel thought he might lick his chops.

She studied her own bowl with a certain amount of trepidation before spooning out a bit, blowing on it, and—inhaling to blow again—catching the aroma. She couldn't fault the aroma. Henry, she saw, had already made a sizable dent in his portion. She took a morsel onto her tongue, held it suspended for a tortured moment, and dived for her water glass.

"Is your tongue asbestos?" she croaked.

Henry's busy jaws stopped in mid-mastication, his beard a quivering exclamation point. "What?" he asked. "Too hot? Blow on it."

Ariel dabbed at her eyes with her napkin. "Who's the man in the last photo? Looks like a diluted version of Lacy."

"Brother. Vaughn Lacy, heads some department at MicroStar. He didn't benefit, on paper anyway, when his brother did a fade."

"Did anybody?"

"Did anybody . . . ? Oh, benefit. Well, the talk was that Lacy was into unorthodox bookkeeping. Had a habit of keeping cash, big bucks, squirreled away in foreign bank accounts and safe deposit boxes, they say. For a fact he had a considerable art collection he'd been amassing over a long time. Speculative—artists he considered potentially valuable. I hear he had a good eye.

"Bottom line, since MicroStar's not a publicly held company, it's hard for anybody except maybe the IRS to know what Lacy had and who, if anybody, makes out with him gone. Having him out in the ether for five non–corpus delicti years doesn't seem to be to anybody's advantage."

Ariel took a cautious bite of her chili, looked at the bowl in surprise, and took another before she said, "Why are you telling me all this?"

"Guy named Richard Cummings was the producer developing the Lacy story for us. Initially, he was gung-ho. Then, bang, he resigned. Said he had an opportunity overseas he couldn't turn down.

"I assigned his projects to other people and, later, when I was following up this particular one, the producer who'd gotten it said it was a no-go. Said Cummings had written 'deep six' on the file and noted that the cops were close to an arrest."

"I don't remember anything about an arrest. For what?"

"Didn't happen. Either Cummings was mistaken or—"

Just then, the waitress showed up with two slices of apple pie. They were the thickest Ariel had ever seen, lofty edifices of crusty, apple-packed pastry, and each had a snowball of ice cream tucked beside it.

Ariel eyed hers with awe. "Did those two fingers you held up include this assault on my arteries—not to mention my hips?"

"Eat, dahling. Enjoy," Henry said in Molly Goldberg's voice, and proceeded to follow his own advice. After polishing off the ice cream and a good chunk of the pie, he said, "We had a spate of hot stories about then—including the one we got the Peabody for—and Lacy went on the back burner. Not just for us. It wasn't the first time, you see, that he'd made himself scarce. One of his biggest successes a few years back followed a stint underground."

"A nine-month stint?"

Henry scarfed down the last of his pie. "No, just weeks, but we didn't know nine months ago it would *be* nine months this time. After a while the police put it on the back burner, too. The trail was as cold as the story.

"Lacy's not a celebrity. He's rich, but he's no Getty grandson; no ears came in the mail. There was no body, no blood and guts, no sex, and no scandal. Maybe in Olathe he'd have been rich enough or weird enough to stay news. Not out here."

"So the man disappears, and everybody just writes him off? Because he's not hot?"

Henry shrugged. "His fifteen minutes of fame were up."

"Is it this conversation that's giving me heartburn?"

"You'll notice we *are having* this conversation. A week ago I overheard one of our researchers—it was Theo Bell—gabbing before a story meeting. He and Richard Cummings used to pal around some, and he was saying that when he was down in Atlanta—when he went down for that Olympics story—he ran into Cummings, who was from there, apparently, and moved back. Anyway, Theo was joking about how he'd love to know more about that 'overseas opportunity' 'old Dick' had, that he'd sure love to get in on one like it. Said Cummings was getting out of a new Porsche in front of some fancy restaurant. Said he was 'dressed to kill,' and the woman with him was a 'fox.' "

"Do you think they'd wrap the rest of this pie for me to take home?"

"Obviously, your devious mind has made some connection between Grant Lacy and Richard Cummings's Porsche—like a payoff. Why does that follow? Maybe," Ariel suggested to Henry, "he already had the car when he worked for you."

She was driving his Oldsmobile—a cluttered, dispirited vehicle as far a cry from a Porsche as it was possible to get—back to the studio. "Some people do like nice cars." She glanced Henry's way. "Or maybe the Porsche wasn't Cummings's. Maybe it belonged to the 'fox.' "

"He didn't drive a Porsche when he worked for me, and it was his car. Theo said it had a vanity plate: CUMN ON."

"I'm so dreadfully sorry I don't remember this attractive-sounding chap. Still, it's a stretch, isn't it, tying that particular story to Cummings's prosperity nearly a year later?"

"Possibly. But I got my blip."

"Oh! The famous Heller early warning device. Well, why didn't you say so?"

"I trust my blip; it's got a track record. When that little sucker hits my personal radar screen, I go with it."

"Do you have anything else—not that you'd need it, of course, since you've practically got the smoking gun."

"At first, no. I tried looking into the much-touted 'overseas' windfall. Talked to some old drinking buddies assigned here and there in Europe and Asia. None of them ever heard of Cummings."

" 'Overseas' isn't limited to Europe and Asia, and there's nothing that says Cummings stayed in the news business. Maybe he had an uncle with emerald mines in South America."

"And maybe my Aunt Becky's a Rockette."

"I have an idea."

"Yeah?"

"Call Cummings up and ask him where he got the money."

"Golly, why didn't I think of that? 'Say, Dick, congratulations! I heard you came into a bundle. Where'd you get it?' 'Thanks, Henry. I put the squeeze on somebody. What's new with you?' I think I'll save that brilliant ploy."

"I still think—"

"Don't. Not until you have all the facts. One or two things have come to light since I started looking into the Lacy file."

Ariel pulled into the empty studio lot, parked next to her van, and turned off the ignition. The engine shuddered to reluctant silence. "What things?"

"I was on the horn to Paris, one of my calls about Cummings, and Theo Bell overheard."

"Theo's got ears like Dumbo and an even bigger penchant for gossip. Not to mention making trouble."

"Whatever. He asked me if there was anything in the Lacy file about a call from a tipster. I looked. There wasn't. There wasn't a whole lot, period. There should've been, given the time Cummings put in on the story.

"Cummings, Theo said, had been contacted by somebody wanting a meeting about Lacy—somebody selling, Theo assumed. Cummings seemed excited but not surprised, Theo thought, and then and there canceled a racquetball game they'd had set up for after work. Next day Theo asked how it had gone, and Cummings said it hadn't; nobody showed. It was a couple of weeks later that he quit."

"But, Henry, if it was a no-show, Cummings wouldn't necessarily have left notes about it."

"Well, see, that's the thing. Theo doesn't believe it *was* a no-show."

"Why?"

"He suggested I ask you about that. It seems he and Cummings happened to be within earshot of your desk when Cummings was complaining how he'd waited at the rendezvous, some bar near Dodger Stadium, for so long he got a buzz on and just went home. Theo said you looked at Cummings 'strange' and started to say something, but then you didn't. Later, Theo asked you what that had been all about. You told him you'd seen Cummings the night before at that open-air market not far from your house—the Brentwood one at San Vicente and Twenty-sixth?"

"Yes, so?"

"Cummings lived in the Silverlake area, close enough to the stadium to hear the boos. The Brentwood Marketplace is all the way across town. That's where you saw him, you said, at one of the tables outside the deli." Into the meaningful pause that followed, Ariel dropped an "And?"

"And he wasn't alone. One might conclude that you saw who the 'tipster'-who-wasn't *was.*"

Henry gave Ariel a wry half-grin. "The only problem, my sweet, is that you don't remember it."

12

"OKAY, I LOOKED AT THE PICTURES UNTIL I SAW THOSE FOUR PEOPLE in my sleep. I still don't remember if I saw one of them with Richard Cummings at the Brentwood Marketplace." Ariel slapped the Lacy file on Henry's desk and said, "I asked dear Theo Bell about the conversation he and I had at the time. You should've heard me trying to pump *him* about what *I* said without sounding like an idiot. He got a real kick out of watching me squirm. Said I hadn't told him 'jack' and something snide about how I've 'never been one to share information.' "

"You weren't exactly a team player, my dear."

"One of these days I'm going to jump onto a desk and announce to the whole bloody room that six months ago I didn't know a sound bite from a dog bite and I'm still learning on the job like an intern. . . . Let me ask you something. Why didn't you take this Lacy thing up with me back then—before my memory went south?"

"Why didn't you bother to tell me 'back then' I had pond scum on my staff? If you'll recall, I didn't know anything about your seeing this 'tipster' and Cummings until last week."

"Yeah, well, I've gone through the notes—such as they are. Cummings wasn't one to knock himself out, was he?"

"Oh, he wasn't bad at his job; I'll give him that. Nervy. Persistent . . . You couldn't insult the guy. Hang up on him, and he'd just show up at your door, with a camera." Henry's mouth turned down sourly. "He'd make a crack private dick, trailing unfaithful wives out for a nooner—and snapping pictures of the action."

Distracted, Ariel lost a few seconds with that image before she said, "So his letting go of the Lacy story so easily is hard to buy. But about the file, I went through it, and I didn't see anything significant. Except for the one obvious thing, of course."

Henry made a tent of his fingers and imitated the Cheshire cat. "Ah, yes," he said, "and that was . . . ?"

"Cummings mentioned a preliminary interview with the wife. There're no notes and no tape and no record of a tape anywhere in the building. I reckon you think he went through the file and got rid of anything important and overlooked that one little entry."

"I *reckon* that's exactly what he did, and I'll tell you what *I'm* going to do. I'm going to make this the quintessential 'open file,' and I'm going to honcho it myself. As sure as I'm sitting here, Cummings is a greedy son of a gun who got so hot and bothered by his 'career opportunity' that he screwed up, and I'm going to nail his sorry hide to the barn door!"

Henry slammed a desk drawer shut for emphasis. "It is a personal insult to me and every person in the news industry when something like this happens. I don't give a rip what happened to Grant Lacy. I don't care if he was murdered or if he's living in luxury in the Cayman Islands. Richard Cummings is not going to get away with compromising the integrity of this business or this show." He gave his beard a quick, impatient swipe. "I hate a thief," he said. "And that's what Cummings is. When a newsman turns rogue, he steals from every person who depends on trust, on his word, to make this profession work."

Ariel let herself down into one of the battle-scarred chairs Henry insisted on keeping. "There are a whole lot of people," she said, "who think integrity and the news business are mutually exclusive."

"If I let this ride, I'd be agreeing with them."

"Well, ever since I inherited this job, I've had reservations. If we're enjoying a bad rap now, it's not entirely undeserved, is it? Actual graft aside, when newspeople pull down salaries like sports superstars, and a person of Diane Sawyer's stature is hustling right alongside Geraldo Rivera for chats with pseudo-celebs about their sex lives, we've got a credibility problem. I'll tell you, with every sensational murder and titillating scandal drawing a media invasion that makes D-day look like a Boy Scout jamboree, we don't exactly bring the same dignity to the job that Harry Reasoner did. Or Walter Cronkite or Edward R. Murrow or—"

"Nellie Bly," Henry cut in, his expression pained. "You're being sexist as well as naive, and I'm not talking about news value here; I'm talking about ethics."

"So am I. How far is it from pandering to fixing?"

"Just about the same distance as a cop letting a kid smoking pot off with a warning as opposed to dealing drugs himself. One's judgment; the other's egregious crime."

"And this is getting us nowhere. Look, I'm not convinced you've got anything on Cummings but, obviously, if he took money to squelch evidence—maybe from a murderer—he should be exposed. So what's next?"

"We're going to find out about Cummings's activities after he left here and, as I said, we're going to very publicly reopen the Lacy story. If we fish enough, could be we'll get a bite."

"If Mr. Lacy met with foul play, could be somebody may get more than bitten."

"Or *I could* get a tipster call of my own," Henry said grimly. "I'd look spiffy in a Porsche, don't you think?"

Ariel snorted. "The very thought's enough to curdle milk. You could still simply call Cummings and ask straight out. I looked him up in the Atlanta directory. He's listed."

Henry rolled his eyes.

"Just a suggestion."

"Actually . . . I want him to know we're back on this, don't I? Calling him's not a bad idea. Not me, though. You."

"And say what?"

"Tell him . . . Tell him you heard from Theo where he was. Say there're new developments in the Lacy story, and we're going forward. Go over the pittance he left in the file. Ask him about the interview with the wife. And ask him, if you can work it in and I know you can, that you know about the 'anonymous' caller."

"I'm beginning to feel the teensiest bit used, Henry. Anything else? How about if I throw in that I saw him at the Brentwood Marketplace?"

"I think we'll keep that to ourselves for now. But, yeah, matter of fact, there is something else. I'd like you to do a little experiment in connection with that anxiety disorder piece you're doing."

Ariel felt herself tense. "What kind of experiment?"

"Try one of the new memory retrieval therapies yourself. Maybe that EMDR thing. What is it? Eye Movement whatever? What if it worked? Wouldn't getting your memory back be to your advantage?"

"And wouldn't remembering who I saw with Richard Cummings be to yours?"

"That would be a side benefit, sure, but I'm thinking about you."

"Sure you are, Henry, and—I quote—'Maybe my Aunt Becky's a Rockette.' I made it clear when I broached this idea that it would not touch on my personal situation, didn't I?"

"What have you got to lose?"

"Didn't I?"

"You're being unreasonable."

"And you're being exploitive."

"Think about it."

"Shove it."

"Ariel!"

Henry mugged shock, his comically round eyes veering from Ariel's face to the door being opened behind her. "What?" he asked Lisa Jolley, a producer whose workstation was next to Ariel's.

"Call for Ariel," the redhead said to Henry, and then to Ariel, "Personal. Sounds like Grandpa Walton."

"Thought you might like to know what happened at the inquest on John William," B.F. said. "They're keepin' the investigation open, and they're probably gon' be callin' you again."

"Why?" Ariel asked, her pulse going into high gear. "What's happened?"

"There's but one thing I know for sure. They found a bruise on his head they think he got not too long before he died. He definitely died from asphyxiation, but there's at least some question whether it was voluntary. Not findin' a note's not settin' well with that cop Newton, I heard, nor the door bein' found unlocked either. I 'spec your sayin' John William was afraid of something or somebody might be a factor, too."

Ariel felt a little shiver between her shoulder blades. "Well, I hope I'm not making too much of that."

"He said it, didn't he?"

"Oh, yes. He said it."

"So . . . ?"

After further brief conversation, Ariel hung up and sat staring into space, seeing in her mind's eye that unreal, middle-of-the-night encounter and trying once again to reconstruct exactly what John William had said about fear.

He'd been talking, she remembered, about the "void" the young Jane had felt, the void he ascribed to separation from her unknown twin. He'd mentioned loneliness, Ariel suddenly recalled, and need, and that's when he'd specifically mentioned feeling "grief, shame, and fear." She rubbed her lower lip reflectively. Were those the emotions of a man about to take his life or a man afraid that someone was out to take it from him?

Later, she remembered, she'd asked directly what either he or Jane had to be afraid of, and he'd said something like, "the fear wasn't Jane's." That could be interpreted only one way. Ariel frowned. There'd been something else. . . . "Murder, like God," John William had said, was "no respecter of persons."

She exhaled in surprise. She'd forgotten that bit. She searched her desk for the phone number the Charleston detective had given her "in case she remembered anything else"—and stopped as a thought struck. Maybe she should go back to Charleston. Wouldn't this make an *Open File* story? She was on the way to suggest it to Henry when she vetoed the idea. This was an open police investigation, too new to qualify as unresolved, and in no need of her interference. *And* she had enough on her plate now.

Still, she couldn't smother the tingle of unease that fidgeted about her innards. It was within the realm of possibility that she'd been the last person to talk to John William. She felt as if that last shared human intimacy obligated her in some indefinable way, as if she owed him something. The courtesy of reasonable doubt, maybe. Like, what if she wasn't the last? What if that distinction fell not to her but to a killer. . . .

Ariel gave herself a mental shake and told herself to stop dramatizing. B.F. had said the Charleston authorities would probably call her again. When they did, if they did, she'd tell them about the mention of the word *murder.* They'd deal with it.

The next call came not from Detective Newton but from B.F., and it came the next afternoon.

It was Saturday, a week and one day after John William's death. Ariel had just put on the dogs' leashes to go to the park when the phone rang.

"I just heard Halley Barron's dead," B.F. said without preamble.

The words were shocking. During the blank, paralyzing second before the name registered, fear blossomed in the pit of Ariel's stomach. Then she let herself breathe. This wasn't bad; this wasn't anyone she knew—it was only John William's sister. As quickly, she was seized by guilt and dawning horror. "What happened?" she asked. "She didn't . . . ?"

"Accident. She and Grace were driving up to Charleston from Savannah last night, to close up the house, I guess was what Grace said. Car went out of control. Halley was thrown out. It was on that two-lane stretch of 64 between Walterboro and . . . well, you don't know the area. Anyway, somebody heard the crash and called the police. Halley was dead when they got there. Funny . . . not having seen her in all these years, I can't help thinking of her as that little girl I knew. Gentle little thing, she was, and quiet. A whole lot more to her than there was to her brother."

"What about Grace?"

"Banged up some. Broke something and got cut up, but I don't think she's all that bad. One thing kind of interesting, though—and pitiful."

Ariel had removed Jessie's leash and was trying to lure the frustrated, dancing Stonewall when she realized what had been bothering her the whole time B.F. had been talking. "What's the matter with your voice?" she asked.

She heard a muffled honk, and B.F., sounding clogged, said, "Catarrh."

"Pardon me?"

"Cold, I reckon."

"Oh." There was some kind of distracting background noise coming over the line, and Ariel put a finger in the ear away from the phone as if that would make it easier to hear. "A bad cold?"

"You ever have a good one?"

Ariel let it pass. "You started to say there was something interesting about the accident?"

"Yeah. It was what one of the cops that answered the call—fellow named Long—told Sarge. He said Grace was out of her head when they got there. Dazed, you know? She was sittin' next to Halley's body, not touchin' it. Just sittin' there and bleedin' like a stuck . . . Didn't even seem to realize she was hurt, this guy said. She was sittin' there and sayin' something about 'You just wait and see' and 'Don't you worry' and such as that, like she didn't know Halley was dead."

"Well, that's not so mysterious, is it? She was in shock—probably *hadn't* accepted that Halley was dead—and she was trying to reassure her that help was on the way." Ariel hooked Stonewall with her foot and, dragging him over, slipped off his leash.

"I didn't say it was mysterious, Ariel Gold, and I wasn't finished. Grace looked straight at the cops, this fellow Long told Sarge, and just as clear and definite as could be, said, 'That's my stepdaughter Halley Irene Barron. She's dead.' "

Ariel murmured a vague lament and, hearing more background noise, a staticky, unintelligible blare, asked, "Where are you?"

"Hangar. We're fixin' to fly down to Charleston to—"

"You're flying with a cold? You shouldn't be doing that!"

"Monroe called and said somebody broke in a house not half a mile from mine. Sarge got distracted by the business with John William last trip, and he never did get in that confounded security system. He's foamin' at the mouth to get back down there and take care of it."

"Well, I don't see why *you* have to go."

"Hattie's still in South Carolina, and I'm takin' some time off. With her and Sarge there, that's the best place to do it."

"You're taking time off? How sick are you?"

"I'm sick of sittin' in two-hour business meetings that ought to last just about long enough to tell a pack of slick mealy-mouthed New York hotshots that I was doin' deals when they were still doin' their diapers." B.F. grumbled. "Wait a minute; somebody's callin' me." After a second, he said, "I've got to go. I'll call you in a day or two."

Ariel left for the park, but all the while she was throwing a Kong toy for Jessie, the latest Barron tragedy played in her mind.

From what she'd deduced from B.F.'s conversations, Halley would have been the last of a once proud family, the end of the line. Why, she asked herself, should that make Halley's death sadder? Maybe old, effete families, like worn-out bodies, were genetically programmed for extinction. That gloomy idea reminded Ariel that she and B.F. were the last of her own family and, with a devil-walking-over-her-grave shiver, she made an effort to let the whole dismal matter go.

Looking around to check Stonewall's whereabouts, she noticed a dog owner she knew, an actress, exchanging air kisses with a middle-aged man. Ariel recognized him as an actor, one who'd had several TV series, none recently. She couldn't think of his name. Just then, a large male Rhodesian ridgeback wandered by the couple and, stopping beside the oblivious actor, lifted a leg.

"Hey . . ." Ariel called out, but it was already too late. The man's charming smile slowly dissolved. Looking like someone who'd received very bad news, his eyes edged down to the dark stain on his khakis, searched the immediate vicinity for the culprit (by now vamoosed), and then flitted further afield to see who'd witnessed his baptism. He turned back to his companion with a weak but valiant chuckle, and called his dog.

As the actor passed, his bichon frise in tow, his name popped into Ariel's mind.

" 'Night, Tony," she said, trying to keep a straight face. He snapped off a jaunty salute and, walking with a stiff-legged gait, made for his Jeep Cherokee.

Ariel began to collect her own dogs. She leashed Jessie, yelled for Stonewall, and decided that Shaw was right: "Life does not cease to be funny when people die any more than it ceases to be serious when people laugh."

13

Ariel was deeply involved in her notes about pop behavior modification and therapy fads—primal scream and EST and I'm OK, you're OK, and so on. She was also intensely aware of the confrontation going on behind the glass walls of Henry's office.

The beautiful woman whose mouth was moving ninety to nothing and whose fist was pounding Henry's desk wore torn jeans, a T-shirt promoting a movie production (and showing an impressive chest to advantage), desert boots, and no makeup. She didn't need any.

Judging by Henry's sleepy-lidded expression and boneless slouch—feet propped up, fingers locked casually behind his head—he was making a monumental effort to appear imperturbable. Ariel knew he was a whisker away from blowing like Mauna Loa. She knew of only one person who pushed his buttons with such unerring accuracy; she guessed that the woman was Emily, Sam's mother.

If she was right, she was also surprised. She'd had no idea that Henry's most recent ex-wife was so gorgeous, or so young. From the looks of her, Ariel figured, she must've had Sam when she was barely out of her teens.

The woman shook her finger in Henry's face, snatched up an expensive-looking leather backpack, and flung open the door. She stormed past Ariel's workstation and out of sight, her departure punctuated by the sound of a crash in Henry's office. Ariel looked back to see muddy liquid trickling down the glass wall. Henry watched the lazily lengthening blotch with satisfaction and, finding a new mug, poured himself fresh coffee. Then, apparently oblivious to the dozens of eyes trained on him, he closed the door and returned to his desk, where he punched a number into the telephone.

Whispered comments and snickers erupted like grassfire throughout the large open room around Ariel. She rolled her eyes at her nearest neighbor, and returned her attention to her notes.

After what she considered an adequate cooling-off period, Ariel knocked on Henry's door, opened it, and poked her head in.

"Safe?" she asked.

"Richard Cummings gave notice on his apartment two days after the infamous tipster call," Henry said by way of an answer. He began to rock back and forth in his chair, and the protesting squeaks almost drowned out his next gloating announcement. "He bought the Porsche, a Carrera, before he left town, and he paid cash. Sixty-nine-five."

"Good Lord, Henry! You sound like Inspector Javert on the trail of Jean Valjean! What's Cummings's current bank balance—or haven't you weaseled that out of anybody yet?"

"I'm working on it. I've also made sure everybody I can think of knows the Lacy story's back open. The bait's out."

"And I'm it. I called Cummings."

Henry's chair squealed to a stop.

"Professed delight that we're back on the story. Said he'd wondered what happened to the arrest he'd heard was imminent. Claimed the wife backed out of the interview at the last minute. Asked me if we had anything new. Invited me to Atlanta. 'Y'all come to see me sometime, sugar pie, now y'hear!' About as appealing as kudzu but, still, you might be off base about him, Henry."

"I'm not."

"Maybe the meeting he had at the Brentwood Marketplace was perfectly innocent, and unrelated."

"Then why did he lie about having it?"

Ariel exaggeratedly stepped over a shard of coffee mug lying in a nasty-looking puddle on the floor and sat down. "You could've broken the glass, you know?"

"I should've thrown Emily at it."

"Ah . . . so that *was* Emily. You never said she looked like a young Ingrid Bergman."

"I don't recall that I ever said anything."

"The operative word, in case you didn't recognize it, was *young.*"

"She's no younger than you. In fact, if memory serves, she's a little older, but her immaturity does shine through."

"It could be argued that only a woman you're still in love with could make you that bitter."

"It could be argued that the welfare system was a boon to mankind."

"Then you're not?"

"Sam's going to be living with me for a while."

Ariel's eyebrows rose. "Has something else happened?"

"Emily's going to be in Oregon location scouting for a few weeks, and she can't take him out of school, but she was insisting on my taking Sam long before she got the job. She can't handle him anymore, she says." Henry played with his beard for a minute. "For once in her life, she's right. It's time."

"When does he move in?"

"Friday," Henry said with a noticeable lack of enthusiasm.

"Well, good luck. I know this is last minute, but I came to invite you to a little dinner party tonight. Are you free?"

A social invitation to Ariel's home was a first, and Henry hesitated before asking what the occasion was.

"It started out to be just having Marguerite and Carl Harris over for a congratulatory dinner," Ariel said. "You remember Marguerite? My neighbor the playwright? They just got word about backing for her new play—the first new one in years—but yesterday I got a call from Win Peacock. He's in town, so I invited him, too, and then I thought, Why not make it a party? So I invited Laya. So how about it? Can you come?"

The Laya Ariel referred to had been a close friend of Jane's. Henry knew that she'd become Ariel's friend, so her inclusion was no surprise. Win Peacock was a different matter altogether.

The ex–*Open File* correspondent had been suspiciously attentive to Ariel before he'd left to take an anchor position on a competitive show out of New York. Of course, there were probably few mortals of the female persuasion to whom he wasn't attentive.

"Why was Peacock calling *you?*" he asked.

"I'm going to overlook the rude emphasis," Ariel evaded. "Do you want to come or not?"

She left smiling, entirely aware of her evasion as well as the pique in which she'd left Henry.

Let him stew, she thought. If he thought Win's interest was professional, it couldn't hurt. If he believed it was personal, she surprised herself by realizing, she didn't mind that, either. She knew Win Peacock's reputation as well as Henry did, and the idea that a dashing (and, to countless women, desirable) man might find her attractive couldn't do her image any harm. In fact, it did her ego considerable good.

It didn't hit Ariel until later that she hadn't been the only one to evade a question; when she'd asked Henry if he was still in love with Emily, he'd changed the subject.

14

Ariel had no known experience as a hostess. From what she'd been told about her pre-amnesia self, she'd seldom been one, and this was her first party in this incarnation, so to speak. Small though the gathering would be, she was nervous.

She lighted the fire in the fireplace, a superfluity on a sixty-degree evening. She didn't care; she'd leave the windows open. Like the candles she also lit, the fire set a cozy mood. She brushed off her hands and surveyed her domain with an eye for any crooked picture, dead plant leaf, or dust ball previously overlooked.

This house was one of the few happy legacies from the past. The sequestered neighborhood in which it was located had come into being during the early thirties and had remained relatively untouched by time—except for sinfully escalating property values. Bought for a modest sum by her adoptive parents in the fifties, the house had been built solidly and with imagination; after it had become hers, it had been remodeled with no less imagination. To coved ceilings and hardwood floors, rounded wall angles and arched doorways, had been added French windows and skylights. The bedroom was almost certainly the result of combining two original rooms, leaving no guest room but creating a large, even luxurious sanctum, and the kitchen was the product of culinary savvy and considerable expense.

It was evident that the indulgence and loving care the old Ariel had denied herself personally had been lavished on the house. It remained unanswered and unanswerable why—when everything else about that ascetic woman was unfamiliar—the present Ariel had felt at one with herself in her house almost from the beginning.

Now, whipping through the dining room, she checked the table setting, again. Encouraging aromas drew her to the kitchen.

The stuffed pork tenderloin was in one oven, potatoes Anna in the other, and fresh green beans were ready to cook, the hors d'oeuvres were set out, and a last-minute check in the mirror told Ariel she was the very picture of a stylish and confident hostess.

" 'Style,' " she told Jessie, who worriedly watched her mistress dart about, " 'is knowing who you are, what you want to say, and not giving a damn.' "

The doorbell rang. Jessie set up a furious barking. Stonewall sauntered into the dining room dragging a pair of pantyhose. Ariel gave chase. Just as the delirious Stonewall disappeared beneath the table, the doorbell rang again. With a muttered threat in the direction of the fluttering tablecloth, Ariel answered the door.

Win Peacock looked even more Hollywood-handsome than Ariel had remembered: blond, chiseled, and just craggy enough to avoid being pretty. The former *Open File* correspondent raised one appreciate (and effective) eyebrow and let out a whistle as Stonewall barreled into the room barking with all the delinquent zeal of a guard dog who'd just remembered his duties. Ariel shouted "Hush!" and wondered where the pantyhose were.

The evening was one of those happy accidents of chemistry no amount of planning can contrive.

Marguerite Harris was at her most eccentric and entertaining. Completing the new play seemed to have charged the tiny septuagenarian with pure, bright-burning energy that crackled from her improbable rust-red hair to her be-ringed, liver-spotted hands which, as eloquently as those of a geisha, held her audience rapt.

Carl, her amused and amusing husband, provided practiced counterpoint. The adroitness of his performance suggested the foreign service; in reality it stemmed from theatrical training undertaken before most of the other guests were born.

As was usually the case, the enigmatic Laya subscribed to the philosophy "Don't talk unless you can improve the silence." Her stillness created its own kind of energy, and the keenness with which the tall, handsome black woman listened seemed to infuse whatever was said with importance.

Win Peacock made it perfectly clear that his legendary technique knew no limits of age, race, or availability. He teased the venerable Marguerite irreverently. Toward Laya, he was respectful, drawing her out in subtle ways. He flirted with Ariel and paid compliments she couldn't construe as mere flattery; his appetite lent credence to praise of her cooking and his anecdotes to regard for her professional abilities.

If his prowess was calculated, it was also fascinating to watch, and, out of left field, Ariel was reminded of the Plains Indians' ritual of counting coup: the warrior dashing into battle, recklessly touching an enemy, and escaping unscathed—just for the hell of it.

Henry was a big surprise. He displayed a hitherto undisclosed talent as a raconteur. Sly, perfectly timed, and probably apocryphal, his tales about famous folks in compromising positions, about the foibles of politicians of his acquaintance, and about his own misdeeds during his years in the news business were, as his son Sam might say, "awesome." They were also funny. If he occasionally gave Win the fish eye (and told an outrageously untrue story about the rakish scar on Win's cheek, which that gentleman had a habit of unconsciously and fondly stroking), he was more civilized than Ariel would have ever expected.

Shortly before the party began to wind down, Ariel went into the kitchen to refill the coffeepot. She was in the process of pouring when she heard a noise behind her and, simultaneously, felt the warm whisper of a breath on the back of her neck. Gasping, she spun to find Win Peacock.

He grinned. "Have I told you how exceptional you're looking these days?"

"You've mentioned it."

"I'm in town until Thursday; are you free any night between now and then?"

Ariel looked Win directly in the eye. "I don't think so," she said. "I know how you *really* got that scar on your cheek, remember? And the one I presume you have on your belly? There aren't many people around who've put their life on the line for me. I don't want to complicate a friendship I value."

Win laughed, showing his perfectly straight, white teeth to advantage. "The sorry truth is, if I'd known the guy was packing a knife, you'd probably have been the one ventilated, and what I want to get together with you about is strictly business. We have a coordinating producer slot coming open on *LifeTime.* I've told the powers that be about you. They're interested. Are you?"

"What were you and Mr. Wonderful talking about in the kitchen?" Henry asked.

The rest of the dinner guests had scattered into the night, and Ariel was saying her last good night, tiredly.

"This and that."

"I see." Henry plunged his hands into his pockets. "Oh, yeah," he said and pulled out Ariel's pantyhose. "My feet got tangled up in these things under the table. I didn't figure you'd want 'em returned over dessert."

Ariel closed her eyes and grimaced. "Stonewall," she said. "You're absolutely . . ."

Her thanks were cut off by the astonishing fact of Henry's mouth on hers. She felt a hand cup her chin, tilting her face, and fingers curling into the hair at the nape of her neck.

Almost before she could comprehend what was happening, Henry's lips moved, playing gently over hers, a whisper, moving to her neck, her ear, to one eye, and then, lingering, to the other. And then they were gone. Ariel swayed as if in a high wind and opened her eyes. Henry smiled.

"I can stop wondering now," he said, more to himself than to her. He picked up the pantyhose that had slipped unnoticed to the floor and placed them in her hands, closing her fingers over them with his own. "Sleep well," he said, "and make sure you lock up."

He was gone.

Dazed, Ariel touched her chin where his prickly beard had been. She was still rooted to the spot like a patch of crabgrass when her phone began to ring.

15

SARGE MCMANUS HAD PUT IT SUCCINCTLY AND AS UNALARMINGLY as possible considering that it was three in the morning in South Carolina and that what he'd said was, in any words, terrifying.

"He's not in ICU, and they're not saying it's life threatening. Now do you understand that? Ariel? Do you?"

"Yes. Okay," Ariel managed through clenched teeth. "But it *is* pneumonia? There's no question?" She crossed her free arm over her chest in an attempt to still the spasms sporadically gripping her.

"If he'd had a shot—like everybody over sixty ought to, according to the doctor—he wouldn't have gotten it. But B.F.'s not one for doctors or shots. Thinks he's invincible."

Ariel took in almost none of what Sarge had said. "But he's having trouble breathing, you said."

"They're handling that. He had no trouble wheezing out the specific command that I wasn't to call you, I'll tell you that. But I figure you're a big girl; you got a right to know. Hattie's down, too, by the way, but it's just flu, which I guess was the problem with B.F. to start with, but then it went into this other thing."

After assuring Sarge she'd be on the first available flight, Ariel called Henry, who hadn't gotten home yet. She left a message. She'd made travel arrangements and was in the process of distinctly muddled packing when he called back. Clearly, the tone of voice of her message had been revealing.

"What's the matter?"

"B.F.'s got pneumonia. I've got to go back to South Carolina."

"How bad?"

"Sarge says his life's not in danger but, Henry, he's nearly eighty."

"You need a ride to the airport?"

"I'm going at the crack of dawn. I've already arranged for a shuttle."

"Cancel it. What else can I do?"

"There's nothing—the dogs! I forgot about the dogs!"

Jessie, who'd been watching Ariel steadily—her head resting on her paws but her ears erect—came to immediate attention.

"I'll take them to the kennel," Henry offered. "Or, wait . . . You want me to stay there while you're gone? Dog-sit? House-sit?"

Ariel sank onto the bed, staring helplessly at the heavy wool pullover she'd been about to pack for eighty-five-degree weather. "You'd do that?"

"Till Friday, anyway—when Sam comes."

When they'd made arrangements for the morning and briefly discussed the most pressing business projects, Ariel fumbled with thank-yous. "And, Henry, about tonight—"

"Not now," he said in a voice Ariel had never heard before. "There'll be plenty of time to talk about that later."

Ariel would have reason to remember that assumption.

16

Ariel's had been the third message on Henry's machine. As he fixed himself a nightcap, which he then set down and immediately forgot, Henry turned over the implications of the first two. They'd both been left by Marty Spitz, a chum down at the county morgue.

It seems that a man hit and killed by a train and positively identified nine months before had been buried with the wrong name on his gravestone. The deceased had turned up alive in Arizona, turned in by a woman who'd thought she was his lawful wife and who, to her wrath, had learned she was second in line for that dubious honor. The erstwhile widow was no more pleased than the Arizona woman.

If a bigamist named Craig Fiore was alive, Henry's friend had superfluously pointed out, the body decimated on a railroad track in Carson belonged to somebody else. The bad news was that the corpus had been reduced to a pulpy jigsaw puzzle by a seven-hundred-ton locomotive and a string of freight cars. The interesting news was that the accident happened the same night Grant Lacy disappeared. Furthermore, the section of track on which the body had been scattered was no more than a few miles from Lacy's Virginia Country Club home in Long Beach.

Marty Spitz had been saying that he'd heard Henry was interested in Lacy, "so I knew you'd want to hear—" when the machine had cut him off.

Marty had called back. Sounding as if the disconnection had been a personal affront, he'd said, "I'm leaving work now. Call me tomorrow if you're interested."

If the body was Lacy's, Henry asked himself, why hadn't the police ascertained it at the time? A prominent man disappears. The same night somebody's hit by a train a few miles from where he's last seen and no connection's made? It didn't compute. Unless the cops *had* made the connection and eliminated Lacy as the victim. But if that was so, why had Marty the Morgue Rat called?

If, on the other hand, it was Lacy, how did the millionaire's walking into a freight train jibe with Cummings's shakedown?

Could I, Henry worried, be wrong about Cummings? Am I losing it that badly?

He scratched his chin through his beard and looked around for his drink. He found it making a new ring on a wooden bookcase. Dabbing ineffectually at the moisture, he mentally probed his gut for his little radar blip, that trusty pulse of right and wrong, news and nonnews. Evidently, it had turned in for the night. Henry swallowed watery scotch and decided to do the same.

He was trying to find his pajamas (the cleaning lady had been in that day and as she did each and every week, she'd put them away in a different place) when the unwelcome thought of Win Peacock drifted into his yawning brain.

He'd give a lot to know why the peerless Mr. Peacock had called Ariel and what he'd been up to in her kitchen tonight.

Ariel was, in a unique way, an innocent. Without a past to guide her, Henry reflected, without the insight gained from a lifetime of remembered experience, she was vulnerable. A virgin of the psyche. A babe in the woods . . . ripe for picking.

Henry could imagine what Ariel would have to say about that mixed metaphor—not to mention his own cynicism. Well, three failed marriages later, he'd earned it.

Something his father used to say when Henry was a smart-mouthed, know-it-all teenager popped into his mind. " 'The best substitute for experience,' " his dad would groan, " 'is being sixteen.' "

Ariel was as green now as he was then. Sure, she'd been married once in the long, long ago, but she had no recollection of it. Ariel remembered zero about her husband, not even his death.

Okay, she was intelligent and she was well read and, even though her own past was erased from her database, she retained an exceptional store of impersonal knowledge. Fine, Henry conceded. But book learning ain't street smarts; it's no substitute for the protective calluses you get only from experience. Ariel had none. Not of the romantic variety. Not to his knowledge, anyway.

Unless you wanted to count what happened last winter, Henry thought grimly, when she'd been romanced by a psycho trying to kill her. That she hadn't recognized him for the headcase he was just went to prove the point. Since then, she'd been too caught up in learning about her job, her new family—herself—to get involved in extraneous personal relationships. A chaser like Peacock could do her serious damage.

Henry found his pajamas. They seemed to have been starched. He crumpled them up and pounded on them. It didn't do much toward softening the pajamas, but it vented a little hostility.

Whatever it was Peacock had in mind, Henry thought with satisfaction, he wouldn't be following through on it in the immediate future. Then he thought of that kiss tonight—something he hadn't known was going to happen until it did—of the worry that had strained Ariel's voice on the phone, of the only relative she had in the world lying in a hospital across the country. He felt guilty. It didn't erase the satisfaction.

17

"I THOUGHT WE JUST GOT RID OF YOU," B.F. COMPLAINED IN A FRIGHTeningly thin voice and turned his too pale face away.

Ariel marched to his bed and took an unresisting hand in hers. "I always wondered what an old buffalo would look like in a hospital gown," she said. She took in the IV feeding into his arm, the oxygen apparatus unattached but ominously available, and gritted her teeth into a moderately convincing smile. All in all, it wasn't as bad as she'd envisioned. "Must be a real peep show when you have to use the bedpan. Don't worry." She gave the hand a quick brush with her lips. "I'll keep the tabloid cameras at bay, and I won't tell a soul how you look with your teeth out!"

That got him.

"The teeth don't come out." There was a wheeze in B.F.'s voice, but he managed testiness. "Pray you were lucky enough to get that sweet little gene!"

"That's more like it. Listen to me, B.F. Everybody gets sick, even ornery buzzards."

"I told Sarge not to call you."

"Sarge has better sense than you." Ariel looked around the room. "The Charleston florists must be sold out. Who're all your admirers?"

"Buncha corporate weasels that woulda rather sent wreaths."

Ariel smiled a genuine smile. "Be your usual contrary self and keep 'em waiting. Now, what can I do? Do you need anything?"

"Yeah. Distraction. Where's Sarge? Did he wait for you?"

"He'll be along, but he can't stay. Monroe's wife—Helen?—is up and about now, he said, and she's sitting with Hattie while he goes to—"

"Halley Barron's funeral. I was goin' but I don't reckon I will now."

"Why were you going? You haven't seen the woman in decades."

"You know us old folks and funerals. Go with Sarge, will you? He's no use at reportin'. You go, then come tell me about it."

"What is it with this place and funerals?" Ariel exclaimed. "I'm starting to feel like a professional mourner!"

"That dress you got on *is* right mournful. You expectin' me to expire on you while you were here?"

"B.F.—"

"It's nice, though—real nice. And just right for the occasion. Go on now. Make haste!"

"What are you looking at?"

Ariel shielded her eyes and directed them to the late-model sedan at which Sarge stared. It was across the street from where he was parking B.F.'s Lincoln, and a man in a dark suit leaned against the driver's-side door. He was silver-haired, fleshy of face and body, and his expression was appropriate for a funeral. His attention seemed to be focused on a black limo just then coming to dignified rest at a side door of the chapel. The car's tinted windows obscured its occupant or occupants. Ariel's gaze returned to the silver-haired man. "Who's he?" she asked.

"Marv Newton." Sarge turned off the air-conditioner and cut the engine. "Detective Marv Newton—the one you said called you. Wonder what he's doing here."

"Would he have known Halley?"

"Not likely. Wouldn't be many around that did since she left town thirty years ago." Sarge unhooked his seat belt. "Well, let's do it."

When they paused in the funeral home foyer to let their eyes adjust to the dimness, a somber man in a charcoal suit approached and directed them to the appropriate room. If a person could be said to chirrup funereally, he managed to do it.

"What on earth am I doing here?" Ariel muttered, almost colliding with Sarge when he stopped in a doorway. She edged around the broad slab of his back and took in the fairly crowded room.

"I thought you said not many people knew her," she whispered.

"I'd guess most of 'em aren't from here. The only person I see that I know is Old Lady Pruitt. She's lived next door to the Barron house since back when I lived there. And Newton, of course." He returned the nod of the detective, who took a seat in the rear pew.

"Why do you suppose she's being buried here instead of—where'd she live? Savannah?"

"For the last ten or fifteen years. Richmond before that, I think was what John William told me one time."

They found seats, and Ariel observed the scene through lowered lashes as muted organ music effused through the air.

There was a respectable showing of flowers: wreaths and sprays and potted plants. The mourners consisted mostly of middle-aged people, more women than men. The casket was closed.

Bending close to her companion's ear, slightly lower than her own, Ariel asked, "Where'd I get the idea that it was customary in the South to have the coffin open?"

"She was messed up bad, I heard," Sarge explained through barely moving lips. "Including the parts that show."

Ariel noticed that a woman was being ushered into a little balcony affair tucked into a discreet corner. She was dressed entirely in black—or at least what could be seen above the waist-high partition was black—and that included the sling that supported one arm. This, Ariel assumed, was surely the stepmother, Grace. The heavy black veil that shrouded her face evoked the woman who'd attended John William's funeral almost exactly a week before, the very woman who now lay in the casket.

Several questions had been bouncing around Ariel's mind, but the sling might just answer one of them. This funeral was being held later than was usual—Halley had been killed on Friday night and this was Tuesday—but perhaps, Ariel decided, Grace was only now able to be up and about.

There were other things that puzzled her. Like why would Grace show up for her stepdaughter's funeral but not her son's?

Because she'd been closer to Halley? No, Ariel thought; even if it was true, it wasn't a rational reason. It was more likely that she was looking at this backward: probably Grace had simply been too devastated by her son's death to mourn him publicly.

Ariel's throat closed. She could feel real pity for any parent outliving both her children—the one she'd borne and the one she'd mothered. It was unnatural; it must be nearly unbearable.

The music ended on a poignant, echoing note, and a man ascended the dais. He was slightly stooped, with gray curling hair and a neat matching beard. Speaking with an accent similar to but not exactly the Gullah-flavored speech of Charleston, he introduced himself as James Salter, dean of Savannah Junior College, where Dr. Barron had taught. It gave Ariel a jolt to realize that, until now, she hadn't even known Halley was a professor. Learning that basic thing here, now, made her presence feel less appropriate than ever.

On this sad occasion, Dean Salter was saying, they were fortunate to have the benefit of Halley Barron's wishes in regard to the services. As always, he said, she'd known her own mind. She'd had the foresight of a practical woman, and it would be his privilege to carry out her expressed desires to the best of his ability. He continued with a brief and, Ariel thought, carefully rehearsed eulogy that she shortly tuned out.

Sarge, she recalled, hadn't attempted to answer her question about why Halley was being buried in a city where she hadn't lived for thirty years and where there'd be few to visit her grave. Had it been her preference or had it been Grace's decision? Or was the answer once again the simplest one: a family plot here in Charleston where all the Barrons expected to be buried.

Ariel saw that a woman had assumed the podium, Halley's fellow professor and friend, she gathered. She tried to concentrate on the tribute. It was short but fervent, touching on the dead woman's uncommon discipline and courage and a selflessness all but extinct in the age of "me." Brevity, too, must have been a trait respected by Halley Barron. The poem read by the last speaker, another woman, was as brief as a limerick.

" 'The friends that have it I do wrong,' " she recited quietly, " 'When ever I remake a song/Should know what issue is at stake,/It is myself that I remake.' "

Ariel hadn't caught the poet's name.

The finale was rendered by a violinist. As the haunting melody of Pachelbel's *Canon in D* filled the room, Ariel was thinking that while it might not be your everyday dirge, it certainly wasn't as provocative a choice as the poem that preceded it.

She watched the woman segregated from the other mourners on her lonely little balcony and wondered what that painfully erect back suggested. Did Grace Barron disapprove of the somewhat unorthodox proceedings? Had she even heard the poem and the music? Ariel wondered, too, about the woman who'd chosen them. She wondered, again, what she was doing here.

She glanced back to where the grim-faced detective Newton sat. His eyes were on the stepmother.

18

"I didn't know that Old Lady Pruitt was up to runnin' around to funerals," B.F. said to Sarge. "I'd figured she'd long since been guest of honor at one."

The old man looked a little feverish, Ariel thought, but the pleasure he was taking in their gossip might account for it.

"Pruitt," she repeated to Sarge. "The neighbor, didn't you say? When you lived in the Barron house. When was that?"

"When Dad married Mama Val, John's mother, we moved into her house. I grew up there. John moved back into it after his mother and then, later, my father, died."

"And that was the same house John William lived in?"

"And died in."

"Ordinary People!" Ariel blurted. Both men looked at her quizzically.

"I wouldn't call the Barrons ordinary," B.F. said.

"No, no. That was the movie the Pachelbel piece was used in—the music they played at the funeral today. It's been driving me crazy trying to remember it." She looked from one man to the other and opened her hands in a so-sue-me shrug.

"What was the story with Grace?" she asked. "Did she stay in the house after her husband died?"

"I wouldn't say she did all that much 'staying,' " Sarge commented, "but, yeah, she lived in the house a few years."

"Place weighed on her, I'd guess," put in B.F. "She did a right smart amount of travelin' once the boy got a little age on him. Halley raised him more day-in-day-out than his mother did—wouldn't you say so?" He shifted his massive bulk uncomfortably, turning toward the radiator where Sarge perched.

"Yeah. Till she left to get her Ph.D. Then he pretty much raised himself. There was always some housekeeper or other, and Grace flitting in and out. He was young when he went off to military school, maybe too young, but it had to be an improvement." Sarge's eyes took on a distant look. "Poor kid was always mixed up. He couldn't figure out why his mother would hang on to him one minute—in ways that weren't that healthy, I don't think—and then go off and leave him the next."

"Unhealthy how?" Ariel asked.

Sarge hesitated. "Look, this is all secondhand—bits and pieces heard through the years, you know? I believe on some level Grace tried to replace John with John William. He looked so much like his father, in some ways got to *be* like him—sensitive and secretive and kind of a loner . . . Who knows? Maybe it was painful for her to be around him. The net result was, he never knew where he was at. He craved affection. Then she'd take a turn smothering him, and even a kid knows when he's being used. He probably felt guilty because he wasn't his father. I wouldn't be surprised if he felt guilty *about* his father—like he was to blame, which is nuts, but nobody ever said feelings made sense."

Each considered the unarguable validity of that statement before B.F. tossed in: "Just to complicate things, there was also the matter of John's will."

"What about it?" Ariel asked.

"He left everything—and it was a considerable estate—to his children; each one got half."

"I thought he didn't know about Grace being pregnant."

"What I said was I didn't *know* if he knew. Made no difference; the will specified everything went to Halley or, if there were more offspring at the time of John's death, it'd be equally divided."

Ariel thought about that and asked, "Did John William still have a lot when he died? Had he held on to his half?"

B.F. raised his eyebrows inquiringly, turning the floor over to Sarge.

"He lived as if he wasn't hurting any, and I have heard talk that he inherited my brother's flair for shrewd investing. Too bad he didn't get his other talents, too."

"You mean as an artist?" Ariel asked. "John William was an artist?"

Sarge nodded. "I always thought it was one of his biggest disappointments, one of the really big hurts, when he finally had to admit he'd never be more than a good technician. He just didn't have the God-given gift John had."

"Who got *his* money?" B.F. suddenly put in. "I never thought to ask about John William's will."

"Halley," said Sarge.

"Mercy," B.F. commented succinctly, pinching his lips together as if he'd just eaten something bad.

"And who got—" Ariel began just as her grandfather said, "Hand me some ice water, one of you, will you?"

Ariel leaped to comply, and while she was filling a glass, she fussed. "We need to get something to eat! Do you realize I haven't had anything since breakfast—*airline* breakfast!"

Ariel sank into the overstuffed sofa and waved a hand in front of her face in an ineffectual attempt to stir the air. Her body should think it was only eight o'clock; how did it know the clock read eleven? She wasn't sure if that day's eighty-seven-degree high still qualified as a heat wave, but there was no question the humidity was an assault: a fair trade for the smog she'd left behind in California but still a burden, heavy as soggy wool. She was worn to a frazzle. She considered sleeping where she sat.

"All done." Sarge came in, flipping a dish towel over his shoulder. "So are you, looks like."

"Done for," Ariel agreed, "between the weather and worry. Not to mention our in-house invalid. There's nothing to wear a body down like playing Florence Nightingale to someone who sees you more as Lizzie Borden." She grinned tiredly. "Somehow I don't think my tender ministrations cut any ice with Hattie the Hun."

"Might be like what I was saying about Grace and John William. You look like Jane. She's dead; you're alive. It hurts. Hattie'll come around one of these days. Meantime, why can't her aunt down in Beaufort play nursemaid?"

"Cousin. She's got grandchildren she takes care of. Hattie won't let her expose the children."

Sarge sat in B.F.'s favorite chair and wiped at a smudge on the piecrust table beside it. "Well, then . . ." he said, "I'll do it."

"Curb your enthusiasm. I'll manage."

The phone rang, a distant shrill from the kitchen.

Sarge went to answer and seconds later summoned Ariel. It was Henry, calling from her house to check on B.F.

"It's not as bad as I feared," Ariel told him, "but I'm glad I came just the same."

"Good. That's good. I thought you ought to know, you just got a call from a detective out there, somebody named Newton. I gave him that number."

"Maybe now I'll find out why we saw him today at a funeral where he had no obvious reason to be."

"You went to another funeral?"

"I did."

"Somebody else you didn't know?"

"Never met her in my life."

"What do you people do down there—go through the obituaries? Don't you have TV?"

"This was the half sister of the man whose funeral I went to last trip."

"My God, this family's like a bunch of lemmings! Don't tell me she did herself in, too?"

"No, Halley Barron didn't kill herself. Car accident."

"You sure there's no story here?"

"I'm beginning to wonder. After I talk to Newton, maybe I'll have a better idea. How're the dogs? Any problems?"

"Jessie's lying by the front door waiting, I think, for you to come home. As for the other one . . . How fond were you of some kind of plant that used to be in your dining room?"

Ariel sighed. "Anything else?"

"Nothing important. I saw Marguerite Harris walking that fossil of a dachshund of hers, and I told her about B.F. She sends love. That's about it. Oh, yeah. Peacock left a message on your machine—something about getting together tomorrow night?"

"Oh, good grief! I completely forgot! Did he say where I could reach him?"

Henry read off the hotel phone number he'd copied down,

made some unsubtle attempts to pry into the nature of their date, and finally gave up the effort and asked how long she planned on staying.

"Two or three days if all goes well. I'd better get off the phone. We don't have such novelties as Call Waiting, and I don't want to miss Newton."

"And you've got to call Peacock, too, I know," Henry needled. "Call me as soon as you know when you'll be back."

Ariel was so used to his habit of abruptly hanging up that she didn't even notice when he did it.

Failing to find Win in, she left her number. She'd gotten as far as the door when the phone rang again.

"This is Marv Newton here. Am I speakin' to Ariel Gold?" The voice Ariel recalled from her previous conversation with the detective was a pleasant baritone, almost musical. It seemed incongruous with the stone-faced man she'd seen at the funeral.

"I wondered," Newton said, "if that just might've been you with Jackie McManus at the mortuary today."

"Jackie?" Ariel cast an amused glance toward the living room. "You're working awfully late, Detective. What can I do for you?"

"Let me ask you something. Don't I know you?"

"Me? Oh, I doubt that." The reply had been careless, purely reflexive, but in an instant Ariel snapped to attention. "Why? What makes you ask that?" The blank book of her past, an abstract of one-dimensional facts, was never far from her consciousness. The pages waited, always, to come to life, to be filled, to be peopled. Had *he* looked familiar? *Could* he know her?

"I've got this memory for faces," the detective said. "Sometimes it's a curse, like when I can't put 'em in context. You're not originally from here?"

"Los Angeles. Were you ever there?"

"No'm. Never mind. It'll come to me. Listen, Miz Gold, I just had one or two more questions about this meeting you had with John William Barron. You mind? Particularly about this 'fear' reference you made mention of? Some things have come up that make us a little more curious about that."

"What things?"

"I believe you said he never did tell you just what it was he was afraid of, is that right?"

Ariel conceded that was so.

"He didn't bring up any particular person, during the whole of your conversation, that could've been the cause of his concern?"

"Like Grace Barron, you mean?"

Ariel heard a sharp metallic squeal that sounded very much like Henry Heller's swivel chair, and when Newton spoke again, his voice was no longer melodious.

"He called her by name?"

"No, Detective Newton, he didn't. That was just a shot in the dark." And a bull's-eye, Ariel thought. "Do you think Mrs. Barron was connected to her son's death in some way?"

"We don't know that anybody was 'connected to his death' but him. We have to look into every possibility, though, and we appreciate your help. Now you didn't see anybody else at all that night on the beach, is that right? Nobody on the dunes? Nobody in one of those public parking lots down there near the inn?"

"Nobody," Ariel said and then, slowly, "but I just remembered . . . John William did make one oblique mention of his mother."

" 'Oblique' how? What'd he say?"

"Well, it's probably nothing, but he said . . . He was talking about when he was young, and he said he'd had 'no mother to speak of.' I think that's how he put it."

"Doesn't sound like he thought much of his mama, does it?" Newton muttered and asked her to repeat it while he wrote it down.

"I've also remembered one other thing he said; although, taken out of context, it may just be misleading."

"If you don't mind, ma'am, you let me muddle through."

" 'Murder, like God, is no respecter of persons.' "

"Say what?"

Ariel repeated the odd comment, assuring the detective that she recalled nothing else of interest.

"You going to be in town awhile, Miz Gold? You think you could come down here and go over this with me? Sign a statement?"

They arranged to meet the following day, and the music was back in the policeman's voice when he inquired after her grandfather ("Your granddaddy's Mr. B.F. Coulter, somebody said? He's doin' some better, I heard?").

Ariel hung up feeling, illogically, guilty and slightly dirty. She experienced the same reservations she'd felt before, as if she were a busybody trying to insinuate herself into a tragedy.

Filicide. The word dropped into her mind like lead. It was unthinkable. People you knew didn't kill their children.

She was quite sure that Marv Newton thought otherwise and, with her help, he was trying to prove it.

Ariel poured iced tea into a glass and took it into the "front room," as B.F. called the living room. There was no one there. She found Sarge on the porch, his chair tilted back on its rockers, his feet propped on the banister.

"It's cooler out here, isn't it?" she said, and settled on the steps. The crickets, which had paused in their concert as if the squeak of the screen door had made them curious, resumed.

After listening for a moment, she said, "That last call was from Marv Newton."

"You get anything out of him?"

"What makes you think I was the one doing the 'getting'?"

Ariel couldn't see Sarge's sardonic glance in the dark, but she could sense it. "Unless I'm mistaken," she said, "he has the notion that Grace Barron is involved in your nephew's death."

"I wondered when he'd get around to that theory."

Ariel peered in surprise at the shadowy mass that was Sarge. "*You* think she was?"

"I didn't say that. John William and Grace had a falling-out a few years back. Old Marv was bound to hear rumors."

Ariel mulled that over before asking what the problem had been.

"John William never said, but the two of them didn't have much contact after that."

"Is that why she didn't go to his funeral?"

"I'd hate to think it ran that deep, but with family feuds you never know."

"But, good Lord, Sarge, even if he didn't . . . even if it wasn't suicide, this 'falling-out' would've had to be the next thing to Armageddon for his own mother to kill him in cold blood!"

"It happens."

"This quarrel . . . Is that why Grace moved away?"

"You got me beat." The rocker creaked as Sarge bent to a

wicker table beside him. He thumbed a lighter into flame, and Ariel watched as he inhaled one of his rationed cigarettes.

"What about Halley?" she asked. "Why'd she leave town?"

"I don't guess there's any mystery there. She just never came back after she went away to school. Probably had a job offer in Richmond or wherever it was and went on from there."

"Tell me more about her," Ariel said, and leaned back against the railing. "How old was she when her father died?"

There was a brief red glow as Sarge inhaled again and reflected. "Fourteen, maybe? Fifteen?"

"You know what I find intriguing? If your nephew did plan to die . . . Here was this man B.F. says tended to dramatize himself, and he not only left no note, as far as I know he left no instructions about his burial, his last appearance on this mortal coil, yet—"

"Most people don't like to—"

"I know. Most people don't like to think about life going on without them. But what I started to say is: Halley, *not* knowing she was going to die, apparently *did* make her wishes known."

"Judging by how she sounded when I called to tell her about John William, she was one tough cookie." Sarge flicked ashes over the porch rail before he continued, sounding as if he were dredging up memories long unexamined. "That's not the way I remember her at all. As a kid she had this . . . fragility. Sort of a shy, old-fashioned way about her. How she talked. How she wore her hair . . . John, her father, was her world. What with her mother running off when she was a baby and him raising her alone till he married Grace, John and Halley were like that." He held up two tightly pressed fingers and after a beat, rather grudgingly, he said, "She was the one that found John's body. Did you know that?"

"No! Oh, Sarge, that poor child!"

"Some doctor sent her away then, for quite a while. Months. Some clinic or sanatorium in, I think, Columbia. I left town around then, so I just got bits and pieces after that. I do know that when she came back to town—right after John William was born, it was—she was a different girl. Serious. Grown up and . . . I don't know."

"Little wonder she was a realist about loss and death! Her mother, her father, and, finally, her brother, too."

"Yeah. And she was nuts about him, I gather. Spoiled him from the get-go."

"Maybe she saw the baby as a continuum. A way to hold on to the father she'd loved." Ariel shifted to find a more comfortable position and looked over at the pale moon of Sarge's face. "How do you suppose her friends got hold of her preferences—what she wanted read and played and so forth?"

"Her will?"

"I guess. About that . . . ?"

She heard Sarge sigh as if he were drained by the whole situation, but he answered.

"There was a sizable bequest for the school where she worked, I understand, with the balance to go to her only other heir—if that person survived her."

"You're not going to tell me . . ."

"Yeah. Grace. And what with the recent addition of John William's estate, with all this happening as fast as it did, it'd be interesting to know if that balance might've been a lot more than Halley intended."

"Round and round it goes," Ariel marveled. "That reminds me of something else I hope you won't mind my asking. Why'd John Barron cut his wife out of his will in the first place?"

"It wasn't a matter of cutting her out. She was never in. My brother was an artist and a dreamer and all that good stuff, but he wasn't a fool. Especially about money. When I heard he planned to marry this girl half his age, I was, let's say, a little cynical? So he told me he'd had a will written up specifying that Grace would come into half his estate—after five years. If they didn't stay married that long, she'd get the minimum the law allowed—in her case, as it turned out, a courtesy stipend."

"South Carolina, I take it, isn't a community property state."

"You take right."

"It doesn't seem entirely fair, does it?"

"It seems smart. Grace did all right. She lived in the house as long as she wanted to, and there was one other 'little' thing. John did leave the *contents* of the house to Grace. She redecorated the place when they married, so he thought it was only right that she get the things she'd picked out. Also in the house, though—in the connected studio—was all his work, so except for a few paintings he expressly left to Halley, Grace got 'em all."

"How nice for her!" Ariel said.

"You have any idea how much those paintings are worth today? I'll tell you something. With hindsight, I've always thought John's not being more particular about the paintings, not taking their potential worth into consideration, said a lot about his state of mind. Like, if he hadn't come to see himself as a failure, he wouldn't have done what he did. And the note backs that up."

"The note? Oh! You mean a suicide note! So your brother *did* leave one?"

Sarge nodded. "Oh, yeah," he said grimly. "No loose ends for John; he left a note."

Ariel sipped her tea and waited to see if he'd elaborate. After a few minutes, he did. It was obvious that he'd long since memorized the contents of his brother's last message.

" 'This is the worst yet,' " he recited as unemotionally as if it were the weather report. " 'The flame seems to have gone out, you see, and that's the pain I can't bear. I've come to the point that I can't keep putting my heart and soul into an effort that seems more and more futile. This impotence, this self-doubt, is corrosive. I hate what it's doing to me.' "

Sarge cleared his throat, took a last drag of his cigarette, and flipped it over the railing in a shower of red sparks.

Ariel was pondering the implications of the words when he said, "You wanna know something rotten? My brother bled over his art. He put his soul into those canvases. And when he was finally 'discovered,' a rumor got around that it wasn't even his work; that he'd signed his name to the 'real' artist's paintings, and it was shame that drove him to suicide. I heard about it on a trip down here. Located the lowlife that started the talk. He wasn't much into gossip about the Barrons when I got through with him."

19

Henry slept like a baby and awakened with the birds—with Stonewall, actually. The dog was standing on his hind legs beside the bed. When Henry opened his eyes, knowing even in his sleep that he was being stared at, forepaws were inches from his face.

He tried, unsuccessfully, to slip back into an elusive, honeyed dream. He stretched, luxuriating in the slow ebb of dream-induced bliss. Ariel's mattress, he decided, was unusually comfortable. Ariel's pillowcases, he noticed—even freshly laundered—bore her fragrance. Ariel, he suddenly recalled, had been in his dream.

Henry got up and took a cold shower.

By eight o'clock he'd already been at his desk for an hour, sorting through the latest development in the Lacy case.

The day before, he'd visited Marty at the morgue—actually on the warmer, brighter, livelier loading dock, where the only smells one had to contend with came from garbage and exhaust fumes.

Marty had little to add to what he'd left on Henry's answering machine. The body buried beneath a righteous epitaph in a Torrance cemetery was not that of a man named Craig Fiore. Mr. Fiore was indubitably alive, and he'd taken a second wife without properly dispensing with the first. As to why the spare body parts on the Carson railroad tracks had been deemed Fiore's, Marty didn't know. He did know they were going to be exhumed.

For more information Henry had gone to police headquarters, Parker Center, downtown. He'd been able to learn only that evidence found at the accident scene had seemed conclusively to ID Fiore. There was to be a hearing but, meantime, the bigamist and his lawyer were saying nothing.

Henry heard an "ahem" and looked up to see his assistant grinning at him.

"Your hair's standing up in a cowlick," Tara Castanera said, and handed him a raft of messages. "From after you left yesterday."

Henry gave his head an ineffectual swipe and foraged for his reading glasses. "What happened to yours?" he said.

"My what?"

"Your hair."

"Oh. Ebony Silk."

"Excuse me?"

"That's the color. You like it? I'm thinking of cutting it, too. Really short and sort of spiky with bangs. Kind of a New Age Audrey Hepburn look."

"Hmm," said Henry, who, accustomed to Tara's personal creativity, had stopped listening. He saw that he'd gotten a callback from Clifford Gilroy. Very interesting. His calls to the MicroStar interim head hadn't been returned before the news broke about the corpse mix-up. Why, Henry wondered, when the press must be on Gilroy like starved pigs at a trough, would he call now?

He had his hand on the telephone when Tara said, "Will you wait? I've been passing Ariel's calls on, but there's some I wasn't sure who you wanted to handle. You probably ought to check these."

Henry sorted through a half dozen additional slips, okaying or delegating as he went. He squinted. "What's this one?"

"Psychologist. Said something about PTSD. What's PTSD?"

"What I experience every night after I leave here. Post-traumatic stress disorder, by name." Henry handed the slips back to Tara. "Tell Theo Bell to field the call."

"I did. He did."

"Then what are you asking me for?"

"Theo tried to reach Ariel at her grandpa's and couldn't. Some question he needs to ask. He wants to know when she'll be back."

"He wants to know because he's a nosy old lady," Henry muttered. He was already punching telephone buttons.

He thought repetition would have polished Gilroy's official statement by now.

The former finance officer's delivery was stilted when he said, "Naturally, we're still holding out hope. Many people were reported missing during the same time period Grant was. This . . . train incident could be entirely unrelated."

"Could Lacy have been in that area? He ever run there?"

"Anything's possible."

"But is it probable?"

"You must know the accident site wasn't far from his home. Grant had . . . I know Grant had several routes mapped out, specific distances he alternated running. I don't know where they were."

"So it could be him."

Henry heard a sigh. "I've always believed that if Grant was alive, nothing could keep him away from here. He invented MicroStar. It's his brainchild."

The frankness took Henry by surprise. Stress, or upset, he thought, must be taking a toll.

"Mr. Heller, this . . . this obscene farce wasn't uncovered until yesterday. I believe you'd left several messages before that."

"That's right, I had."

"Why?"

"An interesting item I'd heard about. Something that, ah, turned up with one of my people."

"What item?"

"Do you know a man—" Henry reconsidered. Some things were better asked face-to-face.

"Do I know what man? This 'item' . . . is this something you should be taking to the police? Or is it some kind of sleazy innuendo?"

This isn't news to him, Henry sensed; because he was the person Cummings met or has he merely heard rumors?

"Well?" Gilroy said.

"I think we should meet, Mr. Gilroy."

"You, me, and your cameras? I don't think so."

"I didn't say anything about—"

"I know what editing can make out of perfectly innocent answers and, frankly, I'm not a glib man. MicroStar's a good, solid company now. Solid money behind us. Solid future. I'm talking to you right now. If you know anything, anything at all that could hurt us—about anybody in this company—I want to hear it, and I don't mean on the air."

"I don't have any hidden agenda, Mr. Gilroy, and we don't deliberately slant—"

"You just keep in mind that we've got top-notch legal talent on call, Heller, and I'm not afraid to turn them loose."

The dial tone told Henry he'd handled things better in his time; maybe that's what the hidden agenda he'd just denied was doing to his technique.

The day went into high gear. Henry issued orders. He made assignments. He insisted on cuts in a death row interview that was coming together with all the trenchancy of suet. Behind the normal, edge-of-precipice panic of putting together a TV newsmagazine, his mind never strayed far from the Lacy file.

He tried and again failed to track down Vaughn Lacy, Grant Lacy's brother. He had better luck this time with Betty Lacy. The wife or widow of the missing man answered on the first ring. She'd just finished a call, Henry thought, or she was expecting one.

Sounding harassed, and as if she deeply regretted answering, Mrs. Lacy said she knew nothing more than he did about these new developments, that "naturally" she hoped the body wasn't her husband's, but that "closure" would be a relief however it came. With that, she began to weep and hung up.

Henry's gut told him the corpse was Lacy's. Whether Mrs. Lacy would get her closure, however, remained to be seen. If she did, the *Open File* segment might be history; closed cases didn't qualify for the show. Of course, there were still some interesting questions to be answered. Like why the tycoon—who, according to the aforementioned wife, had left the house for a twilight jog—was playing chicken with a freight train.

Henry didn't know what state the remains were in at interment (Marty had, enthusiastically, begun to paint a picture for him, but Henry had been in no mood for graphic art). He didn't want to imagine what they'd be like now. They didn't embalm odds and ends, did they? There were always teeth, of course, but why hadn't they checked that out in the first place? And what was the "conclusive evidence" that led the cops to believe it was Fiore they'd found? It was safe to assume the victim wasn't wearing dog tags.

What Henry did know was that whoever had been on those tracks, whether it proved to be Grant Lacy or not and whether the story ever made *The Open File*, he was still on the case. As far as he was concerned, the quarry wasn't Lacy; it was Henry's ex-employee: the extortionist Richard Cummings.

20

" 'I VERY SOON STARTED BACK FROM THERE, FOR THE EMPTY DOG-kennel was filled up with a great dog—deep-mouthed and black-haired like Him—and he was very angry at the sight of me, and sprang out to get at me.' "

Ariel closed the book B.F. had gotten from a candy striper and said, "That's it for now."

You can't stop there," B.F. protested. "Read some more."

"I didn't know you were such a fan of Dickens." She sipped water, covertly scrutinizing her grandfather over the rim of the glass. He'd regained some color, but he was still congested and his temperature was still not back to normal.

"There's lots of interesting things you don't know about me." He sighed dramatically. "David Copperfield and I have a right smart in common . . . hard beginnings and the grit to overcome 'em. I must've read that one half a dozen times."

"What hard beginnings?" Ariel asked with genuine curiosity.

"If you're in such a big rush to get over to the police station and solve the crime of the century—which I still contend is a crime only since suicide's legally considered to be one—you don't have time to do justice to my life story."

"Well, hold the thought. I want to hear the whole uplifting saga, beginning with 'I am born.' Now, Sarge said police headquarters is on Lockwood?" She unfolded a street map she'd found at the house. "He said it was within walking distance?"

"Yeah, turn right when you go out the front door of the hospital. Here, let me show you," he said, and did.

Ariel was shouldering her handbag when B.F. spoke up.

"Newton's on the wrong track, Ariel Gold. You tell him I said so. The Grace Barron I knew couldn't kill anybody." He went quiet, and his eyes lost focus as he sank into memory and sentimentalism. "Lively as a tango, that girl was. Always made you feel like you were the most interesting man alive when she turned those big eyes on you, you know? The truest blue, her eyes. Like morning glories. 'Glory,' " he murmured under his breath.

B.F. caught Ariel's look, cleared his throat, and, with a look of his own, dared her to comment. "That's what I used to call her."

"Listen, my dear, Grace or 'Glory' or whatever, that 'girl' is forty years older, and you don't need me to tell you life can do ugly things to people. Truth is, though, I agree with you. A mother murdering her own child is too . . . evil, isn't it? To comprehend."

She stopped with her hand on the door. "But I will say this. I'm not so sure as you are that *somebody* didn't kill the man."

"You've read it over carefully, Miz Gold?"

Marv Newton squinted at the statement Ariel was about to sign and then removed his glasses and peered at her face. She peered back. One of the detective's eyes was slightly cocked, and it made it difficult to know just where to look. It occurred to Ariel that he was well aware of the discomfort his affliction caused; he used it to advantage, she imagined.

Grateful to have something else to look at, she put pen to paper. "I wouldn't sign it otherwise," she said.

"This is what John William Barron said to you, verbatim, on the last night of his life—is that right?"

"Now, wait!" Ariel stopped midstroke. "Say it like that, and I feel like retracting every word! I hope I've made it clear: this is what was said as I *remember*. I didn't have my tape recorder. I didn't know the conversation might have significance. I didn't even know who he was!"

Troubled, she picked up the photographs she'd been shown to verify that the man she'd met actually was John William Barron.

She was studying them when there was a rap on the door. The man who stuck his head in started to say something, spotted Ariel, and nodded hello. "Marv?" he said, and signaled "outside." The door closed behind the two men, and Ariel returned her attention to the photos.

Minutes later, Marv Newton's fine baritone intruded on her reverie.

"Sorry about that. You doin' all right? You sure I can't get you some coffee?"

Ariel repeated her earlier refusal. She noticed that Newton, who'd left looking merely busy, had returned looking harassed.

"Problems?" she asked.

"You're in a police station, Miz Gold." The detective's fleshy jowls sagged. "You hear about that doctor over on Edisto? Ferguson? Walked in on a burglary in progress? Died," he said. "It's homicide now." He sighed. "You back lookin' at those pictures? You *are* still certain that's the man you talked to?"

"Yes."

"Whoa!" he said suddenly. "That's it! That's where I saw you!" He took a photo from her hand and gave it a perfunctory glance. When he turned his gaze to Ariel, it was anything but perfunctory. A slow smile spread over his face.

"I thought you said you'd never met this man before a couple of weeks ago."

"I've said it more than once. It's true."

Newton nodded. He perched himself on the edge of the table, very close to Ariel's chair. He leaned toward her, using his walleye to full effect.

"In that case, how do you explain a picture in the deceased's house? A picture of you and this man, John William Barron, together—and lookin' very chummy?"

"I don't explain it. I can't because it didn't happen."

Or did it? *Had* she known John William before two weeks ago? The stunning thrill of possibility she'd felt on the phone last night surged again, and rational thought fled as it had more than once in past months when, outside the context of Ariel Gold's life, there'd been the sudden conviction that a face was familiar. It had happened that very morning outside the hospital: a stranger hesitating as if on the verge of hailing her. She'd been sure for the space of a moment that the man knew her, that he was about to call her name.

She wet her lips. "You're sure it was me? What did it look like? Could I see it?"

"Now, that's an interesting reaction. You and he, the victim, were in a boat. You were, maybe, twenty. He looked older, a little older than here." He waved the photo. "Same expression, like an undertaker. You, as I recall, were laughin'."

Ariel's brain, sabotaged by hope, had already kicked in. She let out her breath. "That was my sister," she said. "I told you, he and she were friends. She spent summers here."

"No, ma'am. I told you, I'm good with faces. The girl in that picture was you."

"The girl in that picture was Jane. She and I were twins."

The first sign of doubt flicked across the detective's face. After a moment, his shoulders drooped. "You never said you were twins. Now that I think of it, you never said how it was that she knew Barron and you didn't."

Ariel picked up the statement, trying to absorb the words she'd earlier related. Too much familiarity made them meaningless. "Jane grew up with our grandfather," she said. "I didn't. None of this has any bearing on your case, Detective. Could we get back to that?"

Reluctantly, Newton obliged, but he'd no sooner said "Okay" than his phone buzzed. He picked it up and barked his name. A minute passed during which he said nothing more. "Hold on." He pressed a button, mumbled, "Be right back" to Ariel, and left again.

This time he returned looking preoccupied. He stared through Ariel for several seconds before he gave his head a fractional shake. "You want to read that statement one more time?"

"No."

"It is, to the best of your recollection, what he said?"

"If you believe 'The truth is more important than the facts,' " Ariel said to herself.

"Come again?"

"Detective Newton, I don't want to beat a dead horse, but I also don't want words that were casually spoken to do damage to a woman who must already be desolate. I want to make sure you understand the context in which these things were said."

His head down, Newton pinched the bridge of his nose between his thumb and forefinger. Ariel fancied that she could read his mind; he was calculating how many years remained before he could take early retirement.

"I think I've grasped it," he said. "It was the middle of the night, and there was a full moon and the surf was poundin'. You've explained how you two were talkin' about when your sister and the deceased were children once upon a time and you can't say for sure that he *was* scared but just that he *said* he was scared."

He raised his head, and his expression was that of a man sorely tried. "Miz Gold, I presume that if Barron had said outright he thought somebody meant to kill him, you'd have reported it then. If he'd pointed the finger at some particular person, you'd say so. You didn't. What he said is what he said, whatever the mood of the moment was. It's just a potential piece of a puzzle and, by itself, it's not incriminatin'. I appreciate your . . . scrupulousness. But we're not on TV. You're not goin' to be sued. And—let's be clear on this—we're not tryin' to railroad anybody. Not a soul."

"What about the injury to John William's head—a bruise, was it?" Ariel instinctively went on the offensive.

"I don't believe I mentioned what it was specifically. But you indicated there"—he pointed to the statement—"that you didn't see anything, right?"

"It *was* night. Unless we're talking about a facial wound, something obvious and visible, I wouldn't have seen it."

Newton said nothing.

"I mean if it was under the hairline . . ."

"Uh-huh."

"He didn't say anything about being hurt. He didn't act hurt."

"Uh-huh," Newton repeated. "What about jewelry? You happen to notice if he was wearin' any?"

Ariel was taken by surprise. "Jewelry?" she repeated. "Like what?"

"Like jewelry. A ring, a watch—anything. *Jewelry*."

"I don't remember any . . ." There'd been a gleam on his wrist, she suddenly recalled, when he was writing in the sand. She closed her eyes, picturing the scene. "There was something around his wrist. It could've been a watch, I guess, but I think it was a bracelet. It was wide—and silver."

"Which wrist?"

"The right one."

"You're sure it was the right wrist?"

At Ariel's nod, Newton recalled the stenographer who'd taken her statement. He asked Ariel to repeat what she'd just told him, and they both waited silently while the statement was amended.

Ariel signed it.

When the detective had walked her out to the large anteroom, she lingered where he'd left her, pondering what the bracelet questions signified.

She sensed eyes on her. A middle-aged woman was working at a computer keyboard, but she was staring at Ariel. Ariel smiled; the woman's gaze veered back to the screen.

Ariel was reminded of the exercise in dashed hopes she'd just put herself through. Stop this! she scolded herself. The lady doesn't know you. You don't know her. She's probably deciding whether to tell you your slip's showing. She approached the desk.

"Excuse me. Is there someplace close by that might still be serving lunch?"

The woman turned bright, curious eyes on Ariel as if she'd just noticed her presence.

"Lunch?" she asked and ran her tongue over her front teeth in a darting motion that made Ariel think of her dog Stonewall. "Oh . . . surely." She pointed. "Go one block yonder, turn left. Two blocks down—Bee Street, it is—turn right." She consulted the map Ariel laid out and thumped the location with a confident finger. "Right there. Estene's it's called."

Ariel was turning away when the woman piped, "Are you really on that TV show?"

"Excuse me?"

"I heard Marv Newton sayin' you were from Los Angeles and you're on that *Open File* show. I don't recognize you, though."

Ariel smiled. "I'm just behind the scenes. Do you watch?"

"Well . . . sometimes." The woman patted down a wave of thinning hair. "I really liked that one man—the one that left? Win Something?" She appealed to Ariel. "He looked like Robert Redford?"

"Peacock. Tell you what. You write down your name and address, and I'll get Win to sign a picture for you if you want me to."

The bright eyes widened. "Would you really do that?" She ripped off a blank message slip and began scribbling. "Are you goin' to have something on your show about Mr. Barron?"

"It's possible. Why?"

"Oh, I knew him! Been goin' to his drugstore for years." She made a quick visual check of the door through which Newton had exited, licked at her teeth, and lowered her voice. "Is it true that you people, you know, *pay* people that know something?"

"It's been known to happen."

"Are you goin' to go to Estene's now?"

"I could."

"As soon as Pat—that's the other receptionist—as soon as she gets back from lunch, I can meet you there. In"—she consulted her watch—"twenty minutes."

"Listen . . ." Ariel glanced at the scrap of paper the woman had handed her. "Vera? The Barron death is under official investigation. If you know something relevant, you should be telling Detective Newton, not me." The thought of what Henry would say to that was almost enough to make her choke on the words.

"He already knows."

"Oh. Well, if it's confidential, maybe you shouldn't—"

"It's not."

"I'll see you in twenty minutes."

As Ariel came out of the police station, she saw a man leaning against a car at the curb. He held an open newspaper, but he wasn't reading it. She could see his eyes; they were on her, speculating, she thought. When she looked directly at him, he raised the paper.

Impulsively, acting out of pure frustration, she marched down the steps and stopped in front of him. "Yes?" she demanded.

The paper was lowered by an inch.

"You think you know me, is that it? Trust me, you don't."

Already feeling foolish, before he could utter a word, Ariel said, "Right! I know. Your mistake." With that, she turned on her heel.

Waiting at the café, she mentally groaned. What had possessed her? She knew. She was fed up with not knowing what she knew and who she knew. With waiting for that fantasized breakthrough. With wondering if it would ever happen, if she'd ever remember anything. Hers was a handicap championed by no lobbyists, a handicap for which there was no prosthesis, no rehabilitation, and no cure. Amnesia, she thought, is not for sissies.

She found herself grinning as she imagined what the man had thought. He hadn't been bad-looking. He'd looked startled out of his wits. He no doubt figured she'd lost hers. Maybe she had; she was remembering the man she'd seen outside the hospital that morning. The same man? Following her? Blatant paranoia, she was thinking when Vera Bloodworth plumped herself onto the next stool.

"Do you like vegetable soup?" the receptionist asked. "It's the best thing on the menu."

"Fine," Ariel said. "Look, Vera, I want to be up front with you. I'm not authorized, carte blanche, to pay people for information. I'd have to have some idea of the value, you understand? And I might need to clear it with my boss."

Vera's bright eyes dimmed by a milliwatt, but she shrugged good-naturedly, and her pink tongue flicked out to moisten her upper lip. "Aw, I wasn't really countin' on any money. I'd be tickled to death, to tell you the truth, if I was to hear what I'm goin' to tell you on your show, you know what I mean?"

"I *can* buy you lunch, though." Ariel smiled.

It wasn't many minutes before Ariel was dunking corn bread into a bowl of thick soup and listening to Vera, who, largely ignoring her meat loaf sandwich, had begun to tell her story.

". . . so it's because Corinne told every last person at the missionary meeting what she saw that—"

Ariel held up a hand. "I'm lost already. You're a missionary?"

"Me?" Vera looked startled. "No. My missionary *meeting*. You know, at the church. The W.M.U."

"Oh, yes." Ariel wasn't quite clear on the point but decided it was a tangent anyway.

"Corinne told *all* of us, and *I* told her to tell Marv. So you see, it's because of me he even knows, and it's not a secret because we all know." She took a goldfish-sized nibble of the sandwich and, in a conspiratorial voice, got down to the nitty-gritty.

"Corinne lives across and down from the Barron house. Real early, about dawn of the night Mr. Barron died, she was out waterin' her garden. That's why she *said* she was up that early—you know how you're supposed to water before the sun gets too hot? Well, fine and good, but I know why she really was."

"Really was . . . ?"

"Up. Corinne's about ten years younger than me, forty-nineish or a little better. I remember what it was like at that age, you know? Well, you wouldn't, but I'll tell you, I do. If you're not burnin' up and sweatin', you're cold, and there's some of us can't tolerate hormones. You're up and down all night, and these terrible things come into your mind. Sometimes you just give up and get up. That's why she was waterin', in my opinion."

Ariel scrunched her mouth into a nonsmile and prompted. "Corinne saw something?"

"Well, sure."

"What?"

"A car. Corinne noticed the garage open over at the Barrons', but she couldn't see in from her yard. Then this car came out. Now somebody, somebody alive, was in that garage or the person drivin' had one of those remote controls because the door closed down then." Vera's upheld hand slowly descended, hitting the table with a little plop. "Then the car went off *without* turning on the headlights, and it still not good daylight!"

Ariel had forgotten her soup. "Did she see who was driving?"

"Like I said, it wasn't daylight yet."

"Could she say what kind of car it was?"

"A midsize medium-blue Chevrolet, two-door, not brand new but not old either. She estimated about three or four years old."

"My word." Ariel blinked. "That's . . . unusually observant."

"Corinne's son has a dealership in North Charleston. She gets a new one every three years at dealer cost. That's why. I'd just assumed, you know, that Mr. Barron had taken his life? Because of his daddy and all? But after Corinne told what she saw, well . . ." Vera tsk-tsked meaningfully and then glanced at her watch. "Holy smoke!"

She wrapped her food in her napkin, dropped it into her purse, and pulled out a compact and lipstick, talking all the while.

"Suicide's an awful thing to make folks believe, Miz Gold, and Mr. Barron was a nice man. Both of them were, but him especially. So if somebody made it look like he'd done such a thing to himself . . ." She lifted her upper lip to check her teeth for smudges (and to give them a quick tongue swipe), and her words were almost unintelligible, ". . . I don't mind tellin' you . . ." She snapped her compact closed. "They ought not to get away with it."

"You said 'both of them'? Mr. Barron and who else?"

"The one that worked for Mr. Barron. I can't call his name but like I say, he's nice as he can be." Vera rose and gave Ariel a ladylike handshake. "Thanks again for lunch, and for that autographed picture you promised. I swear, that is *so* sweet of you!"

21

"WHAT ARE YOU DOING WITH THAT THING?" ARIEL ASKED SARGE, whom she happened to meet at the hospital door. She pointed to B.F.'s fat, scarred attaché case. "He's not up to working now!"

"He was doing himself a lot more damage arguing and fretting about not knowing what's going on than he'll do keeping up with business."

"Does his doctor know?"

"He knows. He caved in. Did you go see Marv Newton?"

"Yes. There's new news. It seems John William wasn't alone in the house the night he died."

Sarge came to a halt in the middle of the lobby and gripped Ariel's arm. She looked at his hand in surprise and then at his face. She remembered that she wasn't talking about the stranger she'd met once; she was talking about this man's nephew.

"Marv told you that?" he asked.

"No." Ariel sidestepped, getting out of the way of a defeated-looking man bearing rust-colored mums in a hat basket. As he trudged by, stoop-shouldered, she turned back to Sarge. "He didn't tell me anything. A neighbor saw a car leaving the house."

She rested her hand on Sarge's beefy one. "B.F. will want to hear, too, I expect. I might as well tell it one time."

They found him asleep, breathing noisily through his mouth.

Ariel hesitated in the doorway, uncomfortable with intruding on the old man's vulnerability.

There was a great clatter in the hallway behind her—an orderly dropping a bedpan that, fortunately, was empty—and B.F. jerked awake with a wordless exclamation. He blinked at Ariel and Sarge, drew his bushy eyebrows together crossly, and muttered the imprecations common to every hospitalized person since the days of Hippocrates.

". . . keep you up all night, in and out, in and out . . . wake you up at four A.M. changin' water you wouldn't be drinkin' if you coulda stayed asleep." He pummeled his pillow. "Now they're drop-kickin' number ten washtubs. No place for a sick person . . ."

"Let me do that for you." Ariel reached for the pillow. "Support him a minute, Sarge. There . . . better?" Plumping and consoling, she made the patient even more irritable.

"Enough! That's enough!" B.F. ordered. "Quit takin' on! Next thing, you'll start 'we-ing' and 'us-ing' like that confounded old sow on the night shift. 'Lessus see what our temperature is now,' " he mimicked, pursing his lips as if he were sucking on a kumquat. " 'Oh! We don't want to get our blood pressure up, hon! Lessus cooperate, now. . . . Think positive thoughts.' "

Ariel had met the nurse in question; his version of the pinch-mouthed beehive-haired woman who perpetually looked too busy—as if her mind were already on the next patient—was dead on target.

"Glad to see you feeling better," Sarge commented. "You want to watch the soaps? Play a little gin rummy?"

B.F. didn't dignify the questions with an answer. "Set my grip on that thing," he said, gesturing toward the tray table. "Where I can get at it." He cut off what was clearly going to be an objection from Ariel with: "What transpired down at the station with you and Eliot Ness? Y'all got everything under control?"

Ariel's eyes flicked to her grandfather's burly cook-*cum*-companion and back to her grandfather. "I was just telling Sarge that John William had a visitor on the night he died."

Sarge crossed his arms across his barrel chest. B.F. frowned. Both men waited for her to elaborate.

"A neighbor told the police she saw a car leave the Barron garage just before dawn. Either the driver had a remote device or he or she had an accomplice inside—or John William was still alive at the time. The garage door closed after the car left."

"Who told you this?" Sarge asked.

"A woman named Bloodworth. She works at the police station."

"You've hardly been gone two hours," B.F. said. "I'd be interested to know how you already got that story out of some total stranger under the nose of this detective."

Ariel turned to Sarge. "I've wondered. You had a pipeline to this investigation at first, but now you don't. Why is that?"

The corner of Sarge's mouth did an uncomfortable little jig. "Marv Newton took over the case. He and I go way back, and it wasn't always friendly. It seemed politic to back off."

"Newton," B.F. said, and repeated the name reflectively. "Didn't he have an older sister? Pretty girl—kind of an early developer?" He cut his eyes toward Ariel and away and mumbled something that sounded like "round heels, as I recall."

Ariel again swiveled toward Sarge, her interest piqued.

"Marv's not bad," he said, ignoring B.F., "even if he'd rather have been a gospel baritone than a cop." He went to the door. "I gotta go get some okra for the perloo I'm making Hattie. She's real concerned about you, by the way," he told B.F. "She's even got her cousin doing juju." His smile had an edge of malice. "I'll tell her you asked about her." To Ariel he said, "Helen Monroe wanted me to pick up a new overpressure plug for her canner, and I've got a few other errands. Okay to pick you up in about two hours?"

She nodded and watched him go. She felt as if she'd landed in the middle of some other century, a distant continent, an alien star. However, the months of being a stranger in her own skin had given her plenty of practice adapting.

"Sounds like maybe Sarge had more than one reason for leaving town back in his salad days," she said. "And what, pray tell, are 'juju' and 'perloo'?"

"Sarge can give you the lowdown on all those subjects, though I don't 'spec you'll have much luck with his checkered past. Now get on with this neighbor and what she saw."

Ariel filled him in on what she'd learned from Vera Bloodworth and what she hadn't learned from Newton.

"I'd sure like to know about that head injury of John William's," she said, "and what kind of car Grace Barron drives." The question Newton had asked about jewelry came to her mind. "I was hoping Sarge could find out about those things and some others, too, but I guess that's not going to happen."

"What others?"

"Well, let's assume it was, in fact, murder. I'm sorry, B.F., but that's looking like a given. Who had a motive? Mrs. Barron? What can they possibly think would've made her do it?"

"First off, Ariel Gold, nobody's got to prove motive. Second thing is, where's your brain? You know good and well most killings, even in these perilous times, are done by folks close to the victims, and their 'motives' are nothing but hot feelings. Spur-of-the-moment rage or jealousy or pure old misunderstanding. Somebody gets full of liquor, grabs the nearest blunt instrument or butcher knife or gun and lays into their nearest and dearest."

"I know but . . ." The memory of something Sarge had said sprang to Ariel's mind. When he'd called Grace to tell her about her son's death, he'd speculated that she was "loaded." It was the middle of the day, as Ariel recalled. "People who kill in the heat of passion," she said, "particularly if they're drunk, don't usually engineer elaborate cover-ups. They take off running or they fall on the body weeping and moaning and saying they didn't mean it.

"And think about this: Grace Barron is sixty or better. What do they think this little old lady did? Hit her son on the head and lugged his unconscious deadweight into the garage?"

"I'm sorry I won't be around when you get to be that age. I'd sure love to see your reaction if somebody called *you* a 'little old lady.' "

"Okay, slight exaggeration for effect. But, come on! Do they really think she'd have the strength? Of course, John William wasn't a big man. . . ."

"I'm not the one sayin' she did anything—or that anybody else did! And you, it seems to me, are arguin' with yourself."

"Just playing devil's advocate. Even if she's the fittest sixty-year-old in the South, Grace couldn't have picked him up by herself. If she or anybody dragged him into the garage, I can't believe the police wouldn't have seen a trail. Heel marks or disturbed dust or something."

"You said somebody closed the garage door after the mysterious blue Chevrolet left, didn't you?"

"That's what the neighbor lady said, yes, but before we get into the complication of accomplices, let's go back to motive and who had one. What do you know about John William's short-lived marriage, about his ex-wife?"

"Less than I know about what happened to Amelia Earhart on Howland Island. I got a wedding invitation. Hattie, as I recall, sent regrets along with some pillowcases she embroidered or monogrammed or whatever. Seemed like a month later we heard they'd separated. They didn't send the pillowcases back, I don't think."

"What about the man who worked for him? What was his name?"

"Washington?"

"Washman. No, Washburn. Wasn't that it? Obviously, you're not going to be much help with him, either."

"Well, fortunately, it's not our problem. It's this Newton's, and even Sarge says he's not bad at his job."

"True, but . . ." Ariel considered trying to explain her irrational sense of obligation to her sister's childhood friend. She sighed. "True, no buts. Since I don't have access to the facts and Newton's not being as obliging as the cops always are with Jessica Fletcher, it's just an exercise in amateur deduction. I heard one other thing today. That doctor from up North who got attacked on Edisto died. Now these housebreakers are bona fide murderers. Detective Newton's got that one to solve, too."

B.F. shook his head. "Sickenin'," he said. "I don't envy the man his job. On the subject of jobs, what about yours? Who's handlin' that while you're out here playin' Clara Barton?"

"Not a problem."

"What about that fellow you work for? He's not gettin' anxious?"

"Henry? He can manage for a few days without setting the house on fire."

"The house? He's stayin' at *your* house? Well, well . . ."

"Well, well, nothing. He volunteered. I thought that's what you were talking about."

"You hadn't mentioned it."

"I didn't? Then I don't have any idea—"

"How come you're gettin' nervous?"

"I tell you what. You get better; I go home. Deal?"

22

"DID I TELL YOU I'M A LEGATEE OF JOHN WILLIAM, TOO?"

Sarge guided the Lincoln around a pothole before making a cautious turn into a narrow dirt alley and adding, "No money, just a few odds and ends he knew I admired."

Ariel, who'd been wondering for the last few turns about the unfamiliar route, took in the joyless expression of the man beside her. "This isn't easy for you, is it?"

"You mind stopping by his house with me now?"

He brought the car to a stop beside an outbuilding connected by a breezeway to a tall brick house. A brick-paved walkway curved from the drive to steep steps and a second-level rear entrance. By craning her neck, Ariel could see a cantilevered, railed porch jutting from the third story and a belvedere on the roof.

"Old?" she asked.

"Pretty old—though not by Charleston standards."

Sarge eyed the house with what looked like reluctance and grunted when he saw that the back door was standing open. "Looks like Julian's already here."

"Julian?"

"Lawyer. Executor." He opened the door. "Come on. Keep me company."

The entrance led directly into a smallish kitchen, which, after the late afternoon sunlight, was a dim, cool cavern, tidy but musty smelling from having been closed up for two weeks.

"Hello?" Sarge called out. "Julian? You here?"

From behind the closed door of a room off the kitchen came the sounds of a toilet flushing and water running, and presently a tall, strongly built man emerged, giving his hands a last slapdash wipe on the trousers of his khaki gabardine suit. The grin on his face collapsed into a deliberately comical grimace when he saw that Sarge wasn't alone.

"Well," he said with little apparent discomfiture, "at least I washed my hands." He offered one, still damp, to Ariel. "Julian Taliaferro. And you're . . . ?"

"Ariel Gold," Sarge introduced her. "B.F. Coulter's granddaughter."

The lawyer clasped Ariel's hand in both of his and held the grip while he said, "The mysterious twin from out in California! Well, bless your heart, sugar, of course you are! I heard about you." The grin was back, wide as Joe E. Brown's. "Hey, it's good to meet you. I was buddies with Jane when we were young 'uns. Jackie here didn't say he was bringing a gorgeous woman along."

He pulled a startled Ariel to him, draped an arm over her shoulder, and proceeded to pound Sarge on the back in an extraordinary effusion of high spirits.

"You rascal you—I be dad-gum if you don't look like you could still drive through the middle on fourth and one! He ever tell you," he asked Ariel, "that he's a living legend? I played halfback thirty years later, and they were still holding this tank up as the end-all and be-all!"

Forced to angle his head to address his six-foot-four fan, Sarge asked, "Where's your car? I didn't see it out back."

"Came by shanks' mare. Two-point-seven miles from the office exactly." He patted a middle that looked solid enough to deflect small-caliber bullets and said, "Jog to the Y every morning, work out for forty-five minutes, walk wherever I can during the day—and eat like a hog every night. Hey, Jackie! Did you know you still hold the school rushing record? Two hundred thirty-one yards in a single game," he informed Ariel, "twenty-three carries."

Julian Taliaferro took a breath. "Well, look, you want to go on ahead and get your stuff? I don't need to hold your hand, and you know more about where things are than I do. I'll just pat you down on the way out."

Sarge nodded, not eagerly. By the time the other two followed him into the dining room, he was plodding into the room beyond.

"I heard Mr. B.F. was in the hospital," the lawyer said to Ariel, "but he's doing pretty fair?"

"Pretty fair, yes." It was the first opportunity Ariel had had to open her mouth, but she was more interested in looking.

They were in a formal, high-ceilinged room with elaborate crown molding and slightly faded wallpaper on which pale green vines trailed to wainscoting. The floor was wide planks of honey-colored pine. An Empire-style bench separated floor-to-ceiling windows, heavily draped. Ariel drifted to a walnut sideboard and, caressing the satiny wood, eyed the matching table and twelve chairs tucked around it. The room was museumlike and very still. In her wildest imaginings, she'd never pictured Sarge growing up here.

"Fancy, huh?" Julian asked.

Ariel lifted eyebrows in wordless agreement and moved to one of the windows. "May I?" she asked. Drawing the draperies aside, she breathed sunlit dust motes and looked out.

"There's a sign in the front yard," she said.

"Place is up for sale." Julian joined her at the window. "Damn shame. It's been in the family since I don't know when."

"Does it belong to Grace Barron now?"

"That's the story."

"She obviously doesn't intend to move back."

"I guess not."

"Where is she, by the way? She's not staying here?"

"Went home to Savannah, her attorney said, right after the funeral. Sad business."

Ariel nodded and craned to see the neighboring houses. She wondered which belonged to Vera Bloodworth's menopausal friend Corinne. "Where's the garage?"

Julian's face clouded. "Down there." He pointed to the opposite side of the house, and his voice was considerably less cheerful when he said, "Under the front room." He stuffed his hands into his pants pockets. "Which tragic note reminds me I've been remiss. I heard about your sister, of course. A terrible thing. I was sorry to learn about it."

Ariel turned to face the lawyer, studying his big, open, friendly face.

Although he was probably in his mid- to late thirties, she judged, a contemporary of John William, he looked younger. His skin was fair and peach smooth, and on each cheek was a stain of red, the healthy ruddiness of someone who'd just come in from a cold wind, or of an English schoolboy. He looked like a man who'd never had a worry or a crisis of conscience in his life, who, in the jargon of the sport he obviously adored, took what came and ran with it.

"I'm curious," Ariel said. "You said you and Jane were friends. Most people react to our resemblance. Why didn't you?"

Julian smiled. "Well, truth is, she was just a little ol' bitty kid when I knew her. I was invited out to Kiawah by a buddy of mine this one summer, but after then, I wasn't part of that whole scene. I was a pore boy, see. Had to work summers."

"So you never knew Jane later?"

"I'm sorry to say I didn't."

Ariel nodded. "Is it all right to look at the rest of the house?"

"Help yourself! In here's the front room. Can't say it's much to my taste, but it is fine."

It was that, and big, as were the bedrooms and the one full bath, tiled in old-fashioned little octagonals of black and white and sporting the original pull-chain commode, pedestal sink, and a footed bathtub in which even B.F. could've stretched out.

The library, Ariel felt sure, was where John William really lived. Leather wing chairs bore permanent indentations from many years' worth of comfortable posteriors. The needlepoint cover on an ottoman was almost threadbare in places, and a stand held a cluster of scarred pipes. A faint echo of cherry-flavored tobacco was still discernible. Walls of books, a mix of leatherbound sets and haphazardly shelved hardcovers and paperbacks, were plainly not for show. Ariel fingered a well-thumbed collection of Dickens.

"Not to be tacky, but since Mrs. Barron's selling the place . . . do you think she'll be selling some of the contents? Like books?"

"From what I'm given to understand, she's not interested in keeping anything, so since the stepdaughter . . . You know about that? Her being John William's heir? Since she never got a chance to make out a new will, poor soul, whatever he didn't specifically bequeath is up for grabs. The whole shootin' match'll go on the block in an estate sale."

"I'd sure like to put in a bid on all the Dickens. For my grandfather."

"We can work it out." Slipping two fingers into his breast pocket, he scissored out a business card. The "Tolliver" Ariel had expected to see was, in fact, spelled "Taliaferro"; the firm was Taliaferro and Taliaferro, Attorneys at Law.

"You call me," one of the two Taliaferros said.

"Your father?" Ariel waggled the card. "The 'and'?"

"Nope. I made the other fellow up." It was said deadpan. "Sounds classy, huh? Carrying on the old family tradition?"

Ariel hesitated.

"I'm pulling your leg," Julian said, but he didn't smile. "Actually, they're both me. Split personality. Tell me, is it true what they say? That you met John William? Talked to him the night he died?"

Ariel nodded, wondering if Julian's was some brand of Southern humor she hadn't run into before now. "Let me ask *you* something," she said. "When did John William make out his will?"

The big man's lips curved almost imperceptibly. "Two long years ago. Fellow that went to school with us got killed in a plane crash, and John William finally took my advice and came in. John William, you see, was *not* a 'pore boy.' I'd been after him for years to put something in writing."

"You and he were close?"

"Oh, I wouldn't say that. No ma'am. But we'd known each other all our lives. Went to school together from kindergarten on till he went off to military school."

"Was he close to *any*body?"

Julian sucked his lower lip and considered his answer. "I expect he had some friends."

"I see," said Ariel, who didn't. Just then, however, she did see something and, catching her unawares, it caused her to utter a small, breathless "Oh!"

On a drop-leaf table against the one bookless wall was a grouping of framed photos. Foremost was the blown-up snapshot Marv Newton had remembered. Ariel reached for it, studied the faces, felt the loss.

She'd seen many pictures of Jane. At B.F.'s residences, both here and in California, she'd seen childhood shots and professional ones as well. Presumably, she'd seen Jane on magazine covers even before she knew of their kinship. Neither the little girl nor the expertly posed, professionally made-up model was the young woman in this picture. This smile was wholly spontaneous, a silent crow of delight over the string of fish clutched in an upheld hand. The tiny gap between the two front teeth was the gap Ariel saw in the mirror. The wide mouth and wide-set eyes were her own. The cowlick at the crown of the head, untamed in this moment of abandon, was the same one Ariel struggled with on bad-hair days, and the distinctive longish nose, seldom seen in profile professionally, had once been hers as well. Only the cleft chin, serendipitous bonus of a childhood accident, was the other woman's alone.

How, she wondered, could you miss someone you never knew?

"They stayed friends, looks like," Julian said quietly.

Ariel swallowed. The boat's other passenger was a youthful John William, his expression brooding even then. " 'We are born crying, live complaining, and die disappointed,' " she murmured.

"I didn't catch that?"

"Nothing," Ariel said, ashamed of herself. She was about to replace the picture when she noticed the bracelet on John William's right wrist. She turned on a small sconce and saw a wide band, studded with a dull stone of some kind. Ariel had the impression that it was an American Indian bracelet.

"It's got to be truly weird," Julian said, "to see a picture that looks like you but isn't you. I heard you never met her?"

"People in this town sure 'hear' a lot."

"They do. There's good and bad to having all and sundry know your business. Comes in handy when you got sick folks in the house or when your kid doesn't come home on time, but it does get in the way when you want to park down at the lake without your mama knowing."

"You have children?"

"No, ma'am. Don't have the prerequisite wife. Least it's still considered a prerequisite in these parts. But listen, I want to hear about being a twin. You're the only identical one I ever talked to."

"I can't tell you what it's like since Jane was dead before I knew I *was* one . . . Oh, don't look like you just stepped on a land mine! It's okay!"

They heard a muffled bump from downstairs. Frowning curiously, Ariel said, "I've read about it though, a thing or two."

The truth was she read about it insatiably. There were times when, reading a description of uncanny similarities or looking at a picture of two mirror images, she could feel Jane's presence, laughing, finishing her sentences and reading her thoughts as twins are said to do.

She stole another look at the photograph and in that off-guard instant, the regrets ambushed her.

It was the wasted years that tormented her most, all the years they could have known each other. If only their father hadn't taken only Jane along—for some reason she'd never know, to some destination she'd never know—on the day the State of California took Ariel under its bureaucratic wing. If only her adoptive parents hadn't been so misguided as to keep the facts from her. If only . . .

Ariel roused herself impatiently. If she'd known Jane all her life, chances are she wouldn't remember a minute of it. Amnesia, a perverse thief of time, had robbed her of everything that had been, of everything but now, sucking her past into an abyss.

She became aware that Julian Taliaferro was watching her. His expression was unreadable, but his blue eyes were sharp, and any remaining delusions she'd had about his being some sort of stereotypical good ol' boy, a bluff "Bubba," evaporated. She gave him a bright smile. If there was one thing she should've learned by now, it was not to confuse slow speech with a slow mind; she wouldn't make the mistake of underestimating him again.

Restlessly, she peered into the hall, dusky now with shadows.

"He'll be back directly," Julian said. "Now, tell me what it is you've read about identical twins."

"If you're really interested."

"Speak."

"Okay, well . . ." Ariel paced the room, deciding where to begin her favorite subject. "Naturally, the ones who get separated fascinate me the most. They can be amazingly alike. More so, even, than if they'd been reared together."

"How come?"

"The theory's that when you're brought up together, your parents might tend to stress any differences. To encourage individuality. You really want to hear this?"

"Sit down here. Tell me."

Air squished from the old, stiff leather of the armchairs as they sat, and Ariel said, "There's a famous case of a pair separated at birth, male twins, and when they were reunited later—forty years later—they found out they'd both married and divorced women with the same name, married a second time—again, to women with the same name, and named their oldest sons the same thing. They went to the same place for vacations. Somehow, they'd never run into each other. They had the same hobby and drove the same kind of car. The same color, even." She lifted her hands in a believe-it-or-not invitation. "Did I mention they had dogs with the same name?"

"Is all that true, or did you just make it up?"

"Cross my heart." Ariel kept it light—no mention of twins who'd psychically experienced the exact moment of their brother's or sister's death, some so shattered they'd been unsure whether it was their twin or themselves who'd died.

"Let's see," she said. "Shared pain's always a grabber. Like this twin who suddenly had awful pains. He called his brother halfway across the country and found he'd just injured a muscle in the same place. The groin, actually." She grimaced. "And . . . oh yes, they've determined that if one identical male twin's gay, the other's nearly three times more likely to be gay than if they were fraternals."

Her companion looked uncomfortable with this last tidbit. "I've only known a couple," he said. "Twins, I mean, and they were fraternal. Both those boys were mean as rattlers, though; they had that much in common."

"Surprising. I mean that you haven't run into more. There're two and a half million sets just in the U.S. and thirty thousand more born every year." Ariel held up her hands. "But that's enough of that! Just what did Sarge inherit? He's had time to sack Rome!"

"Wouldn't be surprised if he's taking a last little sentimental journey. It's right rough on him, I imagine, being here where he grew up and where two of his kinfolks . . . well, you know."

Ariel acknowledged the truth of that and wandered back to the table where the photographs were arranged.

John Early Barron she recognized. He looked to be in his early forties. It struck Ariel that she'd been thinking of him as a man well into middle age but, in actuality, this must have been one of the last photos made of him.

The pensive young lady in the over-the-shoulder shot, circa 1950-odd, had to be Halley. Ariel supposed it was fanciful of her, but she thought she could see what Sarge had tried to describe. As a girl, he'd said, Halley had seemed somehow "old-fashioned." Ariel couldn't put her finger on it, but there was a quality of *unwariness* in the clear eyes that was out of place in the latter half of the twentieth century. A certain . . . stillness. Whatever it was, it had nothing to do with the vintage of the photo; this girl could have looked out of a daguerreotype.

Ariel only glanced at the two elderly people she guessed were John Barron's mother and Sarge's father. In this gallery of the dead it was a relief to see someone still above ground: Sarge himself, a very young Sarge in L.A.P.D. uniform.

"Mighty upright looking, wasn't he?" Julian asked. He crossed one leg over the other, making himself comfortable and looking as if he wouldn't mind spending what was left of the day waiting. "Don't let me forget to ask Jackie if he wants any of those, or copies. I'll contact Miz Barron if he does."

Ariel had seen no pictures she judged to be that lady. She was about to comment on it when an angry voice came from behind her.

"What is it that you'll contact Miz Barron about?"

Ariel turned to see someone in the hallway. She had time to see only that it was a woman before Julian Taliaferro bolted from his chair, blurting a startled oath and, with his large body, blocking her view.

"Excuse my language, ma'am, but holy Moses! You about gave me a heart attack!" Julian exhaled noisily, sounding like a winded horse, and moved toward the woman who stood rigid as armor.

She wore black from head to toe: black suit, black hose, black shoes. Strangely, since the light in the room was fading fast, she also wore sunglasses. Her mouth was a flat line. Her chin was thrust forward. Her right arm rested in a black sling. The only thing that wasn't black was the white bandage that covered one side of her face. There was no doubt in Ariel's mind that the woman was Grace Barron.

Her assumption was confirmed with Julian's next words.

"Miz Barron? I thought you might be. I'm Julian Taliaferro, your son's attorney. Come on in here," he coaxed, "and let me introduce B.F. Coulter's granddaughter to you."

He took an unyielding arm, and after uncomfortable, stony seconds, Grace Barron allowed herself to be led forward.

"Ariel, may I present Miz John Barron? Miz Barron, Ariel Gold."

The courtly introduction seemed to fit the occasion, as the short, trim woman by Julian's side held herself as erect as royalty. Victoria in her widow's weeds couldn't have looked haughtier, and Ariel stifled a brief, mad urge to bob a curtsy.

"You said B.F. Coulter's granddaughter?"

Julian smiled his boyish smile, tempered now with the solicitude due the recently bereaved. "Yes, ma'am."

"Then I'm afraid I don't understand," Mrs. Barron said. Hers was the accent Ariel had learned early on to recognize as that of the socially elite of Charleston. The difference was indefinable, at least to Ariel's alien ear, but it was there.

"What is it you don't understand?" Julian asked politely.

"I believe I heard Mr. Coulter's granddaughter died." The dark glasses were trained on Ariel's face. It was impossible to see what lay behind them.

"Yes ma'am. But he had two. Twins!"

"Is that right?" Without turning her head, Grace said, "You haven't said what you two are doing here."

"Well, I can't say I expected you either, Miz Barron. I had understood you'd be returning to Savannah after the funeral?" Julian's tone was respectful as before, his smile still pleasant, but a certain recalcitrance lurked.

Grace Barron finally faced the man with whom she was conversing. Her straight dark hair, cropped unusually short, was speared by a single, dramatic silver streak at the temple. It glinted in the light from the sconce.

"I changed my mind, Mr. Taliaferro," she said.

To that Julian had no reply.

"Why did you say you people are here?"

"Jackie McManus came to get the items your son willed him, Miz Barron. Miz Gold is his friend, and I'm here in my capacity as John William's executor. I notified your attorney that we'd be here this afternoon. Purely a courtesy, of course. I didn't realize it might be an inconvenience, having been told, as I was, that you'd returned home."

"If I understood the terms of my stepdaughter's will correctly, this *is* my home."

Ariel had never heard so much tension expressed so politely. She felt like an invisible audience, watching two actors do excruciatingly civilized stage battle.

"Why, certainly." Julian's smile was downright beneficent. "As I'm certain you can appreciate, however, that will has yet to be probated."

Ariel made a mental note to call Julian if she ever needed a lawyer.

Just then, Grace removed the sunglasses. The skin around both eyes was a palette of purple fading to sickly yellow. What had once been the right eyebrow was now neat black stitches that snaked a crooked trail across the bony ridge and down to the outer corner of a painfully bloodshot eye, swollen almost shut. It was a masterfully timed stroke of visual drama, followed by an even more cunning verbal maneuver.

"Jackie's here, you say? How wonderful! I haven't seen my brother-in-law in far, far too many years. Where is he?" She looked around as if expecting Sarge to materialize from the gloom, then strode to a floor lamp and snapped it on. Her poor damaged face, even more terrible in the light, managed a one-sided smile for Ariel and Julian, both shocked dumb. "There. That's better, isn't it? Why were you two sitting in the dark?"

Amazing Grace. Ariel barely restrained herself from speaking the words aloud. Deftly and impressively, the woman had retreated without losing ground. She was mistress of the house, a sympathetic figure, grievously wounded and vulnerable, yet gracious.

"Ah," said Julian. "Yes, ma'am." He patted the sofa. "Why don't you sit down here."

Grace settled, not on the sofa but into one of the armchairs. She adjusted her skirt with a flutter that was almost a parody of coyness, lifted her remaining eyebrow delicately, and gestured toward the other seats.

Julian and Ariel sat.

"Now, tell me," Grace demanded of Ariel, "how's your granddaddy getting on? He was a great favorite of mine, you know. Quite the Galahad and just the sweetest man! Still is, I expect."

The coquettishness was, in the circumstances, extraordinary. It occurred to Ariel to wonder whether loss and pain had unhinged the woman before her. Her voice was gentle when she finally spoke, extending both her grandfather's condolences and her own.

Grace nodded acknowledgment, taking a handkerchief from her black alligator purse and carefully dabbing at her eyes. Ariel saw no tears, but the fragrance wafting from the lacy hankie almost brought tears to her own eyes. It was White Shoulders, a scent she abhorred.

After Julian added his condolences, his voice brightened.

"Ariel was just expressing an interest in acquiring some of your books as a gift for Mr. Coulter."

"The Dickens," Ariel said, "but now's not the time to bother Mrs. Barron. . . ." She became aware that Grace was staring at her fixedly. With a start, the older woman came to life.

"It's no bother at all! In fact, I seem to remember Halley saying John William had a nice old copy of . . . I don't know, some Dickens book. B.F. must have it, a gift from his old admirer."

She glanced around vaguely before getting to her feet. "Of course, it's been some years since I was here, but I can look. . . ."

She began rummaging through the bookshelves in a rather helpless fashion, talking the whole time—very nearly prattling, it seemed to Ariel, who looked her over curiously.

Mrs. John Early Barron was unbowed by grief. Her carriage was imposing, her figure trim. What the bandage didn't cover of her face, mangled though it was, was enviably unlined, as was her neck. She had subscribed, it seemed, to the old Southern notion that ladies should be fair as lilies and had steered clear of the sun. Even with the gray streaking her dark hair (and even if the "dark" was chemically aided), she was well preserved. If Ariel hadn't known her age, she would not have put it at sixty.

Her manner had become downright girlish.

B.F. had described the young Grace as "lively"; time had

turned her to quicksilver. When Ariel suggested that she let the estate people deal with the books, Grace shushed her, opening and closing drawers and cupboards and chattering as she searched.

"Halley loved this library! Did you-all know her? No? Oh, I wish you could've! She would never have considered coming back here to live, of course. The house holds too many painful memories. For both of us. And she wouldn't have moved without me. She was my lifeline! My health isn't what it was. Nerves, you know.

"Anyway, she did adore this library. It breaks my heart to part with the books, knowing how she would've treasured them, but she was the reader. I'm afraid I was a poor scholar, ignorant as the day is long, if you want to know the truth.

"Hmm," she said. "Maybe the book was more valuable than I thought. It seems to be gone, too."

"Too?" Julian asked.

"You didn't know? I'm surprised. The local gossipmongers must not be as efficient as they used to be."

"Ma'am?"

Grace shut a cabinet door with more force than necessary. "My daughter stopped by here after John William's funeral. She told me some things seemed to be missing. Since she wasn't absolutely sure—couldn't be, really—she didn't report her suspicions. But I did. I called the police myself and told them I wanted it looked into! The door was open for anybody to come in, wasn't it? Those burglars I've been reading about. And that man who worked at the drugstore; he waltzed right in, didn't he? Who knows . . ."

She was peering into one of the cabinets, a frown on her face. "What on earth?" With difficulty, she slid out a gift-wrapped box, awkwardly supporting it against a shelf. She angled her head to read the envelope tucked under the ribbon and then looked at Julian and Ariel as if they might have some explanation.

"This has my name on it," she said, and genuine tears appeared. "Mr. Taliaferro? With this arm I can't quite manage . . ."

The lawyer took the package and he, too, looked at the envelope. "I don't guess anybody could argue that it's meant for you. Did you want me to open it?"

At Grace's nod, he unstuck the flap, pulled out a card, and

handed it to her. She slipped on a pair of glasses. She read the card once, and then again. Her lips quivered and turned inward. She looked, suddenly, quite ill. Laying the card down without comment, she said, "Will you open the gift?"

When the bright paper had come off, Julian poked around in a nest of tissue. His mouth dropped open as, very carefully, he lifted out a gun.

A choked cry came from Grace, the sound of an animal in mortal pain. Ariel tore her eyes from the gun to see Grace pushing herself from her chair. Before anyone could say anything, the woman had grabbed her purse and was gone. They heard the front door slam.

Gingerly, Julian laid the gun back onto its tissue bed. He and Ariel were staring at each other wordlessly when Sarge appeared holding a fishing rod.

"Okay, shyster," he said, "my loot's piled by the back door. Come on and check it out so we can vacate this mausoleum."

23

HENRY HAD BEEN WRONG. THE INDIVIDUAL WHO'D BEEN SCATTERED by an eastbound freight nine months before *had*, in actual fact, been wearing a dog tag. That—among other things—was precisely how identification had been made. Erroneously made.

The error had been compounded by the "widow," the legitimate Mrs. Fiore, who'd needed to see neither dog tag nor remains to be convinced her husband was dead. (The former she'd been shown and had promptly identified; the latter she wasn't asked to view.) Mr. Fiore was a man of consistent and responsible habits, she'd insisted. If he was alive, he would have come home; he hadn't. Of course, he hadn't come home since either; he'd decamped to Arizona.

Some details were fuzzy, but from all Henry could put together in several phone calls, Mrs. Fiore was a fire-eater. One Carson detective—Pete, by name—who'd encountered the lady and bore scars, groused, "If how she acted at the morgue was any indication of her usual charm, it's no wonder the guy took a powder. That woman would make Arnold Schwarzenegger run for the nearest exit—or try to stop a freight train with his face, for that matter! If I was married to her, I'd push *her* in front of a train."

Henry interrupted Pete to ask just what the circumstances of the train encounter had been: "What did the engineer have to say? Was the guy just standing there on the tracks or what?"

Pete didn't know. "I only worked the case a couple of days before there was a restructuring down here. I got put on something else. Anyway, listen to this. This old bag informed us hubby was due home by six forty-five P.M., and he wasn't ever late. I can believe it. He was whipped within an inch of his life. She had his schedule—guy was a salesman, see, office supplies—and she knew where he'd been to the minute because she checked. You believe that? Checking up on the guy like if she let go his leash, he'd vamoose. Which, come to think of it, is just what he did.

"You want to know something unbelievable? I happened to talk to this cop down in Scottsdale? He'd met the other wife, the one this poor schmo married after he cut out? Said she was a holy terror. Is that unreal? He leaves this battle-ax, then goes and gets hooked up with another one just like her. I mean, go figure!"

"So," Henry said, "you guys never looked into the corpse, maybe, being somebody else?"

"Man, we had the dog tag. We had a wallet . . . even had a little money in it and a gasoline credit card. We found it about sixty yards from the largest part of the corpse. And—we had the car."

"The car? You mean Fiore left his car at the scene?"

"Yes, pal, he did. Left the door open, to make it look like maybe something had fallen out the window, and he'd gone back to get it, you know? And didn't see the train coming?"

"He must've driven over the tracks," Henry labored to create logic from the bizarre set of circumstances, "and he saw the train hit the victim and then went back and seeded the scene. Is that what you guys figure?"

"I don't know, pal. Maybe Fiore just saw a window of opportunity and took it. Maybe it was more than that. He hasn't talked yet as far as I've heard."

"What about the dog tag? The blood type. I guess it must've matched Fiore's?"

"The tag wasn't official—I mean, not like a military tag. No blood type on it. It was real silver; jewelry, I guess you could say. I'd bet money it was a present from the wife. Like pinning a note to hubby to make sure he'd get brought home if he strayed."

"What's this bozo going to get charged with?"

"Well, he's nailed in AZ for bigamy. Here? Choose from the menu. Obstructing justice, tampering with evidence, altering a death scene, interfering with an investigation, criminal conspiracy . . ."

"You think his being there might not've been an accident? That he might've 'arranged' for the victim to be his substitute corpse?"

"Anything's possible. Especially if it complicates our job."

"What do you do now about ID-ing the body?"

"Nothing," Pete said. "I'm off the case."

24

Ariel looked up and down the moonlit beach, empty now of tourists, vendors, and sunbathers. She sat down where, as nearly as she could place it, she and John William Barron had talked two weeks before, and she thought.

He'd been an angry man, she now knew, with a cruel streak. She didn't understand the "gift" he'd left behind for his mother, but there was no question it had been intended to cause the gravest pain.

The words from the accompanying card played through her mind; she had no problem remembering them.

"I'm sure you'll recognize this. Perhaps you'll do everybody a favor and use it on yourself. Happy birthday, Grace."

It had been signed: "In hope, John William."

Ariel shuddered. She couldn't imagine what Grace Barron must be feeling now. She couldn't imagine what the whole thing meant. The gun had come from left field; a gun had played no part in any of the dramas connected to the Barrons.

The family did seem to live and die on the crests of high drama, she reflected. Was this last, cruel gesture on John William's part just that? An example of the theatrics to which he'd been prone? If it had been intended as punishment, Ariel wondered what the crime had been.

She was no less puzzled by Sarge's reaction. When he'd been

told about Grace's visit and the gun, when he'd seen the card, he'd gotten really weird. He didn't say two words on the drive back to Kiawah. He'd cooked dinner, making it plain that he welcomed no company, and after they'd eaten, he'd retired for the evening.

Ariel had made an extra effort with the tray she'd taken in to Hattie. She held it patiently while the still-weak woman groped her way to a chair, refusing Ariel's help. While Hattie picked at the food, Ariel straightened the bed.

She knew better than to make small talk, and she had no inclination to do so; she had things on her mind. With a cagy probe here and a leading observation there, she set about learning what the taciturn Hattie knew about the Barrons.

Hattie was cagier. Pretty shortly, Ariel was asked point-blank "how come" she was asking about "those folks."

"You remember I asked you about the man I met on the beach? It turns out he was John William. It was only hours later that he died, and I may have been the last person he talked to and I feel . . ." Tucking the sheets into hospital corners, she struggled to find a way to explain her commitment to the dead man. She stole a glance at Hattie, and the hawklike intensity of the dark, nearly black eyes was encouraging. "He was Jane's friend. If she were here, if she thought he was . . . harmed by someone, I think she'd do whatever she could to avenge her friend. It's something I feel obligated to try to do for her. And, too, if Grace had nothing to do with it, which I believe, I don't want to see her heartaches worsened." She picked up a pillow, plumped it, and clasped it to her middle, waiting to see if she'd made her case.

"You feel 'obligated,' " Hattie said, as if confirming her understanding of the explanation. "Because he was 'Jane's friend.' "

"Yes."

"You come down here callin' these people who're nothing to you by their first names like you know them, like you got some right to their lives, talkin' your big talk about 'harm' and 'avenging' and 'heartaches.' You traipse in here playin' up to me, tryin' to get people's private business out of me like I'm some feebleminded old darky you can twist around your finger."

Hattie paused for breath. When she continued, her voice was quieter and venom dripped.

"Well, you can't. You might fool B.F., but you don't fool me. I don't know what you want, and I don't know how you know things you got no way of knowin' about my Jane, but you're not her. You're nothing like my girl, and you're never gon' be like her or look like her no matter how hard you try." Hattie leaned forward, chest heaving. She all but spat her next words.

"You take your tricks and your meddlesomeness and go back to where you came from. You hear me? You leave us be!"

Ariel felt as if all the blood in her body had surged into the top of her head, setting her ears on fire. She hadn't imagined the depth of Hattie's scorn.

That Hattie was suspicious of her kinship with Jane, being so off target as those suspicions were, was a mere pinprick. It was the lethal accuracy of the rest of the tirade that drew blood.

Ariel knew her reasons for delving into the Barron tragedies couldn't be justified in any sensible way. She was still uneasy over insinuating herself, still plagued with doubts about whether she was being exploitative. Had Hattie been clairvoyant, she couldn't have zeroed in on that Achilles' heel more unerringly.

Carefully, as if she were the invalid, Ariel replaced the pillow. "I imagine," she said, "that you can make it back to bed by yourself."

At the door, she turned. Through stiff lips, she said, "I don't know what I've done that so offends you, but whatever it was, it wasn't intentional. You're wrong about me. You may be right that I'm out of line with the Barron family, but I do know I belong in this family, and I'm not going away. Count on that. And Hattie . . ." With an effort, Ariel kept her voice steady. "Throwing in the fact of your being black was a cheap shot. If you believe that has something to do with our problem, you *are* feebleminded."

She closed the door behind her very quietly.

Ariel went hot again now as anger resurfaced, and she savored the damp salt wind that bathed her face. Hattie hadn't been wrong about the attempt to pump her. But as to the old woman's aberrations, her poisonous, personal suspicions, she could go stuff herself. It's not my fault, Ariel thought, that I'm here instead of Jane, and Hattie's just going to have to work that out for herself. In the meantime somebody else could play handmaiden; it wouldn't be she.

She slipped out of her beach robe, folding it atop her sandals. The water was warm. When it reached the straps of her suit, Ariel began to swim, and when she tired, she turned onto her back. She forced her mind onto a less rankling topic: the Barrons.

Grace, she realized, had made only the most oblique references today to her son. She *had* admitted she hadn't been in his home for some time; apparently, the feud had existed as advertised.

It was a curious twist on the old fairy tales that it wasn't the *step*mother who'd been perceived as wicked. It had been Halley who'd named Grace heir, and it had been Halley's funeral Grace had attended, Halley of whom she'd spoken with affection.

Ariel couldn't help wondering how the relationship had evolved. One would think Halley would have resented the "lively" young stranger who'd usurped her place in her father's affections. But the father, Ariel reflected, had abandoned them both, cruelly. And then along had come his son. Perhaps John William's birth had been a catalyst to affection between the two survivors? A living bond? A bond there must have been; it wasn't by accident, surely, that Grace and Halley had come to live in the same city.

Treading water, Ariel gazed out at the oblivious, endless ocean, seemingly autonomous yet obedient to the pull of the moon's force.

Had Halley been devoted to her stepmother? A willing "life-line"? Or had she been under Grace's thumb? She hadn't had a family of her own, and there'd been no sign of an "other," significant or otherwise, at the funeral. There had been young people; students, presumably. Perhaps Halley had thrown her passion into her work? She was the one principal of the dramatis personae Ariel had never met, and who she had been was elusive.

The Halley Barron of the eulogies had been disciplined, a paragon of selflessness. Sarge called her "a tough cookie." Brooding, Ariel asked herself: since there's nothing to suggest that she played any part in John William's death or that her own was anything but an accident, why am I even curious about her? What is it that's bugging me?

As she began to swim toward shore, descriptions she'd heard of her own past self flashed into her mind. "A loner," Henry had called her. "Reserved," she'd heard said, "uptight" and "private."

She must have seemed, Ariel figured, as dull as rust. But she'd been capable of heartache. Even if she couldn't remember it, she'd known love. And she'd had courage.

That quality had also been ascribed to Halley, the practical, serious woman who sounded as one-dimensional as the old Ariel had appeared to be. And wasn't.

Her feet touched bottom, and she slogged through the surf, plumbing her memory for clues about the dead woman.

Sarge's "fragile, shy, and old-fashioned" girl had, according to Grace, been a lover of books. That suggested imagination. So did the fact that she'd had to be hospitalized after her father's death—a breakdown of some sort, it seemed obvious. But surviving that, surviving even the horror of finding his body, she'd had the resilience to recover. She'd made it home.

Ariel came to a halt, her breathing more labored than she'd have liked. It was late. It was also, she realized as the breeze curled around her wet body, no longer as hot as it had been. Hands on hips, she puffed for a moment, and then reached for her robe. It wasn't as she'd left it. The collar lay partially buried in the loose sand.

Ariel stared. *Hadn't* she placed the robe directly on top of her shoes? She looked up the beach and then down. There was no one in sight. The sand here, well above the waterline, was still churned up from the crowd that had swarmed during the day. She checked the empty beach again and then snatched up the robe and wrapped herself in it, shuddering as she plunged her hand into the pocket. Her fingers closed around the house keys, safe and undisturbed. Ariel listened to the gentle, lulling roar of the sea and began to breathe again. That's what you get, she told herself, for being too preoccupied with what, as Hattie so helpfully pointed out, is none of your business.

She had no access to official information. She had no ideas about how to learn more about John William's former wife, his employee Washman or Washburn, or any of the friends Julian Taliaferro "supposed" he'd had, and, certainly, her speculations about his sister were beside the point.

John William's face appeared before her, vividly, as he'd been on his last night. He was once again beside her on the beach, re-creating a sweet, long-ago time. It was a time she herself would have been part of if blind chance hadn't intervened.

There was no way she could leave the puzzle alone.

I'd sure like to know, she thought, who was at John William's house the night he died. And about the bad blood between him and Grace. And these items that "might" be missing from the house. And the significance of the gun. Her eyes narrowed. Oh, did she wonder about the gun! The depth of anger revealed by that devastating "gift" intrigued her more than anything. And that brought her back to something that had occurred to her hours before.

That surprise package was meant to cause pain, period. It was mighty unlikely, it seemed to Ariel, that anyone would go to the trouble to set up that payoff and then deliberately deny himself the satisfaction of seeing it.

If she'd had any doubts that John William had gone to his death willingly, they'd vanished.

25

THE CALL CAME AT 8:00 THE FOLLOWING MORNING.

Ariel had awakened to find herself alone in the house—well, nearly alone. She assumed Hattie was hibernating in her room; she didn't go look. She was sitting on the back steps enjoying what actually felt like the first stirrings of fall while she ate Cheerios and read the paper (an AP story reporting that a nine-month-old train accident was being linked to vanished multimillionaire Grant Lacy) when the phone rang.

"Well," B.F. said, his voice subdued, "they arrested Grace Barron this morning."

"They didn't!"

He didn't bother to respond.

"Why? What have they got?" Ariel asked.

Her grandfather grumbled out a sigh. "Enough to have the cops down in Savannah pick her up. That's all Ouida knew."

"Who's Ouida?"

"The woman who brought in my breakfast. She used to do for the Bellflowers; I've known her for years."

Ariel shook her head. The local jungle tom-toms were beyond her. "How in blue blazes," she asked, "did Ouida-whoever know that the Savannah police had picked up Grace Barron?"

"She didn't say, but I 'spec she heard it from Bo."

"Oh, well! That clears it right up."

"Bo Rawlins. Her brother. Head mechanic down at the jail. Why are you askin' about all these people? Don't you know I'm upset about this thing with Grace? When are you comin' over here?"

"I don't know how I'm going to *get* over there. Sarge isn't here, and he's taken the car."

"Use the other one."

"What other one?"

"The one in the garage. Keys are on a hook by the phone."

Ariel looked. Keys big and little, each tagged, hung on porcelain hooks. She found the one marked Garage. Beside it, two keys were attached to a ring with a large gold initial *A*. The keys looked like car keys. The initial looked like real gold.

"I didn't know you had another car here," she said into the phone. "Why *A?*"

"Eh?"

"Yes, *A*. Why is there an *A* on the key ring?"

"*A*'s what your name starts with."

"My . . . ? B.F., what are you talking about?"

"The timin' could've been better, but that's life. Hurry up and get on over here."

Ariel listened to a click and a dial tone before she hung up, went out the back door, and walked barefoot through dewy grass to the garage. The padlock was new, the rough wooden door old, the mechanism recently oiled. It slid sideward. The darkness inside was broken here and there by shafts of sunlight that beamed through the rafters and made spangles on the sleek yellow car underneath.

Ariel frowned. Her first thought was that the car was an Austin-Healey. Even before her eyes adjusted to the light, she knew it wasn't; nor was it an MG or Alfa Romeo or any other make she'd ever seen. She circled. It was about the size of her poor destroyed '55 Thunderbird, a roadster, with a white landau top. She tapped one polished, butter-colored fender, tentatively. It was fiberglass. She tried the door, and her frown turned to surprise. It didn't open out; it slid forward.

"What in the world?" she murmured. She sat in the driver's seat and looked at the horn, reached out to touch the *K* centered above a green flag, a checkered flag, and the word *Darrin*. In the glove compartment she found a manual that read *Kaiser Darrin, 1954*, and beneath it was the title, in her name.

"Oh!" It was involuntary, pure reverence, quickly followed by "Oh, no!" She slipped from the car, talking to herself. "He can't do that!" and "He knows better!" she said as she strode to the house. She took a fast shower, muttering all the time.

From almost the first moment B.F. had learned Ariel was his granddaughter, he'd been bent on making up for all the lost years. When he wasn't trying to persuade her to give up her job and move in with him and his quirky entourage, he was pushing sailing trips à deux to parts unknown. He sent flowers—out-of-season peonies or French tulips by the dozen—and gifts, sometimes odd but invariably wonderful. He'd quickly figured out that she wouldn't accept anything wildly expensive, so he'd been sly in his offerings: an Amish quilt; a tiny porcelain keepsake box; the *Our Gang* series on video; an ancient and enormous wooden bowl, smooth with years of kneading bread. On the Fourth of July he'd turned up with sparklers, smuggled into California, and a five-foot-long American flag with forty-eight stars, a souvenir from his war years.

All were a far cry from a rare vintage automobile.

Aware of the untapped power humming under the hood, Ariel drove to the hospital as if a gem cutter were working beside her. She wouldn't have driven the little roadster at all, but she couldn't wait for Sarge to return from wherever he'd disappeared.

"Have you lost your mind?" she challenged when she stormed into the room.

"You don't like it?"

"That is not the point, and you know it good and well!"

B.F.'s mouth turned down. His lips may have quivered a bit. "I'd planned to give it to you in person, but I didn't know I'd be in the hospital the next time you came."

Ariel cocked her head and said nothing.

B.F. tried again. "That van you bought isn't for you, Ariel Gold! This little baby's got a Cadillac V-8 under the hood! It'll do one forty without half tryin'. Okay, all right." B.F.'s face sagged into a hangdog smile. "It *is* a fine little car, though, isn't it?"

Ariel couldn't help noticing that her grandfather's color was good and his breathing no longer effortful. He looked well.

"It's fine," she agreed.

He nodded. "I'd always assumed Margaret would outlive me, actuarial tables bein' what they are. When she fooled me and died, well, I assumed Suzanne . . ." His big shoulders lifted and fell. "And then came Jane." There was no need to elaborate on that.

His voice gathered strength and precision. "Why do you suppose I accumulated all the money? What do you think I planned to do with it? That little car, my girl, is nothing to what I'd do if I could. I wish I could buy the next twenty years of being with you. I wish I could buy the time to know my great-grandchildren. I wish I could buy you the joy of living with someone you love every day of your life. I can't. Drive the car. Enjoy it. If you've got one ounce of loving-kindness in your heart, don't give me a hard time about it!"

Ariel opened her mouth purposefully and then reconsidered her words. "We'll talk about it later," she said. She was fairly certain she'd just been outflanked but was deeply touched nonetheless. She sat on the bed, felt B.F.'s forehead, and smiled.

"Cool!" She made the adjective an interjection.

"Damn right. Now, what're we gon' do about Grace Barron?"

"Us? What happened to Marv Newton being so good at his job?"

"If he's the one issued a warrant for Grace, looks like he needs all the help he can get. You do still think she's innocent, don't you?"

"I haven't changed my mind, no. I met her yesterday."

"You met Grace? Where?"

"Sarge and I . . . Sarge, incidentally, is acting peculiar, but I'll get back to that. We went to the Barron house after we left here, and Grace showed up. I don't know how she looked before the accident, B.F., but she looks rough now. Her face is bandaged, and if what's under there is worse than what shows, I'd hate to see it. Her arm's in a sling and she's . . . Was she always *mercurial?* One minute she's this steely dowager, and the next she's running on nerves." Ariel gave her grandfather a sly look. "She's quite the coquette, aged as she is. She remembers you fondly. 'Galahad,' I believe, was the name she mentioned when she heard yours."

B.F.'s smile was fatuous but fleeting. He adjusted his face into a purse-lipped expression and said, "Stop throwing around words like *aged.* If she's aged, what am I? Doddering?"

"If that smile was any indication, you're getting there." Ariel went on to describe her introduction to Grace Barron and to Julian Taliaferro, whom B.F. didn't know.

"I believe I did know his daddy, though. He was a first-rate carpenter. Big man. Used to keep goats."

Despite herself, Ariel was distracted. "What for?"

"Had a taste for it, I'd imagine."

"Unusual kind of pets . . ." She stopped. "What did you say?"

"They weren't pets."

"You mean . . ."

"Don't knock it till you've tried it. Nothing like goat stew with some light bread to sop up the juices."

A plump nurse wearing nylon track pants and what looked like a pajama top bustled in and, amidst much cheerful chatter, shooed Ariel off the bed and proceeded to take B.F.'s blood pressure.

"You must be plannin' to live to be an old man," she flattered as she ripped off the cuff. B.F. mumbled a question around the thermometer she'd stuck in his mouth.

"One hundred forty over eighty-five. Not too bad." The nurse whipped out the thermometer and squinted at it. "We're gon' get shut of you before long, looks to me like. Soon as you get your strength up."

She fussed around the bed, chitchatting (and becoming at least the dozenth person to ask Ariel "You're not from around here, are you?"), and then left at a brisk clip, her nylon-clad thighs swishing against each other musically.

"Wonder why they don't wear uniforms anymore," B.F. grumbled. "It's hard to have much confidence in a woman wearin' a shirt with little pink balloons on it."

"You're getting well. Don't quibble about fashion statements."

"Guess that means you'll be headin' west."

"Maybe not right away. I'm considering recommending to Henry that we look into the Barron affair, maybe do a show."

B.F. grinned broadly but made no comment, and they both sat quietly, entertaining their separate thoughts. It was Ariel who broke the silence.

"About Grace's innocence, I'm going purely on gut feeling, you know? I'm the first to admit logic's got nothing to do with it." She wandered to the window and, restlessly, bent a slat of the venetian blinds.

There was little to see beyond the overgrown crape myrtle outside and snarled traffic.

"I don't know. . . how to cope with a world where mothers kill their children, where the most fundamental precepts about humankind don't hold true." A city bus had wheezed to a stop at the curb. Ariel watched it take on passengers for a moment before she said, "I *prefer* to believe Grace is innocent, but 'Nothing is more dangerous than an idea when it's the only one we have.' "

"Meanin'?"

"If we were to do this show, I'd have to get a whole lot more objective. You might not like that."

"Honey, if it turns out Grace Barron killed John William by accident or by design, my sensitivities are a pretty low priority."

A very large woman with curlers in her hair and a sagging string bag on her arm climbed from the bus, trudged to a bench, and sat heavily. The bus, sounding equally exhausted, groaned away. Ariel could see the parking lot across the street now and in a distant slot, the Darrin.

She felt a little jolt of Christmas-morning excitement. The man standing beside the car seemed as intrigued by it as she'd been. Ariel bent to get a better look. She found herself smiling as the admirer appeared to do the same, although from her perspective she couldn't be sure. When he seemed to be trying the door, her smile faded. She was certain she'd locked it. Or had she? A cement truck lumbered past and immediately behind came another bus, obscuring her view. It stopped, disgorging a herd of tourists. None was in a hurry.

B.F. stirred behind her. "You were sayin'?"

Ariel let the blind snap back into place. "I'll be right back," she said.

The Darrin was, in fact, unlocked. The man was nowhere to be seen.

The car didn't appear to have been tampered with. After a glance inside, Ariel ran to the end of the parking lot to look beyond the ell of a medical building there. She saw no one but a man in a white lab coat, crouched on the building's back steps smoking furtively. He was slight, and the man Ariel had seen was tall and stocky, and he hadn't been dressed in white. Ariel returned to the car.

A magazine she'd left on the seat was still there, along with the newspaper. Grant Lacy stared up at her from the article she'd been reading that morning.

"Unless that was a personal emergency we'd both be embarrassed to discuss, I'd like to know where the devil you went galloping off to?" B.F. was sitting on the side of the bed, pajamaed legs dangling, one slipper on and one in his hand. He looked as if he were on the verge of forming a posse.

"I went to check the car. I couldn't remember if I locked it."

"Went to check the car," B.F. repeated in disbelief. He dropped the one slipper and toed off the other, muttering, "Thing's insured. Next you'll be puttin' an alarm in it. Bad as Sarge." He jerked the sheet over himself. "Man's got an obsession with . . . What was it you said about him while ago?"

"What?"

"Sarge. Actin' stranger than usual, you said."

"He was last night. See, there was an incident at the Barron house that was . . . disturbing. When we told him about it—he wasn't there when it happened—he clammed up. Like a sphinx."

"What incident? Disturbin' how?"

Ariel related the story of the gift-wrapped gun and the message that accompanied it. "As soon as she saw that gun, Grace took off. That's the last we saw of her."

"The gun . . ." B.F.'s voice was quiet. "What did it look like?"

"A revolver. A Colt, I think? It was a thirty-eight." Ariel looked up to see that her grandfather's face had gone slack, and his eyes were fixed on nothing.

"What's the matter? Are you all right?"

After a beat he seemed to come to himself. "Just seein' ghosts," he said tiredly. "You feel like readin' to an old man?"

"But . . . Sure. I brought today's paper and a *Newsweek*, except I left them in the car."

"Let's give real-life drama a pass for a while, okay? How about some Dickens?"

Ariel found the book and began where she'd left off, but the travails of David Copperfield couldn't drive her grandfather's disturbing reaction from her mind.

"In short," as Dickens's beleaguered Mr. Micawber was wont to say, she intended to corral Sarge McManus and find out what it was about that gun that made everybody freak.

26

It was just before 5 p.m. in Los Angeles, and Henry sat in the parking lot at the main offices of MicroStar. He was looking for an employee named Marcus Black, one of too few names Richard Cummings had left behind. He didn't know what Black looked like nor what he might contribute in the way of information. As Henry had found out, the fact that the name had remained in the file didn't bode well for potential usefulness.

Two other people were mentioned in Cummings's meager notes. An investment banker with whom Grant Lacy had done business refused to talk with Henry, as he said he had with Cummings: "Client confidentiality—you understand." An art dealer had been no more helpful. He'd willingly admitted acting as Lacy's agent from time to time, but said he'd never been contacted by Cummings and couldn't or wouldn't explain why the former *Open File* producer had his name.

Henry had long since digested the clip file of articles about Lacy. Other than the basic facts, the accounts published at the time of the disappearance and thereafter contained mostly background rehash and, in the case of the tabloids, fantasy.

They'd jumped on the story like jackals on a lame wildebeest—"Eccentric Entrepreneur Evaporates" and "Spacey Lacy Beamed Up By ETs?" et cetera—but they'd provided nothing more than entertainment and innuendo.

Henry did have hopes for a meeting scheduled later that same evening. After checking first with the L.A.P.D. and the Long Beach Police, he'd determined that it was not they but the sheriff's department who'd handled the case. One of the missing-persons detectives who'd been in charge was a woman he knew slightly. Marge Luzzatto had said she'd wait for him after her shift ended at six o'clock.

People began to trickle through the MicroStar door. Most were young, and they were dressed as if they'd been working out or washing their cars. Henry approached the most authoritative-looking person he saw, a dark-haired, power-suited woman.

"Marcus?" she asked when she'd heard Henry's question and examined his proffered business card. "I just saw him. He'll probably be out in a couple of minutes." She slung her bag onto her shoulder and eyed Henry curiously. "Does this have something to do with Grant? Are you guys doing a story on his vanishing act?"

Henry's ears pricked up, almost literally. "Act?"

The brunette's red lips curved into a smile, and she tapped Henry's card against small, even teeth as if weighing her answer. "Figure of speech. Although it is possible, isn't it? No body. No ransom calls. Nobody arrested. Grant jogs into the sunset, and life goes on—maybe better for everybody than if he'd hung around."

"You're saying he—or somebody—might've had problems if he hadn't disappeared?"

"Can't help hearing rumors, can you? Heaven knows Grant inspired them. You know, you remind me of him a little. The height, the dark eyes . . ."

Her blue ones did a languid little sideways slide, and she said, "That's the unlovely Marcus over there, by that red Geo." She pointed with the business card and then slipped it into her bag. "I'd love to hear why you want to talk to him, but I guess you'd better hurry or you'll miss him."

"Yeah, but listen . . . Any chance you'd be willing to discuss those rumors you've heard if I gave you a call later?"

"Not later tonight. I've got plans, starting in about an hour. But, sure, call me. Ask for Claudia. Claudia Wynn in sales. Or, better yet . . ." Never taking her eyes off Henry's, she dipped her hand into the purse and, with a speed that suggested considerable practice, produced a silver card case. "My personal card. Feel free to call me at home, most any ol' time."

Henry took the card, tipped his hat, and approached the man Claudia Wynn had pointed out. He could feel her eyes on his back.

Marcus Black was a pudgy man with pale skin, a mustache he ought to forget about, and the bad breath of a heavy smoker who doesn't invest in breath mints.

He gave Henry's card careful scrutiny, glanced at Henry's face, and then looked at some point over Henry's left shoulder as he asked, "What can I do for you?"

"Let me buy you a drink and see if there's anything we can do for each other." It wasn't Henry's usual approach to possible *Open File* sources, but there was something about Black that invited furtiveness. He wondered if this was the informant Ariel had seen with Cummings and wished he had one of the tiny cameras he and his staff occasionally secreted on their persons. He shifted left to put himself into Black's line of vision. Black shifted his eyes. Chewing on his lower lip, he cogitated for silent seconds before agreeing to take up Henry's invitation.

"There's a bar in the Century Hotel two blocks west," he suggested. "Just off the lobby. Follow me, if you want to."

Black drove like a little old lady. Henry rode the brake and fumed and forced himself not to tailgate. When they'd both parked, Black made up for lost time. He all but trotted to the lounge, breathing heavily, and his backside hadn't hit the bar stool before he lit a Salem and started talking.

"You work with that guy Cummings, right?" he asked the air beside Henry.

"I did. Richard's not with us anymore."

"He suggested you get in touch with me, though?"

"Indirectly."

Black's questioning glance ricocheted off Henry's face and returned to the vicinity of his left ear. "I wondered when I'd hear from you people," he said.

"Cummings led you to expect we'd be calling you?"

"Well, he didn't say so, but he seemed interested in what I had to say."

"What you had to say when you two met at the Brentwood Marketplace?" Henry tried, just on the off chance.

"The what?"

"Never mind. We are interested. Very. But we're unclear on some of the facts, so I hoped you'd run over things with me again."

Black exhaled a fogbank and leaned forward eagerly. "I'd be on the show, Cummings said. I mean . . . actually appear, right?"

"That could happen."

Black chewed his lower lip hungrily and then sucked on his Salem with equal appetite.

"So," Henry said, "let's get down to specifics." He patted his pockets as if searching for notes to refresh his memory. Pulling out a piece of wrinkled paper (a request from his son's teacher that they meet to discuss Sam's poor performance), he pretended to study it. "Remind me. Your function at MicroStar is . . . ?"

During what should have been a twenty-minute drive to sheriff's department headquarters, Henry swore at I-405 traffic and considered Black's information.

A MicroStar accountant, Black was also an incorrigible snoop. He'd pilfered through enough files both before and after Lacy left the scene to know (or claim to know) that the missing genius was on the verge of a software breakthrough. It had something to do with Internet security, which Henry didn't fully understand. He had no problem figuring out that the coup would've meant big bucks, and he wondered how reliable Black's "inside dope" was. If Lacy was close to perfecting the product nine months ago, why wasn't it on the market? In fact, Henry thought it likely that a competitor would've scooped MicroStar by now.

Didn't these kinds of developments tend to evolve at a similar rate throughout the industry? Wasn't the industry notorious for moles? He'd get one of *Open File*'s expert consultants on it right away, Henry resolved.

Two CHP motorcycles came up behind him, stuttering with impatience and weaving through the stop-and-go traffic like thwarted hornets. Still some distance ahead was a cluster of blinking lights and sheer gridlock.

Henry gritted his teeth. Spying a break in the lane to his right, he aimed the tired but game Oldsmobile into it, and then made a death-defying dive at an exit ramp. The surface streets were as congested as the freeway. This time of night was agony, he reflected gloomily; it had gotten to the point that any time was.

Marge Luzzatto waited in front of the building, pacing and looking unhappy.

"I just came off a double shift, Heller. Two days of freedom with plans made and you're late."

"Tell it to the rubberneckers. Come on. I'll buy you a burger."

"Raincheck. I've got a candlelight dinner on tap, and the chef's a whole lot better looking than you, so let's get to whatever it is you want."

She directed Henry to her car and when they were closed inside, Henry asked for anything she could tell him about the Grant Lacy case.

In essence, Lacy had left for a run through his exclusive Virginia Country Club neighborhood a few evenings before Christmas the previous year. When he hadn't returned by bedtime, his wife called 911, and officers responded immediately. A command post was set up, and the investigation had commenced.

"What about the forty-eight-hour thing?" Henry interrupted to ask. "I thought you waited a couple of days?"

"Not if the MP, the missing person, is considered to be at risk or if there's reason to suspect foul play. New state law."

"Lacy's being rich put him at risk, obviously."

"Prime target for a snatching, and we were ready for the calls. They didn't come. Well . . ." Marge's glance flicked away. Abruptly, she resumed her story.

"It wasn't only the kidnapping potential. Per the wife, the two of them hadn't fought, there hadn't been any domestic or personal problems that might've triggered Lacy being a 'voluntary,' and he was, to all appearances, a stable citizen with his car still in the garage, his yacht still at the marina, and his money, so far as we could determine, still in the bank—figuratively if not literally, in his case. He'd have been considered at risk anyway."

Marge went on to say that Lacy's name had gone into MUPS, the new statewide Missing-Unidentified Persons System, and NCIC, the National Crime Information Center, and that all other normal procedures had been followed. "Diligently," she added. "He was a rather high-profile 'missing.'

"You know the routine, Henry. We questioned the family. The wife, the brother. Neighbors and associates. Especially the women. He was a pretty sexy-looking gentleman, you know? In a mad genius zealot sort of way. Smoldering passion and all that . . ." Marge noticed that her fingers were stroking the leather sheath covering her steering wheel and cleared her throat.

"Anyhow, we guessed there was at least an even chance another woman might figure in. Wrong. We checked the hospitals. Checked whether he'd been picked up for anything by one of our guys—"

"Stop right there. I heard at one point," Henry said, referring to Cummings's claim, "that you people were close to an arrest. Who'd you have in mind and what happened?"

"I don't know where you got your information, but I hope you didn't pay much for it. It's BS. We never had nothin' on nobody."

Henry nodded. He wasn't surprised.

"As I was saying . . ." Marge looked at her watch, took Binaca from the dash, and squirted her mouth. "We did it all. Checked the airlines, the trains, buses out of town. Kept an eye on his credit card activity—the cards were still in his wallet at the house, by the way. We went through his calendar, appointments lined up and never made. Followed up on all the 'spottings.' "

She slouched in disgust. "We put divers in a pond when some halfwit decided he'd seen Lacy taking a moonlight swim. In December! One time, we really thought we had something. An airline agent in Boston was dead sure she'd sold Lacy a ticket, first class to Madrid. She happened to be an artist, Henry—the airline thing was her day job—and she drew us a sketch that was Lacy in every detail, down to how he parted his hair. Hah! What a goose chase! We got the fax from Boston—"

"Okay." Henry gave her knee a fatherly pat to make up for denying her the relief of complaining. "You went the whole nine yards. But back to the night he jogged into history. Nobody saw him?"

"Only the wife saw him leave the house. Except the helpful crank that 'saw' him taking a dip, no neighbor saw him then or later. That doesn't mean much," Marge grumped. "Houses there are set back from the streets and screened from view. Well, you know the kind of posh area it is."

"You know about the 'train versus pedestrian' incident that happened in Carson the same night?"

"Heard about it this week." Marge looked grumpier.

"Why wouldn't you have heard about it when it happened? Especially being as how it wasn't that far from Lacy's house?"

"Ordinarily, we would've, even with the Carson guys not knowing about our 'missing.' We didn't get the call until late that night, remember? The coroner's office would've made contact with us sooner or later if the victim stayed a John Doe. He didn't. By the time we got involved, they'd already made the one in Carson. Or thought they had. From what I hear, it was one of the fastest body claims on record. That wife—Fiore?—was on the horn about seven seconds after they knew about the train hit, I heard."

"Fiore's route, I guess, took in that train crossing?"

"Not necessarily, but it was a reasonable alternate, say if he ran into traffic. Or if he wanted to put off getting home as long as possible." Marge smirked. "I heard he had good reason to."

"What's happening with the body now?"

"We're hauling it out, I think tomorrow." She made a grimace of distaste. "Yippee."

"And if it's Lacy?"

"Depends. Cause of death was hardly a big question mark and, right or wrong, they didn't do an autopsy—just a blood test for chemicals. There weren't any. But the body was definitely male and white, and the age could be right. Blood type was. It was also A, which about half the country is, Fiore included, and Rh positive, which both those guys and almost *every*body is. We'll see what the dental records tell us. And prints, if we've still got any. Who knows what's in that body bag after all this time?"

"What about his effects?"

"If he was carrying ID, we have to assume Fiore—or somebody—relieved him of it. The clothes got tossed. They were rags. Mrs. Fiore didn't want them."

Marge looked at her watch, pointedly. "Anything else you want's going to have to wait. I hear a chilled bottle calling me."

"One more thing. You almost said something else a while ago about phone calls right after Lacy disappeared, then you stopped yourself. Am I right? Come on, Luzzatto!"

The detective gave Henry a hard stare before she poked a forefinger in his face. "Off the record, you got that? Especially if this turns out to be Lacy! We actually managed to keep this out of the press's greedy paws at the time, and if I thought it amounted to anything, I wouldn't say anything now, but still . . . You let it out, you never get anything from me again. Me or any other cop."

"You know me better than that."

"Two days after Lacy turned up gone we got a call at the house, made from a San Pedro phone booth. The voice was electronically altered. Okay? Mrs. Lacy picked up, and this creepy robot voice said something like, 'We got him. If you want him back . . .' " Marge pursed her lips. "Never mind the details. Robotman never called back. No delivery instructions. No other follow-up."

"You think it was some sickie? The case had already generated a ton of publicity by that time."

"Most likely. The nutcases swarm when these kind of things happen. Or it could've been a hoax—somebody decided to try to cash in on the situation."

"Then why—"

"Mrs. Lacy told this lowlife, per our instructions, that she wouldn't give them a dime until she was allowed to talk to her husband. Could be they believed her. Thought that with no bait they had no chance to collect. Orrr . . ." Marge drew out the word tantalizingly. She pulled a hairbrush from her purse and, looking in the rearview mirror, began to smooth down escaping tendrils.

"Or?"

"There's always the possibility the call was legitimate. The kidnappers could've lost their nerve—the pickup, after all, is always the big risk—and decided to cut their losses." She looked directly at Henry. "Could be Lacy was already in no position to be talking to anybody."

27

ARIEL WAS SPOOKED. SHE'D BEEN FIGHTING THE FEELING SINCE SHE'D discovered the car unlocked. After she'd left the hospital—all the while as she stopped at the library and at a convenience store and at Julian Taliaferro's law office (where, as arranged, she'd used his machine to fax Henry the *Post & Courier* article about Lacy)—the uneasiness had stayed with her.

There was no good reason for it. She'd told herself that several times during the last leg of her long drive home, when she'd been certain she heard the hum of a motor behind her. She'd slowed almost to a crawl, but she'd never even seen headlights. And that's what had reminded her of a certain mystery car, driving blind from a dead man's garage.

The image seemed a lot more sinister in the dark.

She was glad to see the Lincoln in the driveway.

A wonderful aroma assailed her as she opened the back door. She broke left, heading for the stove and the Dutch oven there. She dropped the lid with a clatter when a voice spoke behind her.

"I can hear your salivary glands pumping from over here," Sarge said.

"Could you hear my heart stop?" Ariel snapped. "Don't you know better than to sneak up on people? What's the matter with you?"

"I'd have thought your new car would've put you in a better frame of mind."

"Oh, you were in on that little surprise, were you?"

"You make it sound like somebody played a nasty trick on you."

"Yes, well, *I'd* have thought you . . ." Ariel stopped herself. "Sorry," she said. "I'm a little edgy. That road gets darker every night." She forced a lopsided smile. "What's in the pot?"

"That, my dear, is my own famous version of pilau, known locally as perloo, elsewhere as pilaf or jambalaya or, to you folks from less civilized parts, chicken and rice. You hungry?"

"Famished. But first, can I ask you something?"

"You can ask."

"What was wrong with you last night?"

"Nothing wrong with me," Sarge answered casually, and began to move about the kitchen, gathering first one thing and then another from the refrigerator and various cupboards.

"Really?" Ariel pressed. "You were very quiet."

Sarge cracked an egg into a mixing bowl, measured in buttermilk, and said nothing.

"Did you hear about Grace Barron's arrest?"

"Uh-huh."

Knowing better, Ariel asked, "What do you know about the gun?"

Sarge's hands ceased their efficient movement. He tilted his head to one side and held the pose for several ticks of the kitchen clock, which suddenly seemed very loud. Slowly he turned, his face expressionless.

"Ariel," he said, "just because information might exist doesn't mean you have the right to it."

Ariel flushed and shut her mouth. When the telephone broke the silence, she leaped to answer.

"I've tried that number ten times," said a voice she recognized. "I was beginning to think you'd left it as a joke."

"Win!" Ariel exclaimed. Grateful for deliverance, she gushed apologies for the lack of an answering machine.

"Hey! I'll call all day for a reception like that! How are you, sweet thing? What are you doing down there in magnolia land?"

Ariel got hold of herself. With more restraint, she explained about the illness that had necessitated her hasty departure.

"So," she finished, "I'm sorry to have left you in the lurch."

"No problem for me, but sounds like you could use a friend. Listen, I'm back in New York. Not that far from you, actually. I could just cancel my weekend plans and hop a plane. I can do friendship."

"Yes, well, thanks, but my grandfather's better and I'm fine." She turned her back to Sarge. "Now, what's the story with this job you mentioned? Not that I'm interested; I'm still learning the one I've got."

"Remind me to tell you the story of Jack, a work-obsessed lad who, as a result of avoiding the serious business of play, gained a reputation for dullness. However . . . it's coordinating producer, like I told you. Ron's leaving mid-October—Ron's the current CP—so we've got a month to decide who to bring in. The high-muck-a-mucks at *LifeTime* know about you. From somewhere they've gotten the idea you're a cross between Diane Sawyer and Bob Woodward—her looks, their talent—and they're champing to talk to you. I told them I'd better touch your base first, see what your feelings are. So what are they?"

"As I said, I'm not really—"

"Oh, come on, Ariel. Surely, for enough *dinero*—and I'm talking fairly big-time money here—you could get yourself surgically removed from old Heller?"

"I beg your pardon?"

"You two are still joined at the hip, aren't you? I hate to think what Henry the Hawk would do to me if he heard I was trying to steal you out from under him—figuratively speaking, of course. Well, I'm assuming 'of course'? Maybe I shouldn't?"

"You know, you've got a one-track mind, and it's permanently derailed in the bedroom. Who do I talk to and when?"

Win chuckled, and Ariel's eyes narrowed. She realized, not for the first time, that it didn't do to underestimate Peacock. "What kind of money is 'big-time' money?"

"Whatever you're making plus a lot more. The job's a step up, and this *is* the Big A. You'll have to take all that up with Manny Littell, the executive producer; that's who'll be calling you."

"Win, do they know about the amnesia? I mean, I wouldn't be bringing the experience my résumé says."

"What they don't know won't hurt them, sweetie. Everybody here's seen the segments you've honchoed since I left L.A., and yours, my friend, is not the work of a neophyte. Take my advice; keep your lovely lips sealed about your quaint idiosyncrasy."

Ariel argued, listened, finally agreed to go along. "Thanks, Win." She smiled into the phone. When Win began to croon, she laughed out loud.

" 'Sail on, silver girl,' " he sang in a respectable baritone, " 'Sail on by . . .' "

"You're embarrassing me."

" 'Your time has come to shine. All your dreams are on their way.' "

"Good-bye, Win."

" 'I'm sailing right behind,' " he was singing when Ariel gently replaced the receiver.

"You changing jobs?" Sarge asked, making conversation and, maybe, emerging from the evil spell he'd been under since the night before.

Ariel was setting the table, absentmindedly humming to herself. She refrained from any remark about nosiness, deciding she'd rather have the real Sarge back than fence with him.

"No, but it can't hurt to hear what these people have to say."

They took their seats in lonely splendor at one end of the long mahogany dining table, and for a few minutes there was no sound but that of the cutlery. Ariel was achingly aware of her grandfather's chair at the head of the table. It seemed to echo with emptiness, and his very absence was a presence.

"Did you see B.F. today?" she asked. "He seems a lot better, don't you think?"

Sarge nodded. "I was by late this afternoon. You'd just left."

Ariel had been at the library, consulting the Savannah telephone directory. She'd found Grace Barron's address and, on an impulse, she'd looked up the college where Halley had taught. She figured the distance to Savannah right at a hundred miles. If she drove the Darrin full out, she could be there in a twinkling.

Thoughts of flying down I-95 in the lovely little roadster, the top down, tweaked her conscience. She had to decide what to do about B.F.'s preposterous gift. How could she say no without hurting him? Why did she have to say no?

"I was thinking of taking an afternoon off," she told Sarge.

"Maybe do a little sightseeing and so on. Could you, do you think, sit in for me at the hospital?"

"When?"

Ariel planned to go the next day. She'd miss Grace's arraignment, but she didn't expect any surprises and she didn't know how much longer she could justify being here. She'd get that answer when she talked to Henry, which she planned to do after dinner.

Thoughts of Henry also tweaked her conscience. What if something actually came of this business with *LifeTime?* Henry had been good to her. When she'd awakened without a past, he'd ambled, long-legged and short-tempered, into her void. He'd kept her amnesia to himself while he gave her a crash course in her profession. He'd been mentor, coach, and friend.

The song Win had teased her with had been on the periphery of her mind ever since he'd called. Now, pesky as a mosquito, it surfaced again, mirroring her thoughts. "I'm on your side when times get rough and friends just can't be found . . ."

Ariel mentally clicked Garfunkel off. She couldn't do the same with memories of that last night in Los Angeles, that unexpected kiss. It wasn't the first time she'd thought about it.

Sarge was looking at her quizzically. "What was it you asked me?" she said.

"When did you want to do this sightseeing?"

"Tomorrow? Are you free tomorrow?"

"Fine. Judging by the look on your face just then, those must be some sights you're planning to see."

"I wasn't . . . I don't even have any specific plans," she lied. "I just thought it might be good to get a little distance, to think about things, you know?"

"Oh, yeah. That's what I did this morning. Went down to the Y with Julian Taliaferro and spent two hours sweating and thinking. It's harder than it used to be."

"The sweating or the thinking?" Ariel grinned along with Sarge. It felt good to be on friendly terms again. "The 'chicken and rice'—excuse me—*perloo*'s great. What's juju, by the way?"

"Magic. Voodoo. Local version. Why?"

"And Hattie believes in it?"

Sarge almost choked. "Hattie? Not in this lifetime!"

"But you told B.F. she'd asked her cousin to—"

"That was a joke. Lame effort at irony or whatever. Hattie believes in what she can see. Oftentimes not even that."

Ariel considered how her inexplicable knowledge of Jane's quirks must go down with Hattie and understood a little better why the woman was so suspicious. "Why do you suppose she doesn't answer the phone when we're out? Win said he'd tried quite a few times."

"I don't think the telephone has ever brought Hattie much good news. She pretends she doesn't hear it."

"What's with her, Sarge? What's her story?"

The question netted nothing but an eloquent roll of the eyes.

"Come on! Don't be like that! My interest lies strictly in what she is in relation to B.F. I'm not doing *Roots*. You can skip all the begats. Who is *she?*"

Mildly enough that Ariel hardly realized he'd deflected the question, Sarge said, "First thing you've got to understand is that around here, who you are *is* who you come from." He crumbled corn bread. "Your sister loved to hear people's stories, too. She wasn't so pushy about it, though."

"I can't help it if I didn't get the benefit of a genteel Southern upbringing."

Only half joking, Sarge said, "You jealous?"

"I think I'm experiencing delayed sibling rivalry. Jane the perfect ten. Beauty and breeding, too. You'd think I'd be the polite one. 'Manners are especially the need of the plain. The pretty can get away with anything.' "

"When I first heard you run yourself down like that, I found your modesty kind of refreshing." Sarge let the implication hang in the air just long enough. "Jane wasn't perfect. I knew her when she was a little girl, remember? Circumstances being what they were, she was a spoiled brat at times. B.F.'s doing. Hattie'd bring her back down to earth in nothing flat! She'd draw a bead on Jane with those eyes that seem like they can see right down into your soul. 'You mind me,' she'd say, 'or you'll be pickin' a switch in a minute.' " He chuckled. "She's a caution, that Hattie."

"If you say so."

Sarge shifted in his seat. "I've heard a little from B.F. about *your* childhood. Doesn't sound like much fun."

"No."

"These people that adopted you . . . why did they? I mean, if they were so uncaring."

"The mother wasn't," Ariel said, unconscious of her detached tone, "but she died when I was young. The father was a different story. Pure flint. I picture Lawton Munson as an Old Testament prophet gone bad. A crazed Moses, quoting Scripture and abiding by the parts that suited him—like not sparing the rod."

Ariel's mouth had turned down into a sour, inverted U, and she finished off the water in her glass as if she were trying to wash away a bad taste.

"You really hated the guy," Sarge observed.

"No. I hate what he did to that vulnerable little girl."

"That . . . ? Oh, you mean you. You talk like you were a separate person then."

"As somebody equally nuts once said, 'I can't figure out where I leave off and everyone else begins.' "

Sarge thought about that, decided it wasn't worth the trouble, and said, "How do you remember all that stuff?"

" 'I have a memory like an elephant. In fact, elephants often consult me.' " Ariel snapped her fingers. "Want more? I've got a million of 'em!"

"Jane did the quote thing. You're like her but different, too. I always thought identical twins *were*."

"Genetically, sure. But environment impacts that: nature versus nurture."

"Come again?"

Ariel began to clear the table. "They say some traits seem likelier to be inherited. Imagination, for one. And the way you react to stress. But your upbringing might have more to do with aggressiveness and whether you're ambitious. The need for social closeness—for intimacy, I guess you could say—that's another thing that seems to come more from upbringing. What I'm saying is: your genes program you, but your environment molds you."

"Which means what, using you and Jane as an example?"

"Us? We were both pretty creative, both strong in our own way. But Jane was raised in a loving, supportive home. Given things. She was bred to be confident and outgoing, but she was also, as B.F. said once, 'kind of passive.' My home was a drought. I was no good at relationships, and I had to be aggressive to survive. I was driven to do well, to prove to myself I was worthwhile."

"You keep saying 'was.' How come *was* is different from *is?*"

"Amnesia, so I read, can change people. Maybe it lets them be what they would've been if outside influences hadn't interfered."

"You've got an answer for everything, don't you?"

"No, sir. Not about that subject."

28

THE DRIVE BACK TO ARIEL'S HOUSE HAD BEEN LONG. IT WASN'T traffic; through some aberration of freeway logic understood by no one, cars were relatively scarce. It was Henry's mood. He was unaccustomed to feeling lonely.

The MicroStar saleswoman Claudia Wynn had her evening lined up. Luzzatto was by now dining by candlelight. Even the unlikely Marcus Black had hinted at plans. Henry headed for an empty house. The dogs' dinnertime, he realized, had come and gone. They, at least, would be glad to see him.

When he pulled into Ariel's garage, he looked over at her van, hunkered down beside his Oldsmobile. The only thing that made him feel better was that it was too new to remind him of Ariel.

He managed to deactivate the burglar alarm without bringing gendarmes running. Stonewall was another story; the yellow mutt hurtled in and commenced to climb Henry's leg. Jessie remained planted, as dignified as a New York Library lion. She'd known when she heard the car that he wasn't Ariel; she lowered head to paws and, to emphasize her disappointment, yawned.

"Rough day standing sentry? I could've been a burglar, and you lie there like a lox." Henry made a face, and muttered, "I'm talking to a dog."

He threw his jacket onto a chair and went into the kitchen. At the sound of the refrigerator door opening, the shepherd deigned to make an appearance. She sat squarely in the doorway watching. Her tongue came out, and she began to pant as interest heightened. So much, Henry thought, for dignity.

"Here," he said, putting the dogs' full bowls on the floor. "*Bon appétit.*" He went to the phone and dialed South Carolina.

"Hello," a gruff male voice said.

Henry experienced a moment's disorientation before he realized that it must be Sarge McManus. He got through a polite exchange with the man about whose function he was still unclear and, shortly, Ariel came on the line.

"I was just about to call you." Something wasn't right about her voice. Henry's blip made itself known.

"Don't worry. You're paying for this one. What's the problem?"

The silence wasn't long, but it was too long.

"Just a sec," Ariel said.

He heard talking at the other end, muffled as if by a hand, before Ariel spoke into the receiver.

"Who said there was a problem? I was just telling Sarge to go put his feet up. Listen, Henry, I think I should hang around here awhile. I think there's a story, with the Barrons."

Possibly for the first time in his professional life, Henry couldn't quite focus on the story. He couldn't just then remember what the story was.

"The Barrons," he repeated.

"Henry? Hello? The fifties suicide? The suicide two weeks ago which it now seems *wasn't* a suicide. The accident a week later?"

Henry heard an intake of breath signaling news to come.

"The mother of the supposed suicide was arrested today for her son's murder. Henry, I don't think so."

"Okay, okay. Remind me."

Ariel reviewed the pertinent facts.

"So," Henry recapped, "what we've got that we know the cops know is an allusion to fear and even to murder in a conversation with you the night he died, a head wound of some kind, a car seen leaving the death house, and no suicide note. Pretty strong stuff. Factor in an apparently vindictive gift all wrapped and ready with the giver too dead to enjoy giving it. That about cover it?"

"Such an incisive mind you've got, Grandma!"

"Oh! And despite the fact that the pretty package was for Mommy, we've got your sentimental feeling that she's innocent."

"What about the things Halley said were missing from the house? Mightn't that just suggest that—"

"You mean the things the mother *said* Halley said were missing. Halley didn't say it to the cops. It's just on Mom's word she said it at all. Could be the old lady's trying to scare up a culprit to take the heat off her. Besides, she didn't even say Halley said '*was* missing'; she said—and I quote your quote—'might be.'

"Ariel, the mother was the intended recipient of the gun. The mother was on the outs with the victim—serious outs. The victim slurred the mother in his conversation with you. The mother's got the estate. Just what is it that's prompting your belief in her innocence? A vision?"

"The fact that Grace came into the estate doesn't signify. John William didn't leave it to her; Halley did."

"So, maybe she engineered the accident to bump off the stepdaughter, too."

"And took a chance on killing herself in the process?"

"This family does have a penchant for it, you have to admit."

"Henry, I've met her. She's sixty years old. She's a little Southern lady with gray in her hair and bad nerves."

"Hey! Killing does still make some folks nervous."

"For a man who believes in a 'blip,' you're being awfully hard-nosed about my instincts."

Henry sighed. "I've got as much reverence for motherhood as you do, my little chickadee, but I've seen a whole lot more of the big, bad world than you."

"*You're* the one, if I recall, who kept asking if there was something in this for *The Open File*."

"That was when it was pathos and mystery and artistic genius lost in the mists of time, Ariel. It was before the police decided this latest chapter's murder—with a suspect they've got enough on to charge, obviously. This is an official, active investigation. Why should we get involved in it?"

"Grant Lacy's is an active investigation."

"I've got a personal interest in the Grant Lacy case."

"I've got a personal interest in this one."

"Okay." Henry did an about-face. "Give it a couple of days. Nose around. But keep the term 'steel magnolia' in mind. If the *daughters* of the Confederacy had fought the war, we might all be flying the Stars and Bars now."

"Interesting concept. Like pretending you've been hit by a train. You already knew about that, I guess, but I faxed you an article from the local paper."

"I knew it, I got it, I'm on it."

"Still in hot pursuit of the nefarious Richard Cummings?"

"It's your nickel. You want to hear about it?"

Henry spraddled in one of Ariel's kitchen chairs and went through the litany.

"So," Ariel said when he'd finished. "Cummings lied when he said the police were close to an arrest."

"Like a rug. Sure would be nice if you could remember who you saw him with that night."

"Sure would be nice if you'd stop throwing that up to me. This Marcus Black character . . . If Cummings picked the file clean, don't you wonder why he left Black's name in there?"

"Don't ask obvious questions. I'll know next week whether his information's worth anything, but even if it's gospel, it may have nothing to do with Lacy's disappearance."

"Doesn't sound to me as if the body on the railroad tracks has anything to do with Lacy either."

"Why not? The timing's right; the geography's right."

"Is it? Lacy went for an eight- or ten-mile run? It would've been that, wouldn't it, to the crossing and back? *If* we assume he planned to turn around there. So how much into running was he? What time did he leave home? What time did the train hit the victim? Could he have made it in time? Or, if he was really into running heavy-duty, would he have already been there and gone?"

"I've been in this business awhile, Ariel. I'm not unaware of the logistics."

"You're sounding grouchy."

"And you're sounding . . . Never mind."

"Henry, isn't Virginia Country Club a fine neighborhood? Why would a man who lived there go trotting down into the fumes and filth of a warehouse area for his healthful exercise?"

"If you're suggesting the run was a cover, like for a tryst or something, the cops say he wasn't a womanizer."

"That's not what I was suggesting at all. I'm getting back to what I said in the first place: I don't think the train victim has anything to do with Lacy. Do you know how many people go poof every day in L.A.? How many run away from home? I don't, and I'll bet you don't either. That could've been some poor old soul with Alzheimer's that wandered off and got trapped on the tracks, or a runaway teen. It could've been somebody from somewhere else entirely, somebody who fell *off* the train. You're assuming just because it happened the same day, it's Lacy; I'm saying that every day X number of people disappear. There's really very little to connect Lacy to the train business."

"Replace your X with the following numbers." Henry pawed his pockets for a note he'd made. " 'Roughly four thousand adults go missing each year in the city of Los Angeles alone, as many as forty-four hundred in a recent year. That's a dozen a day, including men and women of all races but not counting kids under eighteen, of which there's an astonishing eighty-five hundred or so annually.' The train victim, however, was no kid and no old-timer, and it sure wasn't a woman." He paused for breath.

"Luzzatto said the victim was a white male adult, that the age 'could' be right. Once they autopsy the remains that remain, we may know if they're Grant Lacy's."

"And you may know they're not."

"That's right. We may know they're not. Furthermore, even if the body's my man's, we still don't know how the accident—if it was one—has anything to do with a bribe paid to Cummings. And if the body's some stranger's, I start at ground zero again."

"Lacy went somewhere. He didn't evaporate."

"Oh, yeah? According to the tabloids he was picked up by a spaceship. He's now designing computer programs for Neptunians."

"The people who design computer programs *are* Neptunians."

Henry changed the subject. "What do you want to do about the dogs after tomorrow? When Sam comes?"

"Are you willing to stay? There's a sleep sofa in the study Sam could use."

"Suits me. You got homeowner's?"

"You talk about that poor boy like he's a doofus. Everything's replaceable except the dogs."

Henry picked at a loose shirt button. "I guess you talked to Peacock?"

"What? Oh. Yes, I did." There was the merest heartbeat of a pause before Ariel, in a different voice, said, "He's fine."

"So I've heard." Henry frowned. "I wasn't concerned about his health."

Ariel changed the subject.

When Henry had hung up, he sat still, twitching his mouth from side to side like a thoughtful rabbit.

"What?" he asked Stonewall, who for once was tranquil. The little dog was perched at Henry's feet, his expression as thoughtful as Henry's own.

"Don't hand me that innocent look." He gave the dog a scratch on the one erect ear before he went to the refrigerator and poked around at the variety of frozen dinners he'd stockpiled. None appealed. He chose one at random and popped it into the microwave.

He wondered what Ariel was feeling self-conscious about and was afraid he knew.

29

ARIEL SAW THE SWIRLING RED LIGHT IN HER REARVIEW MIRROR A SECond before she heard the siren scream to life. With a sinking stomach, she eased up on the accelerator. The speedometer needle was just grazing the legal limit when the patrol car whizzed past.

"Whoo!" Ariel breathed, and felt sorry for the more serious offender somewhere ahead. She kept the Darrin at a more sedate pace until she reached the Savannah city limits.

She had stopped at a gas station to pick up a map when the sky opened. It was a warm, fast-passing gully-washer, and it was already moving on as she entered the original part of the city, which was, literally, from another century.

The rain had hiked up the humidity, and Ariel had the momentary sensation that the historic district around her was suspended in the heavy, languorous air, caught by some trick of time-lapse photography. The buildings were mostly old or older, scarred yet graced by age, and there was a pastiche of styles. Federal here, Regency next door, Greek and Gothic Revival around the corner. Massive oaks dripped with moss in public squares, their monuments shrouded in cloud shadow.

Ariel's memory bank, very nearly photographic and frustratingly extraneous, kicked in. Savannah, she remembered, had been created a couple of centuries earlier by English debtors'-

prison refugees who'd earned redemption under the aegis of General Oglethorpe. She passed the avenue named for that urban planner extraordinaire, and more of the squares he'd designed into the geometric city plan. Ariel had heard someone call Savannah "a beautiful woman with a dirty face." She liked the description. If the city wasn't as tourist-pure as Charleston, it had its own sensual charm.

Consulting her map, she soon found her way to Grace Barron's street. It was a pleasant, oak-lined boulevard of thirties-era bungalows and apartments. Grace's was one of the latter, a three-story brick building with screened, white-painted wood porches at each corner.

The sidewalk leading to the single front entrance was old and buckled where the roots of a huge oak tree had snaked underneath and fought for space. A few tired leaves had already fallen, dotting the grass, a forewarning of the deluge to come.

Feeling like a salesman with questionable wares, Ariel entered a large, linoleum-tiled foyer (recently waxed, her nose told her). Four doors opened onto the entryway, one on either side and two beyond a staircase. Opposite the stairs was a bank of twelve mailboxes, all with names slotted in. *Barron* was printed under 1B, the apartment immediately to the right of the front door.

Ariel knocked on 1A. She waited, knocked again and then a third time. She was about to try one of the rear apartments when the door flew open. A bearded man took up most of the doorway. He wore chopped-off Levi's, a tank shirt commending a rock band, and, hanging on his neck, large black-padded earphones. A pencil rested on his ear. Ariel noticed these details seconds later; at the moment, she noticed nothing but his extremely annoyed expression.

"What?" he said, with an accent that definitely wasn't local.

"Looks like I disturbed you. Sorry."

"Yeah, well, now that you have . . . ?"

"I had an appointment with your neighbor." Ariel gestured toward Grace's door. "Nobody's answering, and I'm a little worried. Could you tell me . . . Does the building manager live on the premises?" She arranged her face into worry lines and tried to look meek. She thought her smile was winning.

"Upstairs. Two B. I don't know who lives there." He copied

her gesture toward the inoffensive closed door. "I don't care who lives there. I'm busy. Okay?" He shut the door in her face.

As Ariel climbed the stairs, she reflected on how quickly she'd become accustomed to Southern ways. That brute had been like a dash of ice water to the face, and she was surprised by how much his alien nastiness disturbed her. People here held doors open for you. They let you go ahead of them, into elevators and onto freeways (or expressways, as they were called locally). Strangers smiled and said, "Hey! How you doin'?"

The manner, she mused, might be influenced by the climate, or maybe it was the lack of anonymity; when people know you, know your family, know your car, you tend to behave better. She hadn't had a driver curse at her since she'd been here—or give her the finger. The brute, she'd bet, had a very quick finger.

The resident of 2B was a whole different kettle of catfish.

"Afternoon," she said, echoing Ariel's thoughts. "What can I do for you?"

Ariel began the spiel she'd attempted downstairs. It was unnecessary. "I'm Ida Barnett," she was informed. "Come on in."

The woman looked too old, too frail, and too refined to be a building manager. Her heart-shaped face was conservatively made-up, and her blue-gray hair was set in soft, albeit dated, waves.

"You caught me in my apron," she said. Carefully avoiding her coiffure, she slipped that old-fashioned pinafore-style garment over her head and smoothed the dress underneath. It was a calf-length frock with a linen collar, at the vee of which was pinned a silk gardenia. Mrs. Barnett looked as if she were about to audition for Blanche in *A Streetcar Named Desire*.

She invited Ariel to sit and took her own seat before an easel at which she'd apparently been working. "You want my husband, Marion, the manager? He's run down to the Piggly Wiggly, Miz . . . ?"

Ariel offered her name into the polite pause.

"I swear, I've hardly seen or heard tell of Miz Barron in the two years she's lived here, and now all of a sudden, it's just . . . You're a friend of hers, did you say?"

"Well, not a friend, exactly. We had an appointment."

"Oh, good!" Mrs. Barnett said on a sigh of relief. "That you're not friends, I mean. The police came here, of all things, and took her off with them. Yesterday morning."

"Oh!" Ariel feigned shock. "What in the world . . . ?"

"We don't know. We'd spent the night out at Tybee Island at our daughter's. When we got back, Huey Noles down in One C said the police had just taken her away. Had on sunshades and a big old floppy hat, he said, and her hand in front of her face like you see them do on TV?" She gave her head a brisk little shake. "Did you ever hear of such a thing?"

"I hardly know . . . But you said you hadn't seen her in two years. How can that be?"

"I was exaggeratin' a little but not by much. Miz Barron is, I reckon, what you'd call curious."

"Curious?"

"*Curious*," Ida Faye Barnett said, as if repetition would clarify. "You know what I mean. She has funny ways. For one thing, she's a pure homebody. Generally had her groceries and what-all delivered"—Ariel noticed a meaningful emphasis on the "what-all"—"until recently. With Hazel not around to do for her, the younger lady must've done what fetchin' was needed."

"Hazel?"

"Hazel . . . Wasn't Parrish her name? A 'companion,' I guess you'd say. Died a while back. I saw her obituary. As I was sayin', Miz Barron seldom went out. She'd call a cab once in a great while but when she did, she didn't tarry to visit. Of course, when a cab's waitin', you don't, and with her bein' right there by the front door, she wouldn't run into folks much anyway."

"Isn't Grace Barron awfully young to have a companion?"

Mrs. Barnett touched splayed fingertips to her bosom and murmured, " 'Nerves' is what Hazel said when I ran into her in the vestibule one time."

The tone left little doubt about her opinion of the explanation. Ariel didn't ask for elaboration. She didn't need to. A few moments of pregnant silence was all the other woman could tolerate.

"I think she drank."

"Ah, is that right?" Ariel had a sudden brainstorm. "She traveled by cab, you said? But what about her car?"

"Her car?"

"That's what our appointment was about. I'm interested in buying it."

"Well, I didn't even realize . . . You know, she *used* to have a car. When she moved in? I declare, I'd forgotten that."

"I haven't actually seen it yet. You don't remember what it, um, what it was like?"

"You're askin' the wrong person about cars! Marion might could tell you."

"Where did she move from when she moved here?"

Mrs. Barnett didn't know and, amazingly, didn't ask why Ariel wanted to know. "The owners of the building would, though, I'd have to think. Johnson and Yawn, over on Bull Street."

Ariel jotted the firm's name and asked another question, although she thought she already knew the answer.

"You mentioned a 'younger lady.' Who was that, do you know?"

"I feel sure she must be the one sent in the rent check every month. POA."

"Excuse me?"

"Power of attorney. I'm *sayin'* she was younger, but I don't know that since I only saw her at a distance. She did have salt-and-pepper hair. Wore it in a . . . a coronet braid, don't they call them? I expect she was some kin. A niece? Never saw another soul visit."

Ariel nodded. "That's sad," she said. "Mrs. Barnett, I don't suppose you might've noticed whether Mrs. Barron made a trip two weeks ago, a trip that would've kept her away all night?"

The answer, regretfully, was no.

Thanking Mrs. Barnett for her helpfulness (and admiring the watercolor on which she was working and declining an offer of tea and admitting that, no, she wasn't "from around here"), Ariel said good-bye. "You come back, hear?" followed her down the staircase.

A stop at a pay phone netted the information that prior to moving into the building owned by Johnson & Yawn two years earlier, Grace had lived in a house she herself had owned. Mr. Johnson didn't seem to grasp who Ariel was (he persisted in confusing her with some local reporter), but he was free with what little he knew about his deliciously notorious tenant. Mrs. Barron, he said, had sold her home to developers. The entire neighborhood had since become a shopping mall.

The college where Halley Barron had taught was fifteen minutes from Grace's apartment. On this overcast but hot afternoon students were much in evidence: couples strolling; purposeful-looking boys and girls moving at a brisker clip; a cluster of girls lolling on the grass studying, undistracted by the boom box that blared beside them. All, Ariel thought, looked astonishingly young.

The administration building was easy to find. Dean James Salter's office was locked tight, dark behind the glass door. The president's office was the same. Ariel was turning away from the latter when a boy appeared from around the corner.

"Excuse me," Ariel said. "Do you happen to know where President Henderson is? Or Dean Salter?"

The boy, a tanned, good-looking youngster in torn jeans and a T-shirt extolling the pleasures of Underground Atlanta, said "No, ma'am" and smiled in a way that took the sting out of the disconcerting "ma'am." Simultaneously, Ariel remembered, one, that in the South the term isn't reserved for geriatrics and, two, that she knew the name of the woman who'd delivered Halley's eulogy. She didn't realize until that moment that she'd even heard it.

"How about a Professor Lissy?"

"She's here. I've got an appointment with her." He grinned. "Come on. I'll show you where her torture chamber is."

Ariel followed him down one flight to a basement hallway bright with fluorescent lighting. Her guide knocked at one of several identical doors, opened it, and poked his head in.

"Hey, Dr. Lissy! Somebody here looking for you." He waved Ariel in and said, "Talk slow, okay? Take all the time you need."

Just then the door was fully opened, and the woman Ariel remembered from Halley's funeral was framed in the doorway. Pudgy, middle-aged, and alert, she eyed Ariel curiously. "You wanted to see me?"

"I didn't mean to break in line."

"Rob!" the professor called down the hallway. "Don't go far! That kid'll go over the wall if he gets half a chance. Come in. What can I do for you, Ms. . . . ?"

"Gold. Ariel Gold. Maybe nothing, and it's just a dumb little ol' thing. Won't take but a jiffy." Ariel smiled, planted herself in the cramped office's extra chair, and tried to believe that her foot-in-the-door story wasn't as half-baked as it suddenly seemed.

In a casual, chatty drawl, she said, "I was at Halley Barron's funeral, and I heard you speak? Mighty touching! But, well, something's been driving me crazy ever since, and here I was today visiting a niece, and I just thought: why not see if I could find you and satisfy my curiosity, you know?"

Dr. Lissy removed the spectacles perched atop her head and put them on.

"So," Ariel continued, "here's the thing. It was that poem, the one that woman after you read? What *was* it, do you know? And who was it wrote it?"

"Interesting. You're asking me rather than the person who read the poem?"

"Well, I couldn't for the life of me recall her name, but I did yours."

"You didn't remember her, but you remembered me?"

"Why, yes."

"I don't suppose the fact that mine was the only black face at the entire shebang has anything to do with that?"

"What?" Ariel bit off the word, molasses mouth forgotten. The reaction was so far removed from what she'd feared—suspicion? a brush-off?—that it had taken her a second to react.

Again, Dr. Lissy's reaction was the last thing Ariel expected. She guffawed, an uninhibited and totally unladylike whoop that set her full chest bouncing. "I thought that might shake you loose from that goofy act," she said. "Lord! That was awful! You're not from around here, are you?"

"I'm from California. Or Sri Lanka! Take your pick! What is it with everybody's preoccupation with where I'm from?"

"It's just that you don't do the flighty Southern belle shtick too well."

"I'll work on it. You weren't serious? You didn't really think I remembered you because you were black?"

"It's not a far-fetched idea. Even if you're color-blind philosophically, you're not blind in fact. But, listen, Rob's making his getaway even as we speak, so why don't you tell me what it is you really want?"

Ariel wasted no more time. "Have you heard that Grace Barron's been arrested for her son's murder, Dr. Lissy?"

"Call me Susan and, yes, I read about it."

"I don't think she did it. I'd like to talk to you about Halley Barron."

"Why? How are you involved?"

"I'm a family friend."

"You knew Halley?"

"No."

"The brother?"

"I . . . met him."

"You must make friends fast. What's Halley got to do with his death?"

"I'm just trying to put some pieces together."

"Why?"

Ariel's mouth twitched. "I work for a TV show, *The Open File*. We might do a segment on the Barron tragedies, but—"

"I see."

"No. Really, you don't. For reasons too complicated to go into, I, personally, need to know what happened to John William Barron. Talk to me about your friend, will you? On the off chance it might shed light on her brother's death?"

"Just a second." Susan Lissy went to the door and bellowed, "Rob!" Ariel heard her tell the boy to go have a cup of coffee. "But don't forget to come back," she warned. When she was again seated, she said, "Halley wasn't, strictly speaking, a friend. She was a colleague. I was surprised, frankly, when I heard about the request she'd left, that she wanted me to do the eulogy."

"Did she have closer friends you'd have expected her to name?"

"Not on the faculty, no. I guess I knew her about as well as anybody. Must be she didn't have closer friends outside school either. I don't know what you want me to tell you."

"What was she like?"

"Halley was . . . principled. A strong woman. I've seen her back some unpopular causes, at a cost, because she believed it was the right thing to do. You knew where she stood. On issues, anyway."

"As opposed to?"

Dr. Lissy propped well-rounded forearms on her desk and tapped her fingertips together as if considering what was appropriate to say. "She didn't exactly let it all hang out, you know what I mean? Southerners tend not to. Not the old line, anyway. Looking back . . ."

"Yes?"

"I've got this idea she was . . . bruised. Deep down. I think that self-containment hid a world of hurt, and the way she distanced herself was to keep—Lord above! Would you listen to me? Halley would hate this!

"Look, one thing I can tell you: she was good to that stepmother of hers. I never met the old gal, but I got the impression it wasn't a bed of roses. . . . Uh-oh! Did I put my foot in it?"

"Pardon?"

"You said you're a friend of the family. By a process of elimination, that must mean the old woman."

"She's not so old. The D.A. obviously thinks she's spry enough to kill. At any rate, I expect you're right; Halley probably had her hands full at times."

"You know what she made me think of? One of those old-time spinster daughters. You know, the dutiful soul that stayed home and tended the parents in their old age while the brothers and sisters got to live real lives? Well, Mrs. Barron's got the law taking care of her now. I wonder if they provide a hairdresser."

"Pardon?"

Susan snorted. "Halley did the woman's hair. And ran her errands. And, I'm pretty sure, tended her finances."

"I thought you said—"

"She didn't confide, but she wasn't mute. We did work at the same place, you know, and Savannah's not a metropolis. A meeting she missed here, a passing comment there. When I had my car detailed, she asked who I'd used; her stepmother's needed doing, she said. And once—"

"But the hair thing . . ."

"Ran into her in the market. She had Clairol, 'Black Pearl' and silver something-or-other, in her cart. Since Halley left her hair natural, mostly gray, I asked. She answered. She didn't say if Mrs. Barron was too vain to let strangers see her roots or if she was just a tightwad." Susan Lissy sighed. "I'm getting depressed," she said. "Halley was one rare woman; had the patience of a saint. I wonder if she ever did let go. Throw a fit or have a few yuks."

"Saints aren't known for it. Why do you think she did it? I mean, why *was* she so good to her stepmother?"

"Might be the most obvious reason. Might be she loved her."

With a wry grin, Ariel said, "Don't confuse my convoluted theories with simple explanations. Tell me, did she ever talk about her brother to you?"

"I didn't even know she had one until he was dead. I'd seen this picture on her desk. A nice-looking blond guy, right? Much younger? An inscription that mentioned 'love'? Tickled me to death. Look out! I thought. This gal's got a whole 'nother life, after all. Come to find out it was just her brother."

"Where'd she live?"

"Over on East Gaston. She'd bought one of those old houses, one of the gingerbready types, and restored it. She had money, I take it, because gentrification don't come cheap. She left the house to the school, you know. As a residence for English Lit scholarship students."

Dr. Lissy didn't know the address, but she was pretty sure it was one of the first two or three houses west of Abercorn.

Ariel had risen to leave when she said, "My pretenses, by the way, weren't all false; I really do want to know about the poem."

"I teach calculus, my friend; I don't know from poetry. I had to read the stuff in college, but I hardly ever could figure out what any of it meant."

" 'A poem should not mean/But be,' " Ariel said offhandedly and thought of a last question.

"What kind of car did Halley drive?"

"A gray Volvo. Safe and solid, or so the poor woman thought. I guess no car's ever safe enough when you lose control of it."

30

"SO WHAT DO YOU THINK, SAM-BONES? OKAY BY YOU IF WE HANG out here a couple of days?"

Henry was putting away groceries picked up en route to Ariel's house after collecting his son. He'd briefly explained the temporary tenancy, reminding Sam that he'd met Ariel at the studio a week or two before. He'd mentioned the benefit of convenience, this house being nearer than his own to Sam's school. He'd emphasized the dog-sitting aspect, knowing the boy still mourned an ancient part cocker, part who-knew-what that had finally succumbed two years back. He'd been deliberately casual; their relationship was too brittle to complicate with erroneous conclusions.

Sam had made no comment about any of it.

"Yo, Sam?" Henry prompted—and was distracted by something unrecognizable he was about to stash in the refrigerator. Bean curd? It had been tossed into the cart by old Silent Sam along with some other kind of gruel. His own eating habits, he reflected gloomily as he put it away, might suffer during this hands-on parenting phase. He wiped his hands on his cords and gave his son a sideways glance. "So, okay? Not okay? What?"

Sam shrugged. Slumped bonelessly in a chair, he continued to scratch the belly of a rapturous Stonewall stretched across his lap. Beside his frayed, size eleven sneakers, Jessie snoozed peacefully. Henry was encouraged enough to venture a mild warning.

"Try to be careful while we're here, okay? There's lots of breakables, so keep your appendages under control."

Sam muttered something unintelligible. "What say?" Henry inquired, on the assumption that the comment might have been addressed to him rather than to the dogs.

"Practice," Sam said into his chest.

The kid looked up long enough to see his father's baffled expression and regained the use of his tongue. "There's not a piano here. You don't have one, either. How'm I supposed to practice?"

Piano practice hadn't been among Henry's many concerns about Sam's coming to live with him. He considered it now. "You could go to your mom's from school. I could pick you up after work."

"Like when? Midnight?"

Henry swallowed the protest that he'd taken that very afternoon off. There was validity to his son's assessment of his work schedule; it would have to become more structured, Henry knew. Another adjustment. "Okay. I'll look into renting a piano when we're back in my place."

"Why don't we just move mine? Or are you going to dump me back on Mom as soon as she comes home?"

"Listen, Sam, I know this is—"

Henry's speech of reassurance died aborning when Sam suddenly pushed back his chair with a loud scrape and, depositing a startled Stonewall on the floor beside Jessie, announced that he was "going over to Kyle's to shoot baskets." The front door slammed while Henry was still issuing the order to be back in time for dinner. He hadn't thought to ask who Kyle was. He folded his mouth into a lipless line and sighed.

Chopping onions for the tacos he knew Sam liked, he tried to figure out a way to storm the barricades of teenage hostility. Every approach seemed too imperious, too circuitous, or too namby-pamby. The problem was, he agreed with the kid: Sam's resentment was justified. Being the bone of contention between two battling parents who should never have gotten past one night of lust was the pits, and not knowing what your address would be next month was no way to grow up. Being a broken-home statistic might be more common than not among Sam's peers, but it was still a damn shame.

Henry remembered when Sam was a bright little kid who thought his dad's every word was oracular. He remembered when, at about age five, Sam had fallen on broken glass and laid open his shin. His grip on Henry's hand while a doctor cleaned the wound had been viselike. Sam hadn't cried; Henry had nearly fainted. And he tried not to remember a virulent argument between Emily and himself, the end of which a pajama-clad Sam had witnessed. Henry wiped his eyes on his sleeve, not sure if it was just the onions.

When the phone rang an hour later, Sam hadn't returned, the tacos were congealing, and Henry was thankful he'd made a point of giving the boy this number. He'd forgotten that he'd also left it with Tara at the office.

"Is that Henry Heller? With *The Open File*?"

The unfamiliar voice was gravelly, nasal, and terse. "My name's Joseph Ross. I'm with Union Pacific. Engineer. They called me from Media Relations and said you wanted to talk to me."

"Ross?" Henry's mind had already changed gears. He reached for a pencil. "The engineer from the Carson fatality last December?"

"Affirmative."

"Hey! It hasn't been easy getting to you. Bert Cannon down there's a friend of mine, but he wouldn't even tell me your name."

"Policy. Not unless I agreed to talk to you."

"Well, thanks. And, Joseph . . . Let me offer my sympathy."

The engineer coughed, a phlegmy rattle. "Yeah. Thanks."

"That kind of thing must put you guys through hell."

"That kind of thing makes us *mad* as hell!"

"Pardon?"

"Forget it. What can I do for you?"

"Umm," Henry probed, "it's got to be hard on you, all right."

"You don't know the half of it!" Ross blurted. He hesitated and then, vehemently, said, "Some guy can't wait for the train to pass; he's just got to try and beat it. To get someplace a minute earlier. Well, he gets someplace all right! He gets dead, and we get the blame. People have got to understand the power of a train! They've got to respect that power!"

"Absolutely. Is that what happened with your train? The man was trying to outrun you?"

Ross was breathing hard and off on a tear. "Maybe you think

I should feel sympathy for anybody stupid enough to try to outrun a six-thousand-ton locomotive moving eighty miles an hour. Well, sorry! I had to get counseling, you know? This was my first time. One guy I know's had five. *Five!* I couldn't work for a month or sleep, either. Then all I wanted to do was sleep. Denial, grief, repression, anger—I went through it all."

Henry heard a sneeze and then another before Ross, thoroughly congested, said, "What exactly did you want?"

"The John Doe in Carson—was he trying to outrun the train?"

"No. I don't know. All of a sudden he was just there, dead ahead."

"What happened?"

"What *happened?* I saw the man. I hit the emergency brake. It took over a mile and a half to stop. I heard they found parts of the body more than a hundred feet away, and I just thank God I didn't have to see what was left of him!"

"But was he just standing there? Was he walking across the tracks? Running? What?"

"He was on his knees."

"Like he'd stumbled and fallen?"

"Yeah. Like he was racing across and got tripped up. That's what I've decided happened. Right at first I thought . . ."

"What?"

Sounding even more wretched, Ross said, "I didn't say anything about this to anybody but my shrink, but in that second I first saw him I had this nutty thought that he was kneeling."

"*Kneeling?*"

"Yeah."

"You mean like he was praying?"

"He was on his knees, with his face down and his rear in the air. It looked like, well, like he was bowing. Kowtowing, you know, like those Arabs do—toward the East." Ross coughed.

Henry worried his beard and added question marks after the word *kneeling*. He was having a problem picturing this bizarre scene. Could Lacy have been a Muslim? A member of some Eastern sect? "Was he facing you?"

"No. He was across the track. Angled. His arms and . . ." Ross sighed, a wrung-out defeated sound. "His arms and his head were on the rails. That's the reason the body got so torn up instead of just being thrown. That's what usually happens, see." A moment passed before the engineer said, "I didn't want to believe he was just waiting! Some nut that decided to do himself in and didn't have the guts to pull a trigger! That happens, you know. People like that, they make us their weapon of choice. They make *us* kill them! And we *got* no choice!

"See, there is *nothing* we can do! Once we get up to speed and we see somebody on the tracks? All we can do is hit the horn and hit the brakes—and then hit whatever's there."

Henry let the silence stretch, and then Ross said, "I won't ever forget seeing him in my headlights. Never in my lifetime."

"You see anybody else near the tracks? Cars? Pedestrians?"

"No. I was, what you might say, focused on what I saw *on* the tracks."

"Could you see what he was wearing?"

"Something dark, some dark color. His shoes . . . I remember a white shoe. There was something reflecting off it."

"Could it have been that fluorescent tape some runners use?"

"Sure, I guess. I was told . . . Bert said you were looking into doing a story, but the accident wasn't the—what? Central issue? That your story might not have anything to do with that at all?"

"I also guaranteed that nothing said to me would be put on the air without clearance from your guys."

Henry just then noticed that Jessie's head had come up off her paws and that her ears had gone erect. Within seconds, he heard the front door open and close.

"You'll get no grief from my show, Joseph. You might even get a forum. Now, you take care of that cold."

Henry turned to see Sam come into the kitchen. He looked tight-mouthed and ready to do battle. Stonewall was clamoring, and the kid was trying hard to ignore him. Henry merely said, "Good. You're back. Let's warm up this stuff and eat. I'm starving."

31

WHEN ARIEL LEFT THE CAMPUS, SHE DECIDED TO TAKE A LOOK AT where Halley had lived, an address even closer to Grace's neighborhood than the school was, she observed.

Gaston Street was presided over by close-set nineteenth-century townhouses, some impeccably restored, some languishing in shabby gentility. Multistoried, they recalled an era when families were large and staffs larger. Tall windows were framed by shutters, and front doors opened from the second level onto steep steps that led down past the kitchen and servants' quarters onto the sidewalk. Ariel quickly guessed which house had been Halley's. She eased to the curb in front of a Victorian, newer than many of its neighbors and recently refurbished.

Her footfall on the porch steps seemed disreputably loud. The bell was one of the old twist types; Ariel could hear its shrill, futile ring. She'd hoped to find a caretaker or perhaps some of the scholarship students, students who'd known their benefactor. She knew even before she rang that no one would answer; the house was heavy with emptiness.

She glued her face to the etched glass of the door, cupping her hands like horse blinders, and peered through lace into the entry hall, which had been cleared of any furnishings it might once have held. Draperies covered the other accessible windows.

Moody with irritation at herself for a pointless trip, she paused at the gate to look back at the house, closed and mute and as devoid of life as its former owner, a woman no one seemed to have known. Halley Barron had vanished as inconsequentially as a hole in water, leaving hardly a ripple.

The mood didn't dissipate during the drive north. Dusk had long since deepened into night by the time Ariel crossed the bridge onto Kiawah, and narrow little Bohicket Road was virtually deserted. On nights like this one when the moon was obscured by clouds, the two-lane road was a black and lonely stretch, smothered under a canopy of branches. It felt like the inside of a shroud.

Preoccupied, Ariel was just coming out of a dogleg curve when she saw something in the road ahead. It was an animal, standing stock-still, pinned by the beam of her headlights, directly in the path of her car.

In a purely reflex action faster than rational thought, she spun the steering wheel. The tires threw gravel as the little roadster screeched protest, skidded, and then righted itself. Ariel's feet hit the pedals and she geared down, heart hammering.

"Stupid!" she hissed. She steered the car off the road, stopped, and got her breath back. After checking both directions, she made a U-turn back onto the shoulder, switched to high beams, and killed the engine. The dog or cat or whatever she'd seen must have been hurt, she thought, to stand there like that.

Gravel shifted and crackled beneath her shoes as she took to the road, searching, thinking that she should have brought the car closer. Then she saw the creature up ahead. It had barely made the edge of the road, where it had halted, staring into the light with beady eyes, mesmerized. The hair on Ariel's neck prickled. She hadn't known rats could be that big. This one was the size of a large cat, gray, with a pointed snout and a disgusting nude tail.

She took a step backward. In that instant she heard the hum of a motor. The car was rounding the bend, and the headlights glanced off the woods before they picked out the lone figure in the road, spotlighting Ariel as if she were on center stage.

Ariel shielded her eyes. Disbelieving, as mesmerized as the rat had been, she heard the car pick up speed. It was moving fast, highway fast, far too fast for a country road. By some contrary trick of time, action slowed. With uncanny clarity, as the car raced directly toward her, Ariel saw the hood ornament and the parallel bars of the grille and the rubber bumper that, dreamlike, seemed to loom bigger and bigger in a series of still frames. She also saw the treads of the front tires as those tires crossed the center line.

While some enthralled part of her mind registered each impression, wondering at the very long time it was taking the car to cover what seemed like inches, Ariel's body prepared to bolt. But which way? She made a mighty leap to the side just as solid metal skimmed past, the *whoosh* a more tangible thing than sound.

The noise of the motor faded, and Ariel was amazed to find that not only was she untouched, she'd actually managed to stay on her feet. Her knees weren't as cooperative. They were having trouble remembering their function.

"Lunatic!" she screamed into the dark. "Moron!" Shaking with rage and fear, she cried, "Stupid jerk butthead!" Or maybe she only thought it. Insanely, she heard herself giggle, but her voice caught and the giggle came out a sob. She tottered to her car and collapsed onto the seat, dropping her head to her knees.

Eventually, she was reasonably certain she wasn't going to lose it—either consciousness or lunch. The shakes had settled into an occasional tremor, no more than a two on the Richter scale. Ariel slid the door shut and locked it, but it was quite a while before she trusted herself to drive. Astonishingly, those details so vivid in the eternal three or four seconds the car bore down on her were now visual gibberish, a fractured montage. The entire incident already seemed like the product of hysteria.

The driver had surely, somehow, failed to see her. Or had accidentally hit the accelerator rather than the brakes. Or had been drunk or had simply panicked. Any one of those possibilities would explain her impression that, even if it had very nearly been too late, the driver had swerved.

If he hadn't, she thought, I'd be roadkill.

Ariel pulled into B.F.'s light-swept yard and, with relief, cut the engine. The music and laughter she heard were as jarring as a shout.

She looked around. No car other than the Lincoln was in sight. Were Sarge and Hattie partying? That fantastic picture brought a grin, and Ariel was almost lighthearted (or light-headed; she wasn't altogether sure which) when she opened the back door onto Willie Nelson belting "Whiskey River" from the radio. The kitchen seemed to be full of people.

"And here's the last one missing!" Julian Taliaferro cried. He must have arrived only moments before because he still held a paper bag that, from the shape of it, contained a bottle of wine.

"You look a little peaked, sugar," he said. "Something wrong?"

Ariel shook her head. She felt as if she were emerging from a decompression chamber.

"Well, can't anybody fault our timing! The catfish is hot outta the grease, and the hush puppies are on the table."

The pretty blonde at Julian's side gave him a sharp, noticeably assessing glance before she deposited her purse and crossed to Ariel, her hand gracefully extended.

"Gail Calhoun," she said. "And since I doubt your name is 'Sugar,' I guess you must be Ariel." Her touch was cool; it matched her tone. "I hear you're in television? One of the tabloid shows?"

Ariel had time to notice the sudden frown on Julian's face but not to reply before they were asked to sit down. "You, too, Hattie," Sarge said from the stove, where he was piling fried fish onto a platter. "Start eating. It's no good cold."

"Y'all go on." Hattie rinsed a pot and stacked it with others on the drainboard. Her movements were brisk; there was little sign she'd been sick.

"Hattie," Sarge ordered, "sit."

"Let me get the slaw."

"I'll get the slaw." Sarge pulled out a chair. "Sit."

Hattie sat, but she had even less to say than did Ariel, who was having trouble switching into a party mode.

The late supper was a last-minute affair prompted by the catfish, caught by Sarge that afternoon. Ariel assumed he'd invited Julian, who'd then asked Gail Calhoun as his date. She soon learned it was the other way around. Gail, it seemed, was a near neighbor and, like Julian, an attorney. Evidently, she felt they had other things in common. Her eyes rarely left him, and her fingers frequently drifted to some part of his anatomy, alighting on an arm or shoulder proprietarily. He didn't appear to notice.

He was asking Ariel how she liked her new car when she

remembered she hadn't seen his parked outside and commented on it.

"You didn't come *here* 'by shanks' mare'?"

"Just from down at Gail's. We walked over. Hey," he said, and brought up the ongoing area burglaries. The latest had taken place on Seabrook Island, and Gail had firm opinions about that and everything. She also had a way of verbally pouncing when she made a point, which struck Ariel as rather predatory. Talk turned to a recent local libel suit. The two had worked the case on opposite sides; she'd won.

"Yeah," Julian grumbled. "You've heard the saying, 'You don't know a woman until you've met her in court'? No doubt whoever said it meant divorce court, but when the woman is opposing attorney in a lawsuit that's dog-eat-dog . . ."

The cannibalistic metaphor, Ariel thought, was an unfortunate one for an attorney dining on fish.

Hattie was by then back at the dishpan. Sarge forcibly removed her, commanding that she have some Key lime pie or go rest. When she opted for the latter, Ariel felt free to bring up the Barrons.

Julian had heard that the arraignment that morning had been short and sweet. He didn't know any details except that a "not guilty" plea had been entered and bail had been denied.

What Gail said then was more intriguing.

It seemed Julian had represented not John William but his ex-wife at the time of their divorce.

"I did," he admitted. "Not to bad-mouth a former client, but she was one of those women I was talking about. That you don't want to meet in court? 'Hell hath . . .' " Ariel saw his eyes narrow and slide her way before he said, merely, "Well, she was loaded for bear."

"But wait," Ariel said. "You're—"

"I wasn't representing John William then. An old gentleman by the name of Wesley L. Candler was. He'd always handled the Barron affairs and did right up until he died at eighty-two."

Ariel let a moment pass, but Julian merely cut himself a second piece of pie and said nothing more.

"What was her name?" she asked. "The former Mrs. Barron."

"Beverly."

"What were the grounds?"

"Incompatibility."

"How long ago was this?"

Sarge, who'd been watching the exchange with grim amusement, said, "Now you two know how witnesses feel when you're grilling them." To Ariel, he said, "It's been seven, maybe eight years. The marriage lasted about as long as it takes a French chef to go through a pound of butter." He held up a hand to forestall her obvious question. "No, John William never told me what the problem was and no, I never met her. What else do you want to know?"

"Does she still live around here?"

"She was from Aiken," Gail supplied, finding a way back into the conversation. "Went back there and remarried within the year, I heard, to somebody named . . ." Her brow wrinkled, and she turned to Julian. "Bernd? Is that right?"

Julian nodded. "It is and she was. Stayed hot, too. Called to let me know alimony would no longer be required, thank you, sir. I swear, the women in John William's life . . ." He broke off.

"What?" Gail asked.

Julian didn't seem to hear her.

The others waited expectantly, but it was a moment before he came back from wherever memory had taken him and, looking startled by their attention, said, "What? It's nothing."

"No fair," Gail teased, nudging him playfully.

"No, really." He saw the faint, quizzical smile on Sarge's face and, obviously realizing that further protestations would blow an inconsequential matter into silly proportions, said, uncomfortably, "Well, it's nothing confidential. It's just . . . I was in the drugstore one day, and I went back to the office to say hey to John William. He was on the phone with his sister, lightin' into her about something. When he saw me, he hung up fussing. Called her an interfering . . . well, he called her a name. Then he said the beatin'est thing. He said, 'I'll tell you something, Julian. The only thing worse than one mother is two.' "

"What do you make of what Julian said?" Ariel asked.

He and Gail had gone and, judging by Gail's manner on leaving, she had something specific in mind for when they reached her house. Ariel was trying to ignore a stab of loneliness as she put away the few leftovers. She was also trying to ignore the last piece of Key lime pie beckoning from the plate.

"Two hundred fifty, minimum," Sarge said.

"Excuse me?"

"Calories per slice."

"If you're such a mind reader, tell me what your nephew meant about 'two mothers.' "

"You tell me."

"Sarge, when Halley went off to that sanatorium after your brother died—where was it? Columbia? How long was she gone?"

"You're talking about thirty-odd years ago, and I wasn't even around at the time."

"But you said she was gone quite a while, didn't you? Months?"

"So?"

"Did Grace stay here in Charleston while Halley was away? I mean, where people could see her?"

Sarge narrowed his eyes, examined the question, and began to shake his head, a slow, disbelieving swivel. "You're not serious."

"It's not impossible. Look at the facts." Thinking hard, Ariel sat across from Sarge and, as each item occurred to her, repeated what she'd been told. "Halley was a teenager; she was past puberty, wasn't she? She was out of sight for months. She came home right after John William was born. She virtually raised him. Hey! I'm not dishing up dirt. I'm not telling you anything you didn't tell me." She waited for Sarge's reaction. It was nothing more than a shifting of the jaw, a sign of stubbornness or consideration of her words; she couldn't tell which.

"They stayed very close, Halley and John William," she added. "He left his estate to her—not to Grace."

"You're forgetting something very important." There was an edge to Sarge's words that didn't escape Ariel. "John William looked like my brother. *His father*."

"Oh-h." Ariel sucked air. "That's not what I . . ." After a long, uncomfortable moment, her voice tentative, she said, "Your brother would've been the boy's *grand*father. Children often favor their grandparents."

"You don't give up, do you? Okay. So what if this garbage is true, that Halley played around and got caught. With some kid,

I mean. What of it? John's dead, John William's dead, Halley's dead. What the hell difference does it make?"

"I don't know."

Sarge abruptly left the table. He halted at the door and, with his slablike back to Ariel, said, "Let this alone. Or if you just have to poke your nose in, keep your speculations to yourself."

32

SAM HAD PLUGGED HIMSELF INTO HIS NEW DISCMAN (WHICH HENRY had made sure was a legitimate purchase) and taken the dogs for a walk. His offer to do so was a pleasant surprise, a gesture Henry chose to view as generosity rather than escape, but the house was awfully still in his absence. When the refrigerator clicked on, it sounded like an Evinrude outboard throbbing to life.

"You act like a man who hasn't been living alone for years," Henry muttered. He heard himself and said, "Stop talking to yourself." He didn't know why that seemed nuttier than talking to the dogs, which he found himself doing regularly. He also didn't know why he felt more alone here than he did at his own place.

He was reaching for the phone when it rang.

"How's it going?" Ariel asked. "Sam settled in?"

"He's in but he's out, walking your dogs, matter of fact."

"Really! Well, terrific!"

Henry laughed. "Relax, mama. It's probably okay unless he goes into one of his music-induced trances. You know, just drops the leashes and bebops off into the starry night—"

"Henry!"

"I'm joking, Ariel. Sam wouldn't let anything happen to the dogs. The three of them are already thick as thieves."

"Great metaphor."

"Yeah. Forget I said that."

"Well, I just thought I'd check in. See if you found everything you need . . . the sheets for the sofa bed and so on."

"I hadn't looked, but I wouldn't be surprised if they're in the linen closet. What's wrong? B.F. didn't have a relapse or something?"

"No! He's fine. I didn't see him today, actually. I drove down to Savannah and talked to some people about the Barron ladies."

"And?"

"I could've saved myself a trip. Halley was her stepmother's good and faithful servant, a saint whose only fault was too much virtue. Grace used to have a car but doesn't seem to now, and I don't know what kind it was. I don't know how they think she got herself up here to commit murder. In a cab, I guess."

Ariel sighed. "She's probably a lush, which I already suspected, but she didn't do her drinking in bars. She's been, it seems, a virtual shut-in for years. Nobody knows nothin'."

"Well, Nancy Drew, every day can't be a bonanza." Henry was standing in front of the open refrigerator. He couldn't decide between light beer and something with flavor.

"It's not that. I'm just . . . Sarge and I had a tiff, kind of, and the silence around here right now is mighty eloquent. I guess I'm feeling sort of lonesome."

Henry plucked a long-neck Corona from the refrigerator. "What'd you fight about?"

"It was something Julian Taliaferro said tonight that—"

"Who?"

"A local lawyer. Julian was talking about a remark—"

"He works evenings, this lawyer?"

"What? No, of course not. It was at dinner. He happened to remember one time when he—"

"It doesn't sound like you're all that lonesome to me."

"Will you stop interrupting! Julian was here. At the house. A group, including a good-looking blonde. It happens that he represented the former Mrs. Barron in the divorce—"

"This Barron guy was married?"

"Briefly. But that's incidental to what I'm *trying* to tell you."

Ariel gave Henry time to make a comment if he had one. He didn't.

She repeated what Julian had told them and what she'd then theorized to Sarge. "I'm not suggesting incest. Although . . . John Barron's suicide note could be interpreted more than one way."

"Man, oh, man! McManus must've loved this! His brother was a pervert, his niece abused, his nephew a product of depravity? You say you had a tiff? It's a wonder he didn't give you a poke in the nose."

"I said there was no reason to think incest was involved, but that *would* explain some things, like—"

"Ariel, back up. You're on pretty shaky terrain here."

" 'Every conviction was a whim at birth.' "

"And every birth's not from some convoluted *Days of Our Lives* episode. So the girl left town for a while. So she loved her half brother. Give her a break! Somebody would've noticed if what's-her-name, Grace, gave birth without ever being pregnant. Find out who her doctor was. If he's dead, check the local hospitals."

"They would've taken steps, Henry. We're talking about the fifties. A small Southern city. Young, very young, women from good families didn't have illegitimate children with impunity. I can't waltz into some hospital and say, 'Tell me who really bore this child!' Besides, I'm not saying that's what happened. I'm merely looking at possibilities. If Halley was the mother, whoever the father was, it's a whole new ball game. Grace would've been no blood relation to John William whatever. She may have had no feeling for him either, or if she did, it might've been resentment."

"That's a motive for murder?"

"I didn't say that. It keeps bothering me that she wasn't at his funeral. Halley was."

"Good God, Ariel, maybe the woman was just too distraught. Sedated. Overcome with grief. Maybe she's just not an aficionado of funerals like the rest of you people down there."

"But if he was her son—"

"Ariel—"

"I've also wondered all along why Halley was so devoted to Grace. A beautiful young stepmother who steals Papa? But if that stepmother stood by you in a personal crisis? And let's say incest *was* involved. Victims often feel like it's their fault, right? Put yourself in the place of a mixed-up kid. Your abuser, your father, commits suicide. Think of the guilt! And to Halley, Grace seems like a victim, too. Her husband's unfaithful to her; he's taken away from her; he leaves you and your child—not his wife—his money. Wouldn't guilt explain lifelong loyalty? And the fact that Halley left Grace a sizable inheritance?"

"Will you listen to yourself? You can't have it both ways. If Grace felt victimized, why would she have stayed around? Why would she have gone to such lengths to protect Halley?"

"I didn't say Grace felt like a victim; I said Halley might've seen her that way. And think about this: Halley never married. No husband. No close relationships. Does that, maybe, suggest the deep psychological scars incest would've left? And this much-vaunted integrity of hers . . . 'The more things a man is ashamed of, the more respectable he is.' "

"Would you stop with the screwball quotes?"

" 'I quote others only the better to express myself.' "

"Can I ask you a question? If John Barron was abusing his daughter, why'd he get married? What would he want with a beautiful woman in the house?"

"The beautiful woman he married wasn't all that much older than Halley."

"Ariel, do yourself a favor. Get back on track. Stop thinking about inbreeding and think about motive, as in who had one to kill this guy. The sister did, by the way—a whole lot of money. You think of that? Your pal the lawyer also overheard the brother and sister fighting, you said, so they weren't lovey-dovey all the time. Maybe she wasn't as saintly as you think.

"Who else had motive? The ex-wife? A disgruntled employee? Friends? Enemies? Lovers? And concentrate on who had opportunity. Did the sister? Did she have an alibi? Did she have a car?"

"She had a gray Volvo, not a blue Chevrolet."

"Did she have a credit card? And access to a rental agency?"

"The car that was seen leaving the Barron house wasn't new, according to the witness. Rental cars are."

"You're thinking again! Good! Find out what kind of car the mother had. What happened to it? And the garage door opener. Can you get back in the house? Is there an opener in there? A wall unit, I mean? Did the cops find remotes? How many? What's the story on that gun? Most important, find out what else they've got on the mother. There's something, believe me, and, Ariel, if it's solid, give this thing up. I need you here."

Silence reigned long enough for both to consider the implications of that.

"Is Sam back with the dogs yet?" Ariel asked.

"They haven't even been gone half an hour. You want me to send out an APB?"

"Give 'em a hug for me."

"I don't hug dogs, and I'm sorry to hear that's how you get your kicks. Go make up with McManus. Tell him romantic deprivation addled your brain." Henry grinned and looked toward the hall. "Hey, wait a minute. I hear the pitter-patter of little paws."

Jessie came in, grinning as if in parody of Henry. She padded to her water dish and interrupted greedy lapping to give a vigorous shake that sent tags jingling and water slinging.

"Well, one's back in the corral," Henry said.

"Jessie."

"Is that your maternal instinct at work?"

"Don't make fun; I heard her tags. Where's Stonewall?"

Sam came in, deposited the leashes, and was gone again before the yellow dog came in carrying a rope toy he'd paused to locate. He dropped it at Henry's feet as if it had been urgently requested and took his own turn at the water bowl.

"Present and accounted for," Henry said as he heard the study door firmly close. "I meant what I said, Ariel. If it looks like they've got the goods on the old lady, catch the next plane."

33

THE ROOM WAS REMARKABLY LIKE THE JAILHOUSE VISITING ROOMS Ariel had seen in movies. She waited in one of a line of hard wooden chairs beyond which was a series of tables partitioned by glass. Bulletproof? she wondered.

The visitors on either side of her were mostly women. One or two talked together in a desultory fashion, but the atmosphere was subdued, weighted and waiting. Ariel felt a small chunk of the heaviness in her skull, making up its mind whether to become a full-fledged headache. She felt in her bag for the little enamel pillbox B.F. had once given her, a treasure because it had belonged to her grandmother. It didn't want to be found, and the search, Ariel realized, was more distraction than need. She was nervous about talking to Grace Barron.

Sarge had arranged it.

After talking with Henry the night before, Ariel had made up her mind to apologize. It hadn't been hard. It was easy to admit she'd been heedless of Sarge's feelings in her pursuit of speculations. To her they'd been abstract; to him they'd been slander.

Sarge had made the call to set up a visit for "B.F. Coulter's granddaughter," assuring Grace's attorney that Ariel was a family friend. He'd had no interest in accompanying her.

A great deal of bitterness simmered in Sarge McManus, and Ariel sensed that his emotions were more complex than he was acknowledging, even to himself. He was a man of formidable loyalty, and his lay with his brother's son. He'd known his brother's young bride only briefly. Any ties that might once have existed had been tenuous; for decades they'd been nonexistent. If he wasn't convinced of Grace's guilt, he was no more convinced of her innocence, and he knew he didn't want his suspicions confirmed. He was afraid of the power of the wrath that would be unleashed.

Grace was the last of the prisoners shepherded through the door. She couldn't have looked more out of place in a bus station men's room.

Her arm still rested in the sling, her face remained bandaged, and her eyes were no less shocking than before, but she seemed to hold herself above her surroundings. She appeared unaware of the gray county-issue dress she wore. Her dark, silver-streaked hair was neat, her carriage erect. She looked as in control as she'd been in the proud old Charleston house that, after so many years, was finally hers. Her eyes flicked over the room, and she came directly to the table where Ariel waited.

"Thank you for seeing me, Mrs. Barron," she said. "I wasn't sure you would."

"I was curious."

The blunt statement wasn't accompanied by any sign of friendliness or even recognition. Grace Barron, it seemed, was in her imperious mode. She waited to be enlightened.

"You remember, don't you, that I'm a friend of your brother-in-law?" Ariel hesitated. "I met your son. The night he died. I was, I think, one of the last people to speak with him."

If Ariel hadn't been watching the impassive face across from her so carefully, she wouldn't have noticed the tiny spasm that shook the uplifted chin.

"I'd like to help you if I can," Ariel said.

"In what way?"

"I work for the television news show *The Open File.*"

Grace's hand flew to her face and hovered there. It was a gesture of protection, Ariel thought, as if she'd announced that a battery of TV cameras were trained on Grace even now.

"No," Grace said, beginning to rise from her chair.

"I'm a producer. We're considering doing a piece, a story, on your son's death. It could be helpful to you. If you're agreeable to the idea, you could use us to help yourself."

"You want me to *cooperate* in sensationalizing this outrage?"

Ariel deliberately lowered her voice in hopes of drawing the other woman back into her chair.

"You don't belong here, Mrs. Barron, do you? Don't you want to see John William's real killer here? Isn't that what you want?"

Grace remained as she was, on the point of flight. "Mr. McCrory, my attorney . . ."

"Your attorney would be fully apprised."

"But what would you do? Why would you do it?"

"We have extensive research resources. *I* am an experienced researcher." Ariel managed the slightly shaded truth with only inner qualms. "The D.A.'s office has a staff preparing their case against you. We can help balance the odds. I don't know how big Mr. McCrory's firm is, but I can't believe he'd be sorry for a team of competent people working on your defense—at no cost."

Grace lowered herself to her chair. The tendons in her neck, taut as piano wire, relaxed, and the rigid lines of her face seemed to melt. She gazed around in confusion, as if only now did she realize where she was. It came to Ariel that what she'd seen as arrogance was a carapace, and a fragile one.

"Did you know," Grace said, "that tomorrow is my birthday?"

"I didn't, no."

"Can you imagine celebrating your birthday here?"

"No. Let's make sure you don't spend another birthday—"

"These people . . . I've led a very private life for many years, seeing no one, really. I have no friends anymore and few comforts."

She licked her lips as if they were parched, and Ariel noticed for the first time a tremor in the hand that rested on the table.

"Tomorrow," Grace said, "I'll be sixty." She turned back to Ariel, and in her face was the ghost of the coquette she'd been at their previous meeting. Her arch expression invited comment.

"I'd never have guessed."

Grace rested her chin on her fingers and tilted her head. "I've never told anyone my real age before. Well, not in thirty years. I've always looked younger, you see."

"I do see, yes." Ariel touched her finger to her temple, pressing gently at the dull throb there. This was beginning, she thought, to be bizarre.

"Do you know if they printed my age in the newspaper?"

"Um, I don't actually remember."

"It doesn't matter." The coquette vanished. "Nothing does, anymore."

"Mrs. Barron—"

"You never answered my question."

"Which question was that?"

"Why are you doing this?"

"It's my business; it's what I do for a living."

"Of course. Everything comes down to money, doesn't it? Money and *breeding!*" Grace's eyes turned mean. "It's never been any different. I was never accepted in this town, never a 'real Barron'! These people just saw a girl from nowhere, from nobody. *'And who are your people, dear?'* Oh, the times I heard that! But I learned fast; I outclassed them all." She pressed her lips together. "I suppose that's why I'm supposed to have done this thing? Money?"

"Is that what your attorney told you?"

"The questions they've asked . . ." Grace shivered. "I gather from what you've said that you *don't* think I did this?"

"That's right."

"Why?"

"It just seems . . . unlikely to me. Did you?"

Grace uttered a cry of disgust and, Ariel thought, despair.

"Of course I didn't kill my son!" she said, and her voice shook with passion. "He was the one thing left of the only man I ever loved! My . . . John Barron was a genius who perished at the height of his powers without ever knowing the fame he deserved and finally earned. He never knew, do you understand? This vital, brilliant man, this man whose work was his soul. He never knew!"

Grace drew herself up, and her jaw worked convulsively. She made a visible effort and said, "John William was his father all over again, serious and artistic. *Sensitive!* I didn't even know about him—that I was pregnant, I mean—until after John died. This child was a gift. You can't know what it meant to have another chance."

Ariel lifted a hand, realized that she couldn't touch or comfort the other woman. She was about to murmur some banality when she noticed people beginning to make winding-up movements. Conversations were growing more urgent or more awkward; eyes darted toward guards; belongings were being apologetically gathered.

"May I ask you something?" She didn't wait for permission. "Is it true that you spent a great deal of time away from home while your son was growing up?"

Grace looked her in the eye. "I'm not strong," she said. "I'm not proud of that. Being with John William was sometimes more painful than I could stand. Sometimes . . . it was excruciating." Her eyes still on Ariel, she asked, "Did he say anything to you that last night? Anything I should know?"

"We just talked about when he was young, Mrs. Barron, old times with my sister. She and he were good friends for many years. Did you know that?" Ariel hoped there were no plans to call her as a prosecution witness; that evasion would come back to haunt her.

Hurriedly, seeing visitors getting to their feet, she said, "I've got a great many questions, Mrs. Barron, and I'm going to be talking to your lawyer, to Mr. McCrory, but tell me . . . What does the prosecution have? What's the evidence against you?"

Grace shook her head hopelessly. "It doesn't make sense to me. I don't even drive anymore; my nerves won't take it." She looked genuinely puzzled when she asked, "How do they believe I got here? How do they think I got up here without a car?"

"How'd you get up here the day I met you at your son's house?"

"How did I . . . ? Oh, well, I hired a car, of course."

The announcement to "Conclude your visits" came then, and Ariel gave what she hoped was an encouraging smile. "I'll be back soon. Try not to worry."

When the prisoners had straggled from the room and the door was closed, Ariel made a serious search for her pillbox. Her mind was a tangle of reactions, and the headache had found a place to perch: just above her eye socket. She found no pillbox—worrisome since she was sure she'd put it in this handbag—but she did find a loose white tablet she hoped was an aspirin. She swallowed it dry and left in search of a phone booth.

34

THE MAN WHO'D BEEN DEMOLISHED BY THE TRAIN WAS GRANT Lacy.

Henry got the word Saturday morning from Marty the Morgue Rat, who'd assisted with the autopsy of the exhumed remains. They hadn't been embalmed. What had been a handsome, gifted, and enigmatic human being was shattered bones now, bone festooned with shreds of muscle tissue and flesh, largely decomposed.

Finally, Mrs. Lacy had her closure. Henry wondered if it brought the relief she'd anticipated.

In the quiet, weekend-deserted *Open File* studio, time passed quickly as Henry made up for his Friday afternoon off. He returned calls (including one from Claudia Wynn, who wasn't in, her machine informed him in sultry tones), viewed tape, and made from-the-hip decisions only time and ratings would prove right or wrong. He wasn't really there. In the back of his mind the questions repeated themselves in constantly changing variations like novelty neon signs. What didn't he know about the accident that Richard Cummings did? Who had something to hide? What was it? What was it worth?

If the entrepreneur had stumbled as he trotted across the tracks, whose misfortune was it besides his own and the train engineer's? To whom *wasn't* it misfortune? Had Lacy been pushed? Then why didn't the engineer see anyone else? If an attacker had time to get out of sight, why hadn't Lacy gotten himself out of the train's path? Had he hit his head, been knocked unconscious? Had his foot caught, trapping him? At least one shoe had been in plain sight; the engineer saw it.

And Craig Fiore . . . ? Was he merely an opportunist, a man desperate to escape a humdrum life with a tyrannical wife? Or was he a killer? Had he and Lacy met there, argued? Had he met Grant Lacy at all, ever?

By eleven o'clock, Henry's normally incisive mind was a twist of conjecture. He had to know what Fiore knew. He'd been chasing the Carson detective in charge of that case since Thursday, and this time he caught him. The cop wasn't one of his pals, one of his quid pro quo sources, and he wasn't in a frame of mind to cooperate with the press. Beyond admitting that Fiore had been extradited back to L.A., he'd give out nothing.

"Look," Henry wheedled, "if you won't talk to me, can you at least give me the name of Fiore's lawyer? Just give me that."

FREY, DONALD J., ATTY AT LAW, had a bold ad in the yellow pages. His was not one of the city's blue-chip firms, and he was probably finding Fiore's case a stimulating break from drunk drivers, bankruptcies, and third-party claims. He was perfectly willing to meet Henry at his office within the hour, visions of a TV interview, no doubt, dancing in his head.

The address was downtown, one at which Frey wouldn't be smart to work after dark. Henry ate his deep-fried lunch en route. The corridor leading to Frey's office smelled as if someone in the building had been dining similarly for years.

The lawyer eagerly admitted Henry and then checked the hall in both directions, clearly disappointed to see no camera crew.

"You won't be doing an actual interview, then?"

"This *is* an interview."

"Oh, well, certainly, but I meant—you know—on the air?"

"That could be next," Henry said, observing the other man as he led the way into the second of two rooms.

Frey was short—he was wearing elevators, Henry noticed—and he had implausibly thick hair that began too low on his forehead. His suit and tie were trendy, but Henry suspected they represented more flash than cash. Of course, Henry wasn't exactly on the cutting edge, fashion wise, himself.

"Could be next," he repeated. "We'd set up the camera here. Have you in front of your power wall there. . . ." Henry straightened a diploma; he wasn't familiar with the school. Beside the diploma a document certified that Frey was qualified to practice in California. The year on this was recent; the year on the diploma wasn't. Either Frey had taken a hiatus or he'd been a while passing the bar.

"Yeah," Henry went on, "we'd put you in front of your pedigrees and this shot of—who's this with you? Pia Zadora, is it? And here you are with Don King. Wow! Look at that!"

He sat on the opposite side of the desk. "So, talk to me, Mr. Frey. What's the situation with Fiore?"

The lawyer's face settled into gravity, and his voice deepened into what Henry imagined was opening-statement timbre.

"My client is absolutely innocent of any deliberate wrongdoing, Mr. Heller. There *are* two recorded marriage licenses, that's true, and no record of divorce. But up until the gruesome accident Craig Fiore had the misfortune to witness, he was a model citizen. A valued employee of C and C Office Supplies for six years. An irreproachable husband and father. What we've got here, unarguably, is temporary insanity. A classic case." Frey paused to gauge Henry's reaction. "Who among us wouldn't be traumatized—*unbalanced*—after the horror he saw?"

"Which was?"

"I'll tell you what he saw. Here we have this exemplary, ordinary man on an ordinary evening. One like any other. He's driving home from work. He comes to a rail crossing. The barrier gate's down, the warning light flashing. He hears the whistle; he sees the train approach. Then he sees something else. A man down. A man prostrate on the tracks—directly in the path of the train! Mr. Fiore watches in horror, a captive audience. He sees the engine crush the man's skull. He actually sees a severed limb tossed into the air. He sees freight cars roll over the body. He sees—"

Irritated by the oration, Henry interrupted to ask if Fiore had seen anyone else on the tracks. Fiore hadn't. Then he asked if the victim had made any move to escape.

"Interesting question. It's one Mr. Fiore wasn't able to answer with certainty."

"Why not?"

"The victim was at least thirty yards away. Mr. Fiore *thinks* he moved, but he can't be sure. The whole tragedy, Mr. Heller, happened quickly. Too, Mr. Fiore was sickened. He closed his eyes."

Henry didn't ask how poor Mr. Fiore had seen all the gore with his eyes closed.

"It was night by then, wasn't it?"

"Yes. Oh, but there're streetlights in that area. And, of course, the headlight of the train. If he couldn't see every detail, he could certainly see enough to be profoundly affected."

" 'Who among us wouldn't be?' What did Mr. Fiore do then?"

"He recalls only that he sat stunned, beyond rational thought. He has no memory of leaving the car, of going to the victim. His hands must have been trembling violently. He doesn't recall dropping the belongings the police say they found at the scene."

"He doesn't recall hanging a dog tag around the neck of a dismembered corpse?"

Frey didn't look pleased with the question.

"I don't suppose," Henry asked, "that he recalls *removing* anything either—like the victim's ID?"

"The next thing he remembers was when he came to himself months later in Arizona."

"Remarried without benefit of divorce."

"Happy with a woman he'd turned to in confusion and need."

Henry didn't care about Fiore's bigamy, but he was finding this tale increasingly funny. "He didn't feel inclined to 'fess up to Mrs. Fiore Two?"

"My client was still disoriented, and plagued by nightmares. Whatever he'd done, he'd done unknowingly, while in a state of shock. There'd been no intention to harm. Now he was on the horns of a dilemma. His new bride loved him. If he told her the truth, he'd cause untold anguish. He couldn't bring himself to hurt her."

"What about Mrs. Fiore One? He didn't think she'd be happy to know he was alive and well?"

"His, uh, legal wife had gone through the mourning process, Mr. Fiore reasoned. She'd put the worst of her sorrow behind her. How could he reopen her wounds? She had his life insurance money. She had her children. With the kindest intentions, he decided to leave things as they were."

Henry wished the lawyer luck. "I've enjoyed this, Mr. Frey," he said sincerely. "I'll be in touch."

He was surprised to find an attractive, very young woman working in the outer office, her fingers flying across computer keys. She looked up at Henry with a friendly smile and shucked her Dictaphone headset.

"Hi!" she said.

"Hi!" Henry pulled Frey's door shut. "Business must be brisk."

"Huh?"

"You work Saturdays?"

"Oh! It's Mr. Frey's manuscript. I couldn't wait to hear what happens next! Are you a fan of his?"

"Mr. Frey's a writer?"

"Tanya Marling."

Henry consulted his beard with thoughtful fingers. "That's his pseudonym?"

"Right," the girl agreed.

"What's the name of this one?" Henry asked as if he were familiar with the rest.

"This is just the working title, you know, but for now it's *Passion on the Amtrak Express.*"

35

AIKEN, SOUTH CAROLINA, INFORMATION HAD ONE RESIDENTIAL LISTening for Bernd. Ariel placed a call, but the former Mrs. John William Barron wasn't in residence.

"Neither Will nor Bev can come to the phone right now," a machine regretted. Ariel left a message identifying herself as a producer for *The Open File.* She didn't mention the Barron name.

The Barron pharmacy was only a four-block detour out of her way. With a glance at her watch, she turned the little yellow roadster in that direction.

It was the type of drugstore, Ariel imagined, that anyone over thirty might remember from their youth. Fans whirred from the embossed tin ceiling high overhead. Chrome stools perched like mushrooms down the length of the marble-top soda fountain, behind which an ornate, dark-stained oak affair of cabinets and shelves and beveled mirrors loomed. Hallmark cards and Whitman samplers were displayed prominently, hot water bottles discreetly, condoms not at all.

Ariel bought a tin of the Swiss pastilles she knew B.F. liked. She was browsing through the magazines for one that might interest him when the lure of the fountain grew too strong to resist. She climbed onto a stool.

"Bobby's run out for a minute," a clerk called out, "but I'll be over in a jiffy to help you."

"I'll get it, Lottie."

The voice had come from the rear of the store, from behind pebbled glass on which *Prescriptions* was lettered in gold. A man in a white coat emerged, wiping his hands on a towel.

Ariel learned his correct name, finally, from the tag pinned to his breast pocket.

Despite a face slightly scarred by adolescent acne, Washburn was a good-looking man. Late twenties, Ariel judged, with dark hair combed back from a widow's peak, strong eyebrows, and full lips. The lips curled up now, but only on one side. Ariel had the sudden conviction that someone sometime had told the pharmacist he smiled just like Elvis, and he'd never forgotten it.

"What can I get you?" Washburn grasped a porcelain dispenser as if it were a throttle and he a pilot at the ready and gave her the full benefit of the Elvis sneer. "Banana split?"

"Something a little less decadent this time. How about a small cherry Coke?"

While he squirted syrup into a glass, Ariel tired to decide what tack to take. A slow buildup seemed right.

"It was your house where we went for John William Barron's wake, wasn't it?"

That earned her a surprised look. "We don't really call them 'wakes' around here, but yeah, that's me." He placed the drink on the counter, dried his hands, and extended one. "Grover Washburn?"

"Ariel Gold. What do you call them?"

"Call . . . ?"

"If you don't call them wakes, what do you call them?"

Washburn laughed. "Darned if I know. I don't think there *is* a name. People just 'come by' after the services. You're not from around here, I take it?"

"No."

"Your husband with the navy base?"

"I don't have a husband."

Washburn raised one of his fine eyebrows. It wasn't, Ariel sensed, a sign of interest so much as an affectation of interest.

"How'd you know John William?" he asked.

"Just happened to meet him." Ariel took a sip of the sweet drink and added, "The night he died."

Washburn's face underwent a series of rapid, indecisive changes. One, unless Ariel was imagining things, suggested alarm.

"Is that right?"

Ariel nodded solemnly, proceeding on pure instinct. "We had a long talk, must've been just hours before . . . whatever happened."

"A long talk . . . ?"

"Long and interesting."

"Interesting." The sneer was back, but now it looked like a sign of heartburn.

"Oh, yes."

"Imagine that."

"The poor man really needed to get some things off his chest, and I was available."

"Is that right?" There was definite challenge in Washburn's voice when he said, "That doesn't sound like John William. You being a perfect stranger, I mean."

"Don't you find it's often easier to confide in a stranger? Somebody with no ax to grind? 'You know,' " Ariel quoted, " 'that if you were for a time in mortal danger,/And are so still, it was not from a stranger.' "

"John William said he was in danger?"

"One of the things about being a confidante is that you keep what's said confidential. If you can."

"What's that supposed to mean?"

Ariel stood up. "It's been nice meeting you, Mr. Washburn. I'll be seeing you again." She took out her change purse.

"Forget it," Washburn said. It wasn't a gesture of hospitality; there was no longer a trace of friendliness in his face.

"Thanks." She smiled. "But I owe you money, and money's one thing I have a great respect for."

"A dollar, then. The drink's a dollar."

He snatched up the bill she laid on the counter and punched a key on the old-fashioned cash register. The cash drawer popped open with a clang.

It rang a bell in Ariel's memory. "Odd place to leave a message," she said.

* * *

"So, they're going to let you out on good behavior?" Ariel said when she heard B.F.'s announcement. He shrugged as if in indifference. Plainly, he was immensely relieved.

"Tomorrow. You tell Sarge I want a fresh pork shoulder on that smoker when I get home. I want to smell those hickory chips from the time I hit the island!"

"That's what you call good behavior?"

"Just tell him. And I want Brunswick stew, too. Tell him to get some over at Toby's place."

"What's Brunswick stew and who's Toby?"

"Stew's what you eat with barbecue, and Toby makes the best in town." B.F. smacked his lips in anticipation. "Now tell me what's goin' on in the real world. You have a good time playin' hooky yesterday? What've you been up to?"

"Just talking to people. I left the last one—Grover Washburn—looking mighty unhappy with me."

"That's the fellow worked for John William? He's keepin' the drugstore open?"

Ariel nodded and described her encounter with the pharmacist. B.F. didn't look any happier with it than had Washburn.

"When I agreed you should look into this thing, I didn't mean go around baitin' people. If John William was killed and Grace didn't do it, somebody else did. Sounds like you worried this Washburn. If he's got something to be worried about, so do you now."

"I wonder if the police have the message he claimed to find in that cash drawer the morning his boss died."

" '*Claimed* to find'?"

Ariel shrugged. "I just think it's intriguing that on that day of all days, John William had, allegedly, planned to come in late. If Washburn looked upset before I mentioned the message, he looked fit to be tied afterward."

"Newton's not stupid. He'd have asked to see it."

"That doesn't mean he did see it. Washburn could've thrown it away. If he didn't know John William was dead when he found the message, he wouldn't know it would be of any importance."

"Just steer clear of the man, you hear me? Who else you been tormentin'?"

"Grace Barron."

"You went to the jail?"

"First thing this morning," Ariel said, and told him all that had transpired.

"She's not the most stable human being I've ever seen," she concluded, "but I'll tell you something I'd stake my life on: that woman loved John Barron intensely and John William, too, if for no reason other than he was his father's son."

Ariel took one of the pastilles she'd brought her grandfather and sucked on it thoughtfully. "Has Sarge said anything to you about what he and I talked about last night?"

B.F. frowned a question.

"About Halley Barron?" she prompted.

"What about her?"

"Never mind. I'm going to use your phone a minute, okay?"

B.F. looked disgusted. "You will find as you go through life, Ariel Gold, that no one—not the first person—appreciates that kind of tease. Put that telephone down."

Ariel hesitantly replaced the receiver. "Don't mention to Sarge that I discussed this with you, all right?"

"What in the world?"

"Do you remember when Grace was pregnant with John William?"

"Yeah?"

"Yeah you remember or yeah what about it?"

B.F. mulled over her questions and their implication and decided the fastest way to get the conversation moving was a straight answer. "I remember knowin' the fact. And thinkin' how wonderful it was—wonderful in every sense of the word, what with John bein' dead."

"Did you actually see her pregnant?"

"What's this all in aid of?"

"Did you?"

"Do you know how long ago that was?"

"Thirty-six years. His birth date's on the gravestone."

"You went to look at the gravestone?"

"I did."

"Why?"

"I'm not sure, to tell you the truth. I just felt like it."

B.F. sighed. "I can't say I actually remember one thing about that time except hearin' that Grace was goin' to have John's child and wishin' he was around to know it. Now wait . . . I do remember how I learned about it. Your grandmother called me wherever I was—London, Rio, someplace—to tell me she'd heard about this baby on the way. Your mother was a teenager then, and Suzanne, Margaret said, was fascinated with the news. She was taken with the 'cosmic mystery' of it or some such thing. 'Fatherhood from the grave.'

"Margaret was amused by Suzanne's romantic notions, but I remember she was plenty relieved they'd already had 'the talk.' " His expression was fond nostalgia when he said, "I know things are different nowadays. You young people can't begin to imagine what an ordeal 'the talk' was for parents back then. I guess there were liberated folks, sophisticated folks, who discussed reproduction and all that with their kids as easy as tellin' 'em to brush their teeth, but not most of us and certainly not Margaret."

He took one of the lozenges for himself and, popping it into his mouth, gave Ariel a devilish grin. "I had to coach her on how to pronounce *spermatozoa*. She had a mental block about that word. There were some others I never could get her to say out loud."

"Like what?" Ariel challenged with a devilish grin of her own.

"You're a little old for 'the talk,' aren't you? Tell me what this business with Grace and her pregnancy's all about."

Ariel's grin dropped. Keeping her tone completely neutral, she said, "Sarge told me Halley went away immediately after John Barron killed himself, that she was gone for months. She came back right after John William was born. You both told me she behaved more like a mother to him than Grace ever did."

B.F.'s reaction surprised her. "I thought that's where you might be headin'," he said calmly. "Knowin' how folks think, I imagine there were more than a few who would've thought the same—if they hadn't seen Grace in maternity clothes. If they did see her pregnant, I'm *sure* there were a good many speculatin' about who got her that way. Then the baby was born. After that, there wasn't any doubt who his daddy was. None. And, therefore, no doubt about the mother either. Like I said, I know things are different now. What you read in the papers that parents do to their kids is enough to gag a maggot." The old man gave Ariel a steady look. "I knew John Barron right well. If I'm to believe he was John William's father—and I do—then Halley was not the mother."

"Forget who the father was. Let me show you something." Ariel went to stand beside the bed. She held out her hands, palm down. "Look at these. Look at yours."

He did. "What's your point?"

"They're the same. You're my *grand*father."

"They are the same, aren't they?" B.F. smiled with pleasure at the discovery. The smile quickly faded. "Yeah, but—"

"You remember Jane's nose? That very same nose I used to have? Who do you think we got that from?"

B.F. screwed his mouth into a stubborn grimace. "You're talkin' about individual features. With John William we're talkin' the next thing to clonin'. Halley, the best I can recall, didn't favor her daddy much at all."

"Traits do skip a generation."

"Oh, bull! You're barkin' up the wrong tree, girl. Who were you fixin' to call while ago?"

"John William's ex-wife."

"Well, do it."

Beverly Bernd was at home this time, and she was both wary and excited about having found Ariel's earlier message.

"You're from a TV show, you said?" she asked when Ariel had identified herself. "This isn't some kind of joke?"

Ariel reassured her, even providing the number of her direct line into the studio. "You're welcome to verify my employment," she suggested.

"That's all right. I didn't mean to be rude, but I couldn't think what somebody from a TV show would be callin' me for."

"Are you familiar with *The Open File?*"

"I know I've heard of it. . . ."

"We're an investigative newsmagazine," Ariel explained, "and we're considering doing a—"

She got no further.

"Now you wait just one minute!" Beverly Bernd said. "This is about John William Barron, isn't it? You should've said so to start with!"

There was a decisive and very loud crash, and Ariel was left holding a dead phone.

"She won't be posin' for your cameras, looks like," B.F. said.

"Looks like," Ariel agreed, and hung up. "I'd say that's a woman who knows how to stay mad." She opened the bedstand drawer and took out a directory. Under *M* she found McCrory, Grace Barron's lawyer.

"I'll give you a few minutes, Ms. Gold," he told her, "if you want to come out to my club. You play tennis?"

Ariel declined a game but took down the address and arranged to meet him at four o'clock "on the patio." A check of her watch told her she had better than two hours to lose or use.

"If all you gon' do is tap your foot, go somewhere else and do it," B.F. said.

She picked up the phone again. Julian Taliaferro sounded puzzled by her request, but he agreed to meet her at the Barron house.

"It is okay for us to be here, isn't it?" Ariel asked Julian as he tried the door leading from kitchen to garage stairs.

"I still don't get why we are, but yeah, I guess." The heavy wooden door was stuck. "These old houses get contrary," Julian said and, after giving the door a few unsuccessful whacks, he put his shoulder into it. With a wounded squawk, it popped open.

He found the light switch, and the empty double-car garage was thrown into sulfurous yellow illumination. "Bug lights," Julian mumbled. The wooden steps creaked as he started down and then came to an abrupt halt, sputtering and swatting at his face. "Damn spiders!"

Amused by the big man's rather frantic reaction, Ariel reached to brush away a strand he'd missed. Julian flinched, and his hand shot out defensively.

"Julian?" Ariel said, as startled by his reaction as he'd obviously been by her gesture.

His hand dropped. It was a moment, though, before his eyes, unreadable on hers, did the same. "Sorry," he said.

He'd been less than enthusiastic about going into the garage; she put it down to unease at being in the actual place where his old friend and client had died. There was, of course, nothing to indicate that murder had been done there: no car, no blood, and no odors, save a rich commingling of pine sap from a box of kindling, the ghost of gasoline fumes, cow manure in several stacked twenty-pound bags, and damp.

The automatic opener Ariel hadn't found in the house was mounted beside the door it controlled.

"That's what you came to see?" Julian asked dubiously.

Ariel gave him an absentminded smile. She wasn't sure what she *had* come to see. "He most likely had two portables," she thought aloud, "assuming he hadn't lost one or given one away." Her footsteps crunched on gritty concrete as she crossed from shelves laden with paint cans and car wax to a metal cabinet. It wasn't locked; there was nothing inside to warrant security measures.

Julian frowned. "Listen, Ariel, I don't care for this. This whole TV show thing. Tell me something. Just what is it exactly you do for that show?"

"Did John William have two cars?" Ariel asked from where she was kneeling beside a dark blotch on the concrete.

After a hesitation, during which he may have been deciding if he'd push for an answer to his question or if he'd answer hers, Julian said, "No. He'd had the same black Cadillac for years. What's that you're sniffing?"

"I don't know. Does this look like motor oil to you?"

Julian swiped a finger across the stain and put it to his nose. "Not much smell to it. Could be transmission fluid. Why?"

Ariel pointed. "That's where I'd guess John William normally parked. There're all manner of stains there. Rusty, like they've been accumulating for years. This is the only stain on this side."

"So what? Unless it was leaked after the murder, the cops would've seen it. Tested it."

Ariel nodded and, with a little creak of the knees, straightened. "I've got to start working out with you and Sarge," she said and brushed her hands together.

"That's it?"

"I guess. This was probably a waste of your time, Julian. I'm sorry."

Julian didn't move, and Ariel couldn't tell if he was relieved or disappointed or simply out of patience. "Whatever," he eventually said, and started toward the stairs.

The bright light of the sunny kitchen had little effect on Julian's mood. He seemed anxious to be out of the house, or to get Ariel out of it, and his edginess was contagious. She found herself thinking of the peculiar joke he'd made about having a split personality; it was no funnier now than it had been then.

She took one last glance around and, on inspiration, asked, "Did John William have somebody in to clean?"

"Have what?"

"A cleaning lady. Don't you imagine he did? A man living alone?"

"I don't know. I suppose."

"I'll bet I know somebody who can tell me."

As Ariel drove to her meeting with Grace Barron's lawyer, she thought over the visit she'd paid Vera Bloodworth's friend, Corinne.

It had required no more than amateur deduction to locate which house was Corinne's. Ariel had gone out John William's front door, crossed the quiet street, bypassed a house with parched, neglected grass and another where a tired-looking young woman pushed a baby carriage to and fro in a lulling journey to nowhere. She'd stopped at the house next door.

In front was a garden glorious with asters and mums just beginning to reach their peak. If you stood in the yard, Ariel had calculated, you'd have an unobstructed view of the Barron garage door and two blocks of street beyond. A person watering the flowers in the gray light of dawn would be able to see a car exit the garage and drive away without benefit of headlights.

From the corner of her eye, Ariel had caught a twitch of curtain movement. Elementary, my dear, she'd thought, and gone up the walk to the front porch.

Corinne looked too old to be in the throes of "the change." Her upper eyelids were heavy, the lower ones pouched. Her throat was softly wattled. The hand-knit dress she wore was pretty, but it was an unfortunate selection for a woman who needed a girdle.

She looked discomposed. She patted at the froth of pink net that didn't quite cover pin curls flattened by bobby pins. Her face was partially made up, suggesting an interrupted toilette. One set of eyelashes was mascaraed, one not; lips were outlined but not filled in. They lifted in enlightenment.

"You're the lady from the TV show! Vera told me about you. Won't you come in?"

"No, no. You're obviously going out. Pretty dress!" Ariel smiled. "I'll call first next time. Oh!" She stopped as if she'd just then been visited by an idea. "I was hoping to talk to the woman who cleaned for Mr. Barron, but I don't know her name. You don't, do you?"

Corinne, unsurprisingly, did.

"Louise," she said promptly and with finality, as if she were naming Colette or Cher.

"Louise . . . ?"

"Uh-huh."

"You don't know her last name?"

"Her *last* name?" Corinne was stymied. Plainly, the concept that domestics had last names was a new one to her. "I know she does for Miz Pruitt. That big ol' yellow house next to the Barron place? You could ask her."

Ariel agreed that was the thing to do and, on impulse, asked, "Does Louise have a car?"

"No, uh-uh, she takes the bus."

Ariel had started down the steps when Corinne added, "Except when her boyfriend picks her up."

Was it possible, Ariel wondered now, that the police didn't know about Louise and her boyfriend? If not, Corinne would take care of that. She'd probably been on the phone to Vera before Ariel had reached the street, gossiping about her visit. How long, then, before Vera mentioned the pair to Marv Newton? Ariel decided she'd better locate Louise posthaste and, she thought, she'd better keep her mind on her driving now.

She made an illegal U-turn and went back to the road she'd missed. Within minutes, she spied a discreet sign that whispered the two words *Ashley Point.* The theory, presumably, was that if you didn't know it was a country club, you had no business being there. Ariel slowed and turned onto the horseshoe-shaped drive.

Bleached seashells crackled under the Darrin's tires as she drove past a columned entrance to the parking lot, tastefully concealed by a hedge. Hers was one of the few American cars in evidence.

She was glad she was wearing flat shoes. She imagined that many an elegant lady had been unhappy with the damage done to high heels by the shells.

A youngster with a golf bag strapped over his shoulder directed her to the tennis courts, and as Ariel hurried down the woodsy path he'd pointed out, she fought impatience. There was so little time. She wished she knew what Grover Washburn was hiding. She wished Beverly Bernd hadn't hung up on her. She wished she knew Louise's last name—and that she'd found "Miz Pruitt" in when she'd called at the "big ol' yellow house."

The woods ended in a dazzle of sunshine. Ariel shielded her eyes, surveyed a complex of tennis courts, an Olympic-sized pool, and the patio bar Grace's lawyer had mentioned on the phone.

Umbrella tables sprouted here and there, and two young children darted between them giggling and shrieking and drawing annoyed looks from the adults. Most everybody, including the kids, was togged out in designer whites from visor to treads.

Ariel found an unoccupied table and looked over the courts, trying to decide which player might be McCrory. She'd pretty much decided on a gray-haired man with skinny legs when she heard her name called.

Chuck McCrory was a young robust redhead, sunburned. Ariel couldn't tell if his legs were skinny; he'd already changed back into khakis. His rust-colored hair was still wet from the shower.

"That *is* you?" he said, reaching for her hand. "I cut my game short so we could have more time. What can I order for you?"

Over iced tea, Ariel answered earnest questions about her grandfather's recovery, how she was enjoying Charleston, and, finally, her interest in Grace Barron's case. McCrory was a conspicuously sincere conversationalist. When she brought up her affiliation with an investigative TV newsmagazine, however, the observe-how-I'm-listening head-nodding ceased abruptly.

"Mr. McManus didn't say anything to me about a TV show," the lawyer said. "He gave me the definite impression that you were a family friend."

"I am. My grandfather and I have had difficulty all along in accepting that Mrs. Barron killed her son. After talking with her today, I'm even more convinced that it's highly unlikely."

"You've got good judgment. She's innocent."

"The district attorney's office must have good reason to believe otherwise."

"I don't know that I'm inclined to discuss that with you."

"I can't say I blame you. You don't know me, and I sprang this media connection on you out of the blue."

McCrory nodded. "Glad you understand."

"Really nice club," Ariel commented, looking around.

McCrory nodded again. "It's one of the newer ones, but I think the members are the real comers in town."

"Oh, I could tell that from the cars in the parking lot. I haven't seen so many Mercedes and Porsches since I left L.A."

"I'm a Jag man, myself."

"Love 'em! What model?"

Ariel suffered in round-eyed admiration until she could appropriately and modestly confide that she drove "a rather sweet little car, too" and say, "Which reminds me of something about Grace. Surely she didn't drive herself up here that night?" She smiled, incredulously, at an idea too silly to entertain. "Her nerves being what they are."

"Her nerves?"

"Being so bad. That's what she told me." Ariel was commenting that Grace was certainly a high-strung lady when McCrory said something under his breath. It sounded like, "At least she talks to you."

"Pardon me?"

"The 'high-strung lady' has gotten two DUIs. They pulled her license."

"Oh! So that's why she got rid of her car."

"What makes you think—" McCrory's eyebrows descended, and he clamped his mouth shut, jutting his lip like a cross child.

He was silent as he and Ariel walked to the parking lot. When she asked if his firm had represented Grace Barron long, she didn't think he was going to answer.

"No," he finally said. "She called me from the jail. She said she wasn't interested in having some 'old fogy' for her lawyer. Said what she needed was 'new blood,' not 'blueblood.' "

36

"WELL, TELL ME ONE *MORE* TIME, STEVE." HENRY PINNED THE phone receiver with his shoulder and searched Ariel's kitchen drawers for a pen. Steve Vanderveer, *The Open File*'s young electronics maven, went back to chattering incomprehensibly into his ear.

"Fascinating," Henry said, "but I'm not looking to build a computer; all I want to know is what you know about some new MicroStar product coming on the market."

He just then noticed a mug full of pens and pencils right in front of him. Taking one, he interrupted the blend of technobabble and streetspeak that was Steve's own peculiar language to say, "Tell you what: I'll become computer literate when you get, *like,* just plain literate, okay? *Like* I don't believe you can utter one entire sentence without using the word *like.* Look the word up sometime. *Like* doesn't mean 'sort of' or 'you know?' or 'uhh.' " He pushed the speakerphone button and dropped the receiver into the cradle. "Talk English!" he ordered.

In words of one syllable, none of them *like,* Steve answered Henry's original question.

Henry made notes, asked a question or two, and finally said, "I get that it's guesswork. Yeah, yeah, yeah. Chill out or whatever you do these days. I'm not quoting you to anybody."

Henry considered the ramifications of what he'd learned.

Grant Lacy had been fanatically secretive in the months before his death, leading to belief within the industry that he was onto something really big. Some speculated that it was a software package that would render the primarily English Superhighway into a dozen languages accurately and instantaneously. Steve favored another rumor mill candidate: that Lacy was working on the ultimate, fail-safe security system. That tallied with what the shifty MicroStar accountant Marcus Black had told Henry.

Whatever the product was—*if* it was—it was strictly Lacy's baby, and it obviously had been nowhere near even preliminary testing stages.

Clifford Gilroy had made no public statement about a product of such potential importance. His style was the opposite of Lacy's, which was always aggressive and often reckless, and his nine-month conservatorship had been precisely that. Conservatism in the computer world, Henry understood, was treading water in the rapids; to stay alive, you had to get the innovations out of the lab and onto the market. What he *didn't* understand was what all this had to do with Lacy's death and Cummings's extortion.

Henry opened the door for the dogs, paced, and thought.

Accident or murder?

If lacy had died accidentally, then whatever Richard Cummings knew had to do with something other than the death itself. That something had to be the product; nothing else made sense. Had somebody stolen the technology? Then where was the product?

Three possibilities occurred to him. One, it didn't exist. Two, it existed, but development had been tabled. Three, it was still in development, with a secrecy comparable to that of the Manhattan Project.

If the third was true, who at MicroStar had access to the technology, the whole picture, as well as the expertise to continue the work? The brother? Vaughn Lacy had been unfindable the week before but now, with a funeral sure to be held, he'd have to come out of hiding or seclusion or wherever he was.

Henry called a friend on the *Times* obit desk, who told him a press release had been faxed in from MicroStar. A memorial service would be held Monday morning at eleven o'clock. Henry jotted the time and a reminder to arrange for an *Open File* camera. He spared a moment's thought for whether his dark suit was clean before his mind turned to murder.

If Lacy was pushed in front of the train or, more likely, since no attacker was seen, struck and left to die, what was the motive?

Okay, it wasn't a healthy neighborhood to be running around in at night. There was always a chance some mugger or vagrant saw Lacy and decided to take advantage. It was also possible that the killing was random: a nutcase who bashed Lacy for fun and let him lie. But . . . where did Cummings come in? He hadn't put the make on a bum or a mugger or a psycho.

Henry thought of the single ransom call Luzzatto had told him about. It was entirely possible that somebody snatched Lacy, got too aggressive, lethally aggressive, with attempts to subdue him, and dumped him on the tracks. But, again, the Cummings connection didn't jibe. Unless Lacy was grabbed by somebody he knew, somebody Cummings could connect to him, that theory, too, was a washout.

Which brought Henry to a motive with which he was more comfortable: greed. Again, he considered technology theft, but the timing bothered him. Why wouldn't the killer have waited? Why not let Lacy finish whatever he'd been working on? His brain had been a natural resource; with no Lacy, there might be no product.

What about an old-fashioned crime of passion? No question, there seemed to be an element of spontaneity; people who premeditate murder don't commit it out in the open where they might be seen, and the average killer doesn't use a freight train as a weapon. So, Henry thought, say it was heat of the moment. Say Lacy met somebody, there was a scuffle, Lacy went down, his adversary panicked and ran. Henry hadn't heard of trouble between Lacy and anybody, male or female; that didn't mean it didn't exist.

The phone at his elbow rang, and so deep in thought was he that he actually jumped. For the first few seconds he thought he was talking to Ariel, and the throaty warmth of her greeting startled him considerably more than the phone had done.

"You don't know who this is, do you?" the voice teased.

"I, uh . . . don't . . ."

"It's Claudia."

"Oh, right. How'd you get this number?"

"Just let my fingers do the walking. Looked it up."

Henry frowned. How had she known to call him here at Ariel's? Off balance, he said, "Well, what can I do for you?" at the same time she said more or less the same. He tried again and, again, both said at once, "You left a message."

Claudia chuckled. "I'll go first. I heard about Grant on the news. Truly grim! Is that why you called?"

"I was returning your . . . Never mind. Maybe you can answer a question. These rumors you mentioned . . . did they involve bad relations between Lacy and anybody? Or, um, good ones, shall we say?"

Claudia was dying to talk about the tragedy. If her late employer had enemies, she said, she didn't know about it, and if he fooled around, it was news to her.

"One thing no woman at MicroStar had to worry about was sexual harassment. Not with Grant. The man was unreal. He'd stare at you with those deep, soulful eyes, and then you'd realize he didn't even see you. Just thinking about some damn equation or something.

"I, personally, didn't find him all that attractive, but I happen to know of more than one woman who tried to get him interested. No sale. They might as well have been androids."

She interrupted herself to say, "Temptation wasn't the only thing Grant was blind to, by the way. This was his company, period. He started it when he was practically a kid, and he couldn't let any part of it go. He'd hire talent—he did have a knack for attracting excellent people—then he wouldn't let them do their jobs."

Henry thought he might be hearing a little sour grapes; he wondered if Claudia was one of those "excellent people"—or if she'd gotten a "no sale" rung up herself.

"Anyone in particular," he asked, "who might've gotten their nose out of joint?"

"Nobody likes having their . . . suggestions rejected.

"Grant was one of those people—you've met them, haven't you? They think because they're experts on one thing they're experts on everything. He'd listen to advice from his product people or finance or marketing—advice he was paying a premium for—and then he might just ignore it. Egomania, pure and simple.

"And the manias didn't stop there! He'd gotten obsessive about the running, too. That's probably why he'd started to look the way running fanatics do. You know, downright skeletal—"

Claudia must have been visualizing the condition of Lacy's remains; she bit off her faux pas with a little squeak of chagrin.

Henry didn't let on that he'd noticed. He asked about the existence of the new product Lacy had supposedly been developing.

"There was never a time when Grant wasn't heavy into R and D on something. It was his life; it was what he did."

"You said no woman at MicroStar had to worry about being sexually harassed, and then you qualified it. Not by Lacy, you said. Does that mean the same couldn't be said for someone else?"

"Oh, not really. Not *harassment,* no." She laughed and, teasingly, danced around answering when Henry rephrased the question. He pretended to lose interest. She rose to the bait.

"I heard Cliff Gilroy had something going with one of the programmers, but he broke it off. I heard he developed other, *extracurricular* interests."

"Is that right?"

"Let's put it this way: maybe Grant was no more inclined toward sex at home than he was at work."

When Henry was satisfied Claudia had nothing concrete to back up the innuendo, he told her that if he thought of other questions he'd give her a call. He noticed she seemed miffed. He put it down to thwarted desire for a TV appearance and forgot about that as well as the fact that she'd called him first and never said why.

He temporarily struck "Enemies?" from his list of possible murder motives and thought instead of "Friends"—or at least business associates—and "Wife."

Obvious questions: Where was Gilroy the evening Lacy jogged into oblivion? And where was Betty Lacy—the last person known to have seen him alive? If it was true that she was unhappy with her husband, Henry wondered, how unhappy was she? Next obvious questions: Had Lacy had life insurance and if so, who was the beneficiary?

Craig Fiore's escapade might've screwed up somebody's timetable—as long as there'd been no body, there'd have been no payoff for five long years—but, as of now, it was a new ball game. And, life insurance or no, Mrs. Lacy was an heir. She owned at least half of whatever her deceased husband had acquired since their marriage—maybe the whole ball of wax, since they'd had no kids.

Henry was dialing Luzzatto when he remembered she was still off duty. Just then, the word *kids* rebounded in his mind.

A check of the time confirmed his worst fears, and he grabbed his keys and tore out the door. The movie Sam had gone to see was over. Henry would be no more than a few minutes late picking the kid up if he broke his personal best speed record. It wasn't that Sam would be upset or surprised to be left waiting; he made it clear he considered that par for the course. It was just that he was insufferable when he was right.

37

Ariel had talked to "Miz Pruitt" of the big yellow house and, through her, found John William's cleaning lady, Louise. She'd also succeeded in getting information about Grace's car. Neither felt like an accomplishment. In addition to being extremely disturbed, she was tired, thirsty, and hungry.

The drive back to the island was endless, and she worried that she should have bought gas before crossing the bridge. Such devices as low-fuel warning lights were nonexistent when the Darrin was built, and the needle was ominously close to the red *E*. She didn't have enough history with the car to know how many more miles it would give her before it died.

When she turned onto the short road that ended at B.F.'s house, she was momentarily disoriented. It was pitch dark; not a single light burned, not even the exterior floodlights. For the space of a second, she thought she'd made a wrong turn. She knew she hadn't. Visions of a waiting feast vanished, and she wondered where Sarge was. Then she thought of Hattie. While the housekeeper was nearly back to her old self, her lungs were still weak, and she had some odd notions about the ill effects of the night air. Ariel was surprised that she'd felt well enough to venture out.

She was within sight of the house when the engine stuttered, strangled, and died. With a silent plea, Ariel pressed the clutch, and the little car continued its forward motion for a few feet, rolling onto the grass beside the front drive. There it came to a defeated stop.

Ariel found her miniature flashlight in her purse. She clicked the button off and on again. She banged the flashlight against her palm. She gave up. She chastised herself for not checking the batteries. She chastised herself for not getting gas. She noticed the utter silence. Even the frogs and crickets were still.

Placing her feet carefully, Ariel managed to get around the house and onto the back porch without stumbling. As she was about to insert the key into the lock, the key ring slipped from her grasp. It dropped with a clatter and just enough of a bounce to take it to the edge of one of the planks and through the space between. Ariel heard a faint clunk as the keys hit the ground. She took a very deep breath.

Quickly, before thoughts of outsize rats could intrude (as well as those of cockroaches, which grew to gargantuan size here), Ariel crawled under the porch. She combed the damp, sandy earth with a hand she couldn't see. Just as her fingers grasped metal, she stopped, listened, decided that the noise had come from a distance if she'd heard it at all. She scurried backward and, this time, clutched the keys firmly.

The quiet of the kitchen was relieved only by the ticking wall clock, the darkness not at all. Ariel felt for the light switch. When she flipped it, nothing happened. Then she realized something that triggered the first stirrings of real fear: she hadn't deactivated the burglar alarm, and it hadn't gone off. The little red light that signaled its vigilance wasn't burning. Her shoe crunched something that sounded very much like glass.

"Oh, Lord!" she whispered.

Remaining there was out of the question. She'd run to the nearest house where there were lights and people, and she'd call the police. She had her hand on the doorknob when she heard a noise—from *outside.* She turned the lock, saw the broken glass pane, grabbed a kitchen chair, and jammed it up under the knob, wedging the door tight.

Ariel clenched her hands into fists, willing herself to reason. First, she thought, a weapon, any kind of weapon, and then straight to the front door and out. She crept to the cabinets and eased open a drawer she thought contained knives. The old wood creaked. She squeezed her hand in and felt a spatula and something she couldn't identify. In that moment a thought flashed through her mind and brought her to frozen stillness. Was it possible that she'd talked to one too many people today? Had she come closer to flushing a dangerous bird than she'd known?

Her fingers made sense of the useless object in the drawer: an eggbeater.

On the counter directly in front of her was a wooden bowl in which Sarge normally kept a rolling pin. Her eyes had adjusted enough to see that the rolling pin was gone. Beside the bowl, however, was the knife block she'd forgotten, and tucked into its slots was a variety of knives Sarge kept honed to razor sharpness.

The rest of the house was darker than the kitchen. All the draperies were closed, and the effect was almost total blackout. Ariel felt her way through the dining room and living room. She'd made the entry hall when she stumbled over something big, solid, and unyielding on the floor. She went down.

She lost her grip on the knife. She sensed rather than heard the figure looming over her. One arm, she could just make out, was raised, and clutched in the fist was something dense, rigid, big. A voice hissed her name.

Who, Ariel thought, in that excruciatingly long moment before the arm came down, had she so angered, so frightened, so panicked, that she had to be eliminated?

She threw one arm over her head, waiting for the blow, a blow that might crush bone. Nothing happened.

"Get up!"

The voice was a whisper, urgent and menacing.

"Move!"

Ariel began to struggle up, her eyes straining to locate the knife.

"Hurry up!"

Where was the knife? Where had it gone?

"Did you see the other one?" the voice wheezed.

"What?" Ariel said stupidly.

"Hush!"

"Hattie?"

The old woman stooped, and in a second Ariel felt the haft of the knife being pressed into her hand. "I called the *po*-lice," Hattie whispered. "They ought to be here in just a minute. Did you lock the back door?"

"Hattie, what is going *on?*"

"There's two of 'em. I got this one, but the other one's outside somewhere."

"You got—" Aghast, Ariel looked down and did a two-step backward, away from the man-sized lump on the floor.

"You didn't see the one outside?"

"Hattie, I can barely see *you!* What's wrong with the lights?"

"I turned off the power. You stay by this door, and I'll guard the back. You hear anybody comin' in by door or window either one, yell out!"

As soundlessly as a wraith, Hattie moved away.

Ariel stood rooted. She held her breath and listened with every pore. She heard the sound of someone breathing, someone very near. Panic very nearly undid her before she realized that the steady, whistling noise was coming from the floor.

The body was alive.

Relief that she didn't share the entryway with a corpse fought with fresh fear. What if he woke up? No wonder Hattie had chosen the *back* door to guard!

She squatted, forced herself to touch the warm flesh. The man lay on his stomach. His hair felt woolly. His arms were pulled behind his back, and they were bound.

Ariel lurched away. She felt for and found a wooden chair and then duplicated her earlier security measure. Crouching beside the wedged door, she lifted the curtain that covered the panes and peered through. She saw nothing but night.

The man on the floor moved. Groaned. Lay still again.

"Would you hurry up!" she begged the absent law. Did they have to come all the way from Charleston? she wondered. Switching the knife to her other hand, she wiped her palm on her dress and got a firmer grip.

She thought she heard noises from the back of the house but getting no alarm from Hattie, she kept her post. After a few minutes—or a millennium—she did hear the sound of a car approaching. Two cars. Headlights flared across the front porch before swerving away. More lights came, and then one short blast of siren. Brakes squealed, there was a loud thump, and from the road came a confusion of doors slamming and men shouting.

Ariel sagged in relief. The lights came on. For seconds she was more blinded by the glare than she'd been by the darkness, and then she saw Hattie.

Her feet were bare. Gray plaits hung down either side of her scrawny chest. Her familiar pink chenille robe was open, revealing a modest white slip underneath. In her right hand she clutched the rolling pin.

Ariel looked down at the large man on the floor. A wool knit ski mask covered his head and face. His hands were tied with a pink chenille belt.

"God bless America!" Ariel said in unconscious imitation of her grandfather and, somewhat hysterically, she began to laugh.

Sarge arrived in the middle of Hattie's story, so she started over. The young police officer taking her statement didn't mind; his expression made it clear that he'd enjoy hearing it all again.

She'd been "feelin' kind of peaked," Hattie told them, and "laid down to rest my eyes." It had been before first dark, she explained; no lights had been on. A noise—breaking glass, probably—had awakened her to darkness.

Figuring the darkness would be to her advantage since she knew the house and the crooks didn't, she'd leaped for the fuse box and then called 911 from her room. When she'd tiptoed to the kitchen, she'd seen flashlight beams in the living room. She'd armed herself with the rolling pin. Crouched behind a counter, she'd watched two men cart various items out the back door. Then she'd heard one tell the other to take a last look around.

" 'I'll go get the van,' is what he said," Hattie told them. "Then he left totin' a TV and I don't know what-all."

That's when she'd snuck up on the remaining robber and "coldcocked him." She'd been tying his hands with the belt from her robe when she heard what turned out to be Ariel, although she'd thought then "it was that other one come back."

"You come close to gettin' your block knocked off," she told Ariel now with no particular sign of concern.

"So that's where the second man was when I got here?" Ariel asked. "Fetching the getaway car?"

"I reckon I know where he was at." Hattie scowled. "I could

smell beer on 'em. You look at the ground by where their automobile was, you'll see right quick what he was busy doin'."

The policeman ducked his head, stifling a grin.

"But where'd they park?" Ariel asked. "I didn't see anything or anybody out there."

Presumably, the young officer said, the men, seeing no lights and no car, had thought the house was empty but had hidden their van down behind the garage in case of a surprise visitor.

"I expect after the one outside finished loading up and the other guy didn't join him, he came back and tried the door. When he saw it was wedged shut, he knew his cohort was in trouble."

"Yeah," Hattie said. "He tried to get it open. Stuck his hand in where they'd broke the glass and tried to shift the chair. I was gettin' ready to break his knuckles when he heard y'all comin'."

The fleeing burglar had been intercepted making his getaway, plowing into a young pine tree in the process.

Sarge had listened to all this with a dazed expression. He asked the officer if he thought these were the men responsible for the string of robberies in recent weeks.

"I'm betting on it, sir. If so, both ladies are lucky to be alive. And, you, ma'am," he said to Ariel. "Lucky you got here when you did instead of a few minutes either way. And that you parked around front. I hate to think what would've happened if they'd heard you drive up."

"Yes," Ariel said, "*lucky*'s not the word. Officer, just a thought and probably a dumb one, but you might want to check out where those two were the night of September second, the night John William Barron died."

Sarge gave her a curious look but said nothing. When the last police car rolled away, however, he had plenty to say to Hattie.

"Why wasn't that burglar alarm on?"

"I didn't think about it till it was too late, and I couldn't of remembered how to work it even if I coulda got to it, which I couldn't."

"It's not a 'security system' if it's not on! I've shown you and shown you how it works!"

"Show me again tomorrow. Now what are we gon' do about supper?"

By then, reaction to disaster averted had begun to set in.

Everything seemed funny to Ariel. When Sarge looked for the rolling pin to make biscuits, she cautioned him about tampering with evidence. That reminded her of a story about a man who'd bashed his victim with a frozen leg of lamb and then eaten the weapon, which reminded Sarge . . . The silly stories flew.

Hattie mainly ate, shrugging off teasing about her heroics. When she declared that "the sorry, low-rent rat" got what he deserved, Ariel told about her recent encounter with a real one. She didn't notice the quiver at the corner of Sarge's mouth when he asked, "What did this 'horrible giant rat' look like?"

"Gray, big as a tomcat, with a sharp . . . What's so funny? What are you two laughing at?"

"If you don't beat all," Hattie said. "I can't feature anybody that doesn't know a possum when they see one. You probably scared the fire out of the pitiful thing!"

She actually smiled in Ariel's general direction and then, almost as surprisingly, admitted to being a little tired. If nobody minded, she said, she believed she'd hit the hay early.

"Oh," she threw over her shoulder to Ariel, "somebody called for you, right when I laid down. Figured I wouldn't get any peace if I didn't answer. Manny somebody, he said his name was, from New York City. I told him I didn't know when you'd be home."

Ariel watched her go and turned to Sarge with her eyebrows climbing her forehead. "Did you hear what she said?"

"That Manny somebody called from New York."

"No! She said 'home.' She didn't know when I'd be 'home.' "

"Yeah. So? Oh . . . It's a start, isn't it? Congratulations."

Ariel was pondering this development when Sarge asked, "What was that about checking alibis for the night John William died? You don't seriously think those clowns had anything to do with it?"

"Those 'clowns' aren't funny. One burglary victim died, remember?" Finger by raised finger, Ariel ticked off facts. "Your nephew had a head wound; the man on Edisto died from a head wound. The robberies began just before they both were killed. John William's door wasn't locked; nobody needed to break in to get in. And . . . Halley believed some things were missing from the house."

"Grace says."

"I didn't see a TV, or a VCR, or any silver in the dining room. Did you? And Marv Newton asked me last week about jewelry. He seemed interested in a silver bracelet—"

"The bracelet John William wore? What about it?"

"It must be missing or he wouldn't have brought it up."

Sarge looked pained. "You think burglars put John William in his car and turned on the ignition?"

"Scenario . . . just for the sake of argument, okay? These men wear ski masks. The Edisto man couldn't identify them, so they left him alive. Fatally wounded, it turned out, but alive.

"Now, what if John William walked in on them as he did? Or he's asleep and, like Hattie tonight, hears them and wakes up? They knock him out. He comes to and tries to get away. Not being as brave as Hattie, that's exactly what *I* had in mind tonight. He could've gotten to his car, turned it on, and then passed out again."

"You've been reading too much Agatha Christie, you know that? You make me tired."

Ariel shrugged. Sarge must be tired; otherwise, he'd have nailed her with the obvious flaw in her theory: The vehicle seen leaving the murder house wasn't a van; it was a blue Chevrolet.

Grace Barron's car was a blue Chevelle, three or four years old, so her building manager had told Ariel on the phone that afternoon, and the only time he'd seen it in at least a year had been no more than "a week or two back." Marion Barnett, suspicious of her questions, suggested that she "might do better to look for another car to buy, ma'am, under the circumstances."

If the men who'd broken in here tonight *had* visited the Barron house two weeks ago, so had someone in a car too much like Grace's to be coincidence. The car had been inside the garage, and the D.A.'s office knew it. Grace couldn't have missed seeing a dead or dying John William. Ariel was having a tough time with that fact. She couldn't see how the presence or absence of burglars would mitigate it.

She realized Sarge had spoken to her. "I'm sorry. What?"

"I said, I'm picking B.F. up in the morning. You want to go?"

"You go ahead, thanks. I'll see you back here."

"Suit yourself," he said and disappeared out the back door.

The sound of a match being struck was a familiar one after a visit Ariel had paid late that afternoon.

When she'd finally reached John William's neighbor, "Miz Pruitt" had assumed Ariel was looking for a cleaning woman for herself. She knew for a fact, she said, that Louise had filled the day left open by Mr. Barron's death, but she'd supplied an address.

Louise Mullis had been in the middle of ironing. Unlike Sarge, she didn't ration her cigarettes. The fiftyish woman, thin and taut as rawhide, kept one between her lips, squinting through the smoke, removing it only to grind it out and, within minutes, light another. The ash would grow to alarming length; not once did it fall onto whatever garment was being ironed to starched crispness.

Ariel wondered whether Louise always chain-smoked or whether the conversation was making her nervous.

When she introduced herself as a friend of the Barrons, Ariel saw a flicker of wariness quickly blanketed by a polite mask. The wariness might only have been a natural reaction to a strange white woman showing up asking questions.

The police hadn't contacted Louise. As far as she knew, she said, they didn't even know she'd worked for Mr. Barron. There wouldn't have been any point in them asking questions, she said; she didn't know anything. She'd heard Mr. Barron had been killed at night. She did her job in the daytime.

"Did you happen to be at his house the day he died?" Ariel asked.

Louise claimed she didn't remember what day that was.

A Thursday, Ariel told her; he'd died on a Thursday night, or early Friday morning.

Louise admitted that Thursday had been "Mr. Barron's day."

"What time did you normally finish up?"

It varied, depending.

"On?"

Some days there was more to do than others.

"Do you remember how much there was to do that day?"

She didn't.

"Mrs. Mullis . . ." Ariel said. "*Is* it Mrs.?"

"I'm a widow."

"Mrs. Mullis, I'm not accusing you of anything. I'm not here because I think you had anything to do with what happened to

John William Barron. I'm just trying to learn all I can to determine who *did* have reason to wish him harm."

"Uh-huh."

"Can you think of anything at all that might help me do that?"

"I sure can't."

"Do you know of anyone he fell out with? Did you ever hear him arguing with anyone?"

"Mr. Barron wasn't hardly ever even there when I did for him. He'd be at work."

"You had a key, then?"

Louise set the iron down in what looked like a pie tin, put out a cigarette, and gave Ariel a direct look. It was almost the first time she'd done so. Her breath was coming shallow and fast.

"I worked for Mr. Barron six years. There wasn't one time in *all* that time he ever thought he couldn't trust me with a key."

"You liked him, didn't you?"

Louise's eyebrows flew together, and her lower lip shot out dangerously. She looked too shocked to answer.

"I mean, you liked him okay? You'd want his killer caught?"

"They got somebody for that already, didn't they? His mama's what I heard."

"Did you ever meet her?"

Louise shook her head and applied herself to her ironing.

"If you had, you'd agree with me when I say she didn't kill her own son."

"It ain't my business if she did or if she didn't."

Ariel sighed. "May I have a glass of water, please?"

Louise sniffed, but she took a glass from the drainboard and filled it from a bottle in the refrigerator.

Ariel sipped it and said, "I noticed a picture of a young woman in the living room. Is that your daughter?"

"Uh-huh."

For a silent minute Ariel had little hope of that or any other conversation, but then Louise said, "Sandra." She couldn't suppress the pride in her voice. "She graduated from the University of South Carolina. She's a teacher."

Ariel asked polite questions about where Sandra taught and what grade, and then she said, "Could you in your worst nightmare imagine harming your daughter?"

The other woman flinched as though she'd been slapped, and

for the space of a heartbeat Ariel thought she'd gone too far. Then understanding lighted Louise's dark eyes. "I don't do my girl like that woman did Mr. Barron.

"I was there cleanin' one day when she called up. Acted like I was lyin' when I said he was at work. Said she'd already called there. 'You tell him Grace phoned,' she said. *Orderin'* me!" Louise's mouth twisted, and in a prissy voice she said, " 'Tell him his sister told me what he said about me, and I don't appreciate it. You writin' this down?' that woman said to me. 'You tell him he's worse. He's a cheap, lyin' pervert just like his father.'

"I'll tell you one thing, miss . . ." Louise reached for another cigarette. "I don't talk about the folks I do for; their business is their business is how I feel. But that woman's a devil. You can believe what you want to, but it wouldn't surprise me *what* she did.

"Mr. Barron was okay, and he wasn't no 'cheap.' When Sandra graduated, he handed me a hundred dollars. Just like that! 'Get yourself something nice to wear,' he said. He went to the graduation, too. There was times he stuck up for me when—"

Louise struck a match and fired up the cigarette. The act seemed to have the opposite effect on her; she was still breathing hard, but she was calmer and she looked as if she'd thought better of whatever she'd been about to reveal.

"I'm gon' tell you one more thing, and that's *all* I'm gon' tell you. I know when somebody's drinkin'. That old woman was."

Ariel was on the front porch, leaving, when she asked, "Do you know if Mr. Barron had more than one garage door opener? If he gave one to somebody?"

Louise was back to her taciturn self. She didn't know anything about that.

"One last thing. Was it you who cleaned the house after the police got through there?"

"No. Nobody called me to do that."

"Then you haven't been there since that last day? You wouldn't know if anything was missing from the house?"

There was no doubt about it; that question did not set well with Louise. She looked angry, and then scared. When a car just then stopped at her gate, her face hardened like a January freeze. She reached into her apron pocket and hurriedly pressed a key into Ariel's palm.

"I didn't know what to do with this here. It's the key to his house. You take it and go on."

Ariel wondered now as she had at the time who Louise's visitor was. No one had gotten out of the car by the time she'd driven away. The last thing she'd seen in her rearview mirror was Louise standing on her porch, arms crossed, feet planted. The expression on her face had not been one of welcome.

38

"HENRY? HELLO. LISTEN, I JUST WANTED TO LET YOU KNOW I'M probably only going to be here one more day. Two at most, okay?"

Henry was watching Sam flip through the swimsuit issue of *Sports Illustrated.* With one part of his mind, he listened to Ariel explain that B.F. would be released the following day; with another he pondered whether he should be doing something fatherly about his son's reading matter.

"Henry? You there?"

He decided the kid could be into a lot worse than wet T-shirts and sandy buttocks and turned his back. "Yeah, okay," he said into the phone.

Jessie set up a ferocious alarm at the front door, and Henry missed whatever Ariel said next. Sam went to answer, and the barking ceased.

"What was all that about?" Ariel interrupted herself to ask.

"Somebody at the door, challenged by our canine friend, returning now to slake her thirst after her exhausting sentinel duties."

Henry heard Sam's voice from the living room, and then a second voice, also male and young, he thought.

As he reached down to scratch the shepherd, he asked Ariel what she'd been saying. Mere seconds later, his yelled "What?"

brought Jessie's ears arrowhead straight. She watched Henry alertly, trying to interpret whether his body language communicated danger she should be doing something about. When he dropped into a chair shaking his head in relieved amazement, she, too, relaxed and positioned her haunch convenient to hand.

Ariel wound up a condensed version of the evening's excitement, making it clear that it wasn't she but the housekeeper Hattie who'd actually done battle with the burglars.

Henry didn't know who Hattie was. He couldn't remember if he'd ever heard Ariel mention her before, and he wondered just how many people the fabulously wealthy B.F. Coulter had waiting on his granddaughter. His imagination conjured up a swarm of faithful retainers scurrying about an antebellum mansion polishing and bobbing curtsies. He shook the deranged image away. Henry didn't have much experience of servants or the people who employed them. Until now, he hadn't associated that world with Ariel either, and a seed of unease sprouted deep in his gut. It was something, he thought, that would have to be analyzed later.

"But you're all right?" he asked. "They took these guys away? You're sure there were just the two of them?"

"Two was plenty."

"You'd better get back here where all you have to worry about is earthquakes and riots." Henry heard a bottomless sigh. "Get some rest," he said. "You sound like somebody ran you over and then backed up."

"Not tonight. He missed, anyway."

"Who missed?"

"I'm too tired to talk about it. Just some drunk driver."

"What drunk driver? What are you talking about?"

"It was last night. I was seeing about an animal I thought was hurt, but it turned out to be a rat. I mean, I thought then it was, but it was actually a possum."

Henry looked at the receiver; was she giggling?

"I told you I was too tired to make sense. Some homicidal maniac—or dipsomaniac—came along. Thought he was Al Unser. I was in the road."

More and more uneasily, Henry pried the details out of Ariel. "Why hadn't you told me about this? Are you sure this guy wasn't *literally* homicidal?" For the first time, he realized he'd been humoring her with this Barron thing. Treating it like an intellectual exercise: the semi-neophyte honing her craft. A melodrama in some time-warped place he knew only from old MGM movies.

A man had been murdered. Ariel, if no one else, believed the wrong person was being held for the crime. "You've been poking around down there pretty recklessly," he said.

"He did swerve, Henry. I think. He—or she—could've turned me into a smear on the road. There was nobody else around. No witnesses."

Henry had no trouble picturing the scene. "Look. Get your granddad settled and get back here. This is Saturday? I'll see you Tuesday morning. At your desk."

"You're overreacting."

Henry considered whether she was right. He didn't have much experience with being frightened on somebody else's behalf. Even his blip chirped with interference.

"Oh," he said. "Hold a sec. I've got another call."

"Yeah, hello?" he said, and then "I heard, yeah. Thanks." And, after a moment, "Well, that's a very, uh, flattering invitation, but I'm on long distance right now. I'll need to get back to you on that. Uh-huh. And the, uh, same to you." He hesitated, finger twitching, before he flashed a cranky Ariel back onto the line.

"This *is* long distance, you know."

"Sorry. I cut it as short as I could."

"Who was it?"

"Woman named Claudia Wynn."

"Who's Claudia Wynn and why was she calling me?"

"She wasn't. She was calling me."

"Oh. How'd she get *my* number?"

"She didn't. My phone's on Call Forwarding."

"Oh." Silence. "I see."

"She was calling to make sure I'd heard about Lacy's memorial service."

"Grant Lacy's dead? I didn't— What's happened?"

"He was the train victim."

"How . . . ? I mean, was it an accident?"

"Maybe, maybe not. I'll catch you up when you get back."

"If it was, you were wrong about Richard Cummings."

"Whether it was or wasn't, I'm not wrong about Cummings."

"Right. You're never wrong, unlike me. Much as I hate to

admit it, I think I've been wasting my time and my sympathy where Grace Barron's concerned."

"Good."

"Good?"

"If the old lady's guilty, nobody's got reason to run you over." Henry heard a snicker from the living room and then his son's voice, sounding irritated. "What made you change your mind?"

"It was almost certainly her car seen leaving her son's garage the night he died."

"You said she didn't have a car."

"Wrong again. I can't guarantee she killed him, but she had to have seen him, dying or dead, and she didn't do anything about it. And she flat-out lied. She said she hadn't been to that house in years."

"Well, that could be shock. She finds the body of her son, an apparent suicide just like her husband? Right on the same spot? She really might not remember it."

"That's not all she lied about. She said she couldn't drive any-more, too nervous. The truth is her license was yanked. But license or no license, she won't have forgotten how, will she?

"Another thing. She had me believing she was mad about her husband. Idolized him. And that, whatever problems she and her son had, she really cared for him. Today I heard she once called him 'a cheap, lying pervert.' *And compared him to his father.*"

Henry was feeling better and better. The right person was safely behind bars. " 'Pervert'?"

"Yessir. The person who told me about the conversation thought Grace had her beak in the corn at the time, but still. What a thing to say about your son! And the man she claims she adored! I was *convinced* of that, Henry. Talk about *lying,* she's pathological."

And guilty as sin, Henry thought. "Just because she destroyed your illusions," he said, "it doesn't mean she killed Barron." He heard the screen door slam, but Sam didn't return to the kitchen.

"I don't like being manipulated."

"Then don't be. Forget the whole thing. Spend your last day relaxing and enjoying your granddad."

"I can't forget the whole thing, and stop treating me like a dilettante. The man who worked for John William is hiding something. The ex-wife's still plenty mad, the cleaning lady's scared, and these burglars tonight—"

"What's that got to do with the Barrons?"

"Maybe nothing. It's a theory."

"Theory's good. You can indulge on a nice, safe chaise longue in the sunshine. And as long as theory's all you're talking, don't forget the sister. She still sounds too good to be true."

"What do you suggest I do? Hold a séance?"

"Just don't forget: her brother died first, and she got his worldly goods."

When he'd hung up, Henry went to see who was at the door.

Sam and another boy were in the yard, barely discernible by porchlight. Henry resisted going out and introducing himself. Sam was here, in more or less plain view, doing nothing that could be faulted. He repressed a slight shiver. It was getting cool.

Closing the door, Henry caught a flash of white arm as Sam made some gesture, and the thought crossed his mind that the boy should be wearing a jacket. A scrap of memory bobbed up from somewhere: him, kneeling and zipping Sam into a red parka. It had to have been ten years ago; it seemed like a few months.

He wandered back to the kitchen and, idly, flipped through the magazine Sam had left open. One of the women looked like a younger version of Claudia Wynn. He slapped the pages shut.

He'd been a boy once; why did he feel so ill equipped to communicate with Sam now? The truth was, he couldn't summon even a vestige of how he'd felt at thirteen: how his mind had worked, what had been important to him.

Hadn't he been in the Boy Scouts then? Getting the next merit badge, he vaguely recalled, had been all-consuming. Or was that when he was younger?

A red-haired girl who lived behind him, a year or two older and stunningly well developed, had been an obsession at one time. He'd spent hours perched in a tree in his backyard, staring at what he thought was her bedroom window. But surely he'd been older then. God knows he felt old as Jerusalem now.

He rolled a perpetually aching shoulder. There'd been too many years of being a part-time father, too many gaps of days or even weeks, and he wasn't going to make up for it overnight.

39

Marge Luzzatto, back on duty Sunday morning, told Henry something that gladdened his heart. In her opinion, she said, Grant Lacy's death had been an accident, pure and simple.

"We looked into the possibility of foul play thoroughly months ago, when we were investigating what we thought was a 'missing.' I don't want to tell you how many man-hours we put in, and we didn't find anything to point us in that direction. Just because we've got a body now, I don't see that's changed. The remains of Grant Lacy, multimillionaire, don't say murder any more than the remains we thought were Craig Fiore, office supply salesman, did."

Henry hoped the official verdict would match the detective's. If the D.A. agreed with her assessment, this personal vendetta might end up being an *Open File*, after all—and an exclusive.

"Of course," Marge was complaining, "since Lacy's an officially dead bigwig, we'll have to go over all the same ground again—plus the ground Carson covered when the body was found. I can't tell you how thrilled that makes me; I just love regurgitated investigations! Nine months later people don't remember what happened; they remember what somebody suggested happened or what they wished happened or what they've dreamed up in the meantime."

"It's not like you don't have enough real crime to keep you busy."

"When you start sounding sympathetic, I start wondering what we've overlooked."

"Hey, Sergeant, has our show been helpful to the people in blue, including the local forces, more than once? In fact, I wouldn't mention this but since it wasn't you guys who handled the body originally, I'm a little concerned about the clothes being tossed or lost or whatever. What were they? What kind of clothes, I mean?"

"If that's the thickest veiled ploy you can come up with, just ask." There was a pause during which Henry heard papers being shuffled, and then Marge said, "We don't have a protocol from then because, like I told you, they didn't do an autopsy, but Carson did list the effects." Her voice dropped to a monotone as she read.

"Dog tag, car keys, wallet containing . . . et cetera and so on. Here we go. One pair gray sweatpants, one gray sweatshirt, one athletic supporter, one pair white running shoes—"

"Did the sweatpants have pockets?"

"Doesn't say."

"Where were the keys and wallet?"

"Doesn't say."

"Did Craig Fiore normally push pencils in sweat clothes and running shoes?"

"You'll be reassured to know I asked Detective Pete Howe down in Carson that question, and he asked the same question back in December. Seems Fiore's last sales call that afternoon fell through. The infamous Mrs. Fiore had found that out when she made one of her regular spot checks on hubby.

"He says now he spent that hour or so in a park communing with nature, but at the time no one knew where he'd been. Frau Fiore supposed then that he'd gone to his gym. He kept workout clothes there."

"And he had workout clothes that fit that description?"

"Doesn't everybody? But wait, you didn't let me finish about the clothes. You'll love this." Marge laughed. "The last item listed was 'one pair black bikini briefs.' Pete said when the wife saw those, she went red as a bullfighter's cape. He figured she'd never laid eyes on them but didn't want to admit it."

"Didn't Pete find it curious that Fiore's street clothes weren't in his car?"

"If he did, he didn't discuss it with me."

"What about Mrs. Lacy? Has she been asked about the clothes?"

"Sure. She was fuzzy back when she reported Lacy missing as to exactly what he'd had on, but she said then it was sweats and she says now he had clothes like these—closets full. And, yes, he did own bikini briefs."

"Where was she that evening after Lacy left the house?"

"On the phone for most of the time, planning a charity golf tournament. Verified."

"Where was Clifford Gilroy?"

"Heller, I'm starting to get insulted. All the key players' whereabouts were checked and rechecked last December. Nobody's come into money since then or done a bunk or in any other way capitalized on Lacy's death.

"We couldn't come up with trouble between him and anybody. His neighbors barely knew him on sight. He didn't mingle with his staff. Some of them hadn't seen him for weeks even before he disappeared, but one and all praised him as a genius. Yeah, we got a few that talked about how he was eccentric and not too democratic in how he ran his company, but even they admitted it *was* his company.

"Other than Fiore, who we've got no reason to believe ever met Lacy, the only person we could place at the accident site is Ross, the engineer. From how he describes Lacy—on his knees, hands spraddled out—it's consistent with a person that's fallen. And, Ross said, Lacy never even looked up. He must have been dazed. Or maybe even unconscious. Who knows? Since a good chunk of his skull was shattered like a watermelon, we never will."

Marge paused for breath. "So, okay, smart guy, find the fallacy there. I want to hear it." Before Henry could open his mouth, she said, "Do you know how many people in our fair land were killed illegally crossing rail property last year? Did you know they're considered trespassers? The answer's five hundred twenty-nine! Do you know how many of those were murder? Guess! Zero, that's how many."

"You're not considering suicide?"

"I just told you what I think. People who decide to end it in that particularly gruesome way don't lie down like a lamb for slaughter. They stand and face the train. They look death in the eye and give the engineer something to see in his nightmares. Quit bothering me, Heller. I've got work to do."

Henry listened to the dial tone for a second before he hung up and sat staring through the window at Ariel's backyard.

There was, in fact, at least one flaw in what Marge had said: someone *had* "done a bunk" since Lacy's death and come into money, too, but the cops didn't know about Richard Cummings. And, evidently, they hadn't heard about the affair between Gilroy and Mrs. Lacy. Or maybe Marge just hadn't mentioned it. Or maybe Claudia Wynn made it up.

They did know one thing Henry hadn't; Lacy hadn't moved in those final seconds. He'd never even looked up.

Maybe Lacy hadn't looked up because he was already dead.

40

The news that Grace had been transferred from city to county jail ran in Sunday's paper along with a photo: a flash of bandaged face behind sunglasses, snapped through the window of a police car. The move was one more ominous turn of the inexorable legal wheel and, as Ariel saw when she visited, Grace seemed to realize it.

The change in her wasn't physical—what could be seen of her face still looked as if she'd lost a fight with a mangle—but attitudinal: a slackness in her carriage and even in her skin, which no longer seemed tight against the bone; minimal eye contact. The ordeal, obviously, had begun to take its toll.

It didn't seem appropriate to wish her a happy birthday.

"Mrs. Barron," Ariel said, "I talked to Chuck McCrory."

Grace didn't respond. She kept her eyes on the hand that protruded from the sling and rested on the table. With her other hand she absently massaged the knuckles.

"I learned from your lawyer and from other sources as well that you haven't been truthful with me."

The only response was a tightening of the mouth.

"It was your prerogative, of course, to tell me nothing at all, but I don't appreciate your misleading me."

Grace looked up briefly, and then dropped her eyes again. "I don't know what you mean," she said.

"You led me to believe you no longer had a car. You do. It matches the description of one seen at your son's house the night he died."

The hands on the table grew still. Grace stared at the white knuckles, slowly shaking her head—a silent, bewildered no.

"And whatever the state of your nerves, if you haven't been driving lately, it's because your license was suspended."

A flash of the old arrogance was in her voice when Grace said, "You don't really expect me to go around telling people that? I wasn't intoxicated. I never had an accident, did I? I was perfectly able to drive, whatever that policeman claimed!"

Ariel sighed with unconcealed impatience. "That's not the point," she said and, hearing herself, stopped. She wasn't a judge, she wasn't a jury, and it had been she who'd initiated contact with Grace, not the other way around. She looked at the dull eyes, the hair lying flat and unstyled on the skull, the pale lips bare of lipstick and chapped, and asked, "Have they impounded your car?"

Grace shifted one shoulder.

"Was there anything in it that might further incriminate you?"

"I don't understand it. Mr. McCrory said . . . The only fingerprints in the car are mine. Mine and some person who—what do you call it when they clean your car? Polish it and so forth?"

"Detailing?"

"Yes. That's it. They found a receipt in the glove compartment. I guess Halley had that done."

"Halley? That's where the car's been? At your stepdaughter's?"

"It's funny. I didn't think of her as my *step*daughter. I haven't for many years."

"Is that where the car's been?"

"Since I wasn't able to . . . Since I was no longer allowed to drive, she kept it . . . away from me. She wanted to sell it. I kept saying I'd need it when I could drive again, but Halley could be very determined. I suppose she had it cleaned in preparation for selling it."

"Had you been in the car recently? Since it was detailed?"

"I don't know when that was but, yes, I was in it not three weeks ago. Halley's car was being serviced, I believe, and I needed a few little things. She came and got me in my car and took me to a shop. But . . ." Grace shook her head hopelessly.

"What is it?" Ariel asked.

"I can't think anymore. It's been at least a year since I drove that car. I don't understand why my fingerprints would still be in it if it had been so thoroughly cleaned. Well, except for on the door handle and maybe . . . Oh, I just can't remember."

"More to the point, why would your stepdaughter's prints not be in it?"

Grace looked momentarily perplexed. "Oh, I see what you mean. But I can tell you that. Halley always wore driving gloves. She felt it was safer." Her face clouded over. "Isn't that ironic? Of all the people in the world to lose control of a car!"

"Yes. Of all people. Mrs. Barron, can you tell me what other evidence there is against you?"

"I don't suppose I should have told you even that. Mr. McCrory doesn't seem to think—"

"Mr. McCrory shouldn't look a gift horse in the mouth."

Grace hesitated. "Well, there was something about a garage door opener in the car. Do you understand why that's significant?"

"Yes."

"I don't, and I don't even care. I'm finding it hard to care very much about any of it anymore. Being here . . ." She looked around the room, her glance falling on one of the guards and quickly veering away. "Today's my birthday. Did I tell you that?"

"Yes, you did."

"You were there, weren't you, when I found that *gift* John William planned to give me today?"

Ariel nodded. Grace had found the gun only days before, yet she was having trouble recalling who'd been present at the time. Ariel wondered if McCrory had a clue about his client's state of mind.

"I didn't know," Grace said, "that he hated me that much."

"Mrs. Barron, that's something else I need to ask you about. The gun obviously had some . . . history. Will you tell me—"

"It has nothing to do with what's happening to me now!"

"Then let me ask you this: it's common knowledge that you and John William were estranged. Why?"

"I can't bear to talk about that."

Ariel swallowed frustration. "All right. Then will you tell me the truth about your feelings for him?"

"I've told you! I was very frank with you yesterday. I won't go through that again."

"Yes, you implied that you cared for him a great deal, if only because you saw your husband in him. I've been told, Mrs. Barron, that you once called your son some pretty nasty names and that you likened him to his father."

"I thought you believed in my innocence. I thought you wanted to help me."

"I haven't repeated what I heard. I may not."

Grace seemed to understand the implied threat. Her mouth twisted petulantly. "I don't know which particular conversation you're referring to. John William could be mean-spirited. Hateful. Sometimes he upset me so that I may have said things I didn't mean." She rubbed dry lips and averted her eyes. "I'd get so upset that I might . . . I might take a drink to calm my nerves. I wouldn't be myself, and then I might say unfortunate things."

"Why would you bring your husband into it? Did he do hateful things, too?"

Grace's head snapped up. "John Early Barron was a genius! You can't apply ordinary rules to extraordinary people!"

Ariel took the opportunity to look the other woman directly in the eye. "Where were you the night John William died?"

"I was in my apartment."

"You were alone?"

"I was seldom not alone."

"You were alone *that* night? No one saw you or even spoke to you at any time? Did you watch TV? Could you have watched something late that night that would prove you couldn't have been here in Charleston?"

With brittle but impressive dignity Grace said, "If that night was like most nights, I had probably passed out long before the eleven o'clock news."

Ariel let out a breath. "Do you know where your stepdaughter was that night?" she asked.

Ariel couldn't stand it. What if Henry had guessed right? What if it really had been Halley Barron who'd killed John William?

In her annoyance, she almost ran a stoplight. She hit the brakes and smoldered. Here she'd spent hours talking to people, hours piecing together facts, and blasted Henry Heller listened for a few minutes and put his finger on the truth? "Don't forget the sister," he'd said. Halley sounded "too good to be true."

The car behind her tooted politely, and Ariel waved apologies, almost choking down in her haste to move along.

How could Henry have zeroed in on what she hadn't begun to consider until now? Not that Grace had endorsed Ariel's dawning suspicions. When asked about Halley's whereabouts on the night of John William's death, she'd grasped the implication lightning fast, and she'd been appalled.

"You will not malign my daughter's name," she'd warned, and there'd been steel in her voice. Halley had been "an honorable woman," and her love for her brother had been unstinting. Her own life, Grace had said, had been ruined by gossip and innuendo, and she would not sit by while anyone, for any reason, slandered a woman who was tragically dead and couldn't defend herself.

Ariel hadn't backed down. "I'm merely asking what the police must already have asked," she'd said reasonably. "They must've been satisfied with the answers or you wouldn't be here."

Henry had observed that Halley and John William had argued, that because of his death she'd been, briefly, a very rich woman. And, Ariel now knew, Halley's Volvo was in the shop at approximately the time of John William's murder. She'd had convenient access to the blue Chevrolet. She'd worn gloves when she drove it.

So why was Grace in jail?

Grace had been of no help. Once she'd delivered her spirited defense of her stepdaughter, she'd withdrawn into sullen silence.

Ariel realized she was tailgating a tanker truck plastered with caution warnings and geared down.

She didn't especially want to believe that Halley was guilty of John William's murder, and not only because she didn't want Henry to be right.

She'd noticed that Grace seldom referred to John William as her son nor as "Halley's brother." She simply called him "John William." And when Louise Mullis had reported the message she'd taken, the words she'd repeated were: "Tell him *Grace* called."

If there was anything to the theory that Halley was John William's mother and if she'd killed him, Ariel was right back where she didn't want to be; she was right back to filicide.

"Mrs. Bernd, if you'll just answer that one question, I won't keep bothering you. Please!"

Ariel had stopped at a public phone and called John William's ex-wife. She was determined to find another suspect. If she was lucky, even the most improbable might surprise her.

Beverly Bernd had demanded that Ariel stop bothering her. When, in exasperation, she responded to Ariel's question—Why had her first marriage ended in such acrimony?—she surprised Ariel only by her wrath.

"You listen to me now," she said, and launched into invective so heavily accented Ariel had to concentrate to understand the words. The gist seemed to be that she'd spent seven years "goin' to church every time they opened the door" and "workin' my fanny off for every charity in this town" to erase all memory of her divorcée status and "wipe those hateful smirks off the faces" of people who thought her first husband dumped her "practically on my honeymoon like I was some kind of tacky joke" and she wasn't about to let "a bunch of strangers drag up the worst time of my life."

Ariel by then had the phone two inches from her ear. "Mrs. Bernd—"

"I haven't seen Mr. John William Barron since then and if you must know, I was down in Destin, Florida, with my family when he died, so I don't know why you're pesterin' me, but if I see one sign of you bringin' my name into whatever that man was mixed up in that got him killed, you gon' have a lawsuit slapped on you that'll make you wish you'd thought twice."

"All I'm asking is—"

"I've got a *respectable* husband now. We've got a five-year-old child. Do you think I want her askin' me about some trashy thing she's heard on TV about her mother?"

"Mrs. Bernd!" Ariel all but shouted, earning a startled look from a man at an adjacent telephone. "I have no intention of using your name without your permission!" She heard heavy breathing but no further ranting and no click. "I assume you didn't consider your first husband 'respectable.' "

"Well," Beverly Bernd sneered, "I don't know what you people in Hollywood or New York City or wherever call respectable, but the people *I* know think men that like *other*—" There was a pause and a "humph" of disgust. Then came the click.

Ariel slowly hung up. She could think of only one likely way that sentence might have been completed.

Ariel was relieved to see that Sarge had replaced the broken pane in the back door before going to spring B.F. from the hospital. Hattie hadn't been idle, either. A tray waited, laden with good china and still-warm gingerbread, and on the stove an old-fashioned percolator gargled coffee into its glass knob. The combined fragrances almost overpowered that of something chickeny simmering.

Hattie was busily polishing ornate flatware that showed no sign of tarnish and when Ariel came in, the old woman bent to her task with a vengeance.

"Not enough to do around here," she muttered to a hapless fork.

"They're not back yet?"

Hattie finished the fork and picked up a spoon.

Ariel tried again. "I'm glad Sarge got a chance to replace the glass."

"He didn't; I did. Figured B.F. didn't need to be hit in the face with the news first thing."

"Oh," Ariel said. "That soup smells good."

"It's not soup. It's chicken 'n' dumplings."

"Ah," Ariel said, just to keep from saying "oh" again, and at that point the scintillating conversation was interrupted by the telephone.

"Ariel Gold? Manny Littell," said the executive producer of *LifeTime*. "You're a hard woman to reach. Win Peacock told you I'd be calling, right? I've heard good things about you. When can we get together?"

Before Ariel could reply, Littell plunged ahead. "Sorry to interrupt your weekend, but we're fighting time here. Got to move forward filling this position. Any chance you could come up this week? Tuesday?"

Ariel found her voice. "I'm afraid that's not possible, Mr. Littell. I have to be back in Los Angeles on Tuesday."

"Next weekend?"

Despite the odd moment spared for nervous thought about a major life change, Ariel had reached no conclusions. She didn't have to troll her feelings now, though, to know she felt steamrollered.

"I appreciate your flexibility, Mr. Littell. I wish I could match it, but—"

"In L.A., then. Can you do lunch Monday the twenty-seventh?"

"Well . . . I suppose—"

"You pick the place. My office will call you to confirm."

Littell quick-fired one or two flattering remarks and assured Ariel that he looked forward to the meeting. Ariel hung up feeling as though she'd been jettisoned from a speedboat.

"That'll be them," said Hattie.

Ariel hadn't heard the car.

"Go on, girl." Hattie scowled and polished harder. "Don't stand there like a fence post. Let 'em in."

They heard the car door slam, B.F. noisily issuing commands, and then the sound of the car leaving again before the old man swept in like gale-force wind.

"Free at last!" he bellowed and lifted one arm heavenward while he enveloped Ariel with the other. "Hey, old woman! Haul your scrawny carcass over here and give me a kiss!"

Hattie marched to the stove as if he hadn't spoken, but she was fighting a grin. "Stop cuttin' the fool. You want coffee or you ruther have some tea?"

"I want barbecue and stew's what I want, but somebody forgot to give Sarge that message, so I sent him after the makin's. Meantime, I'll settle for a toddy."

"That," Hattie said disapprovingly, "you can get yourself."

It was several hours before Ariel had a chance to make a phone call.

Her grandfather had been coerced into lying down, and Hattie was in the laundry room. Ariel made certain Sarge, too, was nowhere within earshot when she dialed Julian Taliaferro's number.

"I asked you once if John William had any friends," Ariel said to the lawyer. "The way you phrased your answer—discreetly, shall we say—didn't register until I talked to your former client, the former Mrs. Barron, today. She wasn't so discreet."

"Good old Beverly."

"You told us she filed on the grounds of incompatibility."

He conceded that he had.

"Incompatibility rather than . . . ?"

"Those were the grounds."

"I put a few things together this morning that add a new facet to John William's life. Do you think his being gay had anything to do with the way it ended?"

"Which 'few things' led you to conclude he was gay?"

"What I've just told you plus something I remembered. When I was at Grover Washburn's house—at the wake or reception or whatever you call it—I noticed he was mighty attentive to one of his guests; not to put too fine a point on it, but he was making goo-goo eyes. The guest wasn't female.

"Washburn said he found the Barron house unlocked when he discovered the body. I wonder if he had his own key, if he didn't want the police to know he had access to the house."

"Seems to me that's a conclusion reached by jumping," Julian said dryly. *"Broad* jumping."

Ariel blinked. Decided not to get sidetracked. "Grace Barron," she said, "once called her son a pervert."

"To you?"

"Allegedly called him a pervert."

"Slander's something we all need to be careful with—even if it's not quite in the same league as murder."

"She allegedly said he was a chip off the old block or words to that effect, and—dumb me—I was so busy trying to figure out the implications as they related to John *Early* Barron that I didn't give any thought to John *William.* Now that I think of it, he said more than one thing to me the night he died that didn't make sense until now."

"The night he died, yes, ma'am. I've been mighty curious about that conversation myself."

"He talked about being a misfit all his life, about feeling ashamed of something. Later, when I knew who he was, I assumed he'd meant the effect his father's suicide had on him, the stigma. Maybe not. I have an idea how homosexuality was viewed hereabouts when he was growing up."

"Trust me, you won't find many mamas out marching in gay liberation parades today. Ariel, whatever John William Barron's sexual predilections may have been, I don't see how they bear on his murder. I would be very . . . disappointed if you intend to stoop to smut on television."

Ariel wasn't listening. "He said something about 'them,' whoever 'they' are, trying to make him into a man. I wonder if he was ambivalent about the whole sex issue. If his marriage was an attempt to fit in, to satisfy 'their' expectations."

Julian chuckled. "It is an amazing thing to me! You meet this man one time. You talk to him a few minutes, and you're an expert on his motivations. Got his whole psychological profile right in your pocket. But we were talking about murder. I suppose you've got a scenario in mind. A lovers' quarrel, is that it? A pickup that turned ugly? What?"

Ariel had no scenario in mind. At the moment she couldn't imagine one sleazier than this conversation was making her feel. Nevertheless, she was more convinced than ever that whatever Grover Washburn was hiding was something she wanted to know.

41

"It's conceivable," Marty the Morgue Rat hedged. As Henry had asked him to, he'd questioned a compadre who'd been on duty the night Grant Lacy's remains had originally been brought in.

"But if the dude *was* dead before the train hit, it wasn't for long; we're talking an hour, a couple, tops. All the blood loss screws up the picture, see, but he wasn't cold when the cops got there. You think he, like, had a heart attack before the hit? Or you saying he didn't make it to the tracks under his own power?"

"Just thinking out loud, Marty. Nothing I'd want you to talk about, okay? Your people didn't see anything that night to indicate the train didn't kill him?"

"All they did was a blood test. If he'd OD'd or, say, died from AIDS, they'd have known. And if they'd seen a stab wound or a bullet hole or something, they woulda been a little suspicious."

"There was enough intact to look for that sort of thing?"

"Iffy. Way I heard it was they had all the parts in one condition or another. Except I think they didn't find part of the skull. The train wheels must've totally—"

Henry tasted bile in his throat. "Marty, could I ask you something? Why do you do what you do for a living? Can't you find anything better to do?"

"What? And give up show business?"

"I'm serious. How can you stand it when they cut into these stiffs?"

"Well, okay, I'll tell you the truth. I was gonna be a lawyer, but I found out I just didn't have the stomach for it. Fainted dead away the first time I had to watch a trial."

After he dropped off Sam and a friend at the mall, Henry kept driving. Without planning to do it, he ended up in Long Beach.

He found himself strolling along a dock near the Long Beach Yacht Club, listening to the gulls wheeling overhead, and idly looking around at the boats. Beyond those moored nearby were endlessly repeated variations, a stretch of white and marine blue. Tarps and flags flapped in the light breeze, restless rigging clanked against masts, and there was an occasional creak of complaint as a hull was nudged against rubber. He was thinking about nothing except how much he was enjoying his impulsive adventure when he knew why he'd gravitated there.

Grant Lacy had owned a yacht, he remembered hearing. This was the marina closest to where he'd lived.

How the work-obsessed Lacy had found time for boating along with serious running and big-time art collecting was a mystery to Henry, who couldn't seem to juggle work and anything else at all. Maybe the man never slept, he thought as he approached the fuel dock operator, who listened to Henry's question and nodded.

"Oh, yeah. That'd be the *Rising Star.*" He gestured toward a distant slip. "Dutch-built job. Seventy-footer."

"Ah." Henry peered again at the scores of yachts, indistinguishable as far as he was concerned. He knew zip about seagoing vessels, but it didn't take Dennis Conner to know that these represented the kind of investments most people feel lucky to be able to make in their homes. "Did Lacy spend a lot of time on board?"

"Never saw the man. Somebody told me about how the missing computer guy had used to own her. Didn't I hear they found him?"

"Used to own her? You mean the boat's been sold?"

"Oh, long time ago—must be a year."

"You're sure?"

"About the time, you mean? No, but it was definitely before this Lacy's disappearance hit the papers. Some big-shot movie producer bought her. Takes her out most weekends."

"Who used to take her out when she was Lacy's?"

"Different ones. Typical country club types, not like now. The producer had—what's his name?—George Hamilton aboard last weekend, and somebody told me they saw—"

"But the same people wouldn't make up the parties back then? From one time to the next?"

The man made a guttural sound that Henry took to mean Who knows? "This one woman was always there. A blonde. About the same age as me, mid-thirties. She was the one seemed to be in charge."

Henry didn't have Betty Lacy's picture with him, but as he described her, the pump operator nodded along.

"Yeah, that sounds like her. Society type."

"How much would a boat like that sell for?"

"Depends how much the owner wants her off his hands. Things being what they are these days, if he wanted to move her, he'd probably have to take down the asking price one or two K. Let's say around a million three, ballpark."

Henry left, mulling over the news that the boat had changed ownership not long before Lacy died—and that Mrs. Lacy had entertained without her husband.

It was Marge who'd told him about the boat, he remembered, and he guessed it was Mrs. Lacy who'd mentioned it to her. Why bring it up at all if it had been sold? Or hadn't she known that?

Henry's next stop was the Palos Verdes Estates gallery named in Richard Cummings's notes. He'd spoken to the owner, Methvin by name, on the phone; he hoped a visit would prove more productive.

The man he took to be Methvin was with a customer, a woman dressed in spandex tights, a cropped fuchsia sweatshirt, and what looked like high-heeled tennis shoes. A mane of silver blond cascaded over a fuchsia sweatband around her head. She didn't look as if she'd been sweating, so Henry assumed the outfit was a fashion statement. He had no idea what it was meant to convey.

He glanced at the nearest painting, a canvas depicting someone's nightmare, and as quickly as dignity would allow, strolled away. A large oil directly in his line of sight brought him up short. He approached it, rapt. For the moment he forgot why he'd come to the gallery.

Huddled by a campfire were three women—the suggestion of

three women. They seemed to be dressed in bright skirts and blouses of some patterned material. The firelight was vivid. Henry could almost feel the heat. A fourth woman was bent to the fire, but her gaze was directed toward the artist. Her dark, broad-planed face was illuminated by the flames, and in it was indecision, as if she were weighing his right to be there.

There was a power in the painting that Henry could feel like the throb of a bass drum, an unheard vibration in the marrow of his bones.

Time passed. Reluctantly, Henry came back to the chichi gallery. The blonde was taking a checkbook from the tiny gold-colored knapsack on her back. She scribbled what took long enough to be a lot of zeroes and ripped out a check, which Methvin discreetly pocketed. He watched her exit before he turned to Henry.

"I noticed you were absorbed by *The Decision,"* he said, and his eyes swept the painting respectfully. "Marvelous, isn't it?"

Henry agreed and tried to make out the signature.

"John Early Barron," Methvin supplied with appreciation of Henry's startled look. "You obviously know the name."

"Well, I'll be . . ." was all Henry said. He was surprised, and not only because of the coincidence. Having read the data collected for Ariel, he knew Barron's work was scarce. He knew, too, that it fetched a premium. "How much?" he asked.

The gallery owner looked profoundly unhappy. "I'm afraid it's not mine to sell. But I'd be more than happy to show you—"

"I really like this one. Who owns it?"

"A British gentleman. Why don't we step into the next room, where I have a—"

"If it's his, why do you have it?"

Methvin sighed. Henry could read annoyance in his eyes, battling the desire not to offend a potential buyer.

"The owner plans to relocate to Los Angeles, but his schedule keeps changing." He looked at the oil again. "The painting's been in my vault for months. Unfortunate, really, that it couldn't be displayed for connoisseurs like you to enjoy until now."

Henry was getting a faint reading from his blip. "Why not?"

Methvin greeted a tourist couple entering the gallery. They looked rich and serious, and his attention drifted in their wake. "Umm . . . I brokered the sale, you see, of a number of items.

The seller's terms stipulated confidentiality in every respect. No work of which he was disposing could be displayed publicly."

Henry gestured toward the prominently displayed painting and frowned the obvious question.

"Right," said Methvin. "As of yesterday, that's no longer a consideration."

Henry's blip picked up speed. "What happened yesterday?"

"The former owner, I regret to say, was found to be dead."

42

JULIAN TALIAFERRO HAD A POINT. HE'D DRAWN BLOOD MAKING IT, but Ariel had to admit: there was no evidence that John William's sexual proclivity was linked to his death. In Julian's opinion it was irrelevant. Ariel would've agreed except that she was fairly sure John William had been gay, she was sure Grover Washburn was, and she was dead sure Washburn hadn't been truthful with the police. The two men's sexuality might not be remotely relevant, but if there had been a relationship beyond that of employer and employee, it couldn't be dismissed out of hand.

She roamed the quiet house trying to decide what she could do with the little time she had left in Carolina. She'd purchased a ticket for a predawn flight Tuesday, and she knew she'd better use it or find a good reason not to.

The back door was open, and the fragrance of hickory smoke wafted in. Sarge had been at work for hours; B.F. would have his barbecue supper.

Ariel watched through the screen as Sarge adjusted the vents on the smoker. From the laundry room came the thrum of the washing machine, a snatch of Hattie's tuneless whistling—what sounded like a hymn—and the faint, clean scent of starch.

It was hard to grasp that in so short a time she'd be leaving Kiawah and Charleston behind. She was struck by the sudden, irrational notion that if this was reality, her life in Los Angeles was something else; that the two totally disparate places couldn't exist in the same time plane. She was sinking into a sentimental funk when she heard the sound of a car, and seconds later a wine-colored sedan slowly rolled up the drive.

Marv Newton looked as if he hadn't seen a bed in a week. With a quick, firm jerk fore and aft, he hitched up his rumpled trousers and trudged toward the smoker where Sarge waited. Ariel pushed open the screen door and stepped outside.

"Miz Gold." The detective greeted her and then lifted his head and sniffed the air like a bird dog.

"Mmmm!" he grunted with what Ariel took to be appreciation. She was caught by surprise, then, when he said, "Well now, Jackie, I heard you'd become a cook—'scuse me, a *chef*. I didn't know you were into real food. I figured you for quiches."

His tone teetered on the very edge of insult and, like the hickory smoke, seemed to linger in the air between the two men. Ariel looked from one to the other and, again, the image of dogs came to her mind. Eye-to-eye they stood, stock-still, each taking the other's measure. She could almost believe their hair bristled. Sarge, she thought fleetingly, was in better shape, but the other man was a good ten years younger.

Then, responding to some code as arcane as if they had been dogs, Sarge grinned and stuck out his hand. After the briefest hesitation, Newton clasped it. The two visibly relaxed and, incredibly (to Ariel), commenced to talk about the best cut of pork for barbecue.

She sank into an Adirondack chair and swatted gnats while Sarge argued for combining a butt with a shoulder. "Hams. Period!" Newton insisted. When a heated debate ensued over vinegar-based versus tomato-based sauce, Ariel resigned herself for a long wait.

Mere weeks before, she'd thought barbecue meant beef or chicken. She'd been in the South long enough to know better—and to know not to interrupt such a serious discussion. Neither man gave an inch and, finally, Sarge promised to drop off a sample of his barbecue at the police station the next day.

"Now you're talkin'," Newton said. As if something had been settled, he turned to include Ariel in the conversation.

"Reason I dropped by was to let y'all know Officer Bollieux, the kid that took your statements last night, passed on your suggestion about lookin' into your burglars' whereabouts the night of the Barron homicide." He fixed Ariel with his good eye. "It turned out to be right helpful."

She stood up in surprise. The burglar angle had been a long shot. Furthermore, far from looking unhappy at having his theories upset, Newton looked serene.

"You're not saying they killed John William?"

"Oh, they did a killin' all right, but not that one. We've got the perpetrator of that one already locked up."

Ariel crossed her arms and glanced at Sarge to see how he was taking Newton's insensitivity. He was shaking out one of his precious cigarettes and staring into the distance.

"Maybe you'd better explain," she suggested politely.

"I was just about to do that, ma'am." Newton was equally polite. "You see, we hadn't been able to get squat out of those polecats. They expected questions about Dr. Ferguson, the assault victim over on Edisto. They 'didn't know a thing.' So"—he smiled—"we decided to put some questions to one of 'em about the night of the second, the night Barron was killed. Threw him right off his game. This character starts to get the drift, starts whisperin' to his lawyer. Compared to premeditated, murder two was all of a sudden lookin' good. Directly, the lawyer was into plea bargainin'. Long and the short, we got a confession.

"We also got a search warrant. Not one thing did we find from the Barron house. Just about every item matched up to a reported B and E, some to one that same night as the Barron murder." Newton paused. "It was quite a ways away—and at the right time."

"You have the time of John William's death narrowed down pretty well, do you?"

"Oh, come on, Miz Gold! There never was reason to believe these boys had anything to do with Barron! Grace Barron made up the burglary thing to get us off the scent. Sorry, Jackie," Newton said with a glance at Sarge, "I don't know if you're close to your sister-in-law, but that's the cold facts of that tale."

"I'm so glad," said Ariel, "that my suggestion worked to your advantage."

"I can't deny it, which is why I stand before you. I am"—he swept off an imaginary hat—"forever in your debt."

He'd turned to leave when Ariel said, "One thing. You must have considered Halley Barron a suspect. Obviously, you dismissed the possibility. Since she's dead, it can't hurt to tell me why."

"She had an alibi."

"Which was . . . ?"

The detective said nothing for a minute, considering, perhaps, what debt, if any, was owed here. "Scotch lady stayin' at her house. Some professor over to lecture at the college, so the dean said. I called the lady in Edinburgh. She was Miss Barron's guest two nights, that bein' the second one. She heard the phone around two-thirty A.M. When she heard her hostess answer, she fell back to sleep."

"It wasn't an answering machine that picked up?"

"She said no."

"And then what?"

"And then came morning. When she went down to the kitchen, at about seven-thirty, Miss Barron was makin' breakfast."

"How did Ms. Barron seem?"

"Oh . . . like business as usual. Talkin', this woman said, about what they had lined up for that day. The '*shedj*ule,' she called it."

"The Scottish woman . . . She was a good friend of Ms. Barron?"

"College arranged for her to be put up. She didn't know her hostess from Adam's off ox before that week. Left that same day to go home. She didn't know about the murder. Fact of the matter, she didn't know Halley Barron was dead until I told her."

"How'd they get to the school that day?"

"You mean because Miss Barron's car was out of commission?" Newton frowned. "My, my. You've been a busy lady. They took a cab."

"A cab? Even though Ms. Barron had a perfectly good blue Chevrolet parked in her garage?"

"Yes'm. Even though. Maybe Miss Barron didn't consider her stepmother's car hers to drive. Since our investigation was posthumous, we couldn't ask her reasons."

"Presumably, she drove it to wherever it was detailed, and then drove it home again."

As if he were making a crowning move in a board game, Newton said, "No, ma'am. Actually, she didn't. Fellow did the job right there at her house. Mobile unit."

Ariel hadn't expected Newton to give her what he had so far, and she was loath to break the rhythm. She did pause for a moment's thought before she said, "I was told that while her car was in the shop, Halley Barron drove the Chevrolet to her stepmother's apartment, that she picked her up for a shopping trip."

"Is that right? I can guess who told you that; she's got a good imagination and no particular respect for the truth. She probably also told you her stepdaughter always wore driving gloves? And that if her own prints—nice, clear ones—were in the car after it was detailed, it was because of this 'shopping trip' nobody witnessed but her and a dead woman." Newton smiled pityingly. "I reckon she also made a big deal about how she just wasn't up to drivin' anymore? Couldn't, wouldn't, didn't ever? And she hadn't been in her son's house for years and years?"

"If she went to his house that night, how did she get over to Halley's house to get the car?"

"How much do you really expect me to tell you?"

The game was over. It was at best a stalemate.

"I don't arrest people without sufficient reason, Miz Gold," Newton said quietly, "and I don't assume a person's innocent just because she's dead."

He had his car door open when he added one last thing.

"I don't much like civilians paddlin' around in my pond, muddyin' up the waters. That doesn't keep me from feelin' bad when, as all too often happens, they get hurt."

Sarge was still staring after the car when he said, "I'd say they found Grace's prints at the house. And they've got more. She wouldn't be behind bars otherwise."

"Well, you know they've placed her car at the scene."

"I didn't. I've made it my business to know as little as possible since the arrest. But obviously you did."

"They've also got John William's garage door opener in the car, and I wouldn't be surprised if the car has a leak. Transmission fluid or maybe windshield washer solution."

Sarge gave Ariel a sharp look. She saw in his eyes a brief flare of interest, his policeman's curiosity. "There'll be more than that, too," he said. "Do you know anything they don't? Have you told them, for example, about the gun?"

Ariel was instantly alert. "Should I? Is it relevant?"

"It says something about the adversarial relationship between Grace and John William, doesn't it?"

"Not really. It says something about John William's feelings toward Grace. You can't infer that the feelings were returned."

"You're splitting hairs." Sarge turned back to the smoker.

"I saw her today." Ariel watched the muscles shift in his broad back and said, "She seems . . . confused. I'm thinking I should call her attorney, make sure he's aware of her state of mind."

"Is that what she's got up her sleeve? An insanity plea?" Sarge's face went heavy with disgust. Slowly, he shook his head. "Where's the gun now?" he asked abruptly.

"Where is it? Julian took it. It's at his office. Why?"

Just then the screen door slammed, and they both turned to see B.F. carefully descending the porch steps. "Who was that leaving a minute ago?" he called out.

Ariel realized she couldn't very well discuss Newton's visit without telling B.F. about the burglary; she decided to do just that before the grapevine took over. With a glance at Sarge, she began, "You missed some excitement here last night."

"Did you get him?" B.F. asked as Ariel returned from calling Grace's lawyer.

"In the middle of his favorite TV show. He thanked me for my concern, said 'certainly' he'd noticed the strain's starting to tell and didn't I think that was to be expected."

"Well?"

"Well, what?"

"Don't you?"

"Of course! Being arrested and stuck in jail's tough enough. But right after the deaths of both your children—being accused of *murdering* one of them! That would send the strongest person alive off the deep end! That's my point, B.F. Grace is not strong. The woman's been shut off from the world for years, and she has problems. I just hope McCrory's got sense enough to get her examined by somebody competent."

"Back up. What 'problems' are you referrin' to?"

"Alcohol, for one."

"Is that gossip?"

"Got it from the lady herself. She's unstable, and I wonder how long she's been that way."

B.F. murmured a wordless "uhmm-uhm" of pity and slumped lower in his chair. He stared into the distance beyond Ariel, and she had an idea that he was seeing the young, untried, and untroubled Grace of long ago. She was only partly right.

"That whole blessed family's reaped John's whirlwind."

Ariel frowned. "What do you mean by that?"

B.F. looked mildly surprised, as if he hadn't realized he'd spoken aloud. He shook his head no. "Nothing," he said, and visibly pulled himself up. "Sounds to me like Newton thinks they can nail Grace on this thing."

Ariel nodded. "Whatever they've got must be so compelling that going in any other direction seemed like a waste of time. Having been there, I can see their point."

"What're you thinkin'? Have you switched sides?"

"I think 'The foolish and the dead alone never change their opinion.' I wanted so much not to believe this woman killed her son. Now I've got doubts they were even related by blood. Even if they were . . ." Ariel turned troubled eyes to the photographs on the mantel: her own unknown grandmother and mother. "I guess, not having much experience of mothers, I had some naive notions."

"Their bein'. . . ?"

"I did a little library research," she said bitterly. "Mothers kill their kids, all right. Every year in this civilized country an estimated seven hundred mothers murder their own offspring."

Ariel gave her grandfather a piercing look to make sure he'd registered the number. "Seven hundred! Granted, what I read dealt with children, not adults, but that doesn't alter the fact that I've been charging around like Don Quixote."

B.F. gave a dismissive wave of the hand. "When you start findin' it easy to accept that kind of corruption, that's when I'll start worryin' about you. I didn't want to believe Grace was guilty any more than you did." He thought for a moment. "I don't reckon you ever heard any more from the druggist?"

"Washburn? No, and I don't expect to." Ariel was emptying her purse, item by item. Her grandmother's picture had reminded her of the missing pillbox, and she was trying to remember the last time she'd seen it. "Short of threatening him at gunpoint, I don't know any way to make him open up to me. Him or Louise Mullis, either."

"Who?"

Ariel recounted her conversation with John William's housekeeper, ending with her conviction that the woman knew something relevant and was afraid to say so.

"Talk to Newton," B.F. suggested. "If either one of those folks knows anything, let the law get it out of 'em."

"What am I going to report? That one acted suspicious and the other scared? Newton would pat me on the head and tell me to go back to California where they encourage overactive imaginations."

B.F. hoisted himself from the chair. "And so you are. What time's your plane Tuesday?"

As they climbed the stairs, they discussed her leavetaking as well as the arrangements he'd made for having the Darrin shipped (Ariel's protests by now being token).

At her door, he said, "Go on home, girl. Much as I'd like to keep you, I 'spec you've been sorely missed."

"Oh, cut that out!" Ariel had just been thinking along the same lines. "You're the one with the overactive imagination!"

"I was referrin' to your dogs, Ariel Gold. Who'd *you* have in mind?"

43

HENRY SLIPPED INTO THE PACKED FOREST LAWN CHAPEL UNCHALLENGED. He'd left his cameraman well away from this particular chapel, one of several in the large memorial park, and that technician was now discreetly shooting stock footage and crowd shots for the *Open File* show that might actually air someday. Henry stood behind the last pew with others who'd arrived too late to find a seat, looking in his dark suit as respectably bereaved as anyone.

He hated funerals. As far as he was concerned he, like everyone, would ultimately have to show up at one too many. He was glad Ariel wasn't here after the hard time he'd given her about being a funeral groupie.

It was, Henry observed, what one might call a generic occasion.

The service and the chapel were inoffensively secular. If, as Henry had once conjectured, Grant Lacy had been into some exotic Eastern religion, there was no evidence of it in the bland words spoken in his memory. There was a good deal of rhetoric about "realization of his gifts" and "faithfulness to his dream" and such pap. Henry stopped listening.

His gaze swept the spectators. He knew Betty Lacy and her brother-in-law Vaughn not only from their photographs but from their first-pew position. He saw that Clifford Gilroy was directly behind the widow. That was interesting, but it wasn't what he was looking for. What he was after was an entrée to the wake he'd heard was to be held at the Lacy house. In short order, he spotted it. A state representative he knew fairly well—a man certain to have been invited—sat four rows behind the family. He was not especially quick-witted, he was up for reelection, and he was a press hound. He was perfect.

When tasteful organ music signaled that the service had ended, Henry made his way to the incumbent, greeting him enthusiastically. Without actually saying so, he implied that *The Open File* was considering a segment that could be politically advantageous. "Love to toss some ideas around," Henry said. "In fact, I'll ride to the house with you. We can talk on the way."

During the drive, the politician rattled on about what he saw as a "powerhouse" exposé of his rivals' flaws. By the time he asked for Henry's "take" on the show, they'd been waved through the gate to the Lacy estate. Henry's unwitting Trojan horse was soon too busy glad-handing to notice Henry drift away.

The house was palatial. The guests were a mixed bag: society guns, minor celebrities, corporate moguls, and kids Henry assumed were MicroStar employees. The bartender was busy; the food was trendy; the atmosphere was sociable. It occurred to Henry that if Grant Lacy were there, he'd probably feel out of place.

Claudia Wynn had just come in, looking around like a woman with a mission. Henry snagged a bite-sized chimichanga from a passing waiter and vamoosed. He found himself in a smallish, unoccupied room of indeterminate function.

It was very formal and decorator spoor was everywhere: in tassels and damask-covered walls and spindly chairs that looked as if no derriere had ever been so presumptuous as to impinge upon their seats. Henry wiped grease from his fingers. He was looking for a place to dispose of the napkin when something caught his eye.

He crossed to a marble fireplace. Above the mantel was a large rectangle of slightly darker damask fabric. There were several similar patches, squares and rectangles, on the other three walls.

In the library old photographs, somebody's grim great-grandparents, adorned the walls. Henry glanced into a solarium where a cluster of people chatted beneath hanging ferns—but no artwork. Henry didn't know whether the dead man was the sort of collector who displayed his trophies or stored them in a vault, but it was curious that the home of an art lover was devoid of art.

Just then he spied the widow. Blond, tanned, and chic in a simple black dress, she was holding court across the room. One of those extending condolences (or discussing the newest hot restaurant—who knew?) was his tame politico.

Henry sidled over. Without introducing himself, acting as if he and Betty Lacy had met on any number of occasions, he looked her in the eye and covered her hands with his.

"A sad, sad day," he said, patting solicitously. "What can I say that hasn't been said a hundred times?"

If she was disconcerted by such familiarity from a man she'd never laid eyes on, the widow didn't show it. She nodded and smiled vaguely, and Henry assumed he wasn't the only stranger partaking of her hospitality. It was when she attempted to recover her hands and found them held fast that she actually looked at him.

"You don't have a drink," Henry exclaimed as if heads would roll for this oversight. "Let's get you something!" He guided her, too startled to resist, toward a waiter.

"We are going to find the person responsible for this day," he told her firmly.

"I beg your—"

"The police may wash their hands of it, but I can promise you I won't. You have my word on that."

Betty Lacy glanced about, seeking rescue. "I'm sorry. I don't believe I—"

"Henry Heller." He reached into his pocket, found the greasy napkin he'd stuck there a few minutes before, and then his card, which he held in front of her eyes. They widened. Anger flashed, and then alarm.

"How did you get in?" she whispered and began to edge away, her eyes again darting around the room. Clifford Gilroy had caught her signal. He was already pushing his way through the crowd.

Henry waited. "Mr. Gilroy," he said. "You and I spoke on the phone." He thrust the card Betty Lacy hadn't taken into the man's hand. "I didn't get a chance to ask you about a former employee of mine. I believe you know him? Richard Cummings?"

The surprise tactic wasn't an unqualified success. Gilroy's face did change. It wasn't possible, however, to know whether it was fear, bafflement, or wrath Henry saw there.

"This is a private affair, mister." Gilroy spoke very quietly. "You get the hell out right now or I'll have you thrown out."

"No need to get ugly. I'd like to talk to you at a more appropriate time, though. About why Grant Lacy was quietly selling off his yacht and a fortune in paintings and so on."

That was a direct hit. Gilroy looked thunderous. He took a step toward Henry, who held up his hands. "Later, then. But do ask your girlfriend to repeat what I told her. I don't care if the cops decide Grant Lacy tripped on the track or fell dead of old age. I, personally, will find out what really happened. Count on it."

Taking his time, Henry strolled away. He knew Gilroy had his eye on him, that he was probably already alerting whatever private security they had in place. What he didn't know was that another pair of eyes had watched the small scene with interest; they, too, followed his progress to the exit.

At the same moment Henry was hoofing it down to the gates where, as arranged, his cameraman waited, Ariel was hanging up the telephone on a surprising call.

She sat still, thinking hard, and then hurried to the kitchen. She found her grandfather snacking on leftover Brunswick stew and reading *Forbes.* When he heard where she intended to go, B.F. balked.

"Nuh-uh! No way you're goin' to meet this Washburn alone!"

"It's at a public restaurant, B.F."

"Where do you think they got Dutch Schultz?"

Ariel snorted. "Somehow I just can't see Grover Washburn wielding a tommy gun!"

"If you're bound and determined, get Sarge to drive you."

"Sarge isn't here. He went fishing. Listen, B.F., Washburn didn't sound angry; in fact, he sounded like he wanted something. He knew who I was—I mean, that I'm your granddaughter. He's not going to do anything to me."

She felt confident of that. Really. As she drove into town, however, she kept hearing B.F.'s parting words. "Keep your back to the wall," he'd said, and he hadn't been joking.

The restaurant was a quaint establishment tricked out to look like an English tearoom. Ariel saw Washburn through a window curtained in lace. The tables were covered with apple-green cloths. Ariel's qualms vanished. She strode to the table where he waited.

"You made it," he said unnecessarily, spilling tea in his haste to rise. He pulled out a chair for her, the Elvis sneer coming and going like a tic. He looked like a man who was very worried and trying hard not to show it.

"Look," he said, "I want to know what that was all about the other day at the drugstore. I found out who you are, so I know you don't need money. I heard you work for one of those exposé-type TV shows. Is that what it is? Are you going to put something on the air about . . . whatever it was John William told you?"

Ariel regarded the man thoughtfully, long enough to make him even more nervous, before she asked, "What is it you're afraid of?"

"What makes you think I'm afraid?"

A waitress approached just then, and after Ariel had asked for tea, she turned back to Washburn.

"You're not all that worried," she said, "just because of being gay."

"So he did tell you about me. About us." He fidgeted, assessing the damage, and then relief flickered in his eyes. "Oh, well." He visibly relaxed. "If that's all it is . . ." he said, his thoughts not yet having caught up to his mouth.

"Mr. Washburn, you know and I know that's not all it is. If you land in jail, it won't be because of your sexual preferences. This is the twentieth century, not Victorian England, and you're not Oscar Wilde."

Every bit of color drained from Washburn's face. "You do know about the note! But I don't get why you haven't said anything."

"The note?" Ariel blinked. "The message he left you!" She leaned closer. "You're right. I haven't said anything about the note, so you know I'm not out to get you. Talk to me, Grover. You do need to talk to somebody about it, don't you?"

Washburn wavered and then made up his mind.

"I want you to understand something. I'm not ashamed of anything about my personal life. I don't make a point of advertising either. I don't know about where you're f ›m, but around here being gay's not exactly a professional asset. Straights—I mean, even if they're not homophobes—get a little nervous about a gay man filling prescriptions for them. Anyway, about John William, let's get this straight. He wasn't *gay.*" His fine, full lips twisted at the unintentional pun. "He didn't know what he was! I'll tell you what his problem was: John William believed in romance. *That* was his problem."

Ariel didn't move a muscle.

"He couldn't accept that every little fling wasn't the love of the century, you know what I mean? That just because *he* felt something, or thought he did, that it wasn't returned. I was fond of him, but the man was just too needy. And he would *not* take no for an answer. He made things impossible. I'd already found another job. I'm just lucky they're willing to wait while the sale of the pharmacy gets settled."

"The message?" Ariel reminded.

"If I'd shown it to the cops, they'd have had me in the slammer in nothing flat. You can imagine what fun that'd be for *me!* After I found John William . . ." He licked his lips. "His body, I mean, I flushed that note down the toilet first chance I got."

"What, exactly, did it say?"

Washburn gaped. "But I thought you already knew. When you said that about Oscar Wilde—about jail . . ."

"John William only alluded to what he wrote," Ariel lied through her teeth.

"Oh. Well, like I said, John William was a romantic. He wrote something about how I was killing him. Lovely, huh? The time the cops would've had with that! He wrote . . ." Washburn's voice dripped sarcasm. " 'As Wilde so eloquently put it,' dear know-it-all John William wrote, 'in *The Ballad of Reading Gaol,*' et cetera. Then he quoted that part about how 'you always hurt the one you love.' "

Ariel felt a bubble of laughter fighting to rise; she swallowed it. The situation wasn't funny. "Do you mean, 'Yet each man kills the thing he loves'—that passage?"

"That's it."

The familiar lines ran through her mind: *Yet each man kills the thing he loves/By each let this be heard. Some do it with a bitter look/Some with a flattering word.* She thought of what

Marv Newton would've made of the last two lines: *The coward does it with a kiss/The brave man with a sword!*

"I can see," she said, "why you disposed of the note. What I don't quite follow, though, is the context. What did that have to do with his not going in to work?"

"That was supposed to be my last day, before I went to my new job. John William wrote he wouldn't be coming in, that I'd know why. Him being hurt and all."

What "all," Ariel wanted to know.

"*I* don't know! He was always writing me little notes. Obviously, he couldn't face saying good-bye in front of everybody." Washburn's expression turned sick. "I keep thinking if I'd found the note the night before, when he meant me to, I might've gone over there. I might've been there to . . . But how was I supposed to know the man would be murdered? And by his *mother!*"

"You're sure about that?"

"She's in jail, isn't she? He despised her, and from what I gathered it was mutual. You know what? She's the one screwed him up, from the time he was a kid. Trying to 'make him a man,' he said, but it was just the opposite. What she wanted was him under her thumb. A ball buster, that one! Fed him all kinds of garbage."

"Garbage?"

"He said she'd needle him about his father, about him killing himself, you know? Say he hadn't been man enough to face life. She'd tell John William he was just the same, weak and spiteful and selfish. Evil woman! Or maybe it was just the booze talking."

"You knew her?"

"Lord, no! He didn't have much of anything to do with her by the time I met him. Except . . ."

"Except?"

"I guess in spite of everything he still cared about her. I saw a present he'd gotten her, for her birthday, he said. Must be about a year ago now."

Ariel frowned. "What kind of present?"

"It was already wrapped. When I asked what it was, he just smiled and said, a surprise she'd get a real bang out of. Even then, though, he didn't actually go to see her. His sister took it."

"Did you know her? The sister?"

"Not likely. She didn't approve of me. Well, that's not really fair to her. It wasn't me, per se, she didn't like. See, she thought like me, or so John William said. She believed he was confused. That he was looking for love, like they say, in all the wrong places. That he was having—what did he call it?—a 'crisis of the soul.' You've got to love yourself first, she'd tell him." Washburn started to drink his tea, but when he saw the milk skin floating on top, he set the cup down.

"*I* felt bad. I did! About John William. About not giving the cops the note. So, later, when I remembered something I thought might help, I called up and told them."

Ariel's attention sharpened. "What was that?"

"You know how when you see something really horrible, really shocking, your mind is kind of like a camera? You can't grasp all the details right then, but later—like after your mind develops the film—you can look at the pictures and see what you missed?"

She knew exactly what he meant.

"I *never* saw John William not wearing his bracelet. I mean, he wore that thing in the shower! It was his dad's, he told me."

"A silver bracelet? A wide one?"

"That's it! Set with a hunk of turquoise. He didn't have it on when I found him. His body was hanging out of that car . . . his arm, you know, dangling, and there was no bracelet. It was right after I mentioned that to the police that they arrested the mother."

So that's what that was all about, Ariel thought. She remembered the day she gave her statement, the call Newton got. The subject of jewelry had come up immediately afterward, and Grace was taken into custody the next day. It was safe to deduce that the police had found the bracelet John William had been wearing only hours before he died—and they'd found it in her possession.

"Grover, what did you mean a while ago? What you said about 'if you'd found the note the night before'?"

"Oh, just . . . John William obviously put it in the cash drawer when he left work that last afternoon. That was a Thursday, our late night; we're open till nine. I worked. I didn't get any fountain business, and I . . . We always check up at closing. Take the money from the cash drawers. But I didn't that night. I was in a hurry. Plans." His sorry little smile looked nothing like the King's. "Who am I kidding? Even if I'd found the note, I wouldn't have gone over there."

Ariel left Grover Washington feeling calmer. She saw no reason to mention what he'd said to anyone. She was at the very end of a long process that, finally, had led her to a conclusion that seemed unarguable.

She was walking back to where she'd parked the car, debating whether to make one last visit to Grace, whether she owed the woman any consideration, when she passed a newspaper stand. The afternoon edition was just in. The headline, huge extra-bold black type, stopped her in her tracks.

"Mother Confesses to Son's Murder!" it screamed.

44

THERE WAS NO WAY TO GET NEAR THE JAIL. ARIEL COULD SEE THE TV vans from two streets away, and an army of reporters. They looked like a lynch mob.

The newspaper story had contained fewer facts than "expert opinions" and background: that the murder had been made to look like a suicide identical to that of the victim's famous father; that the police had been fooled for nearly a week but "certain discrepancies" had persuaded them to keep the investigation open; that the victim's mother, known to be estranged from her son, had been charged two weeks after the discovery of the body.

There would be a press conference, but for now the D.A. had simply issued a statement saying that Grace Barron had changed her plea to guilty.

Lightning bolt that that was, it was the sidebar that most stunned Ariel. A "late-breaking report" stated that "according to a source close to the district attorney's office," the victim's half sister had contacted the police the very night of her own death, exactly one week after her brother's. According to the unnamed source (otherwise known as a leak), Halley Barron had accused her stepmother of the murder only hours before she herself had died in an automobile accident.

Ariel called B.F. If he hadn't already heard the news, she thought, she might as well be the one to tell him.

"Where are you?" he demanded. "Grace Barron's lawyer called nearly an hour ago. He's in a lather to talk to you."

"You know she's confessed?"

"That's all that's on the radio. And what in the world is that business about Halley? Sarge is gonna be fit to be tied!"

"Did McCrory say what he wanted?"

"Nope, but he didn't sound happy." B.F. gave her McCrory's office number, which Ariel immediately dialed.

"Well, you certainly managed to bring things to a head!" the lawyer stated. It sounded like an accusation. "You heard she's changed her plea?"

"I heard. What's that got to do with me?"

"Where are you now? How fast can you get to my office?"

"Where *is* your office?" Within seconds, Ariel was on her way there and within minutes of her arrival, she and McCrory were on their way to the jail. The young attorney was very nearly raving.

"You got me worried, lady, so I saw my client first thing this morning. I told her I'd be arranging for a psychiatrist to do an evaluation. No big deal, right? SOP? Ohh, no! She flatly refused. Like to took my head off! I told her the prosecution would be doing the same. Unlike them, I said, I was genuinely concerned about her. I said even you were concerned about her mental health. She went ballistic!"

McCrory muttered a curse at a slow-moving truck and then sat on the horn.

"Right then and there she insisted on getting the D.A. in. She said if I didn't, I was fired. I did what she asked. Here came the D.A. and a stenographer. There we all are, waiting to see what the woman's gonna do, right? She announces she's changing her plea. Says she's guilty. Says, very emphatically, that she's in full possession of her faculties.

"Boy, was she hot on that point! Said her 'helpless, bereaved female act'—*'act.'* She came right out and said it! That it had been to convince us she was innocent, not deranged. Said there'd be no insanity plea. Period. End of discussion."

McCrory squeezed past a TV van, pulled up to a chained-off "permit only" lot, and identified himself to the police guard. Once they'd cornered a building that blocked them from public view, McCrory parked in a space stenciled *Reserved* and faced Ariel.

"She told Albright, the D.A., she'd make a full confession, but she wanted *you* there. He said no way. She said no confession. I called him from my office and told him we were en route."

McCrory led the way through an old basement corridor to a freight elevator and then down another corridor to another elevator. Despite persistent questions about why Grace had asked that she be present, Ariel learned nothing. McCrory simply didn't know. She asked if he thought Grace was non compos mentis. He said he was no psychiatrist. She asked what he *thought*. He said once she'd gotten over her fit of temper, she'd been cool as a countess.

They emerged in the general area where Ariel had visited Grace previously, but this time she was ushered into a private interview room. McCrory pulled out a chair for her at a long table. Shortly, a craggy-faced man of about fifty stalked in, trailed by another man pushing a wheeled table on which a small machine was mounted. The lead man was glowering. He went straight to Ariel.

"Howard Albright, district attorney." His broad, drawn-out *A*'s and almost nonexistent *R*'s were much the same as Grace's.

He gave Ariel's hand a perfunctory pump. Before she could introduce herself, a superfluity, he leaned over the table, propped himself on his knuckles, and hastened to make his position clear.

"I understand that you're a member of the press, Ms. Gold. You're here on sufferance. You are not to interrupt, interfere, or comment on anything. You are not to repeat nor air anything you hear. You are not to speak to any other member of the press without my okay. Is that understood?"

Ariel considered reminding him that he wouldn't be getting a confession unless she'd agreed to be present. She considered explaining that *The Open File* wasn't interested in resolved cases. She said, "Perfectly."

Albright signaled to a waiting officer and then beckoned McCrory down to the end of the table. Several chairs away from Ariel, the two began to confer in voices too low to be overheard.

Presently, Grace Barron was escorted into the room.

If she wasn't "cool as a countess," she appeared to have her emotions in tight check. She spared the men no more than a glance before seating herself opposite Ariel and thanking her for coming.

McCrory hurried to her side, but she seemed unaware of his

presence. She rested her hands on the table and then, unobtrusively, removed them to her lap. It was her only sign of discomposure.

Albright took charge. "Mrs. Barron, you stated this morning that you wished to change your plea in the homicide of John William Barron to guilty. Is that still your desire?"

"It is."

"You are admitting your guilt?"

"I am."

McCrory began to counsel her, but she interrupted with, "This isn't a plea-bargaining session, Mr. McCrory. We're not here to negotiate."

He subsided, and Albright continued, ascertaining for the record that the admission was made without coercion.

"Tell us, in your own words, please, what occurred during the early-morning hours of Friday, September third, of this year."

"I intend to, sir. Before I sign my life away, however, allow me to explain to this young woman why I requested her presence."

There was a rehearsed quality to her speech when Grace said, "You tried to help me, Ms. Gold. I lied to you. I apologize, but since my motive was obvious, we won't belabor that. You're here because of your sister. I never acknowledged that I remember her. I do, very well. She gave John William affection when, unfortunately, there was a dearth of it in his own home. Their friendship was important to him."

"Mrs. Barron," Albright began. He got no further.

"Just a moment, sir." Grace didn't bother to look at the district attorney. "I don't know much about the bonds between twins, but your being the last person to talk to John William . . ." Grace's mouth twisted into a fleeting, ugly smile. "The last but one, of course," she said. "That you were there seems to me extraordinary, as if their friendship, through you, transcended death."

"Mrs. Barron, I insist—"

"Mr. Albright." Grace addressed the D.A. directly. "I'm beginning to think that you are not a gentleman. I merely wanted to say that it seemed appropriate for John William to be represented here today. Ms. Gold appeared to me to be"—the grimace of a smile was back—"a godsent candidate."

"The State of South Carolina represents your son here today,

Mrs. Barron, and I assure you we take that responsibility very seriously. This is not a social occasion! Your attorney would do well to suggest that *you* take this seriously!"

McCrory's mouth opened and closed again in fishlike consternation, and his client glanced at him with undisguised contempt.

Albright glared. "Now. Will you please answer my question, Mrs. Barron. What took place Friday morning, September third?"

"Did you want the details or a general statement?"

"The details, Mrs. Barron, as fully as you remember them."

Grace again focused on Ariel, as if she were speaking only to her. With no further preamble and in a remarkably ordinary voice, she said, "I walked from my apartment to my stepdaughter's house and took my car from her garage. I still had a set of keys. I drove to John William's home here in Charleston. We had an argument, a long and heated argument. Eventually, he went out to his car with the intention of leaving. I followed. We were both very angry. There were tools, on a pegboard. He was getting into his car. When I saw that I couldn't stop him, I took a hammer and hit him. He fell, unconscious, and I pushed him the rest of the way into the car. I picked up his keys and turned on the motor.

"I went back into the house for a while, perhaps half an hour or longer. Then I got into my own car and drove back to Savannah."

"Was your car also parked in the garage?"

"Yes."

"So you had to return to the garage to get it?"

"Obviously."

"What did you see, then, when you returned to the garage?"

"John William wasn't as I'd left him. He was partially out of the car. His upper body was hanging out onto the pavement."

Ariel felt chilled to the bone, and even Albright looked unnerved. "He was dead at that time?"

"I really don't know. The fumes had filled the garage, certainly. I had to cover my nose with a handkerchief."

Albright cleared his throat. "Why did you do it, Mrs. Barron?"

"I told you I hit him in anger."

"And were you still angry during the half hour 'or perhaps longer' while you left your son to die?"

"I can't say that I was, no."

Despite her best efforts, a small groan escaped Ariel. It was hardly more than a sigh, but Albright gave her a sharp look before he said, "Then I repeat: why did you kill your son?"

"I don't believe I care to answer that, Mr. Albright."

The D.A. abruptly shifted his line of questioning. "You say you struck him with a hammer. This was a claw hammer?"

Grace regarded him, curiously, and not for the first time today, Ariel had the feeling they were dealing with a woman of whom she'd seen only glimpses before.

"Is that what they're called?" Grace asked. "It was a regular, everyday hammer."

"Did you strike him with the solid surface—the head—or with the other side, the prising portion?"

"Neither. I hit him with the shaft. On the back of the head."

"You knocked him out with the *handle?*"

"I hit him very hard."

"I see. What did you then do with the hammer?"

"I threw it into a ditch somewhere between Charleston and Savannah. I have no idea where."

Albright studied the contents of a file folder he'd brought in with him. "What was the time frame, Mrs. Barron?"

"I got to the house between three o'clock and three-thirty A.M. I would guess it was five or shortly after when I left."

"What were you doing in the house during that half hour?"

Grace didn't reply.

"Mrs. Barron, I asked—"

"I heard the question."

"Did you intend to answer it?"

Grace's shoulder lifted and fell in a gesture of resignation. "I suppose so. I was looking for something."

"Looking for what?"

"Letters. Letters that belonged to me."

"Letters." Albright's eyes were slits. "Was it over these letters that you killed your son?"

"They were the last of a long list of reasons."

The D.A. glanced back at the folder. "Did you do anything else when you returned to the garage? Did you remove anything from the premises other than the hammer?"

"Are you talking about the bracelet? Actually, I took that before I went back into the house."

"Why?"

"It had been my husband's. Like the house and the money, it should have been mine when he died, not theirs. The bracelet was a small thing by comparison, I know—a nothing—but seeing it on John William's wrist . . . irked me."

"Irked you," Albright repeated and, momentarily, seemed at a loss for words. "Indeed," he said and, with concentration, shuffled papers. "Your stepdaughter, Halley Irene Barron, telephoned the Charleston police the night she died. She made the following statement. 'My stepmother is a murderess. I'm bringing her up there. She will tell you what she's told me.' " He looked up. "When you were questioned after the accident in which Miss Barron was killed, you said you knew nothing about this call, that you'd said nothing unusual to her about your son's death. She was 'obviously distraught,' you said; the two of you were driving here 'to close up the house.' "

"Yes, that is what I said."

"Were you, in fact, aware that she'd made this call?"

"I was in the room with her. Yes, I was aware."

"You were lying then."

"I just said so."

"Why?"

"Why?" Grace gave a short bark of laughter. "Because I thought I might be able to get away with this then, sir! I'm afraid I overestimated my chances."

Albright's next question was delivered with the sudden force of a rifle shot: "Did Halley Barron die at your hands?"

Grace blanched. In the circumstances, her shock was incongruous. Solemnly, as if uttering an oath, she said, "She did not."

"I see. You lied about your stepdaughter's phone call, you've lied every time you've been questioned about your son's death, but today you're telling the truth. Is that right?"

"Mr. Albright, I've admitted to murder. I can only be electrocuted once. If I'd somehow engineered my stepdaughter's death, why would I deny it?" When the D.A. didn't immediately respond, Grace pushed the point. "How *would* I have engineered it, for that matter? You must've examined the car. Had the brakes been tampered with? Or . . ." She shook her head in sudden agitation. "I don't even know what else to suggest! I'm not a mechanic." Her hand, back on the table, was clenched into a fist. "I regret that Halley had to die in such a way."

Albright let it go. He continued to ask questions, some of which Grace disdained to answer. Some answers—like why her son had been up and dressed in the middle of the night with his bed unslept in—she professed not to know. Finally, he closed his folder. "I think," he said, "that we've covered the most crucial points. We'll have your statement ready for you to sign shortly."

"Excuse me."

Every head swiveled toward Ariel.

"Ms. Gold, I warned you—"

"Just one question, Mr. Albright, please."

He hesitated. Hurriedly, Ariel asked what, it seemed to her, was an obvious question. "Why are you confessing now?"

Grace answered readily. "The people in this place, Ms. Gold, are scum. These few days of incarceration have been hell. There was every chance that I'd be imprisoned a long while. At my age that amounts to a life sentence. If Mr. McCrory had been allowed to maneuver, I'd have been pent up not just with scum but with demented scum. I decided death would be infinitely preferable. They do have the death penalty here in lovely South Carolina, you know."

Directly to Albright, she said, "I didn't kill my son in the heat of passion. I arranged it and I waited for it. I *desired* it! Do you think, Mr. Albright, that there's any chance I'll be left to rot in prison? I don't!"

Albright was still formulating a reply when Ariel said, "How did you get your car into the garage?"

Grace smiled regretfully. "You did want me to be innocent, didn't you? I'm sorry." She genuinely seemed to be. "John William gave Halley an opener years ago. I'm afraid I stole it from her. It was when she saw it in my car and knew she hadn't left it there that she started asking questions. She'd be alive, wouldn't she, if I'd just lied? I should have. I'm good at it. So many years' practice. But . . . I counted on her loyalty to me. I was wrong."

"Her loyalty to her brother was stronger," Ariel thought aloud.

"No." Grace appeared to waver momentarily and then to come to some decision. "No," she said. "Her loyalty to her father was."

Every person in the room, including the stenographer, froze to stillness. They all stared at Grace in bewilderment, and it seemed to Ariel that in some indefinable way she grew younger and lighter before their eyes. There was an odd, almost victorious lilt to her voice when she said, "I think she might have forgiven me John William's death, in time. She knew about his many unkindnesses. But she just had to know why I'd killed him. That was the price of her loyalty. She had to know. So I told her. That he'd found certain letters, letters written to me forty years ago by my lover. He intended to turn them over to the police.

"Most of the letters wouldn't have mattered anymore. People aren't all that particular about adultery these days and, really, how many from that time are still around to care? But one letter, as John William reminded me, included rather specific details about Hugh's and my plans." A tiny suggestion of a smile played across Grace's face. "They were good plans. I've gone scot free for four decades, so they must have been—good enough, I thought, to adapt. Unfortunately, I wasn't as well prepared this time."

Albright found his voice. "Mrs. Barron," he said, "what, exactly, are you talking about?"

"Am I not making myself clear, Mr. Albright? I'm talking about killing my husband."

45

Hattie, her face tense, kept her eyes on B.F. He'd sagged in his chair as though he'd been poleaxed. Sarge was equally immobile. His rigid body looked the way the earth must, Ariel thought, just before the cataclysmic shifting of tectonic plates.

She'd never considered obeying Albright's gag rule where these two men were concerned; they would *not* hear about John Barron's murder via TV or a headline. If she'd ever had harder news to break, she was glad she couldn't remember it. Except for the rasp of B.F.'s breathing and the metronomic click of the wall clock, the kitchen was silent.

"Grace said . . ." Ariel bestirred herself, filling the silence, "that she welcomed death. That she might as well make 'doubly' certain it would happen."

No one spoke. After a moment, Ariel said, "Sarge, I feel very sure that—"

When his fist hit the table, she jumped as if she'd been shot. She was even more surprised—and utterly confused—when he faced B.F. and said, "My God! We helped the murdering bitch!"

Ariel looked at her grandfather. He'd squeezed his eyes shut, and his face was a grimace of wretchedness. Abruptly, he shook himself, lifted the shot glass he'd hitherto ignored, and drained it.

Just as abruptly, Sarge challenged Ariel. "What did she say happened to this Hugh Cross? To her *lover?*"

"That . . . She said that when he learned she'd be getting little of the money, he vanished. That she never heard from him again."

"It was her!" Sarge said to B.F. "It was her that killed that man! She made my brother look like a gutless nothing, a killer and worse! All these years . . ."

Ariel attempted to interrupt. She didn't even get a word in.

"Well, sir," B.F. said, "I imagine we neither one ever bought a hundred percent that it was him did it. Poor, sad John. He had his dark side but . . . God knows *I* always had that little splinter of doubt. Comes at you in the night . . ." To himself, he said, "Reckon why she didn't tell the whole story? Woman can't fry but once."

"That doesn't mean she *won't* say anything. What she's done . . . She's not even human!"

"What is it?" Ariel managed to interject. "What are you two talking about?"

She was ignored. The men continued to act as though they were alone in the room.

"She's a bottom feeder, all right, but looks like she's got a vestigial streak of loyalty." B.F. made a harsh, guttural sound deep in his throat. "If she tells, she tells. That's the last thing in the world I'm worried about right now."

"John William!" Sarge said. "Grace was pregnant then. What if he was this Cross's—"

"You know better than that," B.F. said firmly and then asked Ariel, "What about the letters? Did she say what she did with these letters she killed John William over?"

"She destroyed them. B.F., *please!* Tell me what's going on!"

The two men locked eyes, and some signal passed between them. When the screen door banged behind Sarge, Ariel heard the *scritch!* of a match being struck. Peripherally, she saw Hattie take the chair he'd vacated, but she kept her eyes on her grandfather. His mouth worked as if he were swallowing a bitter pill, and then he began to talk.

"When Halley found her father's body, she found Cross, too. He'd been shot. Twice."

B.F. waited for the information to be absorbed. "I was at Sarge's that night. Poker game. Grace called in hysterics. Even I could hear her. I took one look at Sarge's face and got rid of the other boys. We got in his car and went, fast as we could get there.

"Halley . . . She was in total shock. It was like she was trying to scream, but it came out just this croaking sound, like an animal." B.F. swallowed. "It's the worst thing I ever heard out of a human throat.

"I got her wrapped in a blanket. Tried to calm her while Sarge got the facts—what until now we *thought* were the facts—out of Grace. She'd been asleep, she told us, and thought it was a car backfire woke her. She went downstairs to the kitchen. Said she found Halley huddled by the door to the garage steps. Grace could smell the fumes, she said. She went down and saw both men, John in his car and Cross a few feet away, a gun next to him. They were both dead.

"Grace was . . . Grace was convincing. Crying. Wringing her hands. Said she didn't know why John killed himself, didn't know the other man, didn't know what he was doing there.

"Sarge didn't much like Grace. Even after he saw the suicide note, he wasn't inclined to believe her. He was going to call in—he was on the local force then—when Grace stopped him. Held him bodily, begging him not to let anybody see how things were. It was bad enough people would know about the suicide, she said; he couldn't let people know his brother was a murderer, too. 'He's already punished himself,' I remember she said. 'Don't do this to John. Don't do this to the man we both love most in the world.' "

B.F. paused as Sarge came back inside. If he'd left looking murderous, he returned looking ill. Gray in the face, he stood just inside the door and listened while B.F. resumed.

"I saw sense in what Grace said. I took her side. 'Get your kit,' I told Sarge. 'Print Grace and John, too. Dust the gun. If she's lying, you've got her. If she's telling the truth,' I said, 'then let's get this man out of here.' I didn't want to think about what the scene suggested"—B.F.'s eyes flicked to Sarge and away again—"and there wasn't any purpose to be served, I didn't think, in blackening a dead man's name.

"So . . ." B.F. gave a sad little smile. "That's what we did. The gun was John's. The only prints on it were his, and he was the only one with shot residue on his hand. Not Grace and not Cross.

"Neither one of us had ever seen Cross before. Wouldn't have known his name but for the license on him—Pennsylvania, it was. We wrapped him in this tarp he'd fallen on and put him in my trunk. Sarge called in. That night we took Cross's body out to the middle of nowhere and buried it."

Sarge crossed his arms over his barrel chest. "What now?" he asked B.F. "Just what do we do now?"

"You don't do one damn thing!" Hattie exploded. "That she-devil's took three lives! She's confessed to two of 'em, and that's enough. I won't let her ruin two more, you hear me? God'll see she gets what she deserves, and that's the end of it!"

B.F. gazed at her fondly. "That's the same kind of self-serving reasoning that's let her walk free all these years, Hattie. What about that man buried out there in the woods? You don't think he deserves anything?"

"Deserves what? He *got* what he deserved! He was that woman's partner in adultery and, from what she says, murder, too!"

"Hattie's right," Ariel said. "Grace has lived her own kind of hell all this time. She thought she was going to be a rich, fine lady after she killed John Barron. It backfired. She was just the dubious widow of—forgive me, Sarge—a failed artist and a suicide. By the time your brother's recognition came, she was a miserable, misbegotten woman cut off from everybody and pickling herself in booze. You two did what you thought was the right thing. You've got nothing to blame yourselves for."

"I blame myself she wasn't electrocuted forty years ago," Sarge said. "I could walk into that jail right now and kill her myself!"

"That's enough of that kind of talk!" B.F. commanded. "You're not gonna let Grace befoul any more than she already has. I'll tell you something, my friend, that I should've told you long years ago, but I figured the less said the better. I had Cross checked out. He wasn't missed by anybody, and his passing wasn't much of a tragedy. He was a bum. A low-life grifter who'd served time for every kind of swindle you can name. I don't know where Grace ran into him, but you can bet he was no better than her."

"I'm not worried about him! Don't you realize that if we hadn't helped her then, John William wouldn't be dead now?"

B.F. regarded the other man with compassion that was almost palpable. "Don't you think that's crossed my mind? But think about this. You and I are pretty bright. You were by far the sharpest man on that force. I don't know yet how she engineered it all, but she fooled us. Anybody else fingerprinted the gun would've found the same thing you did. Anybody checked the hands would've gotten the same answers. And the note . . . That note was written by John! The experts agreed. So, what do you think they'd have proved that we didn't? You had a bigger investment in finding out what happened than anybody, didn't you? But you believed her."

"If they'd had all the facts, they might've come to a different conclusion. Somebody more objective would've—"

"The same thing would've happened, man! But say she'd been charged. Been found guilty. Then what? John William would've been born in prison, of a convicted murderess. The authorities wouldn't have let a girl Halley's age have him, you know. At least as things were, his sister could help raise him and love him all his life."

Ariel wasn't sure how much of B.F.'s rationale Sarge was hearing. He looked too grief-ridden to absorb much of anything.

"You don't want to hear this," she said before she lost her nerve, "but I'm going to say it. John William knew what Grace was capable of. It was in the letters. But he acted right in character, the character even you acknowledge, Sarge. He made a drama of it. He didn't turn the letters over to the law; he *threatened* to turn them over. He let Grace into his house and stayed there arguing. He was a grown man, Sarge. Responsible for his actions."

"She was his *mother*, Ariel!" Sarge bellowed and slammed out.

No one moved for what seemed like a long time. B.F. eventually got to his feet. He steadied himself against the table and, silently, he too left the room.

46

THE GRANDFATHER CLOCK DOWNSTAIRS BONGED SOFTLY. THE actual grandfather was fast asleep. Ariel could hear the proof of it from where she lay, down the hall in her own rumpled bed, too tired to sleep. A tree branch fidgeted at the window, and she heard the first, light patter of rain against the tin roof.

The clock read ten, too early for bed, even if she did have a predawn flight. As she reached for her robe, her jawbone creaked in a vain yawn.

She left the kitchen in darkness as she shuffled through to the refrigerator. She was staring into the cold white interior, vacant-minded as a snowman, when the phone began to ring. It was off the hook and in her hand almost before she knew she'd heard it.

"Hello!" she whispered.

"Well, well. The TV lady herself."

"Who's this?"

"You had a big day, I hear. Big break, too."

"Julian?"

"How often does a newsperson get invited to a murder confession? And by a triple murderess! Think of the ratings!" Julian's voice, normally so thick and soft-edged, could have etched crystal. "Your *friend* Jackie ought to especially enjoy the show. Ol' Dirty Harry McManus! Wait'll he hears all the juicy bits about his nephew's 'alternate lifestyle.' "

Ariel stood openmouthed.

"Is he there?"

Tightly, her face flaming as if she'd been slapped, Ariel said, "I'll see."

She went to look. The door to Sarge's room was open. She could see by the light from the window that the bed was neatly made.

"Sarge?" she said quietly.

There was no reply. She went to the window and looked out into the driveway where the Darrin sat alone.

When she got back to the kitchen, she turned on the light. Hattie, wrapped in her robe, was sitting at the table.

"She kill herself?" Hattie asked.

"*What?* No!" Ariel said on her way to the phone.

"Julian? He's not here. Now, what is it? What's going on? Julian? Are you still there?"

"If he comes in, please ask him to call me," Julian said, and hung up.

"Something's wrong," Hattie said flatly. "What?"

"Don't ask me!" Ariel was surprised to feel her eyes stinging. She looked up, blinked back tears, and breathed deeply, listening to the rain. It had settled in, she noticed, not hard but steady. "I'm going to make some cocoa," she said. "Do you want some?"

"No, you're not. There's not any. What did the lawyer want?"

"Did Sarge tell you where he was going?"

"He's not here?"

Ariel considered calling Julian back, but she had the uncomfortable conviction he'd hang up on her again. She gnawed her lip, realizing that he'd been cool, even prickly, the last few times she'd seen him. What had set him off?

It had to do with the show, of which, it was painfully clear, he was no fan. Newsmagazine, Ariel thought, equals investigation equals exposé. Of what? What did Julian Taliaferro have to hide?

And what was all this about Sarge? *Dirty Harry?*

"Hattie, you know Sarge better than I do. He's not likely to do anything stupid, is he?"

"Last one to in the normal run of things."

The two women looked at each other. It didn't need to be said that the events of the day had been anything but normal.

You're overreacting, Ariel told herself; Sarge is probably sitting on a bar stool somewhere liquefying his troubles. Still she asked, "Does he own a gun?"

"He owns one. He hasn't got it."

"How do you know?"

"Because I took it this afternoon and put it where he couldn't find it. Just in case he might think he needed it."

Ariel started to smile. Her face froze. It had been only yesterday that Sarge had asked her where another gun was: the one gift-wrapped for Grace. He'd asked even before he knew what she'd used it for.

Ariel was already moving when she said, "I'm going to look for him."

While she dressed, she tried to think. She was hopping in place, trying to keep her balance as she put on the second sock, when Hattie appeared at her door.

"You have any idea where you're goin' to?"

"Julian Taliaferro's office. If I don't see any sign of him, I'll call you. If he's not back by then, I'm going to the jail."

A good many cars were parked along the street in front of Julian's building and beyond. Many, Ariel assumed, belonged to occupants of a large apartment complex on the opposite side of the street. The law office was dark. There was no sign of the Lincoln. Ariel tried to see beyond a hedge at the side of the building but couldn't tell if there was a private parking lot there.

The windshield wipers swished back and forth. A car passed. Lights went off in one of the complex's topmost apartments.

Of all the fool's errands! Ariel told herself. But she knew Sarge had called Julian or been to see him and worried him enough that Julian felt a need to check up. "Triple murderess," he'd said, so he knew the whole sorry story. The Dirty Harry reference made Ariel believe something had been said about revenge. About the gun, too? Julian wouldn't have given it to Sarge or given him access to it, but Sarge was an ex-cop. If anybody could pick a lock, Ariel was willing to bet, he could. If he had enough motivation.

A light flared behind her. A car approached, slowed, and parked. Her pulse picked up. She waited, but whoever it was didn't come her way. Without being conscious of doing so, she'd been staring at the law office sign. It had been deliberately designed to look old, as if it had served generations of venerable

Taliaferro attorneys. Subtly lighted. "Classy," as Julian would say. And half of it represented a nonexistent person. Ariel cut the motor. As long as I'm here, she told herself.

She'd been in a rush the one time she'd been here before, the day she'd faxed Henry the Lacy article. The building, she observed now, was a genuine antique: old brick, black shutters, and a substantial wooden door that looked as if it might have held against Union forces. It hadn't been so impregnable tonight; it was ajar.

Ariel nudged it. It creaked, as did the wide pine planks of the floor when she stepped inside. Softly, she crossed the reception room into the secretary's office. That was as far as she'd been on her last visit. She saw as she passed into a hallway that the building was bigger than she'd thought.

Light from outside shone through the windows of open doors along the corridor. A different sort of light glowed from a room at the very end. At most, a low-voltage lamp. Maybe a computer.

A sudden, vivid image flashed through Ariel's mind: herself tippytoeing around, surprising a furtive, distraught Sarge with a gun in his hand.

She flattened herself against the wall, slipped into a niche beside a copy machine, and listened. Other than the rain on the roof, she heard nothing. Whoever was here, she realized, might already have left. If it was Sarge, he might've been in too big a hurry to close the door behind him. He could be on his way to the jail right now. The jail, where his old buddies from his days on the local force would know him and let him pass without a moment's hesitation. They'd consider it perfectly normal that he'd visit his own sister-in-law, and Grace would be glad to see him, even if she knew why he'd come.

Ariel came out of hiding and hurried back the way she'd come. She was making no attempt to be quiet. She was simply making tracks. She burst into the reception room.

A man stood in it, a large, solid man outlined by the light of a window.

"Oh!" Ariel gasped and skidded to a stop. The man was far too tall to be Sarge. She'd absorbed that in an instant. And the way he was standing: tense, shocked . . . It was the posture of someone who's come upon an intruder on his private property.

He couldn't have been more shocked than Ariel. "Oh!" she

said again. "Oh, my Lord, it's you!" Her words tumbled over one another in her haste to identify herself, a person who had no right to be here: a trespasser dressed completely in dark colors and unisex clothes. And, not having taken the time to put in her contacts, she was wearing glasses. Julian had never seen her in glasses. If he could see her. All she could see of him was his dark bulk.

"It's just me!" she blurted. "It's Ariel!"

He took a step toward her. She stiffened.

"I know who you are, sweetheart," he said.

Ariel sagged and breathed again. "I was afraid you didn't recognize me!"

He tilted his head and chuckled. He didn't sound amused. He sounded even sharper and more unlike himself than he had on the phone when he said, "At first I didn't. Couldn't believe my eyes! But you're the same old Ariel. A snoop still, now and always."

"Okay, you're mad. I don't blame you. You have to be wondering—" In moving her hand, a gesture of appeal to his understanding, Ariel bumped something on the desk beside her. It fell to the floor. "Oh, I'm sorry!" She knelt, and in her haste to grab the object, knocked it under the desk. "Damn it! I *will* explain, but not now." Even as she was impatiently reaching under the desk, she was declaring, "I've got to get out of here."

"What's your hurry? After all this time? After what you've put me through these last few days, wonderin' what you're up to?"

"What did Sarge actually say to you?" Her fingers found what turned out to be a letter opener, a trifling little plastic thing.

"In and out of police stations. Consortin' with cops and lawyers. I don't have nearly as much at stake as some we could name—or *you* could name." He laughed that nasty laugh again. "But, still, I don't like being screwed with. In a manner of speakin'."

Somewhere between kneeling and standing Ariel knew. The voice she was hearing was thickly Southern, but it wasn't Julian Taliaferro's.

"For days now," he was saying, "you've had us off balance. We knew what you knew. You could point a pretty little finger anytime and cause a certain amount of trouble. But you didn't."

Ariel was almost too bewildered to be scared. She had no idea who he was. Whoever he was, he must be crazy to show himself now. On the very day Grace confessed? When, finally, Ariel was convinced of her guilt?

"At first," he said, "I just planned to confront you. Ask you straight out what the deal was. But keepin' an eye on you got to be kind of a kick, actually, and it's not like I've got anything more pressin' to do."

"You've been following me?" He had to be crazy! Ariel thought—a crazy man who could have walked away with murder, unknown and unsuspected.

"I'd pick you up whenever I felt like it and just watch. Mostly. Tonight . . . Now, that was luck. I'd been partyin' with a little lady out your way when I caught sight of that cute car of yours flyin' down the road."

His hand went to his pocket. Ariel tensed.

"Just think of all the times I could have edited you right out of the picture."

What he took from his pocket wasn't a weapon. Casually, having fun, he tossed something at her. Reflexively, she caught it. Her fingers closed over her grandmother's little pillbox, recognizing it by touch. She still clutched the letter opener in her other hand. She wished it were metal and sharp and a foot long.

"On the beach that night," he went on, "just you and me. You half naked and lookin' fine, by the way. Then there was that night on that dark, lonely stretch of road. I actually considered it then, for about three seconds. It was like . . . a dare. Some kind of high. Tell you the truth, I *was* high at the time, but no way I'd really do it."

He'd begun to walk toward her, taking it slow, taking all the time in the world.

"You know me. I'm a lover, not a fighter. Don't have it in me to kill a fly. And besides, my mama didn't raise no fools. I mean, what's the worst *I* could get, whatever you took it into your head to say? A slap on the wrist?"

Ariel had been taking a step back for every step he took forward. The room wasn't that big. She collided with a wheeled desk chair, lost her footing, and collapsed into the seat, her legs spraddled like a rag doll's. She was jarred into speech.

"Listen to me! This is crazy! You've made a big mistake—"

"So you told me."

"I've never told you anything. I don't even—"

"Outside the police station that day. Stompin' over, tough as a marine, tellin' me straight out you knew all about my 'mistake.' But you still didn't make your move. I couldn't figure it out."

He'd very deliberately positioned himself between her legs, leaning over her, bracing himself on the armrests and bringing his face right down to hers, suffocating her in a haze of musky cologne and the stale, overripe smell of wine.

"But I've got it now. The only thing that makes sense." All she could see was eyes, rings of pale iris and dilated pupils. "You've changed, babe, in spades. You're after a bigger score than a story." His voice had taken on a caressing quality. Soothing and seductive. "Am I right? And now . . . payoff time. You're done here. The old man's home and . . . Oh, yeah, I know about that." The eyes crinkled. "Got my own personal Deep Throat, my old *Open File* bud. I know how you've been 'cooperating' with Heller, with the phone chats and newspaper clippings. And holdin' out on the one thing he'd give his soul to know.

"But tomorrow it's home again, home again. And then, bet you anything, you're off to see my friend."

His face brushed hers; his mouth was against her ear.

"No way, babe," he whispered. "That's my sweet little deal, and I'm selfish." She felt his tongue and then she could feel that he was smiling again. "But not with everything."

"Don't do this." Ariel said it very quietly.

He was folding his fingers around hers, extricating the letter opener as he straightened up.

"You don't need that toy, sweetheart. I've got what you need."

He actually said it.

Ariel felt the plastic blade being slipped through the opening of her shirt, holding the fabric taut as he undid the top button.

"I mean it," she said. "Don't."

"I don't know what you've done to yourself, babe, but I like it." The opener and then his fingers went to the next button.

She began to move her leg. Her inner thigh slid up the outside of his calf.

Another button was undone and another. "Could you have imagined this a year ago?" he murmured. "Me with *you* . . . In your wildest dreams?"

Her knee grazed his as it slipped across, edging inward, squeezing between his legs.

"I used to see the way you looked at me. Well, now! Could *that* be the real reason you've kept quiet?"

Her shirt was open. The opener was poised beneath the center of her bra, playfully, lifting the elastic as if to slice through.

"A little unrequited passion?"

Ariel had reached up and grasped his shoulders.

"Oh, baby, *okay.*"

She was pulling him toward her, sliding down in the chair.

"Daddy's comin'."

Sliding down onto her tailbone, down until she had her knee precisely in position. She didn't have much leverage. She didn't know how much damage she could do.

She gave it her all.

He bent double, howling.

She was upright and almost out of the chair when his fist connected, knocking her back into the seat and sending her spinning. The chair made a half circle. Before it could come to a stop, he'd launched himself after it. She could see his face for the first time—still not clearly, a white blur—because the room was suddenly blasted with light, and then there was an actual blast, ear shattering.

Ariel's whole body went into a tight, defensive clench: shoulders hunched, eyes squeezed shut, hands over ears.

Someone was shouting, coming at her—a mass more sensed than seen—but she was up and moving.

"Are you all right? Ariel!"

A hand grabbed at her. She struggled to throw it off.

"Stop it! Are you hurt?"

She focused.

Julian Taliaferro towered over her. "Did he hurt you?" he was saying. "My God, girl! Look at your cheek! It's red as— I'm sorry. I'm sorry I waited so long!"

She looked down at the man on the floor. He was making an effort to move. One knee bent and weakly unbent. His shoe scraped at the floor and then went still.

"Have you *shot* him?" Ariel cried. "Why did you *shoot* him?"

"Why? Because he was after you with a knife!"

"What knife? He didn't have a knife."

She was already on her knees. The wounded man was breathing, shallowly. He didn't appear to be conscious. She was about to tell Julian to call 911 when she heard him at the phone.

"They're coming," he soon said and then, quietly, "Who is he?"

He was the man Ariel had seen a few days earlier as she was leaving the hospital; the man she'd seen, again, outside the police station. Unremembered even now, he was a man she'd once seen selling his silence, maybe on the subject of murder.

And if he dies, she couldn't keep from thinking, we still won't know who the buyer was.

"I'm pretty sure," she said and began to button her shirt, "that he's a man named Richard Cummings."

"But what . . . Never mind. Tell me later." Julian was staring at the flimsy plastic letter opener that now lay on the floor. "You go on. Take off. No point in you getting bogged down with this."

"I can't go. Except . . . Sarge! Oh, Julian! What time is it? How long . . ." She'd scrambled up. "Has Sarge got the gun?"

Julian's smile was sickly. He held up his hand, with the gun in it. "This one, you mean?"

"Oh! I was afraid that he—"

"Me, too. That's why I came to get it." He let out a tired, ragged exhalation and laid the gun on a desk. "Now go on. Git!"

Instead, Ariel went to the phone. Hattie answered on the first ring.

"He's here," she said. "Come in not ten minutes after you left, not walkin' too straight. He's snorin' away now."

"He's home," Ariel said to Julian.

"Who you talkin' to?" Hattie demanded. "What took you so long to call?"

"I'll talk to you in the morning," Ariel told her and hung up. "What're you going to tell the police?"

"The truth, or as much as I need to. He was trespassing. I thought he had a knife."

They both looked at the man on the floor, who was breathing but not moving otherwise.

"We should be doing something," Ariel said.

"What?" Julian shook his head, helplessly. "I told you to go."

"I told you, I can't go."

"This isn't the time to be noble. I'm the one did it."

"Nobility's got nothing to do with it. I need to be around if he . . . says anything. Why *did* you wait so long to show yourself?"

"I thought at first y'all were together, doing God knows what. You under the desk. Him saying something about snooping. I couldn't see worth . . . And—I couldn't make sense of it—it started to sound like he was mixed up in the murder. I was thinking, What if Grace is protecting somebody? Or, I don't know, if I just waited a minute, he'd name names.

"Then, right when I thought you were in trouble, y'all started whispering, and you were . . . You didn't seem to be protesting. Hell, Ariel! I was ready to go out the back and leave you to it!"

Ariel went to him and laid her head against his arm. Wrapping her own arms around it, she said, gently, "Fool."

After a moment, she said, "Why have you been acting so hateful to me?"

"Oh, for . . . That's not important now. They'll be here any second."

"Then talk fast."

"I despise what you do, that's why. What it does to people. TV tabloids, trash talk shows . . . It's insidious crap. Cheap and destructive and symptomatic of everything that's wrong—"

They heard a siren and, with a scowl, ruefully, Julian said, "I hated, especially, that *you* did it. See, I'd kind of taken a shine to you."

Ariel listened, marveling. "I haven't been right about one thing since I set foot down here. I'd about decided you were gay." In any other circumstances she would've laughed at his expression. "I even thought more than once," she said, "that you had something to do with John William's death."

The predawn flight home was eerie. Ariel had the sensation that she was encapsulated, winging through a silent darkness where time hung as suspended as the plane itself. The cabin lights were subdued. The plane was half empty, and the passengers Ariel could see were dozing. Except for an occasional murmur from the galley, there was little sound but the drone of the engines.

Ariel was wide awake. She'd almost caught her coattail coming through the door, so close had she come to missing the flight.

Julian had followed her home from the hospital, reassured a worried B.F. and Hattie (Sarge had still been asleep), and told them to sit still; he'd be back to explain the events of the night. He and Ariel had hardly a word to say as he drove her to the airport. Then, as they'd hurriedly hugged good-bye, when it was too late to say anything sensible, both had begun talking at once.

Ariel hadn't had even a second to call Henry. There was no point in waking him up now, just to tell him he'd been vindicated in his suspicions about Richard Cummings. It would be different if she could give him the name of the person Cummings had blackmailed. Cummings wouldn't be revealing that or anything else, ever again.

They'd found his Porsche parked on the street, two cars back from Ariel's. Georgia plates. Binoculars along with golf clubs in the trunk. A receipt from the Kiawah Island Inn on the seat. He'd been registered there, no more than a mile from B.F.'s house, for five nights.

Blue-white light had begun to rim the horizon. Ariel leaned her head against the cold window, watching as a fierce molten ball appeared above the blackness, hovering unnaturally as the plane flew west. Slowly, the sky began to be suffused with a rose-tinted yellow.

Poor Julian, she thought. Poor B.F. Poor Sarge. So much pain, so much guilt, and not a molecule of anything but good intentions between them. Even poor old Richard Cummings. If he'd been immoral, he hadn't been evil.

About Grace Barron, Ariel still agonized.

There was no question that she'd killed in cold blood—both Barron men and Cross as well. But, even after listening to the woman describe her atrocities, Ariel still couldn't accept that such corruption could fester inside a perfectly reasonable-looking fellow creature. Could her acts be put down to madness? Was it that frustratingly simple?

She shivered. If finer minds than hers hadn't resolved the question of whether pure evil existed, she wasn't likely to.

The facts were more manageable. Grace knew about the position of her son's body and the time frame. She knew about the head wound, the location, and, apparently—judging from a remark Albright had let slip about microscopic splinters—that a wooden weapon had dealt the blow. Grace knew about the bracelet; she'd *taken* it. She'd been in the car, and she'd been in the house, and her fingerprints proved it.

Ariel dug a seat belt out of her back, stuffed the little airline pillow under her head, and thought about John Early Barron's murder, unsuspected for so many long years and described yesterday in cool detail.

Grace had known Hugh Cross before and after she met the man who was to become her husband. The marriage was a setup from the start, and from the start she knew how it would end. She wooed the lonely artist and won him, comforted him in the dark times when he lost heart over his continuing obscurity, brought gaiety into his fine old house. And less than a year after John Barron married the beautiful and greedy young Grace, he was dead.

She *had* been young, Grace had emphasized, to explain why, after such painstaking planning, she miscalculated financially. Her husband had all the money in the world. In her youthful confidence, in some intimate moment, she ascertained that he'd changed his will to include his wife. Stipulations hadn't been mentioned.

She'd also had no idea of the potential worth of his paintings. She sold them at a fraction of their current value and counted herself lucky to have sold them at all.

She was luckier with a suicide note. Sometime during that year, she came across a letter her husband had begun. In a discouraged moment, convinced that his talent had deserted him, John had poured out his heart to an old mentor. He hadn't signed the letter or even completed it. He'd dragged himself from the slough and gone back to work. But the letter was in his own hand, and the paragraph Grace tore from the page served her plans admirably.

Ariel thought now of those opportune and ambiguous words she'd heard first from Sarge and again yesterday from Grace.

This is the worst yet. The flame seems to have gone out, you see, and that's the pain I can't bear. I've come to the point that I can't keep putting my heart and soul into an effort that seems more and more futile. This impotence, this self-doubt, is corrosive. I hate what it's doing to me.

The law had seen it as despondency over failed hopes, an embarrassing problem with "manhood." Ariel had wondered if there might also be an allusion to child abuse. The truth was that John Barron had indeed been depressed about his work, as the next paragraph would have made clear. He'd feared that his doubts were poisoning his mind. He was beginning to be suspicious of his wife.

Grace had counted on a good two-year stint to establish herself as a devoted wife. She didn't make it through the first winter.

She told about a trip John had taken, driving Halley to a church retreat in North Carolina. He'd planned to return the following day. She invited Cross over, but John returned early. Grace wasn't still in bed with her lover. A half-full ashtray on the nightstand, however, left no doubt about his recent presence.

John Barron was a proud man. Made a figure of pity by a faithless first wife, he wasn't about to forgive the second. The divorce would be handled discreetly, he said. Once he could inform his daughter personally, he would begin proceedings.

In the meantime, he removed himself to his studio, where he worked into the night, sleeping on a cot there. A strained day passed. Then John got a call. Halley had the flu; she was on her way home.

The lovers were ready. While John was at the train station fetching his daughter, Cross slipped into the studio and rigged the propane heater there. Then he and Grace waited.

That night John went once again to lose himself in work. From a third-floor window, Grace looked down into his studio, watching as he uncovered the easel, turned on the heater, and warmed his hands. After a few moments of studying the canvas, he drew the curtains closed and, presumably, began to paint.

John had suffered for years from migraines. When he began to experience the symptoms of carbon monoxide poisoning, Grace imagined, he'd have blamed the onset of one of his sickening headaches. The lethal, odorless gas quickly filled the small room. When John lost consciousness, Grace and Cross were there, she to open the windows and he to readjust the heater and carry John to his car, idling in the closed garage. There, without ever regaining consciousness, John Barron died.

What then took place troubled Ariel a great deal.

According to Grace, once Cross had performed his function, he'd made himself scarce and, later, when he'd found out she wouldn't be a wealthy widow, he'd made himself invisible. Ariel figured, rather, that once he'd performed his function, he'd outlived his usefulness.

She visualized the scene. Grace producing the gun. Cross stunned, disbelieving. She fires once. Her superfluous lover falls. Then she wipes the gun clean, presses it into her dead husband's hand, and holds his finger on the trigger while she fires a second time. There are only two things left to do, and they take no time at all. She goes into John's studio to wash her hands and to place the suicide note where it can't be missed.

Why, Ariel worried, had Grace lied about Cross? And why, come to think of it, had Halley not seen his body?

Halley. Awakened—Ariel now knew, by gunshots—to descend into nightmare.

By the time Grace came to relate the girl's grisly discovery, her voice had lost all inflection. It was, Ariel believed, because the conclusion was spoken with such utter flatness that it so chilled her.

"Something," Grace told them, "woke Halley. I've never . . . I don't know what. She was ill, feverish with flu and lightheaded. She crept down the stairs. She couldn't find her father. Then she smelled the fumes, and she went down, and she found him.

"It's unfortunate that the girl was there that night. I can't answer for what might have happened if she'd come into the garage just a few minutes earlier."

47

IT WAS JUST BEFORE 8 A.M. IN LOS ANGELES. ARIEL PAID THE CABBIE and hefted her bags. She could hear Stonewall barking before she reached her door. When she unlocked it, the little yellow dog made one of his marathon leaps into her arms, his welcome a deluge. If Jessie'd had the time of day, she wouldn't have given it. Contrarily, her tail fanned the air as she sniffed everything of Ariel within range of her nose and then sniffed the luggage, too. Ariel stood inspection patiently.

"Okay?" she asked. "Can I come in now?" She released her wriggling burden and knelt to stroke the other dog. "Where are your keepers?" Ariel looked around, half expecting to see one or both despite the fact that she'd gotten no answer when she'd called from the airport an hour before.

The house was still. She found a note with her mail and a foot-high stack of catalogs and magazines. "Welcome home," Henry had written. "They haven't eaten yet. They were good. We were good. See you at work." There were two postscripts. The first said "Homemade raisin bread from Marguerite Harris in bread-box," and the second, almost illegibly scribbled, was: "Did you have ants when you left?"

While water heated for coffee and the dogs devoured breakfast, Ariel tried Henry's home phone and got a busy signal. Either he was on it or he hadn't yet changed Call Forwarding.

She made a tour of the house. She saw no ants, and it was evident that Henry had made an effort. The cushions on the sleep sofa Sam had used were upside down with the zippers showing, Ariel's own bed was imaginatively made, and some things were out of their usual place, but all had been left neat. When she saw a single gerbera daisy from her garden plunked into a vase beside her bed, Ariel smiled. She hadn't known until that moment how much she'd been looking forward to seeing Henry.

When she arrived at work, she found her desk buried under a paper snowdrift. The studio was already in high gear, at a pace, it seemed to Ariel, that was faster than she remembered. Even while she greeted coworkers, parrying jokes about her absence, she felt out of step, an echo of the isolation of seven months before when she'd bluffed her way around a job in which she was lost.

Henry wasn't in his office.

For a second, Ariel didn't recognize the woman who was depositing a batch of messages on his desk. Tara Castanera had been a long-haired blonde when Ariel left; now she was a brunette gamine.

"Welcome back . . . again," Tara said, and her lips, pouty by virtue of genetics rather than temperament and pale pink today, curved in a friendly grin.

Tara, Ariel had figured out early on, might look as if she'd just danced off a Vegas stage, but she was no bimbo. Hers was an incisive mind that wasted no time going around corners; she cut straight through, occasionally to the quick.

"He's at a breakfast meeting downtown," she told Ariel. "He said he'd be back by ten, but Charles Kuralt's the guest speaker. Don't count on seeing him before eleven, if then. You look pooped."

"Thanks. Constant time off'll do that to you. If he calls in, I need to talk to him. It's important."

Theo Bell wasn't at his desk. Ariel was just as glad. She wanted time to savor thoughts of that confrontation.

Within an hour she was more or less back in harness, if such could be said of a person with one eye on an empty office and ears peeled for the beep of the phone. Twelve o'clock came and went. Tara had been optimistic; Henry still hadn't returned.

"Don't look at me," the receptionist said in answer to Ariel's query. "I gave him your message when he called in, from the Beverly Hills Hotel, to which he gave Mr. Kuralt a lift. He went on from there to a late lunch date. Tough job, huh?"

Henry's lunch date was hardly the cushy expense-account affair Tara envisioned.

When he'd checked in, he'd learned that a man who said his name was Lacy had called. Now he sat on a park bench in Playa del Rey, a beach suburb south of L.A., eating pork rinds and waiting. He assumed the man he'd called back and arranged to meet actually was Vaughn Lacy.

Whoever he was, he was late and, despite an ocean breeze, Henry was hot. He reminded himself that today was officially the first day of fall, even in Southern California. He looked at his watch, slid sideways to where the shade had shifted, and wondered what Grant Lacy's brother wanted.

Except for a few placid-looking ducks meandering around a muddy canal thirty yards from Henry's bench, the park was almost deserted, unusual in a city where everyone seemed to have a great deal of time on his hands, where no matter the hour, every last inhabitant seemed to be in his car or power walking or sipping caffè latte under sidewalk umbrellas. When Henry had first come to town, he'd wondered whether anyone at all had a job.

He crumpled cellophane and lobbed the bag toward a trash can. Air ball. He got up and dropped it in. An ancient VW Beetle chugged past the park, leaving the street quiet in its wake. A Latino woman stood down by the canal, watching a blond child playing with a toy boat. On the path beyond, a cyclist—helmeted, latex-clad, and looking like a refugee from the Tour de France—fooled with the chain on his bicycle. Otherwise, Henry was alone. He considered whether he should be worried by that.

The man on the phone had sounded hostile. "You've been asking questions about my brother's death," he'd said. "Why?"

"Because I want answers," Henry had replied. "You have any I might be interested in?"

The man had pointed out that the cops seemed satisfied that nothing of a criminal nature had taken place. From what he'd heard, they were ready to drop the investigation for lack of evidence.

"I'm not," Henry had said.

He shifted again on the now totally sun-washed bench. The cyclist had pedaled off. The woman was being approached by a man who looked like a vagrant, and she was backing away, chattering and smiling nervously. She grabbed the child's hand and the boat and they left. The vagrant started toward Henry's bench, unsteadily.

"Heller?" The voice came from directly behind him. Vaughn Lacy came around the end of the bench and stood looking down at Henry through mirrored sunglasses.

"You're late," Henry commented, and resisted the impulse to stand. The sun was behind Lacy, blinding Henry. He leaned back unconcernedly, crossing one long leg over the other and angling himself so that the other man's head blocked the glare. "What can I do for you, Mr. Lacy?"

"You can tell me what your interest is in my brother's death."

The vagrant had come to a stop, weaving. He must have read refusal in the men's body language, for he shuffled away.

"I'm not altogether sure," Henry said, "that it's his *death* I'm interested in."

The permanent creases between Vaughn Lacy's eyes deepened to furrows. He was older than Grant, Henry knew, and the lean, dark intensity that had lent the younger sibling a kind of offbeat magnetism was gaunt soberness in the older.

"But just for the record, where were you when he died?"

For several seconds Lacy didn't react. Then, very quietly, he said, "I didn't drive up here to be jerked around, Heller."

"Why did you drive up here?"

"I *am* interested in Grant's death. If it wasn't an accident, if you know something the police don't . . ." Lacy's shirt was wet with perspiration, but he crossed his arms as if he were cold. With his thumb, he began to knead his biceps. "Do you?"

"I'll get to that. You didn't answer me: where were you?"

"The police know where I was."

Henry kept his eyes on Lacy's sunshades. The reflective convex lenses made him feel as if he were talking to a giant fly. "Do you know a man named Richard Cummings?"

"Who?"

"You do or you don't?"

"I don't. What's he got to do with Grant?"

"My show considered doing a piece when your brother disappeared. Cummings was the producer. Right after he backed off the story—told us it was a dead end—he came into money. Quit his job. Moved out of town."

"So?"

"So he misled us about some things. One of them was a call from somebody who purported to have information. That was just *before* he came into money."

"A call from who?"

"I don't know."

"A man or a woman?"

"I don't know that, either."

"You think whoever it was offered him money?"

"I think he *took* the money."

Henry couldn't see Lacy's eyes, but the man's prolonged stillness suggested deliberation. "I don't know . . ." he eventually said.

"I do. Do you know anything about the circumstances of your brother's death that would've warranted paying somebody off?"

Lacy shook his head. "Have you told the cops about this?"

"Nope."

"Why not?"

"I'm not especially interested in publicizing that a newsman, a newsman who worked on my show, was bought."

"But if it keeps them from dropping—"

"You obviously have some suspicions, Mr. Lacy. I'd like to hear them."

"That's all they are—suspicions. I'd hoped that you . . ."

Henry waited.

"Listen, Heller, is there such a thing as 'off the record' with you? That I can depend on?"

Henry watched his own mouth move, reflected in the sunglasses, when he said, "There's no record to be off at this point."

"Okay, it's Betty." Brooding, Vaughn Lacy sat. "There're things about Betty that make me wonder." The man clearly intended to work up to whatever he had to say and, despite the fact that Henry could feel sweat dripping down his back, he didn't hurry him.

"Grant was always . . . different. He probably shouldn't have married, not somebody like her. Social." He glanced at Henry, who nodded. "Likes money. Yachting parties. Doesn't give a damn about art unless it's connected to some charity affair. When Grant was buried in some project, gone night and day, you can bet she didn't sit and twiddle her thumbs."

"She wasn't happy?"

"The old story. Woman marries a man because he treats her like a queen and, in her case, because he made the kind of money to keep her like one. Then she resents it when he spends his time making it and resents it even more when he risks—"

Abruptly, Lacy interrupted himself to say, "My brother was a child emotionally, with the brainpower of somebody who'd lived a dozen lives, getting more brilliant with every one of them. You've probably heard he had a big ego? It was all about his mind, this uncanny machine that was his brain, what it could do. You've read about the running? The obsession with running? It was when 'all the synapses clicked,' he said. When he 'connected with the power of the universe.'

"The universe! He didn't know how to function on this planet! Money meant nothing to him. It was a side effect, a necessary evil to keep his toy shop running. He had no more idea how to function in a cutthroat business world than . . ." Lacy took off the sunglasses and dug at red eyes impatiently. "I don't know where he came from. Our family was ordinary. I'm ordinary. Grant was an innocent. He had no . . . armor."

"You were saying something about his wife?"

"When Grant met Betty, he had no experience with women. He'd been a nerdy kid. Betty was pretty and popular. He couldn't believe it when she wanted to go out with him." Fidgeting, Lacy said, "See, he didn't understand how the rules had changed. He didn't get how irresistible the money and the power made him. To Betty, I imagine, he was this wealthy, mysterious, intriguing Heathcliff type. To him, she was an exotic flower. Prized. He'd give her anything. He *did.* A life most people would envy."

"If she didn't like her life, why didn't she get a divorce? She would've gotten half your brother's estate."

"Yes, well . . ." Henry watched Lacy weigh his words. If anguish had impelled him to talk, he wasn't ready to drop his guard entirely. "She'll be getting *everything* with him dead, including insurance and, more importantly, MicroStar. Sole ownership."

"You haven't said what it is that's bothering you about her."

"I was at their place a lot those first days when we thought Grant was missing. Betty was worried, I could see that. But I began to sense it was *nervous* worry. She wasn't worried about where he *was*. I'd swear to that. I'll tell you what else I'd swear to: she knew he was dead!"

It was Henry's turn to be let down by the other man's less than solid evidence. He was mulling over Betty Lacy's alibi, the confirmed, lengthy phone conversation Marge had told him about, when Lacy spoke up again.

"If I saw any way she could've been involved in Grant's death, I'd be talking to the cops, not you."

"Umm," Henry said. "Tell me, did you ever see any sign that your sister-in-law and Clifford Gilroy were . . . friendly?"

"Cliff? And Betty? No. I never even saw them together—I mean, talking exclusively to each other—until yesterday. When you left the wake."

"What were they saying?"

"I don't know. I asked what the trouble was—asked who you were—and Betty just said you were from the press and that you'd snuck in. It was one of our people, Claudia Wynn, who told me your name and said you'd been asking questions all over the place."

"Where was Gilroy the night your brother died?" Henry asked.

"At MicroStar. Security saw him go into his office early evening. Didn't see him come out. The cops found him asleep on the sofa there before dawn, when they were looking for Grant."

"Does Gilroy often work all night?"

"Cliff's ambitious. As consumed by the business in his own way as Grant was. He lives alone. He could keep any kind of hours."

Henry chewed that over. "Why was your brother in the area where he was hit, do you know? Why would he run down there when he had all those nice residential streets near his house?"

"The cops asked that, and I don't know the answer. Because there's not a lot of traffic there that time of night? And he could run on pavement? Who knows?" Lacy paced away from the bench and back. He made several trips. "He did know the area."

"How's that?"

"We've got an old warehouse not far from where the train . . . Where Grant was hit is maybe a mile away. Two miles tops."

"Did you mention that to the cops?"

"It's one of the ones we've shut down. I didn't think of where it was until now."

Henry felt the first embryonic stirring of his radar. "Can we go there?"

"What for?"

"Humor me."

Lacy glanced at his watch. "I've got a four-thirty appointment, but the warehouse isn't far out of my way." He gave Henry the address. "I'll meet you there in case we get separated in traffic."

They hadn't gone a block before Henry lost sight of Lacy's car in a logjam created by a fleet of movie equipment trucks, gigantic lights and wind machines, loitering technicians—and rubberneckers, the people who on any other day would've been hanging around the park. A policeman was directing traffic, and Lacy got waved through first. Nevertheless, Henry was the first to arrive at the cinder-block warehouse thirty or so minutes south.

It was padlocked and deserted and looked as if it had been for some time. The huge masonry yard next door was bustling. Henry was idly watching double-load cement trucks bump, churn, and grind about their deafening business when Lacy showed up.

"How come you're not using this place?" Henry asked while the other man fiddled with a ring of keys.

"Our stuff goes by truck now, not rail." Lacy tried a key that didn't work. "We put it up for sale a year ago."

"A year ago," Henry repeated thoughtfully. "How far off would I be in guessing MicroStar needed a little cash infusion right about then?"

Lacy glanced up but didn't answer. He tried another key.

"Your brother was reputed to be worth somewhere in the neighborhood of thirty million and yet he was selling off his assets. Warehouses, his yacht, his art collection, whatever he could liquidate. I'm wondering, if the house hadn't been in Betty's name, would she still be living there?"

Lacy dropped his eyes and, without replying, inserted another key. The door squealed open.

The building was cavernous and hot, and the dim light filtering through high, cobwebbed windows did little to dispel the gloom. Except for piles of debris here and there, it appeared to be empty.

"There's nothing to see here," Lacy said, and his voice echoed.

Just then he spied a stack of cartons in a far corner. He frowned. "I thought this place had been cleared out."

He moved purposefully away, and Henry strolled toward the opposite end of the building, poking his head into a defunct office, windowless and grubby. A telephone sat on a water-stained carpet, waiting for calls that no longer came in.

Next door was a rest room and, beside that, a broom closet. A last door, closed, hid nothing but a completely empty room that had probably been a second office. Henry's stomach sank, but his blip was still humming. It was a contradiction in signals he didn't often experience.

Lacy appeared at his side. "Somebody screwed up leaving that merchandise here. I'm surprised it still *is* here." He glanced around. "You ready to go?"

Henry shook his head and pushed the door all the way open. "When did you stop using this place?" he asked.

"I told you, last year."

"Why would you have had this room painted?"

"We didn't." Even as he said it, Lacy's nose twitched as he, too, caught the faint scent of paint. He moved as if to step into the room, but Henry held out a restraining hand. They scrutinized the walls, clean and unblemished, and the floor, dirty chipped linoleum.

"What happened to the carpet?" Lacy muttered to himself.

"Would you know about it if, for any reason, work was done here?"

"I'm in charge of distribution. That includes the warehouses."

"Who has access to this place?"

"Access? My assistant has keys. Grant did, so I suppose Betty. Cliff. The real estate broker. Me, obviously."

"Where are you going from here?"

"Back to work. Why?"

Henry shook his head. "I'm not sure. Give me a few minutes to think."

48

ARIEL WAS IN A SNIT. EVERY TIME SHE PASSED HENRY'S EMPTY office throughout the afternoon, she got more disgruntled, more anxious, and (she acknowledged it) more hurt. The man, she thought, must be on some sort of eating binge. First a marathon breakfast, then (after a tough hour or two swapping war stories with Charles Kuralt, for Pete's sake) he was off to the world's longest lunch. Where was he now? Tea? She looked at her watch. By now he might be having predinner drinks.

Her intercom buzzed. "Mr. Heller on three," Tara announced.

Ariel stabbed the button. "Henry! Where are you? Why haven't you—" She heard the unmistakable jangle of a cash register and, in the background, the even more unmistakable sound of Patsy Cline falling mournfully to pieces. "Are you in a bar?"

"Give me thirty seconds, lady, and I'll be all done, okay?" Henry said, apparently not to her; then, "Do me a favor, Ariel, will you? I'm tied up, and I need Sam picked up."

Before Ariel could utter a word, she heard a distinctly feminine giggle and then "Whoops!" Henry's "Hey! Careful with that!" was muffled, but "So, can you do it, Ariel?" was all too clear.

Ariel's ears went hot enough to singe hair. "Are you drunk?"

"I don't have time to explain. I need you to do this for me."

"You need . . . !" Through the red haze of fury, Henry's urgency penetrated. "Where are you?" she said. "What's wrong?"

"Nothing's wrong. It's the Lacy business, maybe a breakthrough. I'll tell you about it if it works out. So will you? Pick up the boy at his mother's?"

"Listen to me! You were right about Richard Cummings. I don't know who or why, but he admitted to blackmailing somebody. Whatever you're doing, you'd better be careful. Henry? Did you hear me?"

For seconds Ariel heard only tinny music and noise; then, sputtering, Henry said, "When did you . . . ? How . . . ?"

"And, Henry, if getting Cummings is still your motivation in this, you can let it go. I'm afraid he's dead."

"Dead? Dead how? Dead when? What are you talking about?"

"He was killed. In Charleston. Late last night."

"In Charles . . . Killed by who? Somebody connected with Lacy was in South Carolina?"

"No. It wasn't anybody from here, and it was an accident. Why don't you—"

"Ariel! He didn't say *anything* about who he was hitting on? Did he say 'he'? Did he say 'she'? Anything?"

"Just said 'my friend.' "

"And you have no idea what he had? What he knew?"

"I'm sorry."

Abruptly, Henry said, "Then I'll find out," and he was rattling off what Ariel took to be Emily's address. "I'll see you at your house later. Thanks." He was gone.

Ariel stuffed the address into her purse and hurried to Tara's desk.

"Did he say where he was calling from?" she demanded of Tara, who raised the eyebrow she was deftly penciling and gave an exaggerated "pardon me" blink.

"He did not. However, before he called you, he called Freddy. You might want to storm back there and interrogate him."

Ariel was already on her way to the equipment room, but she was too late. The cameraman was on his way to pick up Perc, a sound and light man. An assignment from Henry, she was told.

The condominium building was very nice, and Emily's garden unit looked well kept, if a little short on the "garden" part. In the planter beside the front door one leggy geranium struggled in hard-baked soil. Ariel was reaching for the doorbell when Sam opened the door.

"Where's Dad?" the boy asked through the screen.

"Sam, hi! You recognize me, right? Ariel Gold? Nice to see you. Unfortunately, Henry's tied up, so here I am instead." Ariel had the awful feeling that she sounded like a cruise social director. "I told him I'd pick you up. He'll see you at my house later, he said."

"Why can't I just wait here for him?"

"You could." Ariel adjusted her handbag on her shoulder. "But I'll bet you're hungry. We'll stop on the way and get the makings for dinner. Okay? You want to grab your things?"

Sam visibly wavered. "Yeah, okay." He padded away into the recesses of the condo only to return seconds later. "You wanna come in?" he mumbled and pushed open the screen door. To judge by his conversational gambit, he was even less at ease than Ariel. "Stonewall," he said, "is kind of a wiener, isn't he?"

Ariel stepped inside, grinning. "He's a wiener, all right." She noticed the piano. "You play, I hear."

Sam nodded and crammed a couple of books into a knapsack. "I gotta get my shoes and stuff," he said and left the room.

"You practice every day?" Ariel called out to silence. She shifted her feet, sighed, and wandered to the piano. Softly, she pressed middle C. Her fingers hovered over the keys and then stretched into a chord. She sat down, brought her left hand to join her right, and, haltingly, began to play.

"Für Elise," said Sam from behind her, and she gasped and hit a clinker so jarring they both cringed. "You're not very good, are you?"

"Terrible." She gave the satiny wood of the piano a little pat. "But, then, I didn't know I could play at all."

"I don't get it."

"Henry didn't tell you?"

"Huh?"

"I'm amnesic."

Sam's eyes widened. "No way! Fantastic! You, like, don't remember who you are?"

Ariel laughed. It seemed she was transformed from just another boring adult into an object of interest. "That about covers it."

"You *do* know who you are, though," Sam challenged. "I

thought when people got amnesia they forgot their names and everything."

"Let's go. I'll tell you more than you ever wanted to know about memory loss on the way."

While Ariel had been driving to fetch Sam, Henry had been pushing his old Oldsmobile beyond even its usual long-suffering limits, racing back to the warehouse.

Ariel's news had thrown him. As curious as he was about Cummings's demise, he was more concerned; what the devil had he been doing in Charleston? And how had he known Ariel was there? He must still have been on somebody's payroll, somebody who'd found out what she'd seen. Whom she'd seen. And Cummings, just across the state line in Georgia, had been handy to see whether she was anything to worry about. Did "somebody" now know that she posed no danger?

Henry almost turned around on the spot, but it was too late; tonight's scheme had been set in motion. Vaughn Lacy would by now have made two phone calls: one to his sister-in-law and one to Clifford Gilroy.

"Call no earlier than six," Henry had requested, knowing it would take time to contact a camera crew and have them drive the unpredictable freeway south. "Say you happened to pass by here and see a car, somebody poking around. They know you saw me yesterday, right? Say you think it was me. Ask why I'd be sneaking around, what could I be looking for . . . that kind of thing. Okay?

"Don't tell either one that you've called the other, and make it casual. Act curious, not suspicious; will you do that?"

Once Lacy had left for MicroStar, Henry had his own calls to make, much easier intended than done.

The abandoned telephone in the warehouse was dead as a carp. Next door—at Gibraltar Masonry & Ready Mix Plant, according to the sign—a salesman was glued to the only phone in sight, yelling to be heard over the ear-splitting racket. The nearest public phone turned out to be two miles away and there, in the marginally less noisy depths of a smoke-hazed dive called Jazzbo's, Henry had set things up with Freddy. Then he'd called Luzzatto.

He could imagine what she'd think of his hotdogging this

thing—of what she'd think of the whole plan—but something shifty had gone on in that office, too close to where Grant Lacy was hit to be unconnected. Henry was betting a few hours of his time and some *Open File* budget that he'd turned up a murder scene, and that the killer would return to it. That he, or she, would get nervous about what might have been overlooked. Would take the bait and show up tonight.

It had taken long, aggravating minutes (while staving off a tipsy female anxious to call somebody named "Sweet Thing") to establish that the detective was out on a call. So be it, Henry had thought. He'd get his pigeon on tape, and then he'd get the cops involved. If there was anything at all in that bare room, Forensics would find it.

Henry had been hanging up when he remembered his son.

Now, fretting over Ariel's bombshell, praying that Vaughn Lacy hadn't jumped the gun and that no one had come and gone in his absence, he made the last turn. He was feeling a familiar excitement.

Henry was something of a cowboy, he'd freely admit it. He could go all year without another UFO sighting, another hung jury piece, another man's-inhumanity-to-man horror story that made his gut churn with impotence. *This* was the sort of challenge he thrived on. He was feeling so good that he realized how lousy he'd *been* feeling lately.

A flatbed truck rattled by in a cloud of dust; then the road was empty. The sun had set, but it seemed to have gotten hotter rather than cooler, and a wind had kicked up, a dry, agitated Santa Ana. Blinking away sweat, Henry cruised slowly abreast of the warehouse. The parking lot was vacant.

He parked next door, concealed by the Gibraltar showroom. Listening to the restless *ping-pingle-ping* of his cooling motor and then to silence broken only by the wind, he scarfed tepid coffee and pickled eggs he'd grabbed at Jazzbo's. Gibraltar's security lights snapped to life, startling Henry, but all remained still in the yellow glow.

It would have been just about this time of day when Grant Lacy (or his dead body) had ended up a mile or more down the rail line. Henry could see the tracks from where he sat. Because it had been December then, it would have been fully dark and, he reckoned, as forsaken as it was right now.

Digging through the backseat debris, he located sneakers he'd last worn for a pickup baseball game with Sam and some of his buddies. He changed shoes, picked out a stack of wooden pallets from behind which he could see the road, and hunkered down to wait.

Time dragged. The wind blew cement dust into Henry's face and began to annoy him a lot. He fretted about where his crew was and wished he had something else to eat. Before long his thoughts strayed back to what he'd been thinking about in the car: the unusual malaise he'd been feeling.

It wasn't a feeling he could remember having had before, and it had been with him to one degree or another for the last week or so, for about the same length of time Ariel had been away. He'd experienced it in her absence, in her house, among her things, and now she was back and it was gone, replaced by—what?

Henry's mind tinkered with the "what." It wasn't the curiosity that nudged him toward his first marriage nor the hormone stew that spurred him to the second nor any "romantic" response he could recall before or since. It certainly wasn't the feeling of duty (and certain doom) that accompanied his union with a pregnant Emily.

He *had* once felt something not unlike this, he realized. He dredged his memory. He'd been a little kid, away from home for the first time and miserably homesick. The ache of loneliness had been much the same. So was the anticipation as the last day of camp had drawn near and, at long last, dawned.

Get a grip, putz! he told himself.

The image of Ariel was jarred from his mind as he felt and then heard the rumble of an approaching freight. The single headlight pierced the gloom, and seconds later the train thundered by, sixty feet from where Henry skulked. Car after car passed, clanking and rumbling and striking sparks on the rails. The pallets beside Henry clattered their answering vibration, cement dust filled his nostrils, and the earth shuddered in the behemoth's wake. The weight and devastating power were unimaginable. What they would do to a human body was unthinkable.

The train disappeared into the night, and a long time passed before Henry saw a pair of headlights. They grew brighter, and he found himself gritting his teeth in frustration as a Mercedes nosed its way into the MicroStar parking lot. Where, he fumed, was the camera crew? The car stopped, and for long minutes, no one got out.

Henry expected to see Clifford Gilroy emerge; he was surprised to see Betty Lacy. She hesitated beside her car, and the wind riffled her blond hair as she surveyed the building, the lot, the street. Then, warily, she approached the entrance.

Henry, too, scanned the street; there was no sign of the *Open File* van. He fidgeted while she unlocked the door. When a light came on inside, he left his hiding place and stole to the doorway.

She stood uncertainly, directly under one of the few bulbs that still worked, looking about as though she'd never been there before. She dropped her keys into her bag, and the high-heeled boots she wore clicked and echoed as she walked toward the offices. She glanced into the first before reaching for the closed door of the second. She flipped the light switch and stared into the empty room. Then she went inside. Swiftly and silently, Henry followed.

She was kneeling in the corner when Henry spoke.

"Is that where it happened?"

Betty Lacy gasped, threw out a hand to steady herself, and lurched to her feet.

Henry watched panic round her eyes as the situation was assessed. When she launched herself toward the door, he was ready. He blocked her way, gripping her by the shoulders and dodging her kicks as she struggled.

"Where are you going to run?" he grunted. "Hey, come on, Mrs. Lacy, forget it! It's over!"

The sharp toe of her boot landed squarely on Henry's shin, and he yelped in pain and thrust her away. She fell, landing hard on her backside. Chest heaving, she drew herself up to renew her attack, and then her face crumpled. Her body sagged in defeat.

"People," Henry panted, "will be here any second." He wanted badly to cradle his shin, to dance and hop and howl, but he planted a forearm against either side of the door frame, ready to restrain her if he had to. "So we'll just wait, okay? Till they get here."

When she only continued to cry, Henry took a deep breath and gradually relaxed. He didn't offer to help her up.

"Why don't you tell me what happened? How'd you do it? How'd you kill him?"

Betty Lacy snarled something Henry couldn't understand.

"You want to wait for the cops? Tell them?"

"I didn't!" she cried furiously. Glaring through her tears, she repeated it. "I didn't do anything!"

She made a lunge for her purse, but Henry snagged it with his foot. As he dug through it, finding nothing more dangerous than a nail file, Betty began to shriek at him.

"That's mine!" she cried and slammed the floor with her fist. "What do you want? The same thing as your friend? I'll bet there's no police coming here! You're just Cummings all over again! Bloodsucker! Feeding on people's troubles! Out for anything you can get! How much, bloodsucker? How much will it take to shut you up?"

Henry smiled. "How much did it take for my friend?"

Before the hysterical woman on the floor could do more than hurl another insult, Henry heard a sound from the vast room behind him. He turned, eagerly, expecting to see Freddy and his camera. Clifford Gilroy emerged from the shadows. The man looked badly shocked, and a muscle in his jaw twitched with a life of its own. The gun he held was steady enough.

49

Sam was turning out to be far easier than Ariel had anticipated. She was even enjoying him. He was bright, and his curiosity was relentless. His questions about her reentry into life had been original, if a little startling.

"What if you're allergic to something—like my mom's allergic to shellfish?—but you don't remember it, and you ate it and died?" he wondered. "What if you've still got dry cleaning someplace from before, waiting?" and "How do you know you're not wanted someplace for some crime?"

"Okay . . ." He posed another question obliquely, swallowing the last of the kielbasa Ariel had grilled. "Some things you remembered . . . how to drive and cook and play the piano, sort of. But you forgot everything about work, right? And about when you were young? Weird! What else?" He tried to look analytical. "Did you, for example, still know how to dance? And kiss and things?"

Ariel took his plate. Scraping it over the garbage disposal, she considered what had prompted the last question.

"I haven't had much opportunity to check 'things' out. What about you. Do you know how to kiss?"

"You don't live to be thirteen and not know that," the jaded Sam declared. "You don't have any kids, I guess, or you'd— Hey! What if you did, but you didn't remember—"

"No kids." Ariel smiled. "That much I do know."

"Oh. Well, kids grow up faster now, take it from me. Things are different from when you were young."

"Kissing had been invented even then, you know. I think that predated fire."

"Yeah, but life was easier back then."

Ariel loaded the plate into the dishwasher. She gave Sam a thoughtful look. "I expect you're right about that."

When Sam reached for his CD player, Ariel figured he was bored with sociocultural commentary. He examined the machine intently, as though it had sprouted new buttons since he'd last used it. Casually, he asked, "Were your parents divorced?"

"No."

Sam's head bobbed up and down, and his mouth twisted into a see-what-I-mean grimace. "You guys had, like, the mom that kept house and the dad that came home for dinner, right? The kids and the dog would come running like they hadn't seen him in a week, and then they'd all play Monopoly or something."

Ariel nodded. "Yep. And the moms wore neat little dresses and perfect makeup even at breakfast, and the dads went to work in suits and carried briefcases. That's the way it was, all right."

The irony was lost on Sam. "Yeah, well, almost all my friends' moms and dads are split. I don't know but one whose mom's around—I mean, that doesn't work or anything. Her boyfriend lives there. He doesn't work, either."

Ariel nodded again but refrained from flippant remarks.

"There's this one friend of mine, Eric . . ." Sam hesitated and then, very fast, said, "His dad's the pits. He knocks Eric around." He glanced at Ariel, checking, she thought, to see whether he was believed. "I was over there one time when he did—I saw it—and Eric hadn't even done anything. I mean, nothing! His dad goes, 'Where have you been?' and before Eric could even answer, he went like totally ballistic and slammed Eric into the wall. Then he saw me—he didn't know I was with Eric, see?—and he smiles and goes, 'Hiya, kid,' like he'd been just fooling around or something!"

Ariel was completely out of her depth. "Maybe you got in on the tail end of the story. Maybe Eric had done or said something earlier, and you just saw—"

"No! That's not the way it was, and it's not the first time either.

I've seen bruises. When I think what that jerk would do to Eric if he knew he really *did* do something wrong . . ."

"I think it would be a good idea for you to tell your dad what you've told me, Sam, or your mom."

"Oh, sure! Even if they got involved—which they wouldn't—all that would happen would be to get Eric in worse trouble."

Ariel had a sudden revelation. "It was Eric who stole those CDs, wasn't it?"

The boy's chin dropped and then set sullenly. "*I* took them. I admitted it."

"I see." Ariel wished Henry were there. She looked at the clock and wondered why he wasn't—or hadn't called. Squelching her concern, she asked, "Hey, where'd the dogs go, did you notice?"

Sam clicked his fingers. The signal had brought Stonewall racing to his side several times earlier in the evening, but now neither dog responded.

Ariel found them beside the front door. Jessie was in a voluntary down-stay: forepaws symmetrically aligned, head up, ears antennae. Stonewall sat beside her, in silent communication. He looked from Jessie to Ariel and back again. Jessie just watched the door. Evidently, she associated Sam's presence with Henry's, and she was waiting for the other shoe to drop.

"Is this some kind of instinctive thing?" Ariel whispered. "Do you know something I don't or is it just that old Henry's a sucker for handing out treats?" Both dogs gave full attention to that word, but when there was no action, they lost interest.

Freddy and Perc knew where Henry was.

Ariel went to her study, dialed the studio, and hung up on the recording. Her interoffice directory listed numbers for the three camera vans. Two were no-answers. The third, on the first ring, reaped a relieved-sounding Freddy.

"Henry?"

"Freddy, this is Ariel. Where are you? What's going on?"

"*Man!*" Freddy said, the dam of frustration breaking. "We are *stuck!* We're between off-ramps, we have not *moved* in over an hour, and we weren't exactly making time before that! There's some guy on an overpass up ahead, it said on the radio, with a gun. Threatening suicide and who knows what else, and they've got us blocked. Have you heard from Henry? I don't know how to call him. Do you?"

"Where were you supposed to go?"

Ariel took down the address and asked, "Where are you now?"

"Just west of the one-ten, not eight miles from there!"

"You haven't heard from him since he first called you?"

"Not a peep. We were out of the van for a few minutes—ten, fifteen max—just to grab some burgers. We thought we had time to kill. Then this psycho jumper—"

"Henry knows that number?"

"Oh, yeah."

"Did he say what he wanted you to do? At this warehouse?"

Freddy told her: Go pick up Perc. Bring the M-94, the infrared lens. Hide the van next door. Be there 6:15, latest. (Freddy groaned.) "He said we'd hole up, stay low, and tape any action. And, oh yeah; we might need to stop somebody compromising evidence."

Ariel had a very bad feeling about this whole thing. As she looked for a map, the kielbasa she'd eaten made itself felt.

"Okay," she said. "I've found you." The shortest alternative route looked like a thirty-minute drive. "I'll meet you there," she said. "I'm leaving now."

She grabbed her bag and was already calling Sam's name when she got to the kitchen. She forced a smile. "I have to go out for a while. Stay here till I get back. I'll call you."

"Does this have something to do with Dad?"

Ariel hesitated a second too long.

"I'm going, too."

"What have you told him?"

Clifford Gilroy addressed his question to Betty Lacy, but he didn't take his eyes off Henry while he asked it. Henry didn't take his eyes off the black hole of the gun's muzzle, which was pointed pretty accurately at his heart.

Betty hadn't moved from the floor. She, too, was transfixed by the gun, and she didn't look much happier with its presence than did Henry. When the wind slammed the outer door shut, she—along with both men—jumped. "I haven't told him anything," she said, and swiped at tears with her knuckle. "What have you got that for?"

"I heard him ask about Cummings." Gilroy's voice was tight. In his expensive suit and Brooks Brothers button-down, he looked as if he should be chairing a meeting, not waving a gun. Actually, the gun wasn't being waved; it was steady.

His tie had some kind of ducks on it, mallards. Henry didn't want to be shot by a man with ducks on his tie. Henry didn't want to be shot.

"What did you tell him?" Gilroy pressed. "What have you gone and said this time!"

Henry cut across Betty's protest. "The lady's telling the truth," he began before he, too, was cut off.

"What are you *doing* here, Betty? Did you bring him? Or . . ." Gilroy shook his head impatiently. "You!" he said to Henry. "Vaughn said he saw you here. Trespassing. What are you after?"

"Why don't you point that thing somewhere less personally important to me, and I'll tell you."

"Cliff," Betty said tentatively. She'd pushed herself erect and was gingerly massaging her bruised coccyx. "You don't need a gun, do you? This man probably just wants money, too; otherwise, why wouldn't he have—"

"Would you for once trust me and shut up? He's going to tell us what he wants."

The nuances of this conversation had begun to penetrate Henry's stupefied brain. The lady sounded ready to swap cash for his absence, and Gilroy seemed willing to listen. He didn't look bent on using the gun. But it was still trained on Henry's sternum, at a distance too close to miss, and Gilroy was nervous. Sweating. Henry knew more people died at the hands of panicked shooters than cold-blooded ones. The knowledge wasn't a comfort.

Any number of responses flitted through his mind in the time it took to wet his lips. "We've got a misunderstanding here," he said, "and we can all agree that we don't want to make things worse. Now, there're some people on their way. Police and people from my show, with a camera. You don't want to be pointing—"

"I don't believe that, frankly. As for police, I got word late this afternoon. Their investigation, a formality, at any rate, is being dropped. I don't know what bull you may think you know, but there's nothing *to* know. You've been hanging around an empty warehouse for nothing."

"You make a good point. It *is* empty, isn't it? Cleaned out, slick as a whistle, and cleaned up, too. Even painted, in spots."

For no longer than a heartbeat, Gilroy glanced at the room behind Betty. He shifted his shoulders in the fine suit jacket and wiped his free palm against the pants. It was plain that he was a man with a dilemma. If he let Henry walk, he let anything Henry knew walk with him and, clearly, Henry knew something. If he acted too concerned, he gave away that there was reason to be. He opted to try a little damage control.

"Okay, Heller. Obviously, we know Cummings. With nothing more than vicious, half-baked suspicions, your ex-colleague saw a way to line his pockets. We figured he was less expensive than a battery of lawyers. We made a mistake, but with a man who's so low as to use the rantings of a grief-stricken woman—"

"Cliff—"

Gilroy held up his hand, an order to keep quiet. "We're the victims here. Of extortion. If this Gold woman on your staff was there, she knows that."

"Cummings told you about her?"

"Insisted she was trouble, that she'd cause me trouble. For yet another 'installment,' he went to see about her."

"Who told him?"

Gilroy shrugged, disinterested. "Somebody he called after she called him asking questions. I think Cummings exaggerates. She hasn't done anything at all, has she? Then or now."

"What does 'seeing about her' consist of?"

"I can't be held accountable for what vermin like Cummings might do. The point is, I've committed no crime here; he has."

Henry said nothing. Meaningfully, he let his eyes trail down to the gun.

Gilroy hesitated, calculating. The gun barrel, ever so slightly, dropped. Just then a swath of light cut through the high, grimy windows of the warehouse, sweeping across the rafters. All three heard the sound of an automobile motor.

"Cliff, he wasn't lying!" Betty ran to Gilroy's side and gripped his free arm.

"Who is that, Heller? Who's out there?"

"What are you going to do?" Betty cried as Gilroy eyed the gun he'd reflexively whipped back up. He looked as if he didn't know whether to fire it or wish it away.

As suddenly as the car had arrived, it reversed and departed. Someone had merely been using the parking lot for a turnaround.

Betty whimpered and buried her face in Gilroy's shoulder. "I can't take this anymore, Cliff! After him, who? With their dirty minds and their hands out? Why don't you just tell him the truth!"

Henry began to edge toward the door.

Betty was clutching Gilroy's lapels, her voice rising. "You asked why I came here? To see! I came to see for myself where it happened. To know if I could trust you. If I could *feel* the truth! I can't! So why don't you tell us *both* about that night? I need to hear it again!"

She'd begun to pound his chest with her fists, and Gilroy struggled to extricate himself. "Get hold of yourself!" he was pleading as she cried, "Can I believe you? Cummings didn't, but he didn't care. I do! So tell me again, Cliff! Is that the gun? His gun? Is that what really happened? Is it?"

"Betty, for the love of—" Just then, Gilroy caught Henry's movement. "Hold it!" he ordered, trying desperately to twist toward Henry, who by now was sprinting.

The shot was muffled by Betty's body, but it was loud enough to reverberate endlessly through the vast empty building and to stop Henry in his tracks.

Both men stared, horror-struck. Irrationally, Henry started toward the wounded woman. She cried out once, weakly, in surprise. Interminable seconds passed while she maintained a grip on Gilroy's coat, her lips opened as if to speak. She'd still said nothing when one hand and then the other lost strength, and she slid down his body. Gilroy reached for her, calling her name. He saw the trail of blood smeared down his shirt and froze.

"Betty?" he said. His head snapped up, and he screamed at Henry. "You did this!"

Henry dived straight for the other man's midsection, ramming his shoulder into Gilroy's gut. Gilroy deflated like a beach ball and folded double. Both men hit the floor. Henry got a knee down, braced himself against Gilroy's chest, and put everything he had behind a fist to the jaw. It hurt like hell. When he drew back and did it again, he didn't even feel the pain.

He scrambled to his feet, saw Gilroy's empty hand, and, frantically, looked about for the gun. He hadn't heard it land. Where, he thought wildly, could it have gone in a practically empty room? How far could it have flown?

Seconds ticked by, too fast. Gilroy was stirring. Henry was pawing through a pile of trash when he heard a groan, saw that Gilroy was trying to get up. He considered clobbering him again, but his hand was throbbing like blue blazes. He made for the exit.

When he reached the rear of the building next door, he stopped dead. Directly behind his car was a white Jaguar that hadn't been there earlier. The hood of his own car stood open in a giant yawn.

Gilroy had taken precautions.

Henry pushed wind-whipped hair from his eyes and wasted precious time peering at his motor. The light was too poor to see what had been tampered with. If it had been high noon, Henry wasn't sure he'd know what had been tampered with, and the car was blocked in anyway. He tried the other car; it was locked.

His first thought was to start running, to hightail it down the road as fast as his long legs could take him. Two things changed his mind: the Jaguar, ready to roll and a whole lot faster than his legs, and the faint sound of leather on gravel.

Jump him! Henry thought, but he was already backing into the shadow of the Gibraltar building. What if Gilroy had found the gun? His back hit brick. Dreading every crackle of the loose rocks under his feet, he sidled along the wall. A Dumpster was between him and the cars when he heard Gilroy round the building. Henry stopped where he stood.

Gilroy, too, had stopped. Henry couldn't see him, but he could hear the other man breathing: a raspy, ugly sound.

"Heller? Come out, Heller. Let's talk. You saw what happened. You saw it wasn't my fault. None of this is! I've got nothing against you. I had nothing against Grant, but I couldn't let him ruin me. Destroy me. I've worked too hard. You can see that. You would if you knew the facts. Come on. I'll tell you—all of it." The voice was stretched thin, and desperate. Gilroy, Henry thought, was near the end of self-control and losing ground.

After a moment the footsteps resumed. The Jag's door was unlocked and opened; Henry could tell that the dome light had come on. When the door closed again, a stronger light came on.

"Hey, Heller!"

The end of the building to Henry's right was illuminated in the beam of what he figured must be a powerful flashlight.

"I thought you were so hot to know what happened! Or was Betty . . ." Gilroy faltered. "Was Betty right? You want money? Is that it? I've got money."

The beam moved left, toward the area Henry faced, slow and thorough. A plastic bottle, buffeted by the hot wind, scraped across its path. The beam jumped to the MicroStar building, to the railroad tracks. Gravel crunched as Gilroy walked away, but Henry knew it would be only minutes or less before he returned, before that beam would be turned in his direction.

He also knew that Gilroy wouldn't be coming after him if he hadn't found the gun.

Crabwise, Henry crept to the corner, where the fence met the building's outer wall. Except that they didn't quite meet. The end post was wrenched away from the building, and the chain-link mesh was bent inward—backed into, perhaps, by a careless trucker.

Flattening himself against the bricks, he poked a leg through. Wire snagged his jacket and, as he squeezed through the inadequate opening, stabbed into his chest. Henry bent the metal prong away. He stood on his toes, sucked in his breath, and, feeling the pain, crammed himself through.

He was on a dirt surface now, dirt and mud, and his sneakers made little noise as he hurried around the building. The property was enormous, dotted with piles of rocks and pallet after pallet of bricks and concrete blocks. Far down at the end was a tower of some kind. In between, heavy equipment—Caterpillars and giant sweepers—hulked about like some species of mud-encrusted, hibernating mammoth.

The building was padlocked, as were boxcars lined up beside it. Henry spun in desperation; if he could get through that fence opening, so could Gilroy. He darted behind one of the huge machines and crouched; would Gilroy see the opening? Would he try it?

The flashlight, pallid in the distance, swept the area where Henry had entered the lot. Then, unmistakably, came the sound of a car. The light went out. Freddy! Henry thought. Finally!

The car came abreast and kept going. Henry heard a grunt and a curse, and very shortly the light came on again, brighter now, nearer. Gilroy hadn't given up.

"I'll find you, Heller; you know that." Gone was any pretense of friendly relations. "When I do, you're going to pay for Betty."

Gilroy was moving from one mountain of building blocks to another, from machinery to sand and gravel bins, never turning his back on any potential hiding place. He kept up a steady monologue, thinking out loud from the sound of it. "I came here because I heard somebody was snooping around the property. Vaughn will back me on that. I found you trespassing. You attacked me. I was forced to kill in self-defense."

Fleetingly, Henry wondered how Gilroy was going to explain Betty, shot at point-blank range.

The same thought had occurred to Gilroy. "You pushed Betty in front of me," he said. He didn't sound happy with the scenario. Henry heard what might have been a sob and then an angry mutter, unintelligible, whipped away by the wind. The flashlight ranged over the terrain beyond where Henry hid. It lingered on the tall structure he'd spied earlier.

It was a narrow, vertical shed a good eighty or ninety feet high, taller than the silo that abutted it and only slightly wider. A long pylon-supported ramp zigzagged from the ground clear up to the shed's roof. The thing must have been over two hundred feet long. Henry had only a vague idea what the whole rigmarole was for.

"Would you look at that!" Gilroy said to himself and raised his voice to make sure Henry could hear. "You know how that baby operates, Heller? I do. I drove a cement truck one summer, working my way through school. They call that a 'batch plant.' They dump sand and gravel and cement in there. By the end of the day the weigh hopper's pretty empty. A forty-foot drop. I'll just escort you up there, why don't I? You might die when you hit. If you don't, tons of sand and gravel pouring down on you tomorrow will fix the problem. I can get Betty up there." His voice dropped. "I can do that. I can fix that problem, too."

Moving low to the ground, Henry had been darting from cover to cover. He was upwind of Gilroy, but the next time or the next he was bound to be heard. He couldn't keep retreating forever. He looked at the luminous dial of his watch, astonished to see that only fifteen minutes had passed since Gilroy's arrival, since things had spiraled out of control.

Gilroy muttered an obscenity. From the sucking sound that followed, Henry figured the other man had stepped into one of many mud puddles. He sounded steadier when he spoke again—meaner.

"Let me tell you what happens to the sand and gravel and cement, Heller. It's loaded into trucks, all fed into their tanks. Those tanks have fins, and those fins are kept sharp; they can churn up tons of material—tons!

"The train did a good job on Grant. Those trucks will do as good a job on you and Betty. You'll be pulverized." As if it might be a consolation, he said, "You might be part of an important building someday."

Gilroy was getting closer. He was no more than forty feet away, and Henry was weighing his options. He tried to flex his swollen hand; he wished he hadn't. Charging his stalker was a last resort, way down on the list. Betty Lacy's anguished face was too fresh in his mind to chance a close encounter with the gun. He simply couldn't make himself do it.

The shed Gilroy called a batch plant was twenty feet in the other direction. After what Gilroy had described in such blood-curdling detail, he'd never expect Henry to head there. If he could get there, Henry thought, if he could get inside and secure the door, he was home free.

There wasn't much cover between him and the shed. He scooped up a handful of gravel and, forcing his fingers to work, threw it as far as he could away from the shed. The rocks struck something hard. Gilroy whipped around and dropped into a crouch. Hugging what cover there was, Henry scuttled to the shed. He slid the corrugated tin door shut.

If there was anything to secure it, it wasn't attached. In the pitch black, Henry groped for a lock, a plank, anything. Squatting, he cast about on the floor. He felt something damp and spongy and nasty—no stick, no rock, no weapon.

There was only one thing to do and, pasting himself to the wall beside the door, Henry braced himself to do it.

The door was slammed aside. The damned demonic flashlight scoured the small enclosure: the walls, a large cone hanging from the floor above, an open iron staircase. The doorway remained empty.

"You're being so cooperative," Gilroy said from outside. "Now the only place to go is up."

When he came in, he came fast, pivoting in a tight arc toward the side where Henry waited. Henry brought both arms down hard. They made contact with a forearm, and the flashlight flipped into the air. In the same instant, there was a shattering explosion as deafening as it was blinding. The bullet sheared metal somewhere behind Henry and ricocheted, the most terrifying sound he'd ever heard. Every cell in his body flinched, and his eyeballs felt seared. Seeing little but white glare, blinking, he raised his arms again. Gilroy was blinking, too, rapidly, but he had the gun trained on Henry's abdomen. He raised the muzzle as he retrieved the flashlight.

"The stairs are behind you," he said. "Let's climb."

50

TWENTY-SIX MINUTES EXACTLY FROM THE TIME ARIEL LEFT HER DRIVEway, the van was barreling down the road that led to the MicroStar warehouse. She had more than one passenger. Jessie, in a rare display of outright disobedience, had bolted out the door ahead of Sam and scratched to be let into the van. Ariel hadn't taken the time to reprimand or argue.

"Should be that next block," she told Sam as they passed what appeared to be a graveyard for school buses. "Keep your eyes peeled for his car or the *Open File* van."

It remained to be seen what she'd do if the vehicles were there—other than to chew Henry out for worrying her.

"That's it on the left!" Sam exclaimed. Ariel cut her headlights and slowed to a crawl. Parked in front of the warehouse was a sleek, new-looking car. It definitely wasn't Henry's. The door of the building stood open, and weak light spilled out onto the car's hood.

"I don't see the van," Sam said.

"Henry told them to park behind the building next door," Ariel remembered and said. "That one there: Gibraltar . . . whatever that sign said." She cruised past it.

"Masonry and something."

"Right. I expect Henry's car's back there, too."

"What are you going to do?"

"Turn around, park up the road, and walk back," Ariel said more decisively than she felt.

Both Ariel and Sam craned toward the two places of business when they approached from the opposite direction, but they saw nothing more than on the first pass. Ariel parked on the side of the road fifty yards beyond.

"Stay put," she directed. "I'm going to reconnoiter."

She opened the door against a gust of hot wind and closed it on Sam's disgusted "Oh, *man!*" Wishing she'd changed from her work clothes, particularly her work shoes, Ariel crunched down the road's dirt shoulder.

When she reached the MicroStar parking lot, she tiptoed to the door and listened. She could hear nothing but the wind. Cautiously, she went in.

"Oh, God!" she breathed. "Oh, dear Lord!"

Betty Lacy lay on her side. One arm was bent beneath her body, one crooked in front of her, the hand open. Ariel had only to take a few steps to see the dead eyes and, on the shirtfront, a black-looking stain.

Her eyes flicked from the bare, lighted room at one end of the warehouse to cartons stacked in darkness at the other and, except for a handbag on the floor, to the nothingness in between. When Jessie brushed against her, she shrieked.

Sam stood in the doorway, his eyes huge. "Is she dead?"

"I told you to stay in the van!" Ariel hissed.

She clicked her fingers to the shepherd and herded dog and boy outside, ordering, "Back there. Now!"

Sam dug in his heels. "Let me at least see if Dad's car's where you said." Before Ariel could stop him, he'd gone pounding across the driveway to the building next door. She followed and, together, they took in the disquieting scene: Henry's Oldsmobile, hood agape, and the white Jaguar directly behind it.

"Where's Dad?" asked Sam in a small voice.

"I think we'd better get some help out here." Ariel placed her hand on Sam's shoulder, almost on a level with her own. "Let's go."

They were at the end of the driveway when Ariel noticed that Jessie was no longer beside her. She turned to see the dog sniffing along the fence that enclosed the Gibraltar property.

"Jessie," she ordered, "come!" But Jessie had her own agenda.

Fur up, ears arrow straight, she pointed her nose in the air, nostrils quivering. For a delirious second Ariel thought the shepherd was about to bay at the moon, a *Hound of the Baskervilles* fancy that brought her own neck hair erect. She called out, but Jessie's attention had returned to the fence. She whined once and began to trot along the perimeter, her nose again to the ground.

"What's that?" Sam pointed into the distance beyond the fence.

"What's what?"

"See? On top of that tower thing way down at the end there. Wait. It's gone now."

Ariel looked where he pointed. "What's gone?"

"There! There it is again. See that little light?"

Ariel saw more than the small glow. On the tip-top of the structure she thought she saw the silhouette of a man, and he seemed to be the source of the light.

Both Ariel and Sam moved toward the fence, straining to make out what was hardly more than an elongated black speck. It moved.

Sam grasped the wire mesh. "Could that be Dad?"

"I don't know, but I can't believe there's a legitimate reason for anybody to be up there now, not with this place closed."

Worriedly, Ariel looked for Jessie. The dog had evaporated.

"Sam," she said quietly, "do you know how to drive?"

His mouth dropped open. He recovered quickly, but his voice had risen half an octave when he said, "Dad showed me."

Thinking she might regret this for the rest of her natural life, Ariel handed him her keys. "You remember that bar we passed a few miles back? Go there. Call nine-one-one. Tell them a woman's been killed, that we have a situation. . . . Tell them to hurry."

Sam swallowed, sober but unable to repress his excitement entirely. He started to speak but just nodded again and took off running at top speed.

Ariel didn't waste time watching him go. She took something from her purse, dropped it into her pocket, and dropped the purse on the ground. "Over the top, boys," she muttered. Hoisting her skirt, she stuck the toe of her pump into the chain link and pulled herself up. At the top, she threw one leg over and before she could think better of it, lifted the other. She was over. Her foot slipped and she let go, hitting knees-first.

Fortunately, the surface was soft. Unfortunately, it was mud and filthy water that splattered into her face. Bleary-eyed, she ran for the tower.

Halfway there a shoe was lost to sucking mud. Ariel shucked off the other and looked up at the structure: a silo, she could now see. Behind it was a taller building, like a bell tower, crowned with machinery and encircled by a rail, barely thigh high. From it, an endless catwalk extended, supported by gradually diminishing stanchions as it zigzagged to the ground. It reminded her of a roller coaster; she guessed it was a conveyor belt.

There were two men up there. One stood, holding what had to be a flashlight; the second was seated or kneeling, Ariel couldn't tell which. She couldn't recognize either man, but the one standing looked too short to be Henry.

For the remainder of the way, she concentrated on stealth. When she looked up again, she saw that both men were upright. The tall, thin one was Henry. He was holding the rail for dear life. The other man was holding a gun. Ariel caught the sound of a voice raised in anger or excitement, unintelligible words snatched away by a blast of wind that lifted both men's coattails.

She crouched behind a pyramid of bricks, studying the edifice. The silo portion was nearest her. Affixed to its sheer, curved wall—from waist level to very distant top—was an iron ladder.

Merciful God! thought Ariel; is that how they got up there?

She eyed the rungs that went up and up—and up. The thought of climbing that ladder turned her to jelly. Her arm jerked, an involuntary grasp at an anchor, and a brick clanked to the ground.

Both men looked down. Ariel ducked.

She considered the catwalk. It was far less precipitous, but the base was too far away; it would take forever to get up the thing and she'd be in plain view the whole time. She risked another look at the men. They seemed to be focused on each other again. She dashed to the silo and plastered herself against it, invisible from their perspective.

Was there another way up? she wondered. Inside the building? The portion within her line of sight was only blank, unhelpful corrugated tin—no door.

She couldn't count on Sam's making it to the bar. She didn't know how long it would take help to arrive if he did. She knew only that Henry was up there, within inches of empty air, and the gun pointed at his chest could send him over, dead before he fell.

Saying a prayer, Ariel hiked her stockinged foot up to the ladder's lowest rung and took hold of another. She kept her face to the silo. She never looked down, and she had only a fuzzy, cavalry-to-the-rescue idea of what she'd do when she reached the top.

Pepper spray bought months ago was in her pocket. She hoped the stuff hadn't lost its potency. At the least, she could provide distraction and give Henry a chance to get the gun. She climbed.

When a fresh, howling gust slapped hair into her eyes and sent her skirt flying, she stopped, hugged the ladder until the wind died, and then forced herself to reach for the next rung. She couldn't see the men—couldn't have if she'd looked; the flip side was, they couldn't see her either.

A phrase was ticktocking through her brain, over and over, in steady tempo with her hand-over-hand climb. "Plenty of time. Plenty of time. Plenty of time." It was a silent entreaty. It was what Henry had said the night he'd kissed her. She saw his face in her mind's eye, a breath away. She felt the nape of her neck tingle as if his hand still touched her there. "There'll be plenty of time to talk later," he'd said. It had been scarcely a week ago; it seemed like years. It seemed like years since she'd begun to climb.

The ladder gave a sudden jolt. Ariel felt it and heard it. If there'd been any room left for fright, she would have been petrified, but Ariel was in some benumbed place beyond fear. She made her legs, spongy with fatigue, climb faster.

She passed the place where a bolt had popped free of its mooring. There's lots more bolts, she told herself. When her hands grasped the last rung, she made a far worse discovery. The top of the silo, still above her head, was rounded. There was no flat surface to walk on to get over to the tower and nothing to hold on to, and there was no cover if you were stupid enough to try.

The wind dropped momentarily, and she could hear a voice, Henry's voice, saying, ". . . not going to throw myself down there voluntarily, you know, and I don't believe you can pull that trigger. You can't do it, can you?"

Ariel's grip tightened. If the ladder had combusted, she

couldn't have moved; no more could she just hang there and wait for the shot. Her mind closed down. All the blood that had left her limbs pounded in her ears. Henry! she thought. The scream built like trapped steam.

In that moment the ladder began to tremble, only a little at first but then seriously, clattering against the silo. Rust chips flecked off as the world exploded into turbulence, and both silo and tower erupted into searing, brilliant daylight. Ariel clamped her body to the ladder, fusing herself to the rungs. She heard a scream, a cry of mortal terror that seemed endless. Then she heard a *whumpf!* far below her.

At the same time the light abruptly shifted, and the racket began to subside.

She pried her face loose to see a helicopter settling to earth. A dog was barking and, over the noise, someone called out.

"Dad!" Sam cried, and someone else yelled, "Henry?"

Ariel craned, frantically trying to see the tower's roof. Henry's face appeared, ghost white. "Ariel?" he said. Holding on to something behind him, he leaned to peer over the edge, first at Ariel's face—which was all he could see of her—and then at the distant ground.

"Sam?"

Ariel could hardly hear him. It was unlikely that Sam could.

"I'm okay, son," Henry called. "Stay there. I'll be down in a second." He said it, but he didn't move.

The dog's barking had become a series of anxious yelps, and Ariel could hear a discordant clamor of voices as well.

"Henry," she said, "are you really all right?"

"Yeah," Henry said and then repeated it, trying to convince himself it was true.

"Who was that?" Ariel asked. "That fell?"

"Clifford Gilroy."

A man called from beneath them: "You people okay? Can you get down?" and Sam chimed in with "Dad? Are you coming down or what?"

"I'm coming, son. Right now."

Ariel waited to see how Henry would climb over to her perch. He didn't.

From his higher vantage point, he took in the situation—the slippery, curved metal top of the silo and a two-foot-wide chasm between the silo and the batch plant—and lifted a hand helplessly. "There's no safe way to get you over here, Ariel. Better you go down the same way you came up."

Ariel looked down for the very first time, and, very quickly, looked back. "Henry," she said, "I can't."

"What do you mean you can't? Are you hurt?"

"No. I just can't."

"Okay," Henry said. "Okay. Hold on." The wind took whatever he said next, but then he said, "I can't get over there. Nothing to hold on to. My belt's not long enough, and there's nothing else up here. What if I get the copter pilot to lower a ladder?"

"No!"

"Then I'll go see about a rope to tie to this brace here—or a net. Hold on."

"I'm doing that," Ariel said to nobody. Henry had disappeared. She snuck another quick look down, just long enough to get an impression of activity. Freddy, far below her, Betacam in hand. Uniformed men standing over the inert body of Clifford Gilroy. Jessie at the base of the ladder, whining.

Then Ariel felt the ladder being jostled from below. She heard a pop in the vicinity of her feet. She held on tighter, looking straight through the rungs into the silo, an inch from her nose.

"Miss?" It was a stranger's voice. "I'm going to come up there and help you down, okay?"

"No!"

"It'll be—"

"No!"

"What do you want us to do?"

"I don't know," she yelled, "but stay off the ladder. It won't hold." She waited for inspiration: some other route. "I'll just climb on down," she told herself. "Right now." The hot Santa Ana wind played with her hair; she was freezing. Her hands were frozen to the rungs.

Jessie barked: one sharp demand. "Miss?" the stranger said.

"I'm coming!" She felt distinctly annoyed at being hurried.

" 'The road up and the road down is one and the same,' " she whispered. You've already done this; you can do it in reverse.

She lowered one foot. Found metal. Unglued her fingers and locked them onto the next rung down. Stopped and breathed and did it again. She tried to make her mind a blank. Instead, insidiously, came: "Rock-a-bye baby on the treetop . . ." Herky-jerky, her knees bent and straightened. "When the wind blows . . ." The ladder wobbled where a bolt had worked loose. ". . . down will come baby, cradle and all."

When her foot reached down and found nothing but air, Ariel felt hands at her waist. She jumped as if she'd been startled from sleep and was lifted the last long step to earth. Her knees were shaking so badly she could hardly stand.

"I did it!" she said. Jessie barked in relief or excitement, and a tic at the corner of Ariel's mouth passed for a grin.

The policeman grinned back, nodding, and then Ariel was in Henry's arms. She hadn't known that solid flesh could feel that good. "What in the name of sanity," Henry demanded into her hair, "were you doing up there?"

Ariel just shook her head. She swallowed, convulsively, several times, feeling as foolish as a cat rescued from a tree. Here she was requiring comforting, and she'd accomplished nothing. She hadn't been the one held at gunpoint, and she hadn't been the one who'd fallen. She pushed away. "Is he dead?" she asked.

"Neck's broken," the policeman said.

"My own personal SWAT team! Between the two of you, you saved my sorry hide."

So saying, Henry stretched his long arm across Ariel's kitchen table and gave his son's hair a rough tousle.

"Da-a-d!" Sam jerked away, frowning, a study in indifference.

Because Henry had been required to remain behind to make a statement, Ariel had driven Sam back to her house. The boy had made a big effort to be blasé about the exploits of the night—and suitably solemn about two deaths—but every few minutes, like a cauldron at high boil, he'd erupted with another play-by-play of his solo drive or a question about what happened in his absence.

Ariel felt no such satisfaction. Even while she'd nodded or replied as the moment demanded, she was wondering what she should have done differently. Smarter or faster.

Now, exhausted and hungry, Henry had arrived, and Ariel, just as exhausted, was frying bacon.

"Did you know," Sam asked his father, "that Ariel's . . ." He turned to her. "What is it again?"

"Acrophobic," she mumbled.

Henry regarded her thoughtfully before he said, "The owner of the masonry yard came after you left. Said that ladder's corroded all to hell. Hasn't been used in years."

Ariel felt her insides lurch with a fresh wave of fear. "I feel so much better now." Grease spattered as she slapped more bacon into the pan.

"Tell me about Cummings," Henry said. "What happened?"

With a meaningful glance at Sam, Ariel said, "Later."

"Hey, Dad," Sam prodded, "what did you mean about us saving your life?"

Henry, too, looked at Sam, appraisingly. "Well, son," he said, "when you got there, I was out of time. That man, Gilroy, had wanted to talk. Needed to, to justify himself, even to a man he meant to see dead. But the more he tried to convince me he'd done what he had to do, that he'd never had a choice and still didn't, the more worked up he got. He took me by surprise. All of a sudden, he was coming at me with the butt of the gun.

"Before I saw that's what he was doing, I heard Ariel." He smiled at her. "That was the precise moment you called my name. In that god-awful eerie wind, I thought I was hearing things. Angels calling. Point is, I turned to the sound of your voice. That movement saved me. Gilroy hit air. His momentum took him over."

"Funny . . ." Ariel frowned. "I don't remember saying anything."

"Well, if it wasn't you, it *was* an angel. She said 'Henry' and then screamed bloody murder. If you hadn't been there . . ."

"But, I thought . . ." Sam was clearly disappointed with the story so far.

"Oh!" Henry backpedaled. "Didn't I say? You got the copter there in the nick of time! When that light hit, it must've blinded Gilroy or he wouldn't have lost his balance like that."

"Why don't you tell Henry exactly what you did?" Ariel suggested.

"Yeah, well, I drove Ariel's van, Dad, down to that bar, but the phone didn't work. Some drunk woman broke it, the man said. I jumped back in the van—I didn't know what to do!—and then I saw the *Open File* guys coming down the road, doing about eighty. I started blowing the horn and blinking the lights.

I got them to pull over, and they're going, 'Where's Ariel?' and 'Where's your dad?' and 'What's happening?'

"So I told them about the dead lady and that we thought you were up on that tower thing. That maybe whoever killed the lady *had* you up there."

"And who called nine-one-one from their van?" Ariel said. "And who crawled under the fence to get to his dad?"

Sam hitched one shoulder. "Hey, it was Jessie that dug the hole. She was, like, Super Gopher! If it hadn't been for her, we wouldn't ever have seen you, Dad. She smelled you or something. She stopped us from leaving."

The heroic Jessie, tongue lolling, was eyeing Ariel's every move as she put a BLT in front of Henry.

"Why'd he do it, Dad?" Sam asked. "Why'd that man try to kill you?"

Henry broke off a bit of bacon and held it out to the dog. Very quickly, almost by rote, he related what had happened that day and evening up until the time Gilroy had forced him to the top of the batch plant. Then, more slowly, reflectively, he said, "I'd been suspicious of Gilroy all along, that he'd somehow killed Lacy. He told me tonight he didn't. I believe him."

Ariel frowned. "Mrs. Lacy . . . ?"

Henry shook his head. "Let me tell you what I've learned about Grant Lacy," he said.

"He was a kid that never fit in anywhere, not even in his own family. Too smart, too odd, too introverted. Until MicroStar. Suddenly, he was a silicon *wunderkind*. His company was cutting-edge, and the IQ that had always made people look for the nearest exit was a hot commodity. The dopey-looking duckling was a swan, quoted, courted, and rich. Even considered handsome. He was oblivious to that and the money, too, but the power, the respect, were heady.

"He got dazzled. A kid on a sandlot, trying to function in the big leagues. And the industry was already changing. The eighties megadeal mergers created giants with pockets too deep to compete with, and little by little, Lacy began to slip under.

"He got obsessed with this Internet antiinvasion program. Staked everything on it, convinced that with a little more money, a little more time, he'd be ready with a first test version. Meantime, he was ignoring business in hand. He was alienating retailers and making increasingly irrational decisions. Getting more secretive. And spending money like water.

"He'd spent the proceeds from everything he could liquidate, millions, Gilroy told me, and nobody would talk to him about lending more. Not unless he showed them something solid *and* made major structural changes in his company. He couldn't do the first and wouldn't do the second. He wouldn't go public, and he wouldn't deal with venture capitalists. Said he didn't have time to run around looking for funding, that investors would pressure him to turn out product prematurely. The truth was he believed they'd take control away from him, and he was right.

"Gilroy saw the company going down the tubes. On his own hook, he got an investment group interested, and he finally persuaded Lacy to sit down with them. The terms were Gilroy would run the show fiscally, report directly to them. Lacy was between a hard place and no place. Even he saw he didn't have much choice."

With one eye on Sam, Henry said, "By then his marriage was history, but he'd been too obsessed to notice. His wife saw him throwing good money after bad, saw everything she valued threatened. She wasn't happy. Gilroy wasn't happy. They'd gotten together. When she asked for a divorce, it must've been the last straw. Gilroy and Betty thought Lacy hadn't known about them." Henry stopped and sighed, a weary exhalation. "They were wrong.

"Lacy called Gilroy. Said meet him at the warehouse; he wanted to show him something. When Gilroy got there, Lacy was in one of those abandoned offices. Sitting on the floor, Gilroy said, cross-legged like a Buddha. He had a gun. He was waiting. He wanted Gilroy to see him . . . do what he was going to do."

Seconds ticked away before Ariel got it. "Lacy killed *himself?* That's what Gilroy told you? But why? I mean—"

"He'd flipped. Gone off the deep end. Looked like he hadn't slept in a week, Gilroy said, but he had this big smile on his face, like he was really enjoying the moment, like it was the most fun he'd ever had, and once he had his say, he pulled the trigger."

Sam had been listening intently, understanding that in being allowed to hear this, he was being told something else as well.

"But, Dad," he said, "I still don't get why this Gilroy was trying to kill you."

"I don't either," Ariel said. "And that's just the beginning of what I don't understand. What was with the train? And Cummings—why would he pay Cummings off if it was suicide?"

"Lacy admitted . . ." Henry scoured his face with his palm, stretching it into tired, rubbery distortion. "Development was going nowhere. There was no hope of that or any new product—not from him. He was out of ideas, is what he told Gilroy. 'A thirtysomething has-been,' he called himself and laughed about it. Then he stopped laughing. He accused Gilroy of stealing his wife and his company, too. Said something like, 'Enjoy the consequences because you're not going to enjoy the rewards.' "

"Which meant what?" Ariel asked.

"Mr. Lacy, it seems, wasn't too far gone to want revenge. He'd gotten hold of Gilroy's gun, you see." Henry looked from Sam to Ariel. "It was Gilroy's own gun he used on himself.

"At first, Gilroy didn't get the picture, but Lacy got a kick out of making sure he did. Asked how Gilroy was going to make anybody believe suicide, since it was *his* gun and *his* prints on it."

"If Gilroy wiped off his own prints," Ariel said, "there went Lacy's, too. And Gilroy could hardly get rid of the gun. Not and claim it was suicide!"

"You got it. Lacy said the cops might decide both their prints indicated a struggle, and then . . ." Henry shook his head as if he still couldn't believe this part of the story. "Then Lacy aimed the gun at the wall and fired. Suicides, he said, didn't miss, but when two men fought over a gun, it might discharge just like that.

"He taunted Gilroy with the fact that there was no note and no other witness. 'Who knows you met me here?' he asked him. 'Who did *I* tell?'—that kind of thing. 'Did anybody see you?' and 'Do you have an alibi? Who-all knows you were . . .' " Henry quickly rephrased: 'Who-all knows about your affair with my wife?' "

"What a—" Ariel began.

"It gets weirder. Seems Lacy'd made a study of gunshot suicides. Said he wouldn't put the muzzle in his mouth or against his skull the way suicides do; he'd hold it just close enough 'to do the trick.' Said a downward angle might be 'fun,' like if somebody standing over him had done it. Said maybe he'd even get more than one shot off—wound himself someplace unimportant first. He asked Gilroy if he'd ever heard of a suicide doing that!

"He begged Gilroy to try to take the gun away. Nothing he'd like better, he said, than to take Gilroy with him. Then, daring Gilroy to interfere, he put the gun to his head and fired."

"*Man!*" Sam breathed, and then, more forcefully, "Yuck!"

"Precisely," Henry said. "Well, Gilroy went into a blind panic. He took off. He was in his car when he saw the railroad tracks, and it came to him: not suicide, not murder—accident."

"God in Heaven!" Ariel whispered, and Henry nodded.

"He wrapped the body—less a few missing bits of skull—in old packing material and drove it a couple of miles away. He propped Lacy up, like he'd fallen to his knees, and put his head right on the rail. Some of the body got tossed by the train, but not the head. The head was—"

"Okay," Ariel said. "You don't have to belabor it."

"Then Gilroy snuck back to MicroStar, to the office nobody'd seen him leave, and waited to be called about Lacy's 'tragic accident.' Waited and worried. Claimed he didn't even remember the insurance until then. Another nail in his coffin."

"What insurance?"

"A ten-million-dollar key man policy MicroStar held on Lacy. Gilroy's idea. He insisted on it when he went with the company, too recently for it to have paid off in a case of suicide."

"I guess it hadn't paid off anyway," Ariel said, "thanks to Craig Fiore."

"Yeah, Mr. Bigamy did slow the wheels of progress. Gilroy must've been berserk when nobody called! On the one hand, a missing body lessened the chances of a tie-in to him and the debacle at the warehouse; on the other, you've got a legal snarl and no payoffs."

Henry frowned. "You know, Marge Luzzatto told me they got a ransom call. I wouldn't be surprised if it was Gilroy, capitalizing on the disappearance, trying to throw the cops off and reinforce the idea that it was a kidnapping." He shrugged. "Anyway, Gilroy said tonight that the cops were closing the file on Lacy. His death would've officially become an accident."

Sam didn't know from ransom calls nor did he care. He got to what was for him the bottom line. "Then *you* showed up."

Henry was about to take the first bite of his sandwich when Ariel asked again about Cummings's extortion.

"Seems Gilroy told Betty the true story," Henry said. "Seems she didn't entirely believe him, much as she wanted to. There was still property Lacy hadn't liquidated that would belong to her, including the business Gilroy was now running. There was also the widow herself, free of encumbrance, with substantial holdings in her own name and a life insurance payoff down the road.

"Cummings must've gotten to her at a vulnerable moment. He always was persuasive with the ladies. He pressed her. She broke. She told him what Gilroy said happened, maybe to discourage Cummings from pressing further, or looking for reassurance that it really could've happened that way. Maybe trying to protect herself.

"Cummings saw opportunity. He threatened Gilroy with *Open File* exposure. Gilroy panicked again. He paid Cummings off, with money from Betty. The more he covered up, the more he felt like he had to cover up—just like tonight."

Although it was she who'd asked about Cummings, Ariel had listened with only half a mind to the answer.

"What's with you?" Henry asked when he noticed that she was staring through him, preoccupied.

Ariel blinked. "I was just thinking about being right for the wrong reason."

"Say again?"

"You were sure Gilroy was lying about Lacy's death; he was but, in effect, he was covering up his innocence, not his guilt."

"Innocence? You could argue that if it wasn't for Gilroy, both Lacys would still be alive. But you're right: it's not murder he was guilty of; it's cowardice. He was scared stiff the law wouldn't believe what happened, and after the way he covered it up, they probably wouldn't. Staging the 'accident.' Obliterating evidence. Cleaning up, getting rid of spent bullets . . . He even wiped the powder smudges off Lacy's skin! What would that look like but the work of a guilty man?

"It was easier to let the train engineer torment himself. To pay Cummings off. To sweep everything under the rug, including me. Gilroy saw himself as a victim to the end. He'd done nothing wrong, had no malice toward anybody. He was just doing what he had to do."

Sam had gone ahead to wait in the car when Henry asked what had happened to Cummings. Ariel gave him the barest, most sanitized facts; she had enough horrific images to haunt her dreams. Uncharacteristically, Henry didn't press. Shaking his head, looking punchy, he'd gone to check around for anything he might have forgotten that morning—that very long-ago morning.

Ariel found him kneeling to look under her bed when she came into the bedroom and quietly spoke his name.

"I just wanted to tell you," she said, "you've got a good kid."

"Yeah. He did okay tonight, didn't he? For a J.D."

"I wouldn't worry about that."

"Hmm?" he murmured, his mind on the sock he'd just retrieved. "Is this yours or mine?"

"Yours. Talk to him. We need to talk, too, I think. Soon."

"Something else about Cummings?"

"No."

"Good. I'm beat." Henry was yawning as he stuffed the sock into his pocket.

"It's . . . about us."

Henry's jaw snapped closed with an audible click. He sat on his heel and looked up at Ariel. Even by the soft glow of the bedside lamp, he could see that she was nervous. She stood very straight, and her chest rose and fell in a quick, steady cadence. She looked to Henry like a determined child who'd worked up her nerve for something that might not go well.

"Is there an us?" he asked.

"When I heard Gilroy go off that tower tonight, when I thought it might be you . . ."

"That was fright," Henry said. "Heightened emotion. Whatever. You can't go by that."

"What do I go by?"

"If you have to ask, I don't know what to tell you."

Abruptly, Ariel relaxed. "Never mind," she said and turned to leave.

"Hey!" Henry came to his feet. "We're both knocked out. Sam's waiting. This is too important to talk about now."

" 'Later,' right?" She faced Henry. "That's what you said once before, that there'd be plenty of time to talk later. Well, there almost wasn't a later. Look, obviously, I've misunderstood. I'm sorry if I put you on the spot, but when you're short on yesterdays, tomorrows don't seem all that reliable, either. You tend to put a premium on now."

"I'm not on any 'spot,' and you didn't misunderstand. I simply said the timing's not great."

"And I didn't say now; I said 'soon.' "

"And I don't want to argue. If there *is* an 'us,' it shouldn't require a lot of talking."

Ariel's face closed as did both fists, clenched at her sides. "Fine. Let's just do whatever you've done in the past. That seems to have worked really well."

"Ohh!" Henry sucked air, and angry red climbed his face like mercury in a thermometer. "Hey!" he said. "You're good at this talking! Already you've managed to say the first mean thing I've ever heard out of your mouth!"

"I didn't . . . I simply meant that you might've been better off with a little more talk and a little less action."

"Great! We've established I'm no good at relationships. Or, wait a minute. What are we talking about here exactly?"

"You have to admit, three marriages do suggest a certain . . . impetuousness? Makes one wonder where your mind was."

"Just what are you saying? That it was in my pants? That I was chasing my . . ." Henry let out a sharp bark of laughter. "My libido?" That Ariel was right made him madder. "You must have me confused with somebody, Ariel. I've known you nearly three years. I haven't laid a hand on you, and God knows I've never put the make on you! But, oh yeah! I'm a real stud. If Sam weren't out there, I'd probably be trying to get you into the sack right now!

"This is great, this talking. What would you like to discuss next? Hey! How about the difference in our ages? How about we chew over the fact that I'm more than ten years older than you?"

"Eleven."

"Eleven. Right. I said more than ten, and eleven is more than ten. But, obviously, I'm not bringing up something you haven't already considered, so let's move on. Let's chat about office romances, shall we? How they're bad news and unprofessional and they never work."

"Yes, well, I can fix that problem! Let's talk about that for a—"

"No! You talk. I'm leaving!"

"Henry, you're being—"

Henry halted in the doorway, slammed his palm against the frame, and whipped around. He pointed a finger at Ariel, taking aim, looking as if he was about to explode into another tirade. When he did speak, however, his voice was surprisingly soft.

"Let me tell you something. I *know* I'm a three-time loser, and it's not something I'm proud of. I *know* I'm not exactly every mother's dream for her daughter. I *know* I'm older and tireder and you're young and lovely and you're probably ready to have kids and I don't know how to cope with the one I've got. I'm not unaware of the problems we'd face if you showed one iota of interest, and I don't know the solutions. But I'm a step ahead of you. I know how I feel, even if you don't, and it's nothing like I've ever felt for anybody, ever, anytime before. So even if it's not going to be with me, I want you happy. I want you safe. I want you—"

Henry had stopped talking because he was being kissed, soundly. Ariel's arms encircled his neck. Her body pressed against his like some missing part, found and fitted snugly back into place. The kiss was deep and decisive and chased by short, gentle nips. When, eventually, Ariel opened her eyes, Henry's were a handbreadth away, so dark a brown they were almost black, and red-rimmed with fatigue. They were a little bewildered as well. "You talk too much," she said.

"Umm . . . I must be getting the hang of it, though."

That was the last thing either of them had to say for quite a time. Stonewall wandered in, saw nothing of interest, and wandered out, unnoticed. Presently, Henry touched a finger to Ariel's upper lip, tracing the wide curved line of it, just grazing the little furrow above the center.

"Your timing's still lousy," he said.

"Later."

"Tomorrow night?"

"We've got tomorrow night and Thursday night. Friday night I'm flying to Charleston."

"What?" Henry took a step backward. The bed stopped him, and he plunked down on it. "Are you *commuting* now?"

Ariel smiled. She sat beside him and took his hand. She was

turning it in hers and stroking each long, thin finger when she said, "I've always loved your hands. Did I ever tell you that?"

"You never even told me you liked them or anything else about me. Why are you going back to Charleston?"

"Grace Barron."

"Oh, good God, Ariel! Not that again!"

"I'll be going over the weekend, on my time and my money."

"Money. I guess we ought to talk about that, too—as in, you're an heiress. On the subject of problems, what did you mean about fixing the 'office romance' one?"

"Oh, that . . ." Ariel said. "Definitely later." She touched Henry's fingertips to her face, brushing them against her cheek. "Let's talk about why I'm going back to Charleston."

"Okay. Why?"

"I don't believe Grace killed her son."

Henry swallowed the automatic protest that leaped to his lips and almost strangled doing it. He merely repeated his "Why?"

"Clifford Gilroy."

"Gilroy? What's he got to do with anything?"

Thoughtfully, Ariel said, "Clifford Gilroy turned a suicide into an accident. I think Grace turned one into murder."

Ariel felt the sharpening of Henry's attention down to his fingertips. "I believe John William killed himself," she said. "Grace lied about that. Like Gilroy, she lied to cover up her innocence."

"On what possible basis—"

" 'Clever liars give details, but the cleverest don't.' Grace gave too many. She made herself look as vile as possible. Like she was punishing herself for her son's death. And making sure she'd *be* punished."

"That's it? That's all?"

Ariel thought of Hugh Cross, the body that wasn't there. She wondered again why a woman set on incriminating herself would fail to mention another notch on her gun, but it was a question she couldn't voice without revealing her grandfather's involvement, and Sarge's. "No," she said, "that's not all."

"Well, what? Why do you think Barron killed himself?"

"Why? He was a mixed-up man who didn't know who he was or what he was. His mother royally messed up his mind from day one. He was disappointed in himself and despondent, and he'd been dumped by his lover. I don't know; all the above. 'Men don't seem to jump off the bridge for big reasons; they usually do so for little ones.' "

"I don't mean why did he do it—if he did. I meant what brings you to the conclusion that he did? And if you give me another quotation, I swear I'm going to punch you."

"I haven't told you about a note he left Grover Washburn, his erstwhile lover. Grover thought it was a love note, a broken-hearted good-bye because he was leaving. I think it was good-bye, period. Cruel Grover, cruel world. The fact that it was left the night he died seems mighty coincidental to me. And speaking of good-byes . . ."

Ariel narrowed her eyes as if to see the past more clearly. "The night I met him," she said, "John William didn't express any interest in ever laying eyes on me again. He wasn't all that interested in my existence. He didn't give his name and he didn't even bother to say good-bye."

"So?"

"John William loved Jane like a sister. There was a time when she was the only person in the world who made his life bearable. When he saw me—hope against hope, knowing she was dead—he thought I was her.

"Henry, think about a normal person on an ordinary day. This person comes upon you, the twin of someone he's cherished from the time he was a child. Until that moment he didn't know you existed. You're enough like his loved one—his *dead* loved one—to take his breath away. Okay? Would he say: 'Hello, here's the personal and intimate story of your twin and me'—and then walk away without a parting word? That's the behavior of a man who knows he's not going to be around to see you or anybody anymore, isn't it?"

Henry considered the question. "How would you feel about some company on your trip?" he asked.

51

"DON QUIXOTE RIDES AGAIN," ARIEL MUTTERED AND SNAPPED HER compact shut. The shadows under her eyes attested to another late night and too many air miles. This time she hadn't flown solo. She'd been accompanied by Henry and Sam and a stew of misgivings.

Nervousness about West meeting South had been laid to rest; this morning she'd left father and son mopping red-eye gravy with Hattie's biscuits and planning a beachcombing expedition with B.F. Guilt still rankled because she hadn't told her grandfather the real reason she'd made the trip. Doubt rankled even more, about whether she *should* have made the trip.

Ariel paced, waiting for Grace Barron to be brought to the same dismal room where less than a week before she'd confessed to murder. She stopped to gaze out the barred window where, patch by patch, the grass was turning the color of hay. She knew if she hadn't come, she'd have regretted it the rest of her life.

She was sure now about John William. She was pretty sure how Grace would react; it wasn't every prisoner who'd take umbrage at being accused of innocence.

She'd been locked away for nine days and nights now. Deprived of the cosseted privacy in which she'd lived for decades. Without hope. Without booze. She'd gone seriously downhill within the first few days; what would she be like now? Of course, if Ariel was right and the confession was a lie (or, for that matter, if it wasn't), Grace hadn't been in tiptop mental shape to start with.

When the door opened, Ariel steeled herself for the sight of a thoroughly broken woman.

At first glance, it was worse than she'd imagined. The bandage was gone, and the damage it had hidden was shocking, a grotesque souvenir of the accident that had taken Halley Barron's life.

The stitches had been removed, and the scars were a ragged, raw trail angling across the cheek as if some tiny feral creature had burrowed under the skin, moling blindly on a search for the misshapen eye, which drooped like melted flesh. The effect was sinister and, evidently, permanent.

By force of will Ariel managed not to look away. Grace Barron returned the gaze calmly. She looked perfectly, inexplicably serene and only mildly curious.

"Ms. Gold?" she said. "I hadn't expected to see you again."

"I hadn't expected to be here again," Ariel said.

Grace merely smiled quizzically. Ariel saw no trace of the flightiness or helpless confusion of past meetings. Gone, too, was the tense, cold-blooded woman who confessed to two murders.

"And why are you?" Grace asked. "There's nothing more to be said, you know."

Every one of the speeches Ariel had mentally rehearsed left her mind. "You might try the truth," she said.

"You've heard that, my dear. In detail."

"Yes, brutal detail."

"What I did was brutal. I can't think why you'd want to hear about it again."

"There was too much detail, Mrs. Barron. You oversold. The D.A. loved every authentic word, didn't he? And I'm sure the police were delighted to have their suspicions confirmed."

With her small finger, Grace traced the bony ridge above her eye. The stitches there, too, had been removed, and the brow was beginning to grow back. It looked like the stubble on a man's chin.

"I expect so," she murmured on a sigh. "I'm tired, child. Give up your fantasies, will you? Whatever they are. Leave me in peace."

"I wonder why you were so eager to drive every possible nail into your coffin. Is it guilt over killing your husband? I know it isn't guilt over killing your son because you didn't kill him."

Ariel had expected shock; she was disappointed. Her bombshell fizzled harmlessly. "How provocative!" Grace said. "Who did, pray?"

Softly, Ariel said, "John William killed himself."

"He killed himself," Grace repeated. "And I'm pretending I murdered him." She tilted her head, all long-suffering patience. "Tell me, does this have to do with your TV show? Reluctance to let the story go?" She smiled sadly. "I'm disappointed. I hadn't thought you were the usual sort of media person." Every trace of the smile vanished. "I cannot abide that sort of commonness," she said, and turned to leave.

"I paid Louise Mullis a visit this morning," Ariel said. "She told me how John William really got that bump on his head."

Grace was reaching for the buzzer that summoned her warder. Ariel watched the hand hesitate. When it was slowly lowered, she suppressed a sigh of relief.

Louise had been as recalcitrant as Grace was now. It had taken time but Ariel had made her case, convincing the housekeeper that she had no interest in involving her or her "boyfriend" if he'd done nothing wrong. She'd finally gotten the story.

The man went by the name of Elko. A "no-good," Louise admitted; "bad to gamble." He'd gone looking for her on her last afternoon at the Barron house, after money. He found her, but he didn't find her cooperative. He was in the process of persuading her to his point of view when John William walked in. A scuffle ensued. Elko wasn't big on fighting men. He grabbed the broom Louise had been using, cracked it over John William's head, and took off.

He'd been seen only once since, the day Ariel had first visited Louise. Elko had gotten the message then that if he didn't clear out, the law would hear about his fight with a man who was later murdered. Louise didn't think he'd be coming around again.

"I don't doubt," Ariel said to Grace now, "that you were at your son's house the night he died. Is it because you got there too late? Is that what you're set on being punished for?"

Grace made a show of impatience. "A good imagination must

be an asset in your sort of work," she said. "You must be dying to tell me what flights of fancy led you to these ideas of yours."

Ariel sat down, leaning back in the chair in an effort to look confident. "At first, my belief in your innocence was just naïveté, the notion that you should be able to recognize evil incarnate when you see it. Then you hired the most inexperienced lawyer in town and welcomed a member of the media with open arms. Crazy moves unless you *wanted* bad representation, *wanted* publicity."

"Fascinating," Grace commented pleasantly.

"Three nights ago I witnessed how far a person, an innocent person, will go to obscure the truth. To unbelievable lengths when enough's at stake. I wonder what's at stake for you. Atonement? Do you hold yourself responsible for your son's suicide—"

"There *was* no suicide!"

"I wonder if it wasn't the first time he'd tried it, or threatened it; if he really meant to pull it off even then. He'd expected his lover to find his 'suicide note' that night. He hoped Grover would rush to his side. He must've been shattered when it didn't happen. He went to the shore, maybe to drown himself in nostalgia, maybe to work up the nerve to drown himself in fact. I got in the way. He called Halley. I know she got a call in the wee hours. Maybe she'd heard it all before. Didn't take him seriously. Did he call you then? Were you 'under the weather'? Couldn't get your act together fast enough to stop him?"

Grace had turned her face to the wall. If Ariel's browbeating was having any effect, she was making sure it didn't show.

"Big guilt trip," Ariel said, "and the journey started long ago. I wonder if you believe your husband's murder was the first of many crimes, big and small, that drove your son to do what he did." She kept her eyes on Grace's stiff shoulder blades as she said, "I've even wondered if John William wasn't your son at all."

"You . . . ?" Grace turned, abruptly, in what looked like panic.

"If he was Halley's."

Grace laughed aloud. "Where in the world did you come up with that?"

"I guess I was wrong. About that."

"About that and everything. No matter what you, alone, believe, John William was a victim. No matter what *everybody* believed, so was his father."

"Was he? *Was* your husband a victim?" Feeling her way, Ariel said, "Here, now, we're dealing with a suicide everyone's convinced is murder . . . and forty years ago—so *you* say—a murder everyone was convinced was suicide. I have to ask myself: was your husband's death just exactly what it appeared to be all along? John Barron killed himself, too, didn't he?"

Grace had been very nearly imperturbable, poised just on the well-bred side of condescension. As she listened to this last, however, her face twisted, the derision exaggerated by the impotent muscles of her cheek. "You're an absurd woman," she said. "If one outlandish idea doesn't work, you hatch up another one."

"See," Ariel went on, "I *know* you loved your husband. Most of this bizarre charade has been pure fantasy, but what you said to me a week ago . . . 'You can't apply ordinary rules to extraordinary people.' Remember? The way you defended him, the feelings you expressed . . . They came straight from the heart. I'd swear to that!"

"What did you expect me to say, you fool? I'd kept what I'd done to him secret for longer than your lifetime!"

"And what you did to Hugh Cross, too?"

"What in God's name is that supposed to mean?"

"You know very well what I mean. You shot— Wait a minute . . . You didn't kill Cross, did you? You never killed anybody, not John William, not John Barron, and not Cross, either!

"Just what kind of 'ordinary rule' did your husband break, Mrs. Barron? Murder? Did he kill Cross and then himself just like you said that night forty years ago? You protected him then, getting rid of Cross's body, and you're still doing it. I'd stake my life on it!"

In the next second, Ariel thought she'd done just that. The anger that was suddenly emanating from Grace Barron was an almost audible vibration. She flung herself at Ariel, raising her fist like a wrathful god clutching a lightning bolt. Ariel froze. The change had been so abrupt, so without warning, that in that stunning instant she forgot Grace was twice her age, three inches shorter, one-armed, and weaponless.

"Shut up!" Grace hissed, almost choking on rage. "You shut your filthy mouth! You know nothing about my—" Something clicked in her eyes, and as quickly as it erupted, the fury vanished. "I killed John," she said, her voice flat. "That's all you need to know."

"It's what *you* need, Grace." Even as she blurted whatever came to mind, Ariel did a mental double take; was she losing it altogether or had the mention of Cross caught Grace off guard? "I know why you agreed to see me," she said. "You want to tell the truth! You wouldn't be talking to me unless, whether you realize it or not, you want me to know. Me or someone. Anyone."

"Ridiculous!"

"Then *you* tell *me* why."

"I already have."

"Run it by me again. Your reasons didn't make much sense the first time."

Grace exhaled, a sound of disgust, and she walked to the barred window without answering.

"I won't let an innocent woman spend the rest of her life in prison, or worse. I may not be the 'usual sort of media person' but, with or without your cooperation, I'll air this, and I'll get at the truth. I won't give up until the record's set straight."

"It is. Finally, it is."

The words were spoken so low that Ariel wasn't sure she'd heard them at all.

Bemused, as if fascinated by the dead grass or whatever held her attention, Grace said, "You think the truth's so important. And you're the great torchbearer!" She gave a delicate little snort. "That kind of simpleminded messianic zeal has caused a great deal of mischief down the ages, child. You really should watch yourself until you grow out of it."

Ariel went hot. Red-faced, she had to hold on to the one fact she knew beyond doubt—that Grace had lied about the wound on her son's head—to keep from agreeing with her, to keep from walking out. "The truth *is* a terrible weapon," she said. " 'It is possible to lie, and even to murder, for the truth.' You are a liar. But a murderer? I don't buy it—not for the truth or any other reason."

"Thought-provoking quote. Adler?"

"I have no idea." Like a small but irritating splinter, something lodged itself in Ariel's mind, but she didn't stop to examine it. "Here's another quote you might relate to. 'The broad mass . . .

will more easily fall victim to a big lie than a small one.' Herr Hitler, I believe."

Grace's chuckle was tired, and it was apparent as she reluctantly quit the window that the session was taking a toll. "Ms. Gold, I will say this one last time. I'll tell you so that your fine conscience can rest easy. Murder was committed, and the murderer will finally be held responsible."

"Interesting way to put it."

"I can't put it any plainer." Grace sat beside Ariel, her face close. "Look, I've told you what you came to hear. Put it on TV. Make it into whatever pathetic seven-minute wonder you think will sell your sponsors' products, their cereal or beer or whatever pays the piper. Be my guest. Just go!"

Seconds passed. Brakes squealed in the street outside, a distant sound Ariel wasn't aware of hearing. "Your eyes . . ." she said. "Your eyes are gray."

Grace drew back. Her frown, given the condition of her face, was a paroxysm. "They've never been anything else."

"Your eyes are supposed to be blue. A vivid blue, my grandfather said."

"Your grandfather's wrong."

Ariel was shaking her head. She hadn't missed the suddenly more pronounced rise and fall of the other woman's chest. "No. He made a point of it. In fact, he compared them to . . . He had a nickname for you. What was it?"

"You expect me to remember such a thing as that?"

" 'Glory.' It was 'Glory,' for morning glory." Ariel felt her heartbeat accelerate, kicking in even before her brain knew why. "Nobody's really looked at those poor, messed-up eyes or at your face either, have they? Not since the wreck. Doctors, sure. Strangers. I'll bet everybody else takes one look and then looks anywhere but there."

"Don't be—"

"First, the bandage. Now, the disfigurement. Funny you didn't bother to get it fixed. You could certainly afford it."

"You're insane!" The insult was whispered, cracking on the last word, and almost before Ariel was sure what she was thinking, she knew it was true.

52

"MAN OH MAN OH MAN OH MAN!" ARIEL ALMOST KNOCKED OVER the chair when she sprang up, too agitated to be still. "Almost nobody's laid eyes on Grace Barron in God knows when. Just Halley . . . just Halley!" she repeated, awed. *"That's* why he was always 'John William,' never 'my son'! And John never 'my husband.' You almost said 'my father' a while ago, didn't you? You almost slipped up!"

It was tumbling into place so quickly Ariel couldn't get the words out fast enough. "You *did* slip up! Recognizing the Adler quote. Grace wouldn't, not in a million years. *I* didn't know who said it. Nobody would but a scholar, and Grace is no scholar, no reader. You said so yourself.

"She knows Cross was killed that night, but you didn't, did you? Grace is . . . I mean *was* . . ." Ariel couldn't absorb the enormity of her revelation. "Why didn't I see it before? Getting cut off from the sauce should've been hard; it wasn't. Years of boozing should've shown in your skin, that way-too-youthful skin . . . How old are you, anyway? Fifty-three? Fifty-four?

"How did you do this? No! That doesn't matter! *Why* did you do this?"

The woman before her looked as if she'd stopped breathing. Rigid, still staring at the spot where Ariel no longer was, she betrayed no sign of life whatever for long, paralyzed seconds.

"Halley," Ariel said. Panic seized her. *"Halley?"*

The gray eyes blinked. The lips opened and closed on silence.

"Are you all right? Do you want water?"

"You can't prove anything."

"You know I can, now that I know what I'm dealing with."

"No." The protest was unconvinced and unconvincing.

"Yes," Ariel said, staggered all over again as "what she was dealing with" hit home. She'd thought this woman wasn't mad? "You've carried this off only because nobody had reason to doubt you were who you said you were. When did you decide to *do* this thing?" she cried. "When your brother killed himself? When you and Grace had the acci— Oh, Halley! It *was* an accident? You didn't kill her?"

"I meant to."

"What? I couldn't hear you."

"She robbed me of that, too." Her eyes dull, blinking with the heavy-lidded slowness of some stupefied creature, Halley Barron stared into her own version of hell. After what seemed like a very long time, the words began to come, in slow motion, with pauses heavy as stones between them.

"I'd decided not to let the police have her. She had to die. Like my father. Like my brother.

"I meant to kill her. Make no mistake about that. But she grabbed the steering wheel . . . It was too quick. She should've suffered."

"Why?" It was a central question, and Ariel asked it urgently.

"When I saw she was dead, I knew I'd been wrong. She couldn't be punished if she was dead."

"You did this to punish a *dead* woman?"

Halley's mouth made small, futile movements. It was as if after the weeks of grim, solitary planning and all the years of keeping her own counsel that had gone before, choosing words was beyond her. Eventually, trancelike, she said, "You think it's hard to become someone else? When you know every mood? Every tic? Every story? Her past was my past. What I didn't know, I learned . . . finally."

"But she was older."

"A little. A little grayer, under the dye." She touched the new silver wing of hair at her own temple and shuddered out a sigh. "I should know."

"Well, but Halley! I know she didn't get out much, but—"

"The more she aged, the less she went out. The drink had begun to show. She was a vain woman."

"Someone had to see her sometime!"

"Who? A pizza delivery boy? Somebody soliciting door-to-door? Jehovah's Witnesses? Oh, I'd take her out once in a while, to a meal or a movie. People passing on the street didn't know who she was, and nobody here in Charleston had seen her for years."

"But somebody had to know her. A friend? A doctor?"

"She should've been dead from cirrhosis; she never even caught cold. There were no friends. Acquaintances long since drifted away, died . . . There was just me."

"Her affairs . . . Didn't she have to sign something sometime?"

"I took care of all that. She couldn't be trusted to."

"Her driver's license?"

Halley didn't answer; they both knew what had become of that.

"You, then! *You* have friends. You have . . ."

Ariel was floundering, and she knew it. Halley smiled. It was meant to be wry; it was a twisted grimace too painful to look at.

"You think anyone would recognize me now? Even if they looked? They don't. People avert their eyes. They can't help it. The doctor . . . So concerned. He wanted to call in a plastic surgeon." Halley made a sound something like a laugh and stopped, wound down.

"But . . ." Ariel said and then, reluctantly, let it go. She was curious about all the details of the impersonation, the minutiae of a freakish masquerade, but she knew Halley would have answers and she knew, obviously, that it had been successful until now. "Tell me why," she begged instead. "What in the name of reason had Grace done that you were willing to sacrifice your life—"

At that, Halley reacted. "What life?" she snapped. "It's null! A dried-up, sucked-out husk! *What had Grace done?* You can ask that after what she did to my brother? To—"

"Your brother turned on that car engine himself, Halley."

"Grace might as well have, and locked the garage door! She crippled him. He couldn't get free of what she'd done to him even after he got free of her.

"You know why she had him? She couldn't be sure of me. A

son would be her means to the money, her ace in the hole! Through him she'd control half my father's money!

"I always made excuses for Grace. She was so young when she married, to a man who wasn't easy to live with. She wasn't strong. She'd had a tough life. She didn't know how to be a mother because she'd never known her own. She needed me. John William needed me. I needed to be needed.

"Well, I've come to see the truth. Grace wasn't particularly bright, but she was cunning enough to bind me to her from the day my father 'deserted us both.' Her words. She'd loved him so, she'd tell me. He was a genius, oh yes! But 'troubled.' As if she were protecting his memory. She'd hint at mysterious 'grown-up' problems I was too young to understand. Oh, she was too sly to make direct accusations. I was traumatized then and misguided later, but I had *known* my father. With John William, though . . .

"There were too many years when I wasn't around enough. She poisoned him with half-truths. Out of self-pity or a need to control him or . . . I don't know. Ignorance! He wouldn't repeat the things she'd say. He was ashamed, afraid they were true. They'd be at each other . . . I didn't know whose side to take, a difficult boy who tended to fantasize or the woman I believed had befriended me. I know now. Grace had no more maternal instinct than some animal that eats its young, and she devoured him.

"John William looked like our father, but he was Grace's son. That's why he understood her, and hated her." Halley's mouth twisted. "As he came to hate himself."

"You went to his house the night he died?"

"He called, just to talk, he said. Maudlin. Rambling. Obviously depressed. I got more and more worried. I told him I was coming there, then. That night. I got to him as fast as I could. He was half out of the car when I found him. He must've tried to . . . Oh, my soul!"

Ariel fell silent, picturing the scene, and, one by one, she thought of the incriminating clues that, unplanned on that terrible night, later pointed inevitably to "Grace." The fingerprints: on her car and on John William's, in his house, probably on his body. The garage opener left on her car seat. The fluid leak.

"How did you know," she asked Halley, "about the head wound?"

"He told me on the phone. He was proud of it, I think. He'd never been much of a fighter."

"The gun," Ariel said, thinking aloud. "He meant her to have that 'gift' a year ago. But you didn't give it to her, did you? You didn't know its significance, but you knew it was trouble. You hung on to it, and you saw a way to use it." After a moment, she asked, "Were there really any letters? The ones you said he found?"

Halley shook her head.

"Why'd you take his bracelet?"

"It was my father's. It was like finding him all over again! I don't remember taking it. Or taking the note. Or anything about the drive home."

"What note?"

"My father's. He left my father's note. Grace must've given it to him at some time for God only knows what sick purpose. And the gun, too. If Cross died the night my father did, I'll bet she found a way to turn it inside out, to make it into something obscene!" Naked pain came and went in Halley's face. "John William left the note in the same place. He signed . . . he signed his name to it."

Goose bumps tingled on Ariel's arms at the queerness of the situation. "Halley, why?" she said. "I still don't understand."

"I couldn't leave that note behind. To be found again. To start the talk all over again. Not again."

"Lord," Ariel said. "My grandfather had it right. Your whole family's reaped the whirlwind of what your father did."

"What do you mean by that?"

"The suicide that began this spiral of—"

Halley stared at Ariel as if she couldn't credit what she'd heard. "You still think my father killed *himself?* What in God's name do you think this is all about? My father was murdered!"

53

ARIEL WALKED OUT OF THE JAIL INTO A BRILLIANT AFTERNOON. PREoccupied, it took her a moment to remember where she'd left her rental car. She'd intended to drive straight back to Kiawah, but she found herself heading downtown. She parked on Meeting Street and, feeling as if every muscle in her body was tied in a sheepshank, she began to walk.

The old city went about its business all around her. A placid horse clopped by, glancing back with a jaundiced eye at the carriage he pulled. At the City Market tourists swarmed thick as fleas, and silent black women swiftly and ceaselessly wove sweetgrass baskets, seemingly oblivious to the hordes.

Blank-minded, Ariel strode through long shadows cast by church spires, past a marker designating the site of South Carolina's secession. She heard the bells of St. Michael's begin to peal, melodious with the practice of centuries. She trekked on, past a house that was new when Beethoven wrote his Fifth Symphony.

At the Battery she collapsed onto a bench facing Charleston Harbor and, only then, let the final chapter replay itself.

At first, she hadn't believed Halley's claim of murder.

She should have remembered every description she'd heard about the woman she thought until today she'd never met. She should have realized that anyone who could plan and execute her own fate, who could lead the police bit by bit like a hunter laying bait while all the time denying guilt, who could get the story she wanted told on the front pages of every newspaper in the country, would have her facts straight.

"My father was murdered," Halley had said, stunned by Ariel's misunderstanding. "Grace killed him. Grace and Cross! Just exactly as I said. And, don't you see? Obviously, she killed Cross, too."

"Now, Halley," Ariel had tried, "wait—"

"No, ma'am! You had to know everything! You listen!

"I admit I didn't know about Cross. Don't you think I would've used that, too, if I'd known? I didn't see him. Once I saw my father's body, I didn't see anything else. I didn't *know* anything else for weeks!

"No, I didn't see Cross, but I did hear things . . . This is a small town, Ms. Gold, in some ways. Secrets seep out the open windows, carried on the air like a bad odor. I heard the whispers, the rumors. If I did, so did John William. Who knows what he thought all these years, what he must've believed!"

Halley's laugh was brittle flint. "Do you know what Grace did when I broke my brother's death to her? She let me comfort her! Wallowing in self-pity, that woman *allowed* me to be strong for *her!* And I was. I was bedrock. I was *focused!*

"I *focused* on things like whether I'd watered the plants or turned off the stove or needed new panty hose for the funeral. On when I'd eaten or slept last. I spent a lot of time *focusing* on the words of a sonnet. 'But what a shining animal is man,/ Who knows, when pain subsides, that is not that,/For worse than that must follow . . .'

"And I coped. Grace lived in her own reality at the best of times. That week she was mental. Watching me. One minute sullen, like she expected to be accused of something. The next, wringing her hands like Uriah Heep."

Halley had begun to pace. "Usually, Grace didn't get drunk. She'd take just enough to keep a buzz. I knew it, but I denied it. At a certain point of saturation she'd simply go to sleep, harmlessly. She had so little, I told myself—poor, poor Grace!

"The day they buried John William I found her out cold. Too drunk to go to her son's funeral. Nice, yes? I left her snoring. For two days she kept herself anesthetized.

"That last night I went to see about her. She'd been drinking, heavily. I could see something was eating at her. She was incoherent, talking all around what was on her mind and crying.

" 'It's my fault,' she whined. 'But I didn't know I was pregnant then. I didn't know my baby was inside me, absorbing my sin!' Maudlin nonsense, I thought. The way drunks get. 'If not for what happened with John, my boy wouldn't have done this thing.' I thought that was fairly obvious. I thought she meant the method. I tried to comfort her, thinking grief had miraculously spawned empathy! I told her not to torment herself; if John William hadn't gassed himself, he'd have found another way. 'Oh, no!' she said. 'He wouldn't have done it at all.'

"Well, Ms. Gold, it wasn't empathy and it wasn't grief. It was guilt and fear. Primitive, gut-deep fear of divine retribution! I grilled her. Poured coffee down her. I kept at her, and I pried out of her what she did to my father thirty-seven years ago.

"It was she who was reaping the whirlwind, Ms. Gold. Even that sorry excuse for a human being knew that if she hadn't cold-bloodedly murdered John Barron, his son wouldn't have been the maimed creature he was. Born to shame, cheated of the chance to know his own father, and, God pity him, doomed to her tender mercies from the day he came into the world."

Halley's face was wet. She seemed unaware.

"Grace didn't just kill, Ms. Gold. She was a thief. She robbed me of my father. She robbed me of my faith in him. She tried to rob me of my *love* for him. She stole my brother's childhood. His manhood. His desire to live. She stole our lives, Ms. Gold, as surely as she stole my father's."

"Oh, Halley! As much as you hate Grace for what she did—"

"Hate has nothing to do with it."

"Nevertheless . . . You can't punish a dead woman."

"What I can't do is give my father back the years that, finally, brought vindication of his work, but I can undo some of the harm Grace did. I can expunge the shame."

"I don't understand."

Impatiently, as if it were a verdict of some kind, Halley said, "You're not from here."

"I don't see how my origins come into it."

"Then talk to your grandfather. He can explain."

"Why don't you try?"

Halley considered the request. A long moment passed before,

very softly, she said, "The worst thing Grace did, Ms. Gold, was something she could no more grasp than you have."

As if she were explaining the simplest thing in the world, she said, "This city was my family's home. Our name stood for something here. It had for a very long time. I'm not talking about wealth or status; I'm talking about decency.

"Does that sound old-fashioned to you? Foolish? It doesn't to me. It wouldn't have to my father. He was a proud and private man. The respect of his neighbors mattered. His self-respect mattered more."

Halley leaned across the table, willing Ariel to comprehend. "Grace made my father's entire life a lie. Polite people changed the subject when his name came up; they were ashamed for him. Others sniggered and speculated. What had he done that was so contemptible he couldn't face people? So low he couldn't live with it? He was a coward, of course, but was he crooked, too? Had he cheated somebody? Or was it something *dirty?*

"Grace stole my father's name, Ms. Gold. She stole his honor."

The words lay between them, immutable as an epitaph. Then Halley straightened. Unbelievably, she smiled. "When did you last hear that word spoken aloud? Just think. A man's honor was always his dearest possession, dearer than his life. Today, if one even knows the meaning of the word, it's . . ." She shrugged. "A quaint anachronism."

"What I still don't get," Ariel said quietly, "is why you didn't simply tell the police that Grace confessed to your father's murder. Why didn't you just tell them the truth?"

"With no proof whatsoever? Hearsay from a dead woman? Oh, my dear, please! You can guess how far that would've gone. After what happened with John William, what do you think people would have believed? Oh, there'd be plenty of talk before it all fizzled out to nothing. More gossip, more speculation . . . and pity. The pity that made my adolescence hell. Do you think, Ms. Gold, that I would endure that pity again?"

"So you gave them a live murderess."

Halley nodded. "A confession they could see with their own eyes and hear with their own ears. And it worked, didn't it? I gave them the woman who'd executed her husband without a shred of remorse. I gave them the woman who—because men like them hadn't done their jobs—got away with murder. But just to make certain, just to make certain, I went one step further. I gave them a woman capable of committing the most reprehensible of acts.

"You, Ms. Gold, like all humankind, abominate the idea of a mother killing her child. Unlike you, most people have no difficulty believing the worst.

"So, Ms. Gold, what now?"

For the moment Ariel had no answer.

"You must see that this was the only way. The only way to make sure the truth was heard and believed and remembered. To make sure justice was served." Halley hadn't been looking at Ariel when she said, "You're such a fan of the truth, Ms. Gold. Surely justice must mean something to you, too."

Ariel stood and turned back toward the city: the live oaks, the war monuments, the mansions' piazzas, stacked like so many fancy cake tiers facing out to sea. She sensed she'd never fathom the soul of the place if she lived here the rest of her life.

The hike back to her car seemed longer. At last, exhausted but unwound, she spied the tall, stately palmetto beneath which she'd parked. She was unlocking the door when she noticed whitish blotches on the roof. The stately palmetto had had winged visitors in her absence, and they seemed to have singled out her car. "Same to you," she muttered, and got in.

She hadn't decided what she'd tell Henry, but she planned a long talk with her grandfather, who of all people, she believed, would understand the decision she'd been forced to make. She wouldn't be looking for validation. She knew in her heart that, like Halley, she'd done the only thing she could.